TAKE 2

MARIAN
MURPHY

POOLBEG

Published 2000
by Poolbeg Press Ltd
123 Baldoyle Industrial Estate
Dublin 13, Ireland
E-mail: poolbeg@iol.ie
www.poolbeg.com

© Marian Murphy 2000

Copyright for typesetting, layout, design
© Poolbeg Press Ltd

The moral right of the author has been asserted.

A catalogue record for this book is available from the British Library.

ISBN 1 85371 918 8

All rights reserved. No part of this publication may be reproduced or
transmitted in any form or by any means, electronic or mechanical,
including photography, recording, or any information storage or
retrieval system, without permission in writing from the publisher. The
book is sold subject to the condition that it shall not, by way of trade or
otherwise, be lent, resold or otherwise circulated without the
publisher's prior consent in any form of binding or cover other than
that in which it is published and without a similar condition, including
this condition, being imposed on the subsequent purchaser.

Cover design by Slatter-Anderson
Printed by Omnia Books Ltd, Glasgow.
Set by Pat Hope

Author Biography

Marian Murphy moved from Dublin to Wicklow three years ago, and lives there with her husband and two young sons. She always loved reading, and did a B.A. in English, and later an M.A., when she ran out of books to read at home.

Marian worked in the Civil Service for fifteen years and then returned to college to qualify as a social worker.

She began writing two years ago after she attended a creative writing class, and recently won second prize in the Francis Ledwidge Poetry Award competition (traditional section).

Take 2 is Marian's first novel and she is currently working on her second.

Acknowledgements

This is the part you read when you think you might be mentioned. Otherwise, fast-forward to Chapter One.

It takes a lot of people to write a book.

The writer who – if she has any sense – puts her bottom on the chair and her fingers on the keyboard and keeps on going . . .

And then everyone else who knows and loves and encourages and supports her.

My "thank-you" list is long.

And it starts, as it must, with Liam – who is there for me, always.

And my boys, Luke and Michael, who probably watched far more television than was good for them in the past year – but who assure me it's educational (isn't it?).

Everyone in the family – Liam's and mine – who helped me to hang in there – especially Dad, who got me reading in the first place.

Eileen Casey, poet, who taught a creative writing class that got me started, and the members of the writing group that evolved from there – Deirdre Nally, Helen Dwyer, Jane Keane, Kevin Moriarty and Patrick Foley, who give me invaluable support and excellent criticism – and they're all busy writing themselves, so watch this space.

My friends and colleagues in SJH, particularly Sinead, who read the manuscript. Oh, and Eileen and Mary – they know why – and Maeve, for her very interesting contribution.

Bernadette, who introduced me to Connemara, and Mary, who spent some great holidays there with me. Jacqueline, who went to explore New York for me (that was why you went, wasn't it?) and Karen and Kevin who met me there for a truly wonderful weekend. Thanks, folks, I'll never forget it. It only took a week to recover.

Everyone at Poolbeg, particularly Gaye Shortland, my editor, who is just lovely (and a damn good editor).

All my friends – who are still my friends in spite of not seeing me much while I'm writing (maybe it helps).

And you, the reader, without whom there wouldn't be any books. Hope you like this one.

For Liam – first, last, always.
This one's for you.

Chapter One

Clare looked around her apartment one last time, took a deep breath and left. The click of the door behind her had a satisfying finality. She ran lightly down the stairs and out into the garden, stopping when she got to the Stag's Horn tree just inside the gate. Now, at the very beginning of February, the tree was absolutely bare and she felt a moment of sadness that she wouldn't be there to see it burst into life again in summer.

"I'm doing the right thing," she told herself as she headed for her battered blue Ford Fiesta. The little car was packed to capacity with everything Clare possessed. Her rucksack and two suitcases filled the boot, while boxes of books, her mandolin and an ailing cheese-plant battled for space on the back seat.

She headed along the canal and out to the Galway road, suddenly anxious to put Dublin, and Tony, behind her.

"I'm doing the right thing," she repeated like a mantra as she picked up the first sign for Galway. Not

1

that she needed signs. She'd been doing the journey since her mother first let her hitch-hike when she was seventeen.

Once safely past Maynooth she heaved a sigh of relief. Tony wouldn't have stopped her, she thought. But she herself might have lost the courage to go. She needed to escape from what had happened and from what might happen. And 'escape' meant only one place – her little cottage near Clifden, in the heart of Connemara.

This time it wasn't just for the weekend – it was for real, maybe for good. She would have to wait and see. She hadn't quite burned all her bridges. She was on a career break for a year from the civil service, and her cousin had agreed to lease her apartment in Ranelagh. She didn't have a great deal of money but she had enough, and she had time, a precious luxury that was usually in short supply for her.

Now all she had to do was find a life she might want to live.

* * *

As she crossed the Shannon at Athlone Clare felt an exhilarating sense of freedom. She turned up the radio. The Saw Doctors were singing ". . . stone walls and the grass is green . . ."

"And I'm on my way!" she thought.

She found herself smiling for the first time in what seemed like ages. Suddenly, everything seemed possible. Even the sun was on her side. It felt unseasonably warm, until she realised that it was St Brigid's Day – the first day of February, and of spring. She remembered the blind poet Raftery from a long-ago classroom. Two centuries ago he had headed for Connemara at the beginning of spring and left that lovely poem behind him as a sort of road-map. It felt absolutely right to Clare to be doing just the same.

It was just half past one when she pulled into a space outside Hayden's Hotel in Ballinasloe, feeling more than ready to enjoy her lunch.

She ate quickly, relaxed enough to stay there all day, but wanting to reach the cottage while it was still bright. It was fifty miles beyond Galway but worth every penny she had paid for it and every inch of the journey.

Clare remembered the first time she ever saw it, during her last year in College. She desperately needed a break from the pressure of studying for finals, so she decided to go to Connemara one August weekend, just her and her well-used Raleigh bike. She wasn't quite sure what the plan was, just that she would see how far beyond Galway she could travel without getting bored, saddle-sore or totally exhausted.

She had cycled steadily, enjoying the exhilaration and the challenge, until she wasn't too far from Clifden. Impulsively she had turned off the main road and headed in the direction of the sea. She followed a boreen for about a mile before she turned off again and stopped to rest in the sweltering heat. She sat on a big rock by the roadside drinking from her water-bottle and looking around.

A short distance away she saw a small, whitewashed

cottage with red windows and doors, and gleaming thatch. "Picture-book stuff," Clare had thought, wrinkling her nose. She had found it enchanting, all the same, and when an old woman emerged to offer her tea and soda bread, she was more than happy to accept.

In the little cottage, with its one big living-room, the small room "behind" and the loft bedroom, she had felt a rare sort of peace.

"I belong here," she thought.

She left reluctantly, promising the woman, and herself, that she would call again. She went on her way feeling touched by the woman's open generosity, the hospitality to a stranger.

When she passed that way again the following year Clare persuaded her companions to make the slight detour to visit the cottage. She was saddened to find that the lovely place looked neglected, and an old man passing on a bicycle told her that the woman had died in the winter. The cottage, he said, had been lying empty since, because the distant relative who inherited it had no interest in living there and hadn't got around to selling it.

Clare, who had never before thought of buying a house, knew that she had to have this cottage. It didn't make sense on any practical level. She was about to start her first job, so she had neither time or money to spare. The cottage was in poor shape and needed work and money to restore it. It was too far away, really, to get there every weekend – and there was no way that she could afford it.

But Clare, normally practical, just had to have it. She

scrimped, and borrowed, and tried to talk friends into buying it with her. Nobody was interested. They had all sorts of sensible objections to the idea – and they were right. But they hadn't seen it, they didn't love it as she did.

And then, when she was beginning to despair, her father reminded her that he had put away several thousand pounds for her, towards the day when she would buy her "real" house. If she really wanted it, he said, she could have it.

Wanted it? He had offered her the moon and the stars. Clare flew to the door, came back to hug him, and dashed off to ring the cottage's new owner yet again, to say that finally she could buy it.

She learned more than she ever wanted to know that summer about thatching and whitewashing, and the mysteries of well-water and septic tanks. And in ten years she had never once regretted buying it. Now it was going to come into its own, and be her home for the next year. She hoped it would all work out.

It was almost four o'clock when Clare reached Galway. She drove easily through the city, taking the road to the west out past Moycullen and Oughterard. She didn't stop until she reached Peacock's at Maam Cross where she could pick up a few groceries.

She got out of the car, eyes fixed on the mountains in the near distance. That first sight of the Twelve Bens, purple and blue in this light, breathtaking as ever, lifted her spirit and filled her, as always, with a kind of reverence.

Passing through Recess she wound down the window for a moment to smell the rich turf-smoke on the evening air. The peaty smell reminded her of holidays in the Gaeltacht as a child. She used to struggle to manage in Irish for a whole month, loving everything about it nevertheless – the music, the dancing, the walks on the beach. Even the classes, which only lasted for a few hours in the mornings anyway.

She wound up the window again and checked her watch. Not long now.

The final few miles passed quickly. She rounded the bend and drove up the little boreen, delighted to see the smoke drifting up from her own chimney. Thank God for Jack! He had been slow enough to warm to her when she first began coming down, but by now he was both friend and willing caretaker.

Her phone call yesterday was enough to make sure that everything was ready. Her cottage, solid and snug at the foot of the mountain, was waiting to welcome her. She was home.

* * *

She woke next day to the sound of someone banging on the door and calling her name. The sun slanted through the little window, reaching the far wall of her loft bedroom – a sure sign that it was well past eleven.

"Clare Delaney, get out of bed!"

"Niall," she thought, grinning, suddenly awake.

"Coming," she called back.

She dressed quickly and scrambled down the steep

little stairs, still pulling her sweatshirt on. She threw open the door and grinned again in sheer delight to see him there. He smiled back, his brown eyes meeting her green ones almost on a level. He was in his early thirties, just older than Clare. Like her, he was slim, and a bare inch or two taller than her. Even dressed in casual clothes he had a certain air of assurance about him.

"It's safe to come out now, Clare. The day is well aired."

She threw a mock punch at him. Laughing, he ducked as he caught her around the waist and hugged her.

"Am I coming in, or are you coming out? We could walk to the beach."

"Coffee first," she said. "I haven't woken up yet."

He followed her in, settling himself in one of the armchairs by the still warm range as she filled the kettle. He looked around, his gaze resting on a shining blue jug placed in the deep recess of the window. That was new.

Clare had done so much with this place, he thought. Gradually she had added a rug here, a wall-hanging there. It was all done with delicacy and an eye for colour that added warmth to the simple room. Soft white walls, a beamed ceiling – not quite authentic, but lovely – and stripped pine floors made the room glow.

Sunlight through several small, deep-set windows picked out the rich blues and greens of a piece of pottery here, a lamp there. A few small paintings, mostly of sea and boats and mountains, hung on the walls. The yellow sofa was heaped with patchwork cushions, one having fallen to the floor beside an open book and an abandoned coffee mug.

But there was something different. Clare seemed to have brought a lot of stuff with her this time. A cardboard box of books and a big suitcase, open but still unpacked, filled the space beside the big pine table. More books were heaped on the old oak mantle above the fireplace, and the deep bookshelves carved into the wall beside it looked fuller than usual.

Clare followed his gaze. "I know, it's a mess, isn't it?"

She hoped he wouldn't ask any awkward questions until she felt ready for them. Wisely, he didn't.

"You'll get around to it. You've done a great job, Clare – I love this room."

"So do I," Clare replied.

She handed him the cup of coffee and sat down with her own on the chair opposite him.

"I was exhausted when I got here last night – I fell asleep after dinner and had to drag myself up to bed after midnight when I woke up. I'm still wrecked."

"So I noticed," he grinned. "Sorry to get you up, but I was dying to see you."

"How did you . . . ?"

"The smoke."

She laughed. "God, you can't keep anything secret around here, can you? Jack had the place all ready for me."

They chatted easily while they drank their coffee. Then he jumped up, taking her empty mug and rinsing it with his own at the sink.

"Come on – I'll race you to the beach!"

And he was gone. Clare pulled the door after her, not bothering to lock it, and ran through the gate and down the laneway leading to the strand, still protesting that she was too tired, that it was too early . . .

She was laughing as she said it, putting on a spurt to try and catch up with him. He stopped, waiting for her at the top of the lane, watching as she fell into an easy stride. Her long dark hair was blowing about her in the slight breeze. He thought, not for the first time, how beautiful she looked. And how little she knew it.

When she reached him he took her hand and, laughing like children, they ran the final few yards until they got to the top of the little hill looking over the bay. They stood together, hair blowing in the breeze, looking out to the horizon where a Galway hooker was tacking its way back to shore.

"I love those boats!" she said. "They always remind me of some giant prehistoric sea bird with their big black sails. Like a marauding creature or something."

"Why do you love them, so?"

"Oh, I don't know. The power of them, I suppose, and the sense that they've always been here, sailing on the bay since the beginning of time."

"I think I know what you mean," he agreed after a moment. "I prefer the ones with the red sails, though."

"You're a romantic at heart, Niall Devlin. I'd never have guessed it!"

"You never gave me the chance, Clare!" he teased.

They laughed easily together. They both knew they

had had their chances, but that their friendship now had settled into something different.

They watched as a man in a dark sweater, cloth cap pulled low against the morning sun, headed towards a currach which was lying up-ended on the strand. There was no sign of any other living creature in the landscape apart from the distant figures on the far-off hooker and the gulls that swooped, screeching, down over the blue, choppy waves.

Clare put her head back, closed her eyes and took a deep breath.

"You know, Niall, I don't think there's anywhere in the world more beautiful than Rossdarra Strand. I couldn't imagine wanting to be anywhere else right now."

"Not even Dublin?"

"No," she said. "Especially not Dublin."

They stood in silence for a few minutes more, enjoying the peace, the scent of salt, the soft splash of the waves below.

Finally Niall spoke. "I'd better be getting back, Clare. I'm expecting a few people down tonight, in fact I was wondering if you'd join us."

"Thanks, Niall, but I wouldn't be great company at the moment. Friends or customers?"

"Friends, this time. Why don't you come in during the week, then? I'm in Galway tomorrow but I should be back early on Tuesday. Will you still be around?"

"I'll still be around," said Clare.

"So, maybe Tuesday or Wednesday evening?" he asked.

They began to walk slowly back up the lane. "I'll see. No, I'll come on Wednesday, definitely. I don't want to turn into a hermit down here!"

Niall was about to question her further but thought better of it. It was obvious that Clare didn't want to go into detail just now.

"Fine. Do you want to drive in, stay overnight? Or will I call out and pick you up?"

"I'll drive in myself. That leaves you more time for slaving over the hot stove. I'll be expecting great things!"

"Slave-driver!" he laughed as they reached the gate. "I'll see you on Wednesday, so, about seven."

Giving her a quick hug, he hopped into his Volvo and drove off.

Clare stood at the gate, watching him go. The car was gorgeous. Niall must be doing really well, she thought. And he deserved it – he had worked hard enough to get there.

She remembered how much encouragement he had needed to open the restaurant in Clifden. It had seemed risky, since the little town was full of good places already. But Niall loved Clifden just as much as she did once she persuaded him to come down and see it, and he decided to take the chance. From the look of things it had definitely been worth it.

The day passed quickly as Clare finished unpacking. She cooked some pasta, humming to herself, pleased with the cosy feel of the cottage and the silence broken only by a blackbird outside. In the city there was never absolute quiet, but she remembered how she had missed the noise of the traffic when she first started coming here, how she couldn't sleep for the first few nights without the comforting drone of cars outside and the sense of neighbours just a few feet away if you needed them.

Now she loved the stillness, the space that was not quite isolation.

She ate with one eye on a book, the radio on in the background. Afterwards she settled on the sofa with her book, coffee beside her, but suddenly found she couldn't relax. She was used to being busy at weekends. Even at the cottage she usually went walking or cycling, or drove into Clifden to meet friends. Now, suddenly, it felt unnatural to have no definite plans. As if she was in suspended animation, just waiting.

She knew, of course, what she was waiting for – she just didn't want to think about it yet.

Getting up and stretching, she reached for her anorak and went out to the shed where she kept her bike. The day was noticeably cooler now but she relished the idea of speeding along in the slight breeze that was still there.

The bike was a bit rusty but still in fine shape. Better shape than herself, Clare thought ruefully. In the year she spent with Tony she hadn't had time for some of the things she really enjoyed, like hiking and cycling, and she felt sorry she had given them up. Something else to regret, she thought.

She wheeled out the bike, heading up the laneway and back towards the road. Once there she started pedalling furiously, determined to put Tony out of her mind for as long as she could.

Soon she was thinking of nothing but the wind on her face, the smell of the turf, the bleating of the sheep on the hillside. She loved the exhilaration of cycling, the way she felt part of the landscape, out in the elements, instead of sealed off in a car.

She went on for several miles, pausing finally at the top of a steep hill overlooking the bay. The boats were still out. It was perfect weather for sailing, unusually calm for the time of year, but with enough wind to fill the sails. The sun, in the late afternoon, was beginning its descent behind the mountains, making them glow pink and lilac in the soft light.

She turned for home, freewheeling down the hill, thinking she might call over to Jack.

As she rounded a bend three miles or so from the cottage she caught sight of a figure in the distance, pedalling towards her. She squinted slightly in the fading light, thinking she knew who it was.

There were several people around here who rode the big old bikes known as 'High Nellies', but only one had it painted in rainbow colours instead of the usual black. It had to be Kate Kavanagh.

Although Kate had a car she preferred to use the bike for shorter journeys, saying that it kept her fit. It was hard to put an age on her. Clare had the impression that she was in her early fifties, but she might be older. She was a tall, angular woman with black hair that was beginning to turn grey, deep-set blue eyes and a cheerful, no-nonsense manner that Clare found refreshing.

As they drew closer Clare could see Kate smiling in her direction. They both pulled to the side of the road and stood holding the bikes.

"Hello there! I called in when I saw the car at the cottage, but there was no sign of you. I was going to call around again tomorrow."

"Great," said Clare. "I'm on the way over to Jack now, but I'll be around all day tomorrow. Why don't you come for lunch, about one or so?"

Clare thought she saw a distant look in Kate's eyes for a moment, but it was gone instantly.

"Lovely," she answered. "I'll bring some of my brown bread."

It was well after six o'clock when Clare knocked on Jack's door, so she expected to find him at home. She knocked twice before realising that the lambing season had started, and he was probably out around the farm. Suddenly cold, she mounted the bike again, deciding to call again later if she felt up to it.

It was very dark as she drew towards the cottage.

"Good job I left the lamps lighting," she thought, looking at the soft glow in the windows.

The absolute dark of the countryside was lit only by the lamp on her bike, the lights shining from other windows dotted about the hillside and the stars that seemed brighter, closer and more numerous than they ever were in the city.

She shivered as she put the key in the door, feeling

the sudden chill of the February evening and anxious to be inside in the warmth. And then she shivered again as she heard the ringing of the telephone. She hesitated for a second before forcing herself to go and answer it. She lifted the receiver with a sense of dread, knowing who it would be. And she wasn't sure if she wanted to talk to him. Not now, not ever.

Chapter Two

Kate continued her journey quickly, wanting to get home before it grew dark.

Her house was small and nondescript, about two miles from Clare's cottage. There was nothing beautiful about it except the fact that it was hers. Kate often thought how lovely it would be to have a conservatory at the back, where she could sit in the sun and look out over the mountains and the sea, instead of having to make do with a kitchen chair at the back door. A different woman might have envied Clare, who had that lovely cottage as a holiday home, as well as her Dublin apartment. But it was not in Kate's nature to be envious, and she had long since taught herself not to dwell on what might have been.

Still, it didn't stop her looking wistfully around the plain little room that was her main living area. She had plenty of energy but not much time, and certainly not enough money, to do anything much in the way of improvements. Even though she worked from time to time, whatever money she had after paying for the necessities – including her car, and her paints, which were vital to her – went on Kevin. She knew that, at twenty-seven, he should be well capable of earning a living.

She also knew that she spoiled him, but it was hard not to. She gave him what she could, too aware that she hadn't been able to give what he really needed. And besides, he seemed to appreciate whatever she did for him. In recent years she had finally grown closer to her son. Not before time, she thought.

Thinking of Kevin as she heated some stew for her evening meal, she realised that it was only eight or ten weeks now until he would be home from the States. She wasn't sure what his plans were but it would be lovely to have him around again. His year in America had been wonderful for him but she had missed him even more than she had anticipated.

It could be lonely here in winter. Although she had been born and reared not twenty miles away she had no family around now, and not many friends.

Sighing, she placed two dishes of milk just inside the back door.

"Here, puss puss," she called softly.

She heard the purring from the bedroom as two slinky shapes eased through the door, Mishka in the lead as usual. She'd be lost without her cats, she thought.

Sighing again, she put her plate on the table and sat down with a glass of water in her hand. She forced her thoughts in a different direction. She absolutely forbade herself to dwell on the past. She had made choices, she had made mistakes, but dwelling on them would do no good now.

She thought again of Clare. How old was she? Thirty, thirty-two? Young enough to be her daughter. That thought brought an immediate stab of pain, and she stood up and turned on the radio. She picked up the fork again but the food was suddenly tasteless. She abandoned her dinner, throwing it almost untouched into the bin.

She made some coffee, thought about doing some painting. She was finding it hard to stay with it at the moment.

The dark, brooding image emerging on the canvas in the small front room seemed to have a life of its own. She never used to paint like that. Landscapes were her forte, soft mountains, gentle rolling hills, the sea with its sparkle and colour, boats scudding cheerfully along, careless of the powerful, dangerous undertow, the hidden depths.

Now it was as if those depths were forcing themselves to the surface, refusing to be contained any longer. It scared her. No, in fact, it terrified her.

Now what appeared, almost in spite of her, were amorphous shapes in blacks and greys and jagged, violent purple. Frightening shapes that seemed to be creating themselves with no help from her, shapes that found no resonance in her careful thoughts.

Her painting, which had long been a refuge, was

starting to be outside of her control. And Kate, more than anything else at this point, needed to assert control over her life.

Now, while she still could.

Now, before it was too late.

The shrilling telephone interrupted her train of thought. She reached for it, glad of the interruption.

"Mrs Kavanagh?" the caller asked.

She recognised Ned Coyne, who owned the shop in Clifden where she worked occasionally.

"I wonder if you'd be free to come in tomorrow? I know it's short notice, but my wife has to go in to Galway and we're a bit short-staffed."

Kate agreed readily, glad of the money and the distraction of being busy. She liked working in the shop, selling art materials, paintings and pottery to the regulars who lived locally and to the tourists who thronged the little town in the summer. She would have to ring Clare, cancel lunch tomorrow.

Or maybe they could meet in Clifden.

She looked up Clare's number, dialled, hung up when she heard the engaged tone. She busied herself for a few minutes washing dishes, then tried again. Still engaged. She went into the bedroom to select her clothes for the morning, glad to have something to do.

The shop was very informal but Kate was aware that lately she hadn't bothered much about her appearance. She had never been particularly interested in how she looked, but she was vaguely aware that now she had let herself go, which was a different matter. She had always loved bright colours, soft floating skirts, long vibrant shawls.

Relics of my hippy days, she thought.

And relics they were. It seemed, looking into the curtained alcove that was her wardrobe, that she had nothing that matched, and nothing that was less than four or five years old. Losing patience, she grabbed a mauve top and swirly purple skirt that more or less matched.

She would have to think about her wardrobe. Were her clothes really appropriate for a woman of almost fifty-seven? Did she care?

Deciding that she didn't, she added it anyway to the growing mental list of things she must review in the very near future and went downstairs to ring Clare again.

This time she got an answer.

"Are you all right, Clare?" she asked, concerned because the voice at the other end was low, hesitant, very different from how she had sounded just an hour or two before.

"Fine," Clare answered, but Kate had to repeat her message twice before Clare, with an apparent effort at concentration, agreed to meet her at Niall's restaurant the following day.

Kate, hanging up, was worried. Something had happened to upset Clare, that much was certain. But what?

It could be anything, Kate realised. She'd known Clare over the past year, but didn't actually know her very well. Perhaps she'd find out tomorrow what was wrong. She'd have to wait and see.

* * *

Clare woke late again the next morning. This time she had a slight headache, and a sudden sinking in her stomach when she remembered last night's phone call. Then quickly she put the thought from her mind, focusing on the later phone call and the arrangement to meet Kate for lunch. She showered quickly, tied her long hair back and put on her favourite red sweater, so that she looked bright and cheerful in spite of how she felt.

She reached Clifden just after twelve thirty. Her spirits lifted as usual at her first sight of the little town nestling in the mountains. It had changed considerably since Clare first went there but it had managed to keep all its friendliness and charm.

As she drove along looking for parking she became aware of more recent changes – a shop-sign here, new paint there. The town, always busy, looked prosperous and alive, even in February. There were some tourists around already, she noticed, well wrapped up against the slight drizzle.

She parked just down from Niall's restaurant, standing to admire it as she locked the car. The sign had been freshly done, blue flowing script on a yellow background She had laughed when she first heard the name.

"Albatross? You can't call it that!"

"Why not?" he'd grinned. "It will have a maritime

21

theme. And it'll be hanging round my neck for a long time! And besides, it'll come near the top of the telephone listings. That *has* to be good for business!"

She'd laughed again, telling him he'd thought of everything. And it seemed he had. Albatross was now well-established, after several years' hard work, and was fully booked every weekend and most nights in the summer.

She went through the bright blue doorway, remembering how she had dismissed his choice of colours – vibrant blue and green and yellow – as gaudy.

Fortunately he hadn't listened, because he had been absolutely right. The restaurant was cheerful and welcoming even on a wet day in February, and in summer it looked absolutely wonderful.

She went into the warm, pine-panelled lobby, glancing with interest through a doorway to her left where she could see workmen busy with saws and paintbrushes. She must ask Niall later what was going on.

Going into the restaurant she caught sight of Barry coming through the door from the kitchen. He was a compact young man with a neat dark moustache whose warm smile and general air of merriment affected everyone around him. As soon as he saw Clare he dashed over to give her a kiss on the cheek and a big smile of welcome.

"Clare! Niall told me you were around but he wasn't expecting you 'til Wednesday. He's gone into Galway for some supplies."

"That's okay, Barry. I'm meeting somebody for lunch. So he abandoned you for the day?"

"Right – I'm left doing the donkey-work as usual."

"And very good you are at it too!"

He burst out laughing. "Thanks a bunch. I wouldn't want to be easily insulted!"

"Don't think about it too much," Clare laughed.

They always bantered like this. Barry had been here for two years now, since Niall decided he needed an assistant, and he and Clare had got on well from the very start. He was some three or four years younger than her and she enjoyed his energy and his sense of humour.

"So what's good on the menu today?" she asked, taking a seat at her favourite table beside the window.

She was lucky to get it, she noticed. The restaurant was filling up quickly and was obviously going to be busy for lunch.

"The spaghetti carbonara is good. Or cassoulet, if you'd prefer something a bit different."

"So what's that?" Clare asked, interested. She had never heard of it, but she loved trying out new dishes.

"Mainly duck and butter-beans, with about four other types of meat thrown in for good measure."

"Sounds – experimental." She pretended to look horrified. *"You're* not cooking it, are you?"

"What do you think?" he replied, and they both grinned.

Barry was a terrific "front-of-house" man, a good manager and excellent host. But they both remembered only too well the episode last summer when Niall was away overnight and the relief chef had rung in sick. Clare had arrived – luckily – to find Barry struggling with a lasagne recipe and on the point of putting in eight bulbs of garlic where the recipe had called for eight cloves. She had never let him forget the potential disaster she averted.

Clare had taken over the cooking that night. She knew her way round the plainer dishes on the menu, and amid great laughter and much consulting of recipe books – and only one panic-stricken phonecall to a friend in Dublin who actually *could* cook – they had concocted what they called the "Beginner's Luck" menu, consisting of just three different dishes.

Barry, pushing his charm and persuasive powers to the limit, had told the customers of their plight, and offered the meals at half the normal price.

And, to the great relief of both novice chefs, it had been a huge success. Nobody left, nobody was poisoned, and when Barry rang a friend of his to come and bring his guitar, the atmosphere became so lively that everyone wanted to stay and they practically had to push people out the door at three in the morning before collapsing in front of a mound of washing-up, absolutely exhausted and delighted with themselves.

The "Beginner's Luck Supper", music and all, was a monthly fixture ever since, and Barry and Clare had become firm friends.

Barry excused himself now to get back to his work just as Kate came rushing through the door looking slightly flushed.

"Sorry I'm late, Clare – I had a rush of customers just as I was leaving. Would you believe it, a tour bus in February? And nobody wanted to buy anything until I was putting up the 'closed' sign!"

Clare laughed. "Seems like a good way of concentrating people's minds for them!"

Kate didn't look convinced.

"I hate rushing people," she said. "But they were all going for something to eat, anyway, so I told them I'd be back to open up again in an hour. I hope you don't mind?"

"Not at all," said Clare. "That's plenty of time for a chat."

They sat for a few minutes, making small talk, Kate fiddling with the salt and pepper mills. Over the past year they had dropped into each other occasionally for coffee, but they were not on intimate terms and this lunch-time arrangement suddenly seemed too formal.

They were relieved when Michelle, one of the waitresses, arrived to offer them menus. "Barry says the spaghetti's good," Clare said.

Kate considered for a moment. "I think I'll just settle for a chicken sandwich and some minestrone. I love minestrone – I used to nearly live on it when I was in Italy."

"When were you there?" asked Clare, interested. "That's where I first met Niall."

"Really? When was that? And where did you go?" Kate asked, and they slipped readily into an animated discussion about various holidays, laughing more and more freely at each other's anecdotes, so that by the time they had finished their meal some of the other customers had begun to smile in their direction, sharing a little in their pleasure.

"You know, Clare, I never expected to enjoy myself so much! I don't know when I last laughed like that. And after I hung up the phone last night I was afraid I'd made a mistake, because . . ."

Her voice trailed away, suddenly uncertain.

"I know," said Clare "I was a bit down, but I'm grand now."

She didn't elaborate, and Kate didn't press her.

Clare paused, and then seemed to make a decision. "I'd just spoken to my ex-boyfriend. I left Dublin to get away from him. I wasn't sure that he'd actually ring me here."

"And did you want him to?" asked Kate softly. She waited while Clare considered this.

"No," she answered after a moment. "No, definitely not. But I still felt confused afterwards."

Kate nodded.

"I know I did the right thing in leaving," Clare continued. "But knowing doesn't make it any easier."

"Does it ever?" asked Kate, smiling ruefully.

Realising the time, she became more business-like, saying she had to go. "I'm sorry, Clare, because I'd really like to stay another while. But maybe I'll see you again before you go back. When are you leaving?"

"For Dublin, you mean?" Clare asked.

Kate nodded again.

"I'm not," Clare said. "At least, not for a while. I meant it when I said I'd left. I'm staying here right through the summer."

Kate bit her lip. "Look, I really have to go, but – "

"I'll ring you," said Clare.

Kate smiled, squeezed her shoulder briefly and was gone, stopping at the cash desk on the way out.

Michelle brought some more coffee and Clare sat sipping it, enjoying a sense of well-being. The lunch had been really great fun. Unexpectedly so. But she had felt an unusual urgency in Kate just before she left, and she decided not to wait too long before phoning.

Clare finished her coffee and decided to drive home by way of Roundstone rather than lingering in town. The rain had eased off, the afternoon had begun to look more promising and she had nobody to please but herself. It was a wonderful feeling, one she'd have to get used to again.

She got home at about four o'clock when it was already getting dark. She stoked up the fire and tidied the kitchen, a small job when she only had to clean up after herself. She settled down to read for a while with some music in the background, then decided to ring Ruth, her sister, to let her know where she was.

Her friends Mary and Dee knew already, of course, and her brother Dermot. But Ruth had been away on a course in England and Clare had decided to wait until she got back before filling her in on what had happened.

"You should have left long ago," was Ruth's succinct analysis. "I'll be down to see you for Patrick's Weekend – if you last that long."

"Great idea!" Clare answered. "And I'll last. Just watch me!"

Chapter Three

Tuesday was bright and clear, but cold. Clare woke to the realisation that she had better stop counting the days, as if this were just a long holiday weekend.

She went for a walk in the late morning, wandering around her field at the back of the cottage. When she had bought it she had wondered why she could possibly want four acres of stony land, but it came with the cottage and there were several outbuildings. She had had a vague notion that she could use the outhouses for something or that she could maybe sell sites, but there wasn't really enough access from the road.

She had applied for, and got, permission to convert the outbuildings some three or four years ago, but hadn't given it much thought since.

She felt a glow of satisfaction as she walked around. Maybe she wasn't quite sure what to do with it all, but it was lovely to know it was all hers.

Late in the afternoon she decided to walk over and see if Jack was around. She put on rubber boots, because the shortcut through the field could be very wet at this time of year. She took her anorak from the hook on the back of the door, putting a torch in the pocket in case the light had faded before she came back.

Jack was out working in the field when she came towards his house.

"God bless the work!" she called out the old greeting. Strange, she'd never use it in the city but here it came naturally.

He straightened up and she could see his delighted smile. He waved, took one more look at the sheep he had been examining and came over to meet her. He was a tall, spare man of about sixty, with grey hair and kind blue eyes. Clare couldn't remember him ever wearing anything but a cap and a dark suit, even working in the fields.

He touched the cap now as he reached her. "You got here!" he said. It was the way he always greeted her.

"I got here! Thanks for looking after the place – it was great to have the fire lighting. You're kept busy?" Clare asked, turning her attention to the sheep in the field beside them.

"Busy enough," said Jack, predictably.

It was always either 'Quiet enough' or 'Busy enough'.

"Six lambs born today," he continued.

"I'd love to see them."

Jack looked up towards the sheds. "Give it a day or so, let them settle."

"I'll do that," she said. "Have you time to take a

29

break? I bought some soda bread in Clifden yesterday, I thought you might like some."

Jack smiled again. "Come on in, so. I'll put the kettle on."

He led the way into the house, Clare following. She was struck again by the two-storey house, unusually big for one of that age in the area. She remembered Jack saying it was sixty years old, just a bit older than himself, built by his grandfather. There were numerous outhouses behind the house, some of them empty for as long as she had known the place.

Jack did his best, but he was no housekeeper, and there was an air of neglect everywhere that reminded her. almost, of a house that had been standing idle. The remains of his dinner sat on the kitchen table, beside a half-full milk-bottle with a hole poked in the red foil cap, and an open block of butter in its gold wrapper.

The room could have done with a good clean-up, but at least it was warm. There was always a big blaze in the kitchen stove, winter or summer.

They sat by the fire and chatted, drinking tea and eating the soda bread, which Jack spread with thick marmalade.

"I'm down for a while this time," she told him.

He nodded, pulling on the pipe which he had lit from the fire, waiting to see if she'd say more.

Clare hesitated. There was always a slight distance between them, but she decided to take the plunge.

"In fact," she continued, "I might be staying six months or more. Maybe even a year."

If he was surprised he didn't show it. He sat waiting, not pressing her.

She took another sip of tea. "I got fed up with Dublin and thought I'd try living here for a while. You know I love it here."

He laughed quietly. "You mightn't love it in November!"

Clare grinned back at him. "Ask me in November – if I last that long!"

Jack sat silently again, looking into the fire.

"You're doing the right thing," he said suddenly.

Clare was surprised. It wasn't like Jack to offer an opinion about something personal. What's more, he was echoing what she had told herself.

She wasn't sure if he would say more, but he looked at her with an intense expression, unusual for him, and continued.

"If you want something enough you have to go after it. You mightn't get another chance. And there's no use spending the rest of your life being sorry you didn't do it."

He lapsed into silence and she realised he was unlikely to say more.

When she left he offered to accompany her and they set off across a field already white with frost. She only allowed him to come half the short distance, knowing he was anxious to get back to the sheep. At half-past-six on a February evening it was pitch dark, but she had the torch and she'd be home in a minute or two.

She walked along the dark roadside, mulling over

what Jack had said. What had he meant? Or, rather, why had he meant it? She had always taken him to be what he appeared, a kind, simple man concerned about his sheep and running the farm, but with little experience outside of that. It troubled her to think that he had regrets.

"You mightn't get another chance," he'd said. And it didn't sound as if he had taken his. What had it been? She was well aware that for Jack's generation of men on small farms in the west, there had been few opportunities for marriage once the women started going to the big towns to work. Maybe he'd had the chance to go away himself? As far as she knew, he had rarely travelled even as far as Galway, went up to Dublin only once and had never in his life gone outside the country.

She'd probably never find out what chance he had missed, she told herself as she reached the cottage. He was a private man and might never again refer to it. She was all the more touched that he had opened up to encourage her.

She opened the door, glad to be home, but she had no sooner taken off her coat than the telephone rang and her heart begin to beat faster. She hesitated, then reached for it resolutely. She would *not* let Tony rule her life like this. If it was him, she would tell him to stop calling.

"Hello," she said tersely.

She was relieved when she heard Niall's warm voice answering.

"Hi, Clare, it's me. I'm stuck in Galway trying to sort

out some furnishings that have been held up. You don't want to come in and meet me here tomorrow, do you? There's no chance I'll be back in Clifden in time for dinner."

Clare considered. She wanted to see Niall, but she also wanted to get into a slower rhythm than she was used to – and traipsing off to Galway wouldn't help.

"Think I'll give it a miss, Niall – you don't mind? You'll be back in a day or two, won't you?"

"I'd better be! That new dining area I'm opening – did you see it? Barry said you were in."

"I saw some workmen – "

"Well, at least *they're* doing their job. Nothing else is going right. I need the place ready by Easter, and half the furnishings I ordered from Dublin either didn't turn up, or they were the wrong design, or – I'm going *mad!*" He paused for breath. "Sorry, Clare, you know I don't deal very well with frustration!"

"You deal pretty well with most things. Anything I can do? Maybe I *will* come in . . ."

"No need – I'm just letting off steam. I should be back for definite by Thursday night. Feel like coming over then?"

"Great. Ring me when you get back."

"I'll do that. And Clare?"

"Mmm?"

"Thanks for letting me sound off."

"No problem. I'm used to it. "

She put down the phone, laughing at his protests, and went to put on the kettle. She wandered over to the window and looked out towards Jack's house. She switched on the television after a minute, sat down, got up again to check the kettle. She made an exasperated noise when she realised she hadn't even lit the gas ring.

"Concentrate, Clare!" she told herself, lighting the gas, putting the kettle back on the ring. Jack's words had unsettled her more than she had realised. She stretched, took a deep breath, tried to let go of the edgy feeling that had crept up on her.

Back in the living-room she went over to the bookshelves and started rearranging the books. The kettle finally began to whistle on the hob. She removed it from the heat, reached for the tea-bags, changed her mind and took down the coffee instead. She rummaged in the fridge, wondering what she'd have for supper, realised she wasn't really hungry. She sat with her coffee and her book, one eye on the television, not really interested in either.

It was impossible to relax. Maybe she should have gone to Galway after all. She was used to being busy when she was at the cottage.

She found herself wondering for the first time, in spite of her conversation with Jack, whether she should be here at all. She felt that she would go mad very, very soon if she didn't find something to do.

The knock at the door startled her. Suddenly fearful that it might be Tony, she went to the window and peered out. The knock came again as she made out the outline of a bicycle parked inside the front gate. Kate! Thank God. She hurried to open the door.

"Come in, Kate! I'm delighted to see you! Come on in."

Kate smiled, relaxed visibly, came into the room. Clare closed the door quickly against the sharp breeze, taking Kate's coat and hanging it behind the door. She motioned Kate to one of the armchairs beside the fire, watching as she sat down tentatively. The ease of yesterday's lunch-time was gone.

"Would you like coffee? Or have you eaten?"

"I didn't bother cooking," Kate said. "Sometimes it seems like too much trouble when I'm on my own."

"I know," said Clare, struck by how different Kate seemed from the previous day.

"Is something bothering you, Kate? Or did you just call in for a chat?" She put her hand on Kate's arm and felt the slight trembling. "Do you mind me asking?"

"No, no. Is that coffee still going?"

"Sure," said Clare. She went back to the kitchen, glancing at Kate through the open doorway. The older woman was gazing into the fire and for a moment Clare was reminded of Jack. "Sugar, milk?"

Kate glanced up, seeming for a moment not to notice her. "Hmm? Oh, milk, no sugar. Thanks."

Clare brought over the coffee for Kate and a fresh mug for herself. She waited as Kate took the first few sips, wondering what had brought her a distance of several miles on an evening like this.

"I had to get out of the house," Kate said, as if Clare had spoken aloud. Then she paused, seeming preoccupied again.

"Did something happen, Kate?" Clare prompted.

"No, it was nothing like that, nothing happened. It

was just that my thoughts were driving me mad. I decided to cycle a mile or two and see if I could calm myself."

She paused, took another sip of coffee and looked across at Clare for a moment, as if weighing up whether to continue.

"I have to make a decision," she said. "Soon. And I'm not sure I'm brave enough to do it, I've let things lie for so long . . ."

She paused, looking around the room, her gaze resting on two of her paintings which Clare had bought last year.

The smaller canvas, showing two men carrying a curragh down to the water's edge, was one of her own favourites. She remembered the day she had started that, sitting in the sun with the slight breeze off the sea, and the salt scent, and the cries of the gulls. And the fishermen greeting her, highly amused that she should be doing a painting of them.

"I can't paint any more, Clare. You know the kind of things I love to do – paintings like those ones there. But I just can't do them any more. It's as if there's something churning inside me, and what comes out onto the canvas is different entirely to the images in my head. I don't know what's happening. It's all a bit frightening."

"Did that ever happen before?"

"No." A pause, then Kate looked startled. "Actually, it did," she said. "And I'd completely forgotten. It was a long time ago."

She said nothing more for a few minutes. Clare sat

holding the coffee mug, feet curled up under her in the big armchair, looking across at Kate, waiting.

"You know, I never saw the connection," Kate continued at last. "It was so long ago. But it happened, all right. At a time when I had another decision to make."

"And you could paint again after you made the decision?"

"Well, yes. I suppose I could. But for a long time I didn't really want to. It lost its meaning for me. Everything did."

It seemed as if she was going to go on, but then she sighed and remained silent.

"Would you like something to eat?" asked Clare after a while. "I'm beginning to feel hungry now – it must be nearly nine." A thought struck her. "Kate, why don't you stay tonight? It's very cold to be out on the bike and to be honest I'm going mad with just myself for company."

"Are you?" asked Kate, surprised. She was used to seeing Clare laughing and talking and full of plans, always in good humour.

"Yes," Clare said. "I couldn't settle to anything. I'd love you to stay, if you can."

"Well, the cats are fed, so they can manage without me for tonight – but are you sure? I must say the thought of cycling back in the cold doesn't appeal to me."

"Stay, in that case. You'd be doing me a favour."

Kate agreed, smiling, looking relieved, and together they went into the little galley kitchen. Clare opened some wine and put on water to boil for spaghetti while Kate prepared a salad. They chatted away while they cooked, relaxing again into the easy companionship of yesterday's lunchtime, their tension gone for the moment.

They set out the food on the big pine table in the living-room and Clare filled the glasses, the wine glowing a rich, deep colour in the soft light of the lamps.

Kate picked up her glass, smiling. "I think it was one of my better ideas to come here tonight."

"Absolutely!" Clare answered.

They talked easily as they finished the spaghetti and Clare went back to the kitchen for crackers and cheese.

"And are you really going to stay here for the whole summer, Clare?" Kate asked as Clare sat down again.

"That's the plan, anyway," Clare answered. "I'll have to see how it goes. I needed time out to think, and this seems like the best place to do it."

"As long as you don't find it too quiet," Kate said.

"I can always go back if I do," she said lightly, filling their glasses again. "Have you plans for the summer yourself?"

"I haven't really thought beyond Easter. Kevin is coming home then, with a friend – and my nephew Donal will be down with his two little boys. You've met Kevin, haven't you?"

Clare nodded. She had met Kate's son briefly, two summers ago, and had guessed immediately who he was. He had her curly black hair and blue eyes with their direct gaze. The resemblance ended there – he was as outgoing as Kate was private. A likeable guy, Clare remembered. About twenty-four or five.

"Yes, I met him," she replied now. "He's in the States now, isn't he?"

"That's right, New York. I'm dying to see him. Phone calls and letters are no substitute at all. Though in fairness to him he was better at writing than I expected."

"Is he coming for a holiday – or for good?"

"I don't think he knows himself. I'll have to wait and see."

The two women relaxed as the evening wore on, intimacy building between them as they finished their meal and the last of the wine. Clare suggested Irish Coffees to round off the evening.

"I don't usually!" Kate protested, not saying 'no', all the same. Her head was spinning slightly but she was enjoying herself too much to stop.

Clare came back from the kitchen about ten minutes later, balancing the two glasses with their careful blend of coffee and whiskey, topped off with cream.

"I could live on these if they weren't so lethal!" she said. Kate moved over to sit in one of the armchairs by the fire that crackled and flickered in the grate. Clare handed her a glass, placed her own on the hearth by the other armchair and added more turf to the fire.

Kate gave a deep sigh of contentment. Clare smiled at her and sat down, feeling a sense of wellbeing for the first time in ages. Relaxed from the wine and the chat, she felt ready to talk about anything, even Tony.

She was just about to say something when Kate spoke.

"I'd forgotten what it's like to really enjoy myself," she said. "To be able to talk to someone as a friend."

Clare hesitated, took the risk.

"But you have other friends, surely? I mean, you've always lived here . . ."

"No, not always. I was in England for years. And in a way, you know, I've never been sure I did the right thing in coming back here. I'm not sure who I did it for – myself, or . . . someone else. And in the end, coming back didn't really do much good for anybody."

Kate was beginning to ramble a bit, and Clare realised that she – in fact, both of them – were beginning to feel the combined effects of alcohol and tiredness.

"Is this anything to do with the decision you talked about?" Clare asked.

Kate continued as if she hadn't heard. "Did you ever feel, Clare, that you did something for the best of reasons, only in the end it didn't turn out like that? And you keep thinking that one day you'll wake up and it will all fall into place. Only it doesn't, and you realise that you have to do something about it. Or else it will be too late, and for the rest of your life you'll regret it."

Clare nodded. In a way, Kate could be talking about her.

"Am I making any sense, Clare? Sometimes I don't make sense even to myself . . ."

She sat looking into the fire, as if there were answers there.

"And now you have to decide – ?" Clare prompted.

"Now I have to decide whether to let things be, or do what maybe I should have done long ago. I tried leaving things alone and it didn't work. I feel I have no peace – I can't think, I can't paint. So I need to settle it all in my mind, one way or the other. I need to decide what I'm going to do."

She paused, reached to put more turf on the fire, looked again at Clare.

"I have a child." Another pause. "I have a child, Clare. A son."

Clare looked at her, puzzled. "I know that, Kate."

"No. Not Kevin. Another son."

"I didn't – "

"You didn't know, and he doesn't know himself. And that's what I have to decide, Clare. Whether or not I should tell him. And what will happen to everyone if I do."

Chapter Four

At breakfast next morning Kate was subdued and there was a slight awkwardness between herself and Clare as they made coffee, cut the brown bread, put out orange juice. Neither of them could face cereal and Clare was regretting the Irish Coffees – she really wasn't used to drinking so much. But, she reflected, it had been a wonderful evening to begin with and she felt closer to Kate. She just hoped Kate wasn't sorry now for confiding in her.

"Clare."

She looked across the table at Kate, who sat with her food untouched.

"Clare – about last night. I don't know what came over me. The wine, I suppose. And the Irish Coffee. I'm not much of a drinker. And I'm a bit embarrassed that I bothered you with all of that."

Clare reached across and touched Kate's hand.

"Kate, you know, don't you, that I wouldn't tell anyone? It's your own business, and it's for you to decide. I'll help you if I can at all, but I'll never mention it again unless you do."

Kate smiled, seemed to relax. "Yes, I know you won't tell anyone. It's just that, when something is bottled up inside you for so long, and then you finally say it . . . well, it makes it all the more real, somehow."

Clare nodded and Kate continued. "I've decided I'm going up to Dublin today. I'll stay with my sister Molly for a week or so – it might give me time to sort out a few things."

Clare laughed. "You're going up there to sort things out, I came down here. A bit like that Christy Moore song – what's it called?"

And Kate laughed with her, and again the tension was gone, and they made some attempt at breakfast. Afterwards they brought the dishes out to the little kitchen where they washed up together.

"I'd better get home and pack a few things," Kate said when they were finished. She took her coat from the hook on the back of the door, put it on, then came back over to Clare.

"Thank you," she said quietly. "Thanks for letting me talk about it."

She smiled, looking considerably calmer than when she arrived the previous evening. The two women hugged briefly and Kate, to Clare's surprise, kissed her on the cheek.

"I'll ring as soon as I get back," she promised.

Clare stood at the gate, feeling a sense of anticlimax, as she watched Kate begin cycling up the hill. The day stretched ahead of her with no plans at all and suddenly she felt at a loss again, with no definite purpose and nothing to occupy her. She decided to examine the garden and see if she could begin making plans for it.

Walking round to the back of the cottage, she leaned against the stone wall that separated the garden area from the paddock beyond. There was about half an acre of garden here, surrounding the cottage, most of it to the side and at the back, running away from the road. At the front were beds where roses had grown and would, she hoped, grow again. She wasn't sure what other sort of flowers she'd like – vaguely she thought of daffodils, irises on their long slender stems.

She wandered about, stopping here and there to take a closer look at some of the plants, reflecting on what Kate had told her.

Maybe most people have a secret somewhere along the way, she thought. Something they don't often bring into the light of day, something they've done, or maybe not done. Some time in their life when their courage failed them. It was true of Jack, it seemed. And Kate.

And, of course, it was true of herself. She put away that thought. She wasn't ready for it yet.

Instead she focused on the task in hand, running back in to search for a gardening book she remembered packing, returning with it and a spade. She spent most of the day digging, working hard to get the garden into some kind of shape. When the light went she put away the spade and went in to prepare a meal, well-satisfied with her work and needing nothing more from life than a hot bath and an early night.

She woke late next morning and had a long shower to ease away the slight twinges in her back.

Then she rang Albatross, checked that Niall was back, and arranged to meet him for dinner there that evening. Then she spent most of the day relaxing, pottering around the garden – no heavy digging this time – before having another shower and putting on her favourite ankle-length green velvet skirt and crocheted, soft-white top.

She stood back for a moment to examine her reflection in the small mirror in her bedroom.

Her long dark hair, captured in a gleaming French Plait, was tinged with auburn where the light from the bedroom lamp caught it. She turned on the brighter overhead light and carefully began to apply some make-up, keeping it subtle as usual, suddenly aware that she hadn't bothered with any at all in over a week. It was great to have the chance to dress up and go out on the town, she thought, putting on teardrop earrings and a matching emerald pendant her grandmother had left her.

She arrived at Albatross just after half-past-seven and paused for a moment in the doorway, looking quickly around the big, open room with its rough, white-painted walls festooned here and there with fishing nets, its blue-tiled floor and the stone fireplace in which a fire was already blazing. One or two of the early diners glanced at the tall, elegant young woman before returning to their meals.

She went through the restaurant, cheerfully greeting the young waiters and waitresses as she passed, hanging her cloak on one of the hooks near the cash-desk and pushing open the door to the kitchen.

Niall and Barry were both there, peering into a big pot which had steam rising from it. Niall stirred the pot, took a small spoon and tasted the soup, then nodded with satisfaction and was putting the lid back when he glanced up to see Clare standing by the door.

"My God, Clare, you look stunning!"

"Don't I always, Niall?" She opened her eyes wide and flashed him a smile, making a pretence at flirtation.

For a moment neither man said anything, each thinking that Clare Delaney really had no idea how attractive she looked.

Barry recovered first, grinning as he bowed low. "Good evening, Madame. Would Madame care to inspect the kitchen? Or perhaps Madame would care for a drink before her meal? I've reserved the best table . . ."

Now Clare and Niall were grinning too.

"Back off, Mr Murtagh," Niall said. "Madame is *my* date for tonight!"

Giving the soup a final stir and turning the heat down to leave it simmering, Niall removed his chef's apron and hung it behind the door, putting on the jacket he had left there. "You're on your own, Barry," he teased, knowing that Dave, the weekend chef, had just arrived.

He guided Clare from the kitchen through a door she wasn't familiar with, leading into the room where she had seen the decorators on her last visit. One of the waitresses, obviously sent by Barry, came through from the door to the hallway carrying two glasses of kir on a tray.

"Great, just what I need," Niall said.

Clare smiled, taking the glass from Niall, remembering his reaction when she had first introduced him to 'that funny French drink' all those years ago.

"You've come a long way, Niall," she said, half-joking.

"Haven't I just?" he said, taking her seriously. "And a lot of it is due to you, Clare. You know that."

He raised his glass towards her, and she touched hers to it gently.

"Don't give me a big head, Niall! You're the one who's had to work all the hours God sent. Now," she said briskly, changing tone as she looked around the room, "tell me about this new idea."

"Well, as you can see, we've a long way to go yet. The painting is finally finished, though, and we've got the new sash windows in. " He indicated four tall windows in the front wall. "And look here – "

He led her around the corner of the big L-shaped room and she gasped. It was beautiful. Oh, yes, there was a lot of work to be done yet, but the painting was finished, in soft cream and deep turquoise, there was a fire lighting in a fine mahogany fireplace halfway along the wall to her left, and a deep bay window in the rear wall looked out over a small garden with views of the sea in the distance.

"Niall, it's wonderful!"

"Well, it will be," he said. "There's still a lot to be

done, as you can see. The floor is sanded, but it hasn't been varnished yet, and I still have to find the right light-fittings."

They laughed as they glanced up at the bare bulbs dangling from the high ceilings and the bare wires hanging from the alcove walls, incongruous against the elegant paint-work and the fine plaster mouldings above them.

"A detail," he said. "The important things are here – the curtains are upstairs, ready for hanging, and most of the furniture has arrived – finally. It's in the store-room upstairs. Well, all except this."

He indicated the round mahogany table with its two Victorian chairs, placed cosily near the fire although the room was warm anyway from the radiators along the walls. The table was set with silver cutlery and crystal glasses, an ornate menu standing in the centre beside the small vase of fresh flowers.

Clare had assumed it was set up to suggest what the room would eventually look like but Niall was pulling out a chair with a flourish.

"Allow me," he said, and she realised for the first time that they were going to eat here and not in the main restaurant.

Niall moved around the room, turning off the harsh light directly over their table and lighting some tall lamps which stood near the fireplace.

"I just moved them in for tonight," he explained as he sat down. "I couldn't bear to eat with that glare overhead. And I can tell you what's on the menu if you can't see it – I wrote it myself today!"

"Thanks, Niall – I think I can manage!"

As Clare was looking at the menu the waitress came in again, bringing a bottle of Chateau Musar. Clare was delighted.

"Brilliant! You know I love it," she said, as Niall indicated to the waitress that Clare should taste it. She sniffed the heady bouquet in the large crystal glass, savouring it, going through the little ritual that had become a game with them.

"That's fine for me," she said. "So what are you having?" He grinned, took the bottle from the waitress and poured for both of them.

"Thanks, Maura. Now, I'm going to try the potato soup, followed by rack of lamb. You know how I like it cooked."

"I should, at this stage, Niall." Smiling, Maura turned to Clare. "Do you need another minute or two?"

"No, it's fine, Maura. I'll have the soup as well – and the beef casserole."

"You won't try the lamb?"

"No way, Niall. I was over at Jack's the other day, and he was busy with the lambing. I wouldn't have it on my conscience."

"Well, I guarantee they're not –"

"Don't even say it!"

"Well, what about the beef casserole?" he asked, reasonably enough.

"That's different. At least I don't eat veal and little woolly lambs."

He debated whether to tell her all the wool would be

49

removed, then, seeing her expression, thought better of it and changed the subject as Maura went away with the order.

"So, do you want to hear the plan?"

And he began to explain, as their meal arrived. They sat and ate, talking, laughing, discussing some of his ideas. The wine ran low in the bottle and sparkled in the glasses, and Clare realised that she was enjoying herself hugely, and she could see that Niall was, too.

He wanted something elegant, he said. The older restaurant with its pine tables, its white walls and blue floor had a Mediterranean feel to it, and was the perfect ambience for the style of food they served there, and for their 'Beginner's Luck' suppers, and for the 'Try It – You'll Like It' nights that Niall had introduced the summer before last. For these he chose a different country as his theme each week, and presented its food and its music and put posters of it all over the walls.

She had helped him with that, she remembered, writing to the national tourist agencies, getting posters for Spain, Mexico, Greece, Morocco . . .

But now Niall wanted something stylish as well.

"You're getting old," she teased, when he had finished explaining the concept.

"Maybe," he laughed. "But so are a lot of other people, and they'd welcome the chance to eat in a quieter place, with good crystal and silverware, and soft music – maybe classical, maybe live, there's room for a piano – and we'd have a more sophisticated range of food and wine. And maybe we could do weddings – it's big enough – "

"Niall, Albatross isn't the only restaurant around. People already have sophisticated places to choose from," she reminded him gently, reluctant to dampen his enthusiasm.

But Niall wasn't having a bit of it.

"Of course there are. But I *want* them to choose here. It'll be like having two restaurants really, and they can choose depending on their mood. The walls are good and thick, so any loud music won't carry over from Albatross, and here in Kingfisher it'll all be more refined, a little bit more sedate – "

"Kingfisher? It's a lovely name. I like it," she pronounced, noticing again the paint-work that she had taken to be turquoise.

It was indeed, she supposed, kingfisher in colour.

He noticed her glance. "You see that the chairs are covered in kingfisher tapestry? And the curtains – now, they're *really* beautiful. Cream and soft pink with a pattern of diving kingfishers on them."

Maura brought in their dessert – Baked Alaska – and as she moved from the light of the remaining overheads to the soft light of the lamps they watched, entranced, as the small blue-purple flames flared upwards from their plates. Maura smiled at them, enjoying *their* enjoyment, asked if they wanted coffee and went to get it when they both nodded.

"It's a lovely dessert, Niall. The whole meal was lovely."

He looked at his plate, frowning slightly.

"I have to say I'm never quite sure about Baked

Alaska myself, but it *looks* impressive and people seem to like it. They often ask for it, so I thought I'd try it on the menu tonight."

Clare took another spoonful and Niall tried his own just as Maura arrived back with coffee and two glasses – Armagnac for Niall and Bailey's for Clare.

"Good for you, Maura!" Niall said. "Busy out there?"

"The place is hopping, Niall, but we're managing fine. Only they all want the Baked Alaska. I hope we have enough of everything."

"We should have, the amount I paid yesterday for supplies! Call me if you need me."

"Be sure we will, Niall! You're getting off lightly tonight!"

He laughed. Maura and himself got on very well. She had been there with him since the very first night he opened.

They sat sipping their drinks, feeling lazy now and a bit tired. Niall suddenly moved forward, elbows on the table, hands cradling his glass, as a thought struck him.

"How long did you say you're staying for, Clare?"

She could see that he was remembering the suitcase, the piles of books all over her cottage living-room. She played for time.

"Why, Niall?"

"Well, it looks as if you'll be around for a while, and I'm going to need someone to organise Kingfisher, maybe help me run it – and Barry has his hands full – what d'you think?"

"It's a great idea, Niall. But I'm not really sure . . ."

"That you'll be here long enough?" he prompted.

"No, it's not that." She paused, took another sip from her glass. "I intend to be here quite a while. Right through the summer, in fact."

He waited. She glanced at him, trying to decide how much she would tell him now.

"Big decision?" he asked after a moment, when she still hadn't said anything.

"Big decision," she confirmed. "But an inevitable one really."

Maura came with more coffee, saw their empty glasses and brought in two bottles, Armagnac and Bailey's, which she placed discreetly beside them, sensing their mood. As she left the room Niall poured for both of them, and Clare, taking another sip, continued.

"You never actually met Tony, did you?"

Niall shook his head, then took a sip of his Armagnac. "No, if I remember rightly I was away the one time he came down last summer, and then when I stayed with you last November he was abroad."

"He does a lot of travelling. It's a very demanding job . . ."

Her voice trailed away, and Niall nodded but said nothing. Privately he thought that nothing he had heard about the man impressed him. He knew that Tony worked in the financial services sector and seemed, from what Clare let slip occasionally, to have plenty of money to spend. But on his terms. Niall knew that Clare had given up her favourite activities – swimming, horse-riding, even going to music sessions with friends –

because Tony preferred her to be around in case he was free to see her.

Niall had seen a photograph in Clare's apartment of an attractive, arrogant man who seemed altogether too sure of himself, and he had wondered what Clare saw in Tony. She didn't usually fall for men like that. And lately Niall had found himself becoming more and more concerned as he sensed a change in her. But, he had reminded himself, she was thirty-two years old and well capable of deciding what she wanted from her life. Even if what she wanted was someone like Tony.

And then she interrupted his thoughts in a quiet voice. "It's over, Niall. I've left him."

He looked at her again, noticing how vulnerable she suddenly seemed. Clare, who had struck him from their very first meeting as an independent woman, fun to be with, confident in a relaxed sort of way. Who could and would talk to anyone, and was usually cheerful and fairly sure of herself. Tony had done this to her, he thought, feeling an unexpected surge of anger.

"Good for you, Clare," he said. "What happened?"

"Oh, a lot of things." She paused, began again. "He had a lot going for him. He really had," she insisted, seeing the brief look of doubt on Niall's face. "I loved being with him, he was fun and he was witty and he told great stories. And he brought me to places I might never have seen otherwise."

She looked up, tears glittering in her eyes.

"I loved him, Niall, I really loved him, you know? And I could never understand what he saw in me."

Oh, Clare, he thought, but said nothing.

"And then – well, I just couldn't ignore what was going on any longer, even though I wanted to. Can you believe that – I wanted to?"

She was talking quietly again, almost to herself, tears beginning to course down her cheeks. And he had to strain to hear her, strain also to keep himself in the chair instead of going to her, putting his arms around her, holding her. He didn't think she'd want that, not now, just at this moment. She took out a tissue, dried her tears, looked at him again.

"I found him with someone else. A cliché, isn't it, a horrible cliché. I had the key to his apartment, and I went – he wasn't supposed to be there and I thought I'd surprise him, leave some champagne for when he came home – he loves champagne – only when I walked in, there he was. And he was . . ."

She shook her head, as if trying to escape an image she couldn't bear to see.

"He wasn't even sorry. If he'd been sorry, or even if he was angry, I could have forgiven that . . ."

Niall raised his eyebrows slightly, said nothing.

"But he was – he was so bloody *blasé* about the whole thing. *'Clare, what a surprise! I suppose I'd better introduce you –'* I didn't wait. Can you believe he *said* that?"

Oh, yes, thought Niall. Yes, I can believe it.

"And I was so upset, so humiliated. I don't know how I managed to drive home. I felt devastated. And angry, bloody angry."

She looked up at Niall again, her expression a

mixture of hurt and anger and something he couldn't quite name.

"I used to trust him. I *let* myself trust him. Fool that I was."

She looked down, fidgeting with the napkin, folding it in and out through her fingers, hesitating.

"Niall, the worst part, worse than anything – "

She stopped abruptly as Maura burst through the door, cheeks flushed, decorum gone.

"Niall, come quick, you're needed in the kitchen. There's been an accident!"

Chapter Five

Clare drove into Galway just before lunch-time the following Friday, uncertain for the first time ever that she wanted to be there, but quite certain, on the other hand, that she didn't want to stay alone in the cottage that day.

She had woken early in the morning with a pounding headache and a sense of dread that she couldn't quite explain for a moment. Then it came to her – Valentine's Day. A day which, just a month ago, she had hoped she would be spending with Tony in some romantic hide-away.

So much for that, she thought. So much for love, and trust, and all her foolish romantic notions. So much for men, and all that went with them.

She had got up and showered, went for a walk after a breakfast she didn't enjoy, and came back to the cottage at about eleven deciding that she really couldn't stay there all day or she'd just get more and more miserable.

She thought she might ring Ruth, arrange to meet her in Dublin or maybe somewhere en route, but dismissed that as a mad notion, knowing that Ruth would already have plans.

Nothing for it but to drive into Galway, and on her own. She wished Niall was here, but he was in Paris, probably strolling on the Champs Elysée at this very minute with Nicole Gautier.

She hardly noticed the journey into Galway, engrossed as she was in her thoughts. She wondered how young Jim, the trainee waiter, was recovering from the slight burn he got when, carried away by enthusiasm, he had tried setting the Baked Alaska alight, and had nearly set himself alight instead. Niall had been distraught, blaming himself for not being in the kitchen, though Barry and Dave told him it had all happened in a split second anyway. He swore he'd never again have Baked Alaska on the menu. He knew well, as she did, how very serious it could have been.

He had arrived back from the hospital late that night, dog-tired after staying there for hours with Jim. And that was when he told her that he was going to Dublin on Wednesday and flying out on Thursday to be with Nicole in Paris on Valentine's Night.

Clare remembered Nicole from her visit to Clifden last year – a lovely woman whom Niall had begun to mention more and more. Clare knew that Niall had kept in touch and had planned to visit her. But for Valentine's Night?

Clare wondered why she had felt so upset, hoped she

hadn't shown it. But Niall would hardly have noticed anyway in his exhausted state. And it wasn't as if she and Niall had felt anything in the way of romance for each other for a very long time, she reminded herself. Even then it had been fleeting, a brief summer interlude that had settled into a more steady, and permanent, friendship.

Snap out of it, she told herself as she reached the outskirts of the city. She owed Niall more than to begrudge him whatever happiness he could find, simply because she had expected him to be around at a difficult time. She knew he might even have stayed if she had asked, but she couldn't have done that. She would have to get through this on her own, even without his support.

But Galway, for once, was not a good idea. Everywhere she looked there were couples, walking hand in hand, laughing, along Shop Street or standing outside the jeweller's shops there, gazing at trays of engagement rings and Claddagh rings, heart-shaped love symbols just like the one Tony had given her, that she no longer wore.

A flower-shop she passed was crowded, and she noticed men, young and old, carrying elaborately-wrapped bouquets – some shyly, some with a panache born of practice. Like Tony, she thought bitterly. That would be a good word for him, *practised*. Practised at cheating, at using people –

She forced her thoughts away from him and decided to try out some of the new shops that had opened since she was here last. She ended up, over a period of several hours, spending money she couldn't really afford on clothes she didn't really want.

Finally realising how tired she was, she headed for her hotel, just off Eyre Square. Her spirits lifted slightly as she entered the foyer. She liked this hotel, had stayed in it once or twice before.

Once in her room, though, her mood changed again. What had she expected to do tonight? If she couldn't face Barry's suggestion of helping in Albatross for the evening, how had she thought she could cope with all the romantic couples here in Galway, and on her own?

Tired, she lay on the bed and, after a while, fell into a restless sleep.

She woke around eight o'clock feeling disoriented. She showered again, put on her dressing-gown and ordered dinner and a carafe of wine from room service.

Afterwards she took out her novel and tried for about half an hour to read, but found she couldn't concentrate. She put the book away and turned on the television with a swift prayer to whoever dictates such things that there would be something on apart from romantic films. It turned out to be a choice between *Love Story*, a documentary on chimpanzees, or *The Late Late Show*.

She settled for Gaybo, glad that there was a lively discussion in full swing. She drank the last of her wine and was doing fine until Gay handed out little bouquets and heart-shaped chocolates to every woman in the audience . . .

She switched off the TV and then the light, got into bed and sobbed into the pillow until finally, exhausted, she fell asleep.

The sun slanting through the window woke her just after nine the next morning. She got up and showered quickly, knowing what she had to face later in the day but determined, nevertheless, to make the most of her morning.

She decided to begin by enjoying her breakfast – she felt she had hardly tasted anything she'd eaten since the night with Niall – and she lingered for an hour or so, drinking several cups of coffee and finding that she was in much better form, as if the tears of last evening had helped purge something deep inside.

After breakfast, leaving her bag at reception and the Fiesta in the hotel carpark, she wondered back down Shop Street towards Market Street with its Saturday morning crowds and its little stalls piled high with all sorts of wonderful goods – knitwear, and home-made marmalade, and strange bread with strange-sounding names, and dozens of kinds of olives, and the Dutch cheese she loved, a type of Edam with cumin through it, that was made, she thought, somewhere near Tuam and brought in every week for the market.

She refused a sample of the cheese, laughing, saying she couldn't face it so soon after breakfast, buying a kilo of it nonetheless. She wandered back for some olives and some tomato bread, then started towards some of the other stalls to see what they had on offer.

She stopped at one stall selling 'antiques', entranced by a child's wooden sleigh, knowing no-one who could possibly use it. She wondered for a moment what it would be like to have children, seeing the stallholder's little girl huddled in beside him, hunched into her heavy anorak against the cold. The stall-holder was blowing on his hands, and Clare, in spite of her warm coat, began to feel the bite of the stiff breeze coming in from the Claddagh.

As she passed a stall selling knitwear she paused briefly to buy a soft, dark crimson hat that matched her coat. Putting it on, she pushed some stray strands of hair up into it and was immediately glad of its comforting warmth.

Nevertheless, she felt she had been out in the cold for long enough and she headed back again towards High Street and Kenny's Bookshop. She spent a wonderful hour there just browsing, loving the atmosphere of the place, enjoying the books and the paintings.

Finally, reluctantly, she left. She knew she couldn't postpone it any longer. She took a deep breath, braced herself against the wind, and turned in the direction of the Cathedral, and beyond it, Galway University Hospital.

* * *

She'd go out of her mind, Clare thought, if she didn't have something to distract her in the coming months. As she drove back from Galway late on Saturday afternoon she thought fleetingly of Niall's suggestion that she run

Kingfisher, but she dismissed that idea after a moment.

She wanted a project of her own, something that would absorb all her energies. It was all very well, she thought, giving up work for a year and taking time out down here, sorting herself out. The problem was that she had *too* much time now, and nothing to do except worry herself silly.

Back at the cottage she lit the fire and put on the kettle, peering out at the garden in the twilight, barely able to make out the shape of the outhouses and the trees on the hill beyond. She had great plans for it, but that certainly wasn't enough to keep her going.

She brought a mug of coffee to the table along with the delicacies she had bought at the market and sat eating, deep in thought, making plans. She wanted time to herself, wanted other people around too . . . tall order, she thought, as the telephone rang and she reached for it.

It was Ruth, and Clare was delighted to hear the cheerful "Hi, sis!" Suddenly she could think of no-one she wanted to talk to more.

"How're you doing, Clare? I was thinking about you last night. I rang, but there was no answer."

"I went into Galway. No, don't ask – I was on my own and it was desperate, a real bummer. Not the best idea I ever had – "

"Now, Clare, stop feeling sorry for yourself! You got rid of that fella, didn't you? That's the best idea you've had for a long time!"

Clare smiled. Ruth was always a great one for looking on the bright side of things. If the roof fell in she'd tell you the fresh air would do you good, and it was nice to have so much sun in the house.

"So how did the course go?" Clare asked. "You survived it, anyway!"

The family had been highly amused at Ruth's idea that she and Conor, her long-suffering fiance, should go on a self-build course in preparation for the time when they just might have enough money together to get married and think about building their own house.

"Don't remind me!" Ruth answered. "It was great fun, but you'd want to have seen the state of me. But I'd do it all over again – I'm just not sure Conor would!"

Clare could imagine poor old Conor, who barely knew which was the business end of a hammer, struggling to keep up with Ruth. They hadn't even found a site yet, but from the sound of things Ruth was all set to supervise the placing of every nail herself, if they ever did get as far as building. She was determined to learn the rudiments of it, and Conor, like it or not, was learning too. Trust Ruth to find someone who was lovely, and easy-going, and besotted enough to do anything for her!

They talked for about half-an-hour. Rather, Ruth talked, and Clare listened, enjoying her sister's blow-by-blow account of finding themselves with ten other would-be self builders in an old manor house in the Lake District, faced with the unexpected prospect of helping to convert some old byres and coach-houses to holiday apartments.

"Slave labour, that's what it was! The instructor told us the very best way to learn was to have to deal with difficult renovations instead of building from scratch. Renovations, my eye! We had to practically dismantle them stone by stone! And what I don't know now about plumbing, and mixing concrete, and installing windows – "

Clare listened, highly amused at the flow of anecdotes, knowing better than to try to get a word in once Ruth was into her stride.

"Is Patrick's Weekend still on? You can line up any jobs you have, and we'll have a go!"

Clare laughed. Any work needed on the cottage had long since been done, the easy way – by tradesmen who knew what they were at. She wasn't sure she'd rely on her younger sister on the strength of a two-week course, no matter how enthusiastic she was. They arranged that Ruth and Conor would come for a few days and Clare hung up in good humour, some of Ruth's cheerfulness having rubbed off on her.

She decided to go to bed early and banked up the fire for the night. Then she had a quick bath, putting lavender oil in the water for the sheer pleasure of its scent. She went to bed feeling relaxed, switched off the bedside lamp, and fell into a deep, untroubled sleep the minute her head touched the pillow.

She woke early next morning feeling refreshed and eager to get out into the garden. The weather was still cold but it was dry, so after a quick breakfast she put on a heavy Aran sweater, tucked her jeans into some wellingtons and was attacking some nettles with a rusty scythe when she glanced up to see Jack standing just outside the boundary wall, leaning on his bicycle.

He was smiling, and she wondered how long he'd been standing there watching her. "Are you coming in, Jack?" she asked.

"Looks like I'd better!" he responded, climbing carefully over the stone wall. He took the scythe from her and examined it.

"Who was it told you you could cut nettles with a rusty blade?"

"Ah, Jack, it's not *that* bad!"

"Bad enough, girl! And what d'you want doing it for, anyway? There's easier ways to spend your time." He stood looking at the nettles, rubbing his jaw with a rough hand. "I know a young lad who'd do them handy enough, and cheap. And he'd bring his own scythe, a proper one that you could cut with!" This last he said smiling, but with a sideways look at her, gauging her reaction, making sure he wasn't offending her.

It took Clare only a moment to decide.

"Would you mind asking him, Jack? Then I could concentrate on plants and things – though I don't know the first thing about them."

He nodded in sympathy and she remembered the geraniums she had given him last summer. They were dead in no time from lack of water, and he hadn't even seemed to notice.

"You need someone who knows about these things," he declared now. "Someone who'd enjoy helping you."

"It's a thought, Jack. I could do with some advice – but I wouldn't want anyone taking over – I just need someone who could put me on the right track."

Jack rubbed his jaw again, looking over towards the hill, back at the nettles, finally at Clare. "There's Kate. She could do it."

Clare looked back at him, surprised. She'd never heard him mention Kate before, and wondered how he'd know such a thing about her.

"I might ask her. It would be great if she could do it."

He nodded. "I'd better be off. I'll send the young fella, so?"

"If he'll come. What's his name, anyway?"

"Jody Kinsella. And he'll be happy to come."

Touching his cap to her, he climbed back over the wall, reached for his bike and began cycling away, not looking back.

Clare returned the scythe to the shed and leaned against the door, looking across to the outhouses and the big field beyond. Kate! She'd never have thought of her. She hadn't been particularly struck by Kate's own garden the one or two times she had visited. But Jack had seemed very sure. She must ask her, next time she saw her.

She hoped again that Kate would decide to stay for the summer. She'd be glad of her company and if she really did know about gardens and wanted to help, they could have great fun doing it together.

Clare moved from the shed doorway where she had been standing, musing. She crossed to the small courtyard that was bordered on two sides by outhouses, the cottage itself standing a little bit away, its back to the courtyard. It was wildly overgrown, but she saw how lovely it could be with a bit of work. As the sun slanted in from the open side she imagined sitting there, surrounded by heaps of pots filled with flowers, and maybe an old wheelbarrow with fuchsia growing in it, and lobelias trailing over the side. She could paint that old pump bright green, and clean up the outhouses, and –

She stopped, blinked, looked at the buildings again as if for the first time. She laughed out loud, said "No, Clare!" but she was running across, first into one of the buildings and then the other, noticing the size of them, the thickness of the walls.

Was it possible – ?

She ignored the piles of rubbish here and there, the dirt on the floor. That could all be cleaned up, sorted out. The roof seemed intact, she thought, looking up. And they were both wired for electricity, though she hadn't bothered replacing the bulbs – hardly able to contain her excitement, she ran inside to ring Niall and see what he thought of the idea. She needed a project, something to keep her busy, and she knew, she just *knew* that this would be perfect . . .

The phone was already ringing when she got there. It was Kate, asking her to dinner that evening. "I just got back late last night. I'd love to have a chat. And I need to pick your brains. Donal told me he wants to come down at Easter, himself and the twins. But he knows Kevin might be here, with his friend, so I haven't really the room to put them up, and he asked me to find someplace. It would have to be good for children, with a bit of space for them to run around – and Donal would probably prefer to be a bit out of the town. You'd imagine I'd know *somewhere*, wouldn't you? But I just can't think of anywhere, and I thought maybe you'd help me have a look –"

"Kate," Clare said, a huge grin of delight on her face, "I think I might know the very place."

Chapter Six

The next four weeks passed in a blur of activity, beginning with dinner at Kate's that evening. Clare talked non-stop over a meal of spaghetti bolognese and Chianti, hardly able to eat in her excitement as the ideas came to her. She could see it all and she loved what she saw. The outhouses converted to holiday apartments. Seats and a built-in barbecue in the courtyard. Maybe guests in the house – or maybe not. She'd see.

And the big, three-acre field – she'd find a use for that, too. She could extend the shed and use it as stabling, keep one or two horses in the field, offer horse-riding.

And a gypsy caravan – oh, she'd love one of those! She could imagine it sitting at the far end of the field, painted red and yellow and blue –

She paused for breath as Kate burst out laughing at her.

"So what do you think?" Clare asked, holding her breath as she waited for Kate's answer.

"I think it sounds great. Though I don't know why

you want to bring all that on yourself. There wouldn't be any money in it, you know, at least not for the first couple of years."

"I know. But it's not about money – not really. It's about – oh, I don't know. Creating something of my own. Having some kind of vision, seeing it take shape . . ."

Briefly Kate thought of her art, abandoned for the present.

"I understand that," she said.

She looked at her plate, took some spaghetti on the fork, twisting it round and round before looking up again. She could feel the flush of excitement in her cheeks as the idea struck her.

"I'll help you, Clare. If I can, that is. If there's anything you'd like me to do."

"That's brilliant, Kate! If you're sure? I didn't know if you'd be around – "

"I will, at least until the end of the summer."

Clare looked at her, sipped some wine, hesitated. "Have you . . ."

She paused, unsure, but Kate continued for her. "Decided? Let's say, I'm in the process of deciding. And I'm giving myself the summer to think about it, trying to make sure my decision is the right one. So I'll be around all right. And I'd love to be part of it all."

"Well, what I really need – along with everything else! – is some advice about the garden. Jack said you'd be the best person to ask, and – " She stopped as she saw Kate's surprised expression.

"He said that, did he? Well, I suppose I do know a bit

about gardening, but it's been a long time . . ." She thought for a moment, seemed to make her mind up. "Right, I'll have a go. *And* I'll paint your gypsy caravan for you – if you can find one!"

"I'll find one!" said Clare.

Right now, anything seemed possible.

* * *

When she called into Niall next day in his little apartment above Albatross she was still bubbling with enthusiasm, hardly waiting to sit down before launching into her plans. Niall, pouring coffee into the two mugs, looked doubtful.

"It will cost a fortune, Clare. And the work would be harder than you think. And the season is fairly short –"

"Niall Devlin!"

She frowned at him as she took the mug. Her tone was one she rarely used, but he knew from experience that she meant business.

"Niall, who was it that supported you when you had the daft notion of opening a restaurant and you hadn't two pennies to rub together? Who encouraged you, and told you you could do it, and helped you get the whole thing going, and believed in you even when *you* didn't believe in you?"

"My bank manager?" he teased, grinning in spite of himself.

"Thanks," she said dryly, grinning back at him. "But seriously, Niall, where's the problem? I thought it was a great idea."

"It's a terrific idea, Clare – but a lot of hard work, with no guarantee of success. Apartments aren't like restaurants, where there's some chance of customers nearly all year round. If you want something to keep you busy *and* make a few bob, why don't you come and work with me in Kingfisher?"

"Is *that* what this is about? I don't believe it, Niall!"

"Come on, Clare!" He smiled at her and she relaxed a little. "What d'you think I'm trying to do, sabotage you? I'm just trying to save you hassle, that's all."

"Sorry, Niall." She smiled back as a thought struck her. "Maybe I *want* the hassle! At least it will keep me from being bored . . ."

He got up, came around the table and kissed her cheek.

"I think you're cracked! But if that's what you want, I'll help in any way I can. Now, come on, I want to show you what we've done to Kingfisher."

Clare was just about to leave an hour later when Jim arrived, his arm still bandaged but looking relaxed and eager to get back to work.

"I'm never going near Baked Alaska again, though, Niall. Baked Catastrophe, they should call it!"

Niall and Clare glanced at each other. Jim had no idea just what a catastrophe it might have been.

"You're right, Jim. Steer well clear in future!" Niall said, trying to make a joke of it.

Clare glanced at him again, knowing how upset he was still. She decided a change of topic might help.

"D'you want to hear about my latest mad notion, Jim? Have you time?"

"You'll only need about three hours!" Niall said, rolling his eyes in mock horror at Jim as he sat down.

"I think it's a brilliant idea, Clare." Jim said much later, when Clare paused for breath.

Niall smiled, knowing that Clare could do no wrong as far as Jim was concerned. She had covered for him once when he wanted to see a football final that was on in the middle of his shift, and now, whether she wanted to build holiday apartments or sail the Atlantic, that was fine by him. "You should talk to my brother Eddie," Jim continued. "He's a builder, himself and his mate Seamus can build anything!"

Clare took Eddie's phone number and drove home singing along to the radio, feeling a surge of anticipation as the ideas flashed through her mind. She was halfway home before she remembered that she hadn't even asked Niall about his weekend in Paris. She stopped singing, exasperated with herself, hoping he wouldn't mind.

He didn't. Watching her go, he was delighted at the change in her. For the first time in a long while he saw the old Clare again, the exuberant, enthusiastic woman he'd known before she met Tony.

Clare got back to the cottage early and was busy in the little loft store-room when Kate called that afternoon. She opened the small window, giving it a good push because it was stuck through long disuse, and called down to Kate to let herself in, the door was on the latch.

She emerged a few minutes later, grubby but triumphant, clutching a large roll of dusty white paper.

"What's that you have, Clare? You look delighted with yourself!"

"Plans, Kate!"

"More plans?" asked Kate, raising her eyebrows.

"*Real* plans. Look, I'll show you!" She spread them out on the table in front of them, the architect's drawings she'd had done four years ago, when she had first thought of converting the outhouses.

"You always meant to do this!" Kate said wonderingly, gazing at the detailed designs in front of her.

"No, not really. Well, it was just a notion I had years ago, when I thought I might fix up the place for when friends came to visit. But there was plenty of room in the cottage, so I just concentrated on that." She laughed. "I'd nearly forgotten I had these, it's so long since I put them away. Saves me all the hassle of applying for planning permission all over again!"

They made coffee and brought it back to place it carefully beside the plans, still spread out on the table. Kate was entranced looking at them. She imagined she could see it all taking shape, the two apartments, a large one with two bedrooms and a big kitchen/lounge area ("That'll be for Donal," she thought, delighted) and the other with one bedroom and, again, a kitchen/lounge.

"I thought one could be for families," Clare explained, "and the smaller one would be just for couples."

"Hmm," said Kate, peering intently at the plans as she took a sip of her coffee. "It's a good idea, but a bit limiting. What if you have two families wanting to book at the same time? And will couples want to stay in a place that's overrun with kids?"

"God, will I ?" said Clare, looking a bit panicky. Kate laughed at her

"You'd better, if you're set on doing it! But I imagine you'll cope."

Clare looked doubtful for the first time, then she smiled.

"I'll do better than cope, Kate. If I'm doing this, I'm going to *enjoy* it!"

They finished the coffee, rolled up the plans and took them outside, relating what they had on paper to what they could see in front of them. They walked through the two big old buildings and the smaller one – at a slight distance beyond the courtyard – examining as they went, peering at the plans in the dim light of the open doorways before Clare ran back to get some light-bulbs from the cottage.

She balanced precariously on a small stool, holding a torch under her arm for light while she attempted to replace the bulbs. Kate stood anxiously beside her.

"At least let me hold the blessed torch. I can't bear to look at you!"

"No, I'm fine," Clare replied, apparently determined to do things the hard way.

"Ah, that's better," she said, hitting the switch and blinking as the three bare bulbs flooded the outhouse with light.

She heard a scurrying sound in one of the far corners and decided not to look. If there were rats, she didn't want to think about them. She glanced towards Kate, who didn't seem at all bothered – she just commented that Mishka was about to have kittens and this might be as good a time as any to think of having a cat around if Clare was interested.

"Why not?" said Clare. "I was thinking of getting a few animals anyway – maybe a goat or two and a couple of lambs and some rabbits . . ."

She was scrambling up the ladder to the loft as she spoke, and Kate urged her to concentrate on getting there safely, and never mind her animals.

"Come on up, Kate, I want you to see this. The view is fantastic!"

And Kate, though protesting, climbed nimbly up the ladder to join her at the little window high up in the gable wall, and stood looking out at the sea in the distance.

"It's really beautiful, isn't it? You can see right across the bay."

"It's lovely, isn't it?" Clare said. "I should have a few satisfied customers up here, anyway!"

"Yes," said Kate, looking around doubtfully. "You'll have to give them a bit more than a view, though."

They walked through the loft, examining it, treading gingerly on the floorboards.

"Look, this space here would make two bedrooms," Clare explained. "There'd be a proper staircase coming up, and a little bathroom – "

She was still talking as they climbed back down the ladder and moved towards the back of the outhouse, kicking straw and debris out of their way. They went through a doorway about halfway down that brought them into a dimly-lit area with a few cattle-stalls, and passed through another space beyond it leading to a small room with, to Kate's surprise, a fireplace at the far end.

"I know," said Clare, seeing her expression. "I think maybe it was living quarters for a workman at one stage. Or maybe even for a family who lived here, before the cottage itself was built. It's very old. I think it was the fireplace that first gave me the idea of converting the buildings." She paused, looked around. "Can't you just imagine it, Kate? A lovely big space with lots of little windows, just like the cottage, and the fireplace at the far end to make it cosy and give the room a sort of focus."

Kate looked around again, taking in the stone walls, the bare bulbs, the floor that was part mud, part concrete.

"Clare," she ventured, "who is actually going to *do* all the work?"

Clare looked at her. "But you said you'd help, Kate – I'm depending on you!"

"Yes, but – " Kate looked alarmed, and Clare laughed.

"Okay, I'm joking. I know you meant all the artistic bits, the finishing touches."

Kate seemed embarrassed but greatly relieved.

"I rang Jim Flaherty's brother Eddie, the builder" Clare continued. "He's going to come and have a look, and my sister Ruth is only dying to come down and tell us how to do everything, on the strength of a two-week building course she did."

She grinned as Kate raised her eyebrows. "I'd trust Eddie, I know him well. But are you sure – ?"

"About Ruth? Don't worry, I have no intention of letting her loose on her own! And if all else fails I'll try to get Coley to come and rescue me – you know him, he did the cottage for me."

"I thought he'd retired," Kate said.

"He has, more or less – but I'm hoping he'll come if I need him."

"And you really think you'll get it done in time? I know Eddie is good – but Easter is only seven or eight weeks away."

"I know, but if we get started fairly soon, and if Ruth and Conor and Dermot come for Paddy's Weekend, maybe we have a chance. I have a good feeling about this, Kate. I really believe it'll all work out."

And, almost like magic, it did. It just took a while.

Eddie and Seamus came, and spent ages looking around, and drank loads of cups of tea, and made suggestions, and took measurements, and came back with a quotation that gave Clare palpitations. She didn't sleep much that night as she went over and over figures in her head, telling herself it wasn't worth it, telling herself she had to do it, telling herself again it just wasn't worth it . . .

She rang Eddie early next morning to tell him she just didn't have that kind of money.

"No matter," Eddie said. "Have a think about it, anyway."

Clare hung up the phone, biting back tears, and sat going over the options again and again. She knew Ruth and Conor would be delighted to help. Well, Ruth would be delighted, and Conor would do it to please Ruth. And Dermot would come and bring some friends.

But what could they do, really, in a few days? It was all very well Ruth converting someone else's outhouses under professional guidance, but they couldn't go it alone, no matter how easy it might seem to Ruth. The place would collapse on someone, and Ruth would be visiting them in hospital telling them how great it was that they had the chance to stay in Galway a while longer, and it could have been far worse, at least they only broke one of their arms as well as the two legs.

And Clare would be paying compensation for the rest of her life because the insurance wouldn't cover amateur builders who hadn't a clue what they were doing . . .

No, she decided, she couldn't bear it. She'd never again get a night's sleep, worrying about it.

And then the phone rang and it was Jim Flaherty, telling her what he thought of his brother's bargain-basement price, and how he had got him to reduce it by several thousand pounds, and now Clare should ring him and get him to take a bit more off because he wasn't very busy anyway, and besides he'd made pucks of money over in England and he shouldn't be trying to con her. And Jim had threatened never to speak to Eddie again, never to so much as *look* at him, if he didn't do it for a decent price.

And Clare, laughing, but feeling a glimmer of hope, rang Eddie and negotiated as he had apparently expected her to do in the first place, and offered him some free labour in the shape of her sister and assorted male relatives and friends.

"God between us and all harm!" Eddie laughed. "I might charge you extra for that!"

But he brought the price down another bit, and it all began to seem possible again, and they agreed that he would start in two days' time.

Clare crossed her fingers and prepared to ring Anne, her bank manager, and throw herself on her mercy. She sat with pen and paper doing some final calculations, and as she reached for the phone it rang, and Niall was on the other end offering whatever financial support she might need.

"Clare? What do you think? Come on, say 'Yes'!"

She bit her lip. "Niall! God, you're a dote, you know that? But no – I couldn't."

"Why not, Clare? I told you I'd help, and believe me, I'd find it a hell of a lot easier to pay the builders than to heft lumps of concrete around!"

Clare had a sudden image of Niall in his chef's uniform, running up and down a ladder with a bucket of cement. She laughed, and he laughed with her, not sure exactly what was so funny but loving the sound. He must remember to tell her sometime how lovely her laugh was. He wondered if she knew, was sure she didn't.

"Well?" he prompted. "Come on, I need something to invest my money in, and a dream's as good as anything. Better than most things!"

"Not better than a nice healthy balance sheet," Clare laughed. "What would your accountant say?"

"Probably the same thing he'd have said to a young lad barely out of his training, with nothing much going for him but a vision of a restaurant, and a mad friend who believed in him!"

Clare felt sudden tears and quickly brushed at her eyes.

"I was going to ring Anne Maguire. I'm sure she'd give me a loan."

"I'm sure she would, too. Only the bank charges interest, and I wouldn't."

"If I accepted the money, Niall, it would have to be strictly a business arrangement, at commercial interest rates."

"In that case, you might as well go to the bank."

"Well, that's what I was saying."

"God Almighty, was there ever such a woman! Who ever said you had to be so bloody independent, Clare? Come on, if you're worried about my money, think of the phone bill! Say 'yes' and be done with it!"

Clare burst out laughing. Niall wouldn't go into liquidation over one local call.

"Okay, but –"

"Good. Talk to you tomorrow."

Clare sat for a long while after she hung up, tears in her eyes again, a smile on her face. It was going to happen, it was going to be great. As she put on the kettle she was singing, and she knew, she just knew, that she was doing exactly the right thing, that it would all work out wonderfully. And in the back of her mind she had a notion, though she wasn't sure why, that somehow this project of hers was going to change her life.

Chapter Seven

These early morning runs were the very best part of the day. Even in the biting wind of early March it was exhilarating to force the pace, breath coming fast as he struggled along the uphill path through the trees. One more mile and he would have done his quota for today. It was no hardship to him. He loved being out of doors, loved the space and the silence broken only by birdsong, the sense of having the whole world to himself.

As he passed the Rose Garden the illusion was shattered by the sight of another runner in the distance and the roar of a motorbike engine below on the Clontarf Road. He glanced in the direction of the road and the sea beyond, down to his left but invisible in the grey morning mist. He used to love the sea, had spent most of his free time as a teenager down on Dollymount or at Howth, watching the boats, loving the sounds and the smells. He really should start going to the beach again. It wasn't fair on the twins to keep refusing. Maybe Molly would come with them, make it easier for him. But, God, he hated the water now, really hated it.

Shivering as a sudden sharp breeze caught him, he flicked the dark hair back from his eyes, bent into the wind and turned towards the gate that would take him out of St Anne's Park.

"Donal, how's the form?" The other runner's words were nearly blown away as he passed.

He barely had time to greet Mick Flynn before he was gone, heading for the pathway that Donal had just left. He hadn't known Mick was into running. Didn't know much about Mick at all, he realised, though Mick was at St Cronin's nearly six months now. He'd have a chance to talk to him this evening, though God knows why he had agreed to go to the Abbey with the other teachers. He loved the theatre, had always loved it, but it brought back too many memories. When he went now, which wasn't often, he preferred to go alone.

Donal turned into his own road and noticed, as he passed McDermott's house two doors down, that Ursula's car was parked outside. He still felt slightly embarrassed around Ursula, avoiding her if he possibly could. She was his age or thereabouts, an attractive, intelligent woman, but he had no interest in her at all. It had nothing to do with her – he had no interest in any woman, didn't know if he ever would again.

He had gone to Ursula's office party with her at Christmas, not knowing any polite way of refusing the invitation, and it had been a disaster. She had been on edge, over-anxious to please him, while hinting to colleagues at a relationship they didn't have.

And Donal, who could hold the attention of a class of thirty teenagers with no problem, had been tongue-tied and unsure of himself, and though he tried his very best to make the evening enjoyable for Ursula, he had spent most of it wishing he was at home.

When they got to her house just after midnight he had refused her offer of coffee, and his excuse that he needed to get back to the twins was feeble. She knew well that Molly was with them, and Donal knew that she knew, and stumbled over some kind of apology which only added to their embarrassment.

He left her at her door and got back into his car to drive the twenty yards to his own house, feeling like a rat and vowing not to get involved with anyone again. It wasn't fair to them. He wasn't ready for another relationship, didn't think he ever would be. And now he seemed to spend most of his time avoiding Ursula when she visited her mother at the weekend, and avoiding her mother when she enquired whether he had anything planned, and did he know Ursula loved going to the cinema?

Sighing, he let himself in the door, cheering up immediately at the sight of Nuala supervising the twins at the breakfast table. It was still early, not yet half past seven, but then the little villains were always up early.

Nuala, thank God, had plenty of energy for them. She was a large, warm, loving woman in her early fifties who had moved from Sligo some twenty years ago when her mother died, and though she never married or had children of her own she was mad about them and was wonderful with the twins. And Donal, who had resisted the idea of a live-in housekeeper, feeling he couldn't bear to see any other woman in Jenny's kitchen, had given in finally to Molly. And when Nuala had arrived and enveloped the twins in a big hug, and the little boys who had been so shy and insecure since their mother died had laughed up at her and hugged her back, well, the decision was made.

And now, he thought, smiling across at her as he bent to drop a kiss on the top of each little dark curly head, he didn't know how they would ever have managed without her. The two boys beamed up at him, both talking at once, and he laughed and put his hands over his ears, promising them his full attention once he'd had a shower.

After breakfast Donal sat chatting to them, making plans for the day. He loved Saturdays, when he had the whole day to spend with them. Sundays often seemed rushed, preparing for the week ahead, but Saturdays were just for them. Well, except for nights like tonight, but that was unusual.

Nuala was washing the breakfast dishes at the sink. The dishwasher sat like an ornament to the right of the sink, because Nuala would never use it and wouldn't let him fill it either.

"I don't trust them things," she often said. "They'd break all the delph on you, and sure amn't I as fast doing them with my own two hands, the way God intended?"

Donal had given up arguing with her at this stage. Nuala had her own way of doing things, and seemed to enjoy being busy around the house, so he just left her to it. She consistently refused all his offers of help, sharing the attitudes of a generation older than herself about men and housework, and the inadvisability of any encounter between the two.

He should feel relieved, he thought. Instead, it made him feel slightly redundant in his own home, but at least it gave him the chance to concentrate on his work, and his children.

She turned from the sink now to ask, "What play is it you're going to see, Mr Mac?"

After three years she still refused to call him by his first name, though she mothered him nearly as much as she did the twins.

"It's called *The Plough And The Stars*, Nuala. Do you know it?"

Her face lit up. "Oh, I know that one all right." She frowned slightly. "It has a very sad ending though, hasn't it?"

"You're right, Nuala, it has."

He was mad, he thought, to be going to a play with a sad ending. He knew enough about sad endings to last a lifetime.

"Still," she said brightly after a moment, "it'll be grand for you to get out, and the boys will be delighted to see their granny."

Donal nodded. Molly was happy to look after them whenever he needed her, and on the rare occasions when he and Nuala were both out she came and stayed overnight.

"What are you doing yourself tonight, Nuala?"

He was never sure how much to ask, not wanting to intrude, but she seemed to welcome the interest.

"I'm meeting my cousin Cissie Daly – she's on her way back to London from Sligo. I'll have time for a chat with her before she has to go for the boat. It's years since I saw her last."

The twins were getting impatient at this stage, clamouring for his attention, so he turned back to them.

"What's it to be, lads? It's a bit cold for the Zoo yet. What about the model railway in Malahide? Or a film?"

Donal's mind wandered as he sat watching *The Lion King* with an enraptured little boy eating popcorn on either side of him. He remembered the first time he and Jenny had brought them to the cinema as little three-year-olds, and had to fight hard to shake off the memory for fear that he would start crying, as he still did from time to time, in the most awkward places.

He still flushed with embarrassment remembering the day, about a year after her death, when he was discussing one of Robert Herrick's poems with his Sixth Year students. Tears had come suddenly to his eyes as he read the lovely poem about another, long-ago Jenny, and he'd had to take out his handkerchief and mumble some excuse, and leave the classroom.

Now he forced his attention back to the film but there was no escape there. The Lion King was telling his son, Simba, that the stars were his dead ancestors, and Donal remembered that awful night of Jenny's funeral, when he found the twins crying at their bedroom window, hours after he had tucked them up for the night. They were trying to pick out the new star that was their mammy, because some well-meaning adult had told them that she'd be up there looking down on them.

His tears came in the darkness now, and he wished to God that he could get up and leave, and then he heard the slap of the seat on his left as Michael stood up to climb into Donal's lap and cuddle against his shoulder, wet tears running down the warm little face, and Donal had to forget his own sorrow yet again and concentrate on the little boy. On his other side he felt a hand slip into his and he pressed it gently, knowing that Luke would be struggling to keep a brave face.

They left the minute the credits started to roll and went straight to McDonald's, and as they ate their 'Happy Meal' the boys seemed in good enough form, playing with the little plastic toys that were just like the hundreds of other such little toys they had at home. They never threw anything out and wouldn't let Donal do it either, even toys that were broken beyond repair. He sometimes thought that they had already had so much loss in their young lives, they couldn't bear to lose even those useless little bits of plastic.

And Nuala, God bless her, seemed to understand, and though she made them keep the playroom tidy she turned a blind eye to the little pile of broken stuff that was kept on one of the high shelves.

"You're not eating your burger, Daddy."

Donal glanced down at the untouched food in front of him.

"I'm not really hungry, Luke. Are you two finished?"

"Finished, Daddy," they chorused. They hopped down from their seats, put the toys into their pockets and carefully placed the crumpled food wrappers in the bin. As they walked back to the carpark, one on either side of him, he marvelled at their resilience, at how quickly their mood could change. He wished it was as easy for him.

They called to collect Molly on the way home, and Donal, helping her into the front seat, felt a slight pang as he noticed how pale she looked. His mother was only in her late sixties, not old in this day and age, but she hadn't been well in the past few years and Donal wondered for a moment whether she was keeping anything from him. He'd talk to her when he got home tonight, though he knew she was unlikely to tell him if anything was wrong. Molly had always been very private about some things, a bit like his Aunt Kate.

And like himself, he realised, knowing how closely he guarded his feelings about Jenny. Even David Malone, his oldest friend and a teacher at the school with him, had given up any effort to get him to talk, knowing by now that it was futile and that Donal would talk, if he ever did, in his own time.

He brought his attention back to the conversation between Molly and the boys. She was really good with them, he thought. Between the three of them they had kept him going, even on the worst days when he had wanted to die, just to be with Jenny again. It was Molly who had told him, in that direct way of hers, "There are always at least two choices, love. You know that. And giving up on life is only one of them. You can give up, or you can go on. And maybe someday you can do even better than that."

So he had tried, tried hard, for her sake and for the boys. Often he felt he was just going through the motions. But from time to time he found himself laughing out loud, as he did now listening to Michael telling his granny a joke. And at such times the pain diminished, and he felt as if life without Jenny might almost be possible again.

He left Molly and the twins busy at the kitchen table doing a jigsaw and went upstairs to change. He knew he'd be in town too early, but he wanted time on his own before meeting the others, just to relax a bit.

"Cool, Daddy," said Michael, looking at Donal.

That was his latest word, he used it to describe everything. Molly laughed.

"If that's meant to be a compliment, he's right, love," she told Donal. She thought he looked better than he had for a long time. The casual jacket and trousers looked well on his tall frame, and his face had lost the haggard look, filled out slightly. It suited him.

"Those morning runs are worth it, you know. You look great!"

"Easy for you to say, Mam! You're not the one who's up at the crack of dawn."

"I'd be up like a flash, if I could look as fit as you!"

They laughed as he bent to kiss her cheek, and with a warning to the twins to be good for Granny, he left.

Molly was smiling as she got the boys ready for bed. Maybe things were finally beginning to get better for him. After all this time, she thought, he was due a bit of happiness.

Donal met the others in the foyer of the Abbey just before the play was due to start. They were a mixed bunch, all from St Cronin's, and he knew them well with the exception of Mick, who greeted him now like an old friend.

"The man himself! I was just talking about you, Donal! I thought I was the only eejit who'd be out running at that hour of the morning!"

Donal laughed, looking around the little group and joining in the banter. He was relieved to see David there, coming towards them with Rory, half-finished pints in their hands. Most of the others knew his situation and were very good to him but only David knew the ordeal it was for him to go out socially, even now, and he always found it easier when David was there.

He was wondering where Sarah, the young art teacher, was just as she came tearing through the door, dark red hair flowing richly over the deep blue of her satin cape. She stood gazing over the crowd trying to spot them, and Donal waved to her.

"God!" Mick said, never having seen Sarah in anything other than the long skirts and baggy shirts she wore for work. Dressed for the theatre she was stunning and he couldn't take his eyes off her.

"Forget it!" muttered Rory, draining the last of his pint. "She doesn't see anyone else when Donal's around!"

The bell rang before Donal could react and they moved through the inner door to take their seats.

"God, these bloody bells rule our lives," Rory muttered.

Donal glanced at him, wondering about the earlier remark. There was nothing at all between himself and Sarah, though they got on well and often enjoyed a laugh together in the staff-room. He put it out of his mind and sat waiting for the curtain to rise.

The play left Donal feeling unsettled. The production had been impressive, and he had tried to concentrate on the external elements – the acting, the scenery, the lighting – not letting the emotion of it touch him.

But it was no use. He remembered too well the first time he saw the play, with Jenny beside him, pregnant with the twins. The gunshots at the end had alarmed her and she put her hands protectively over her stomach, wondering if the babies had been frightened. And he, knowing her thoughts, had turned to her in the darkness and touched her gently, to reassure her.

Later in bed she had told him, as she lay curled against him, "When the shots rang out, a goose walked over my grave. I was afraid."

And he had held her close and kissed her, and whispered in her ear that he would never let anything happen to her. God, what a fool he'd been, so bloody sure of everything. When she had really needed him he was able to do nothing, nothing at all for her.

"What do you think, Donal? Mulligan's or O'Neill's?"

Rory had suggested going for a drink and they were standing outside the Abbey.

"Actually, Mick, I was thinking of heading home. I'm running again in the morning."

"So am I, but I never let it stop me yet!"

Sarah joined in, smiling at him.

"You have to come, Donal, or Rory will bore us all to death talking about the play. We need someone who can keep him in his place!"

They all laughed, Rory loudest of all.

"Oh, in that case I've no choice," Donal said, smiling back at her.

He ignored the look that flashed between Mick and Rory, and turned with them in the direction of Mulligan's in Poolbeg Street.

They were a lively bunch, he thought, listening as they bantered back and forth across the two little tables they had taken over at the back of the pub. Rory was indeed at his most opinionated, lubricated by several pints, and Donal enjoyed fielding some of his more outrageous statements. His heart wasn't really in it, though, and he had to force his attention back to the conversation from time to time.

David, across from him at the other table, noticed his mood and nodded imperceptibly towards the door. Donal, grateful for the support, gestured that he would leave in a few minutes. Then the conversation changed as the barman called 'Time' and Anna, Mick and Rory tried to persuade the others to join them in Leeson St. Rory was fairly drunk by now, and beyond taking 'No' for an answer.

"What about you, Donal? This other fella," He indicated David. "says he's a happily married man."

Rory's laugh had a bitter edge and Donal remembered the rumour that he was recently separated. "You've no excuse, though. Are you on?"

The pain was sharp, like a knife in his belly. Rory didn't notice even as the colour drained from Donal's face and David moved to his side. Rory was standing now, swaying slightly, but carrying on relentlessly.

"Come on, Sarah will come too. She'd give anything for a chance with you!"

David moved towards Rory as Sarah turned, eyes blazing.

"Would you get out of here, Rory, now!" she said, barely controlling her anger.

Mick and David each took him by the arm and led him out to the street in search of a taxi. Donal looked stunned, while Sarah, still flushed, said nothing. The other three, after a few words to him and a brief touch on the shoulder from Eilis who told them what she thought of Rory, went home, leaving the two of them there, sitting in silence.

Sarah was the first to speak.

"He's a fool, Donal. No real harm in him, but he never knows when to keep his mouth shut."

Donal looked at her. "Is it true?"

"What bit of it, exactly?"

"That you . . ."

"Oh, Donal!" She sounded exasperated rather than embarrassed. "Don't make me say it!"

"You know I like you, Sarah. We've always got on. But . . . well, what Rory suggested . . ."

Sarah picked up an empty glass, toyed with it, looking

at the dregs as they swirled round its base, forming a pattern. Her voice was low. "It could be true," she said.

She looked directly at him, clear blue eyes startling against the white of her skin. Her voice, too, was clear.

"We could give ourselves a chance, Donal. Who knows?"

"Sarah."

He took her hand impulsively, ignoring the barman who was now clearing the glasses with a slight clatter to hurry them up.

"Sarah. God, I'm sorry if I gave you the wrong impression." He paused, lips tight, brow slightly furrowed. "I'm very fond of you, Sarah. You're great fun, and witty, and you're so good with those kids, even the ones who don't know one end of a paint-brush from the other. You're really great. But . . ."

"Go to hell, Donal!" She snatched her hand away and his heart sank as he saw her flushed cheeks and the tears on her lashes.

"It's not you, Sarah. It's – no, wait!"

He stood to block her way as she snatched her cape and bag and brushed past him, crying openly now, going through the door that the barman, his face carefully blank, held open for her.

He followed slowly out, worried but knowing she wouldn't want him tearing after her, and bumped into David who was waiting for him at the door.

"She'll be okay," David said. "Her car's just around the corner, she said she'd go on her own."

He hadn't seen Donal look so upset for a long time.

"Come on. Back to my place for coffee." He ignored Donal's protests, telling him the house would be quiet, everyone would be in bed and it was obvious he needed to talk.

So they talked, long into the night. About Jenny, mainly. And about the future, which seemed to Donal to be like a high hill, which he had to climb with no map, a small child in each arm.

"It's awful, David. So bloody awful. Unfair. Isn't that really stupid, to expect things to be *fair?* But I never thought – and now – God, you can't imagine . . ."

The tears were running down his cheeks, and David sat, giving him space to talk it out, cry it out, if that was what he wanted. Donal never talked much at all about Jenny, keeping everything under careful control as if it was the only way he could hold himself together. The dam burst now as he held his head in his hands and sobbed, seeming unaware of David who stood behind him, a hand on his shoulder, as he let go some of the pain and hurt and his thoughts about God, or life, or whatever it was that had deprived him of Jenny.

Finally the sobbing stopped.

"Would you like a drink?" David asked quietly. "Or some more coffee? You could stay the night."

"Thanks, but I'll get back. A coffee would be good."

David made the coffee, brought it back to the table.

"Why now, Mac? Why is this all coming up now?"

"You mean, I should be over it?"

The flash of anger, so out of character, startled David.

"You know I don't mean that. It's just . . ."

"Sorry. I know. I never talk about her, do I?" He was silent for a moment, sipping the coffee. "I'm afraid to, Dave. Afraid . . . well, afraid of this, I suppose. Making a fool of myself. Crying like a child, for God's sake!"

"What's wrong with that?" David asked gently. "And as for making a fool of yourself . . ."

"It's her birthday next week. Did you know that?" Donal said, cutting across David as if he hadn't heard him. "She would have been thirty-seven. Two months younger than me. I always used to tease her, you remember? Telling her I that I was older, I knew better . . ."

His voice trailed away. Again David waited.

"Remember in college, before I met her? All I ever dreamed of was getting through the exams, taking a year out, heading off on the motorbike, just going, stopping when I wanted to stop, feeling the wind on my face, seeing what was out there."

David nodded, remembering.

"And then I met her, and the dream changed. She became all I wanted. And when she died, that was it. Part of me died with her."

David sat quietly, straining to hear the words, feeling almost as if he was eaves-dropping.

"You know, Dave, sometimes it takes everything I've got, just to get up in the morning." There were tears in Donal's eyes again as he looked up.

"God, I'm a wreck, David. I used to think I could cope with anything, but this . . . this is different from any bloody thing you could imagine. Sometimes, if it wasn't for the kids . . ." His voice trailed into silence.

"Donal."

He looked up, surprised at David's tone.

"We go back a long way, Donal. School, UCD, all that craic. I know you more than twenty years."

Donal nodded, waiting.

"And I know what she meant to you," David continued. "God, you only had to look at the two of you . . ."

He paused, caught by the anguish on Donal's face.

"And you're right, it's not fair. Only maybe fairness doesn't come into it. And maybe now . . . God, how can I put it? It's been nearly three years, Mac. That's a long time. Maybe it's time to . . ." He paused, rubbed his cheeks with the tips of his fingers, looked at Donal whose face had begun to flush.

"To move on? Is that what you mean? To forget her, as if . . . God Almighty, Dave. You, of all people!" He stopped suddenly, aware of what he had said, but too angry to take it back.

"Yes," David answered, anger written all over his face. His voice, like Donal's, was quiet, conscious of his family asleep upstairs, but he too was furious. "Yes, me, of all people. Because I lost her, too. No, wait!" he continued, as Donal made to interrupt. "I loved her, Donal, you know that. And when I couldn't have her, I blew it. You know all that. I'd never have told you only you came after me when I failed the exams, pushed me to know what the hell was going on, made me stop drinking myself stupid, helped me with the repeats."

Donal nodded.

"And do you remember what you said?"

"It was a long time ago, Dave."

"Yeah. But I still remember. You were sorry it happened. But it *had* happened, you couldn't change that. None of us could change it. And you said – and I remember I hated you for it, but you were right – you said I could let it destroy the rest of my life. Or I could pick myself up, try to move on. Remember?"

He looked at Donal, seeing that he did remember. "So I moved on, Donal. Because you were right, I had to. There was no other choice."

"But . . . you're happy with Sue?"

"Very happy. Happier than I ever expected. I wouldn't be without her . . ."

He stopped as he saw Donal's expression, the look of pain that flashed across his face.

"Sorry," David said. "But, if I *were* without her – if anything happened to her, or to me – we'd try to move on. We've talked about this. It wouldn't be easy, we know that. But for our own sake, and the kids . . . because what else can you do? Spend the rest of your life thinking about how it might have been?"

"That's how I see it, Dave."

"You're wrong, Mac. I'm sorry, but you're wrong. You only get one chance, you told me that yourself. It's not a rehearsal. That's what Jenny used to say, isn't it?"

He watched Donal carefully, afraid of hurting him, more afraid that Donal would close up again into that guarded space where it was almost impossible to reach him. Then, to his relief, he saw Donal nodding, the ghost of a smile on his face.

"You're right, Dave. That's what she used to say, all the time. Every time she took some crazy risk, every time we skipped lectures to head for the mountains on the bike. That's what she used to say. It was as if she couldn't get enough of life, as if . . ."

"As if she wanted to live every minute. I know. I watched her doing it," Dave said. "And it's what she'd want you to do, Mac, you know that."

"It's easy to say, Dave."

"I know. But look at the alternative."

They sat for what seemed like a long time, one at either side of the kitchen table, lost in their own thoughts.

"I'd better get back," Donal said finally. "David . . ."

"Mmm?"

"Thanks." He was smiling now, a bit ruefully, and David smiled back.

"For being a bastard?"

"For saying what you did. I know it wasn't easy."

"Easier than watching you waste your life."

"Dave?"

"Yeah?"

They spoke quietly now, exhausted.

"Have I made an awful balls of things? First Ursula, now Sarah. I made fools of them, and myself. I never meant to. I don't know, I must be giving out the wrong signals, or something – I mean, Sarah's about ten years younger than me!"

"No law against it. And I've seen the way she looks at you. You never noticed?"

"Never. If I had – what the hell do I do now?"

"Anything you like, as long as you start by going home, or bedding down here." He rubbed his eyes. "Sorry, Donal. I've had it. I'm shattered. D'you want to stay?"

"I'll go. And thanks again."

"It'll get better," David said at the door, touching Donal's shoulder.

It couldn't get worse, Donal thought as he drove along the Howth Road. And then he reflected that that wasn't really true. He had the twins, and Molly, and his work. He loved them all. And he had a good friend in David.

God knows, he was lost without Jenny and had never thought of looking for someone else, never saw Sarah in that way, and didn't now. He's have to talk to her, let her down gently.

But maybe Dave was right. He'd never forget Jenny. How could he do that? But Jenny had taught him to love. Jenny would want him to be happy. And in time, if he let himself . . .

Maybe, just maybe, there was someone else out there for him.

Chapter Eight

It was a kind of magic, Clare thought as she gazed around the little courtyard. You dreamed of something, worked for it and then there it was, just as you had imagined it.

"Does it pass?" Eddie asked as he came up beside her, smiling, enjoying the expression on her face.

"Pass? It's wonderful!" she said.

They had worked like slaves, himself and Seamus, spurred on by Kate who kept reminding them that her nephew would be the first guest so it had to be perfect.

"Oh, if it's only perfection you're after, that's no bother, Kate," Eddie said. "I was afraid you might be expecting the impossible!"

And now, with three weeks still to go 'til Easter, it very nearly *was* finished. They had cleared out the outhouses and knocked down walls and put in plumbing and wiring so that all the basic work was done on the three buildings. The largest of them – which Kate always thought of as Donal's – was nearly ready to be lived in.

"We'll be back in the morning to finish a few things," Eddie told her on the Friday of St Patrick's Weekend. "But you won't see us for a day or two after that. I haven't been inside a pub for a month!"

"No harm!" she laughed. "But maybe you're as well off out of it – my sister is coming down for the weekend to make sure you're doing everything right. She's an expert on building after a two-week course she did in England."

Eddie winked at Seamus.

"That's great, isn't it? Maybe we won't need to come back at all, so."

He headed towards the gate, saying, "C'mon, Seamus!" and was gone before Clare could open her mouth.

Ruth and Conor arrived about two hours later, while Clare was getting dinner ready. Ruth gave her a quick hug and disappeared with her bags into the small spare bedroom. She emerged about two minutes later wearing, to Clare's astonishment, a pair of bright red overalls that had clearly seen some use.

They were covered in hardened cement and splatters of green and yellow paint, and fitted her to perfection.

She stood for a moment, hands on hips, dark hair curling about her face, looking the essence of femininity in spite of the outfit. Clare could just imagine her on a building site – there wouldn't be a man there who could resist doing whatever she wanted.

Just like poor old Conor, she thought. Ruth dragged him outside before he even had a cup of tea, calling Clare to come and show them everything. Clare could only laugh and follow them out, telling herself dinner could wait another half-hour.

When she caught up with them Ruth was carefully picking her way towards the outhouses in the light from the kitchen window, warning Conor to be careful.

"Do you have a torch, Clare?" she asked.

"Better than that," Clare told her, stepping past and flicking on the big yard light Seamus had rigged up.

They crossed to the first outhouse and spent about twenty minutes there. Clare watched, highly amused, as they moved about carefully in the half-finished building, thumping walls, examining sockets, talking about trusses and joists and stud partitions as if they were born to it.

They were enjoying themselves hugely, and Clare was impressed in spite of herself. They had all the terminology, though she suspected they didn't know much more about actual building than she did herself, which was precisely nothing. Except that you put it up and hoped to God it stayed up.

Ruth was all set to get stuck in there and then, and it took all Clare's persuasive powers to get her to leave the place alone.

"You'll have Seamus and Eddie to deal with if you touch anything, don't say I didn't warn you!"

Ruth looked disappointed. "Well, maybe we'll just have a look at the plans, we might have some ideas."

"Why don't we eat first, and then I'll show them to you."

"Ah, come on, Clare, I'm dying to see them."

"Ruth, if I don't have something to eat very soon I swear I'm going to drop down dead!"

They took one look at Conor's face, decided he was probably right and headed for the kitchen to crack open some wine and finish preparing the meal.

They sat up late into the night, catching up on gossip, looking at the plans which Clare felt were emblazoned on her brain at this stage, and Ruth made some suggestions that Clare had to admit made sense. Then she got some paper and a pencil and started making sketches of alternative layouts until Clare, laughing, begged her to leave it until she could at least see the buildings in daylight.

Conor finally gave up the struggle to stay awake and went to bed, leaving Clare and Ruth comfortably curled up in the armchairs beside the fire, finishing the wine and looking as if they'd talk until morning.

Which they very nearly did, except that Ruth wanted to be fresh for the following day. She couldn't go to bed, though, until she'd asked Clare about Tony.

Clare didn't answer for a minute or two. She sat gazing into the fire, twisting her empty glass round and round in her hands, and then she sighed, and told her sister all that had happened.

And Ruth, who normally took everything so much in her stride, Ruth, who found the good in every situation, just looked at her with an expression that Clare had never seen on her before.

"I could kill him, Clare. I could strangle him. He had no right to do that to you."

In spite of her tears, Clare had to smile at her sister's ready, warm protectiveness. Ruth crossed over to her and sat on the side of her chair, arms around Clare, holding her older sister as Clare had often held her, and Clare let herself cry for the first time since coming back from Galway.

They sat like that in the half-dark of the flickering firelight for a long, long time, until finally the fire had burnt out and they roused themselves, and went to bed.

Ruth was already in the kitchen next morning, dressed again in the overalls, making coffee and warming the croissants they had brought, when Clare emerged bleary-eyed at the top of the stairs to the loft. Conor glanced up at her from where he sat at the pine table, newspaper in front of him, looking relaxed and rested.

"Mind your step," he warned. "You look like you're sleepwalking!"

"I very nearly am," Clare answered, her voice raw from tiredness. She made it to the table and Conor offered her the Weekend section of *The Irish Times* as Ruth put coffee and croissants on the table in front of them, beside the orange juice and Bewley's brown bread.

Clare gazed at the food, feeling better already, then glanced at Conor.

"Today's paper? Did you go into Clifden?"

"Two chances! I'm only out of the bed myself and I never go anywhere before breakfast if I can help it! Someone called Kate sent it over with the young lad."

"Jody?"

"Don't know. He's out there."

Conor nodded in the direction of the back of the cottage as he helped himself to a croissant, just as Ruth joined them at the table.

"He didn't say much," Conor added. "Just that he was doing some gardening for you. We thought you were expecting him."

"Sort of," said Clare. "He comes and goes. He's great, he cleared all the nettles from the back field and now he's taking the weeds from the courtyard and digging out the flower-beds."

"Maybe I could help him with those, start planting some shrubs and things," Ruth said, helping herself to some brown bread.

"That's Kate's department – we'll need you for the building," Clare said hastily, hoping Eddie would forgive her but remembering the havoc Ruth had created in their mother's garden during her mercifully short-lived horticultural phase.

"You're right," said Ruth, brightening up at the mention of building. "I'd prefer that, really. What time are they coming, anyway?"

"They didn't say. About eleven or twelve, I suppose."

"That's ridiculous, half the day will be gone."

"Ruth, it's St Patrick's Weekend. I'm lucky they're coming at all!"

Ruth ignored that and picked up the plans and Clare saw, to her horror, that there were fresh pencil-marks here and there.

"Maybe it's as well they're not here yet," Ruth said. "It'll give me a chance to show you a few ideas I have. I've been out there already – I'm up since eight."

Clare looked at Conor, hoping for support, but he was buried behind the newspaper. He knew from bitter experience what it was like to try and talk Ruth out of an idea once she got going. He'd let Clare deal with this one.

"Could I finish my breakfast first, then I might just be able to concentrate?" Clare asked, but it was already too late.

Ruth was in full flow, and in spite of herself Clare began to listen with interest.

"You know, it makes sense!" she said at last.

"Of course it makes sense," Ruth said. "Why wouldn't it? You'd be far better off finishing all three apartments now, when the groundwork is all done. What's the point in just doing two and leaving it?"

"Well there's the cost, for one thing – "

"It wouldn't cost much more, Clare, and we'll help with the work – won't we, Conor? And then you'd have the three buildings up and running, and if you broke through into the shed beside that one – " she paused to indicate the plans – "it would be big enough for a hostel, with six or eight beds, and you could use that small building, way over there, for couples."

"The old forge? I was going to use it as a studio, or something – *hostel???*" Clare's voice went up an octave as she took in what Ruth was suggesting.

"Hostel," she repeated firmly. "Well, why not? We

stayed in a brilliant place in West Cork, didn't we, Conor, and really it was just a converted outhouse too, with space for eight or ten people to sleep, and the showers and toilets in another building, and cooking facilities in the main house. And it was lovely, it had a great atmosphere. Come on, Clare," she said impatiently. "You've stayed in hostels!"

"A long time ago," she said, still looking doubtful.

Ruth took no notice. "Come on, it'll be great! And if the hostel didn't work out, you could use it as another apartment. We'll just have to figure out where to put the showers . . ."

"Maybe the builders could suggest something?" Conor asked innocently, winking at Clare.

"I won't tell you what they'll suggest," Clare said, as a dark blue van pulled into the yard and Eddie and Seamus got out.

What they might have suggested didn't really come into it, because Ruth was out introducing herself to Eddie before he could set foot inside the door, and she led him away by the arm in the direction of the outhouses, leaving Seamus to join the others for a cup of tea. And Ruth talked and talked until Eddie was beaten into submission and even began to believe that all these new ideas had been his in the first place.

"We're going to do *what?* asked Seamus, nearly choking on his tea as Eddie told him the revised plans about twenty minutes later.

Ruth sat there beaming, thrilled with herself. Clare and Conor cleared the dishes off the table, listening from the kitchen as Eddie overruled all Seamus's objections.

"That poor man doesn't know what hit him," Conor whispered.

"I know," said Clare, laughing softly. "He never really stood a chance."

They didn't stand a chance either, because Ruth came in to hurry them up, and drafted in young Jody to help as well, and they all worked harder than they knew they could, only stopping when Clare had dinner ready.

"Jasus, Eddie," Seamus muttered as they took their boots off at Ruth's instructions, before going into the cottage. "I don't know if I ever worked as hard in me whole feckin' life!"

Eddie grinned at him wearily. "Didn't you? What am I paying you for, so?"

"At least you let me stop to eat me sandwiches, not like Her Ladyship. She nearly fed them to me herself for fear I'd stop what I was doing and not get back to it in time!"

Eddie would have laughed, but he hadn't the energy.

They were all drinking tea and eating apple-tart, beginning to relax and chat a bit at last, when Kate arrived with some brown bread and fruitcake and a dozen bottles of beer.

"Mrs K!" exclaimed Eddie, eyeing the brown bottles with delight. "Where were you when we needed you?"

Kate sat down at the table and smiled easily at him. "Oh, if you don't need me now, that's fine. I'll just go away again." Smiling, she removed the beer from where she had left it on the table.

"Come on, Kate!" Eddie groaned. "We need something to keep up our strength. We thought we'd be doing the rounds by now, on the right side of a few pints!"

"You're better off!" said Kate, caustically. "How's it going, anyway?"

They told her the revised plans and she was careful to show no reaction, lest they realise just how much extra work they had let themselves in for.

"You know, it's my birthday in two weeks' time. You'll all come, won't you? We could have the party in one of the apartments." Ruth was innocence itself as she sat by the fire, taking a sip from her glass.

"But you can't!" Seamus said.

"They wouldn't be ready in time," Eddie added apologetically.

Ruth looked at him, all big blue eyes in an elfin face.

"God Almighty!" Clare thought, watching the eyelashes flutter. She was flirting with him right there in front of everyone. And, to no-one's surprise but Seamus's, it worked.

"Well, we'll do our best," Eddie said, looking doubtful.

"That's brilliant," Ruth said, giving him a huge smile. "I know you can do it!"

He smiled at her in spite of himself. Maybe she was right. It would be a great achievement to get it finished in time.

"Do you never get annoyed, Conor?" Clare asked later as they cleared up in the kitchen. Ruth, for once, had pleaded exhaustion and gone to bed early. "I mean, you have to admire her, but she manipulates all round her. Does it never drive you mad?"

"Only sometimes," he answered. "Mostly I think she's great and that I'm lucky to have her."

"You're right, she's great. But Eddie and Seamus will never talk to me again!"

They hardly had time to talk to anyone for the next two weeks, but to Clare's delight, and their own astonishment, it was all completed by Ruth's deadline.

They had worked right through St Patrick's Weekend and every day that followed, even getting their entire football team in for two days which made Clare panic even more about the cost, until the lads told her they were doing it for nothing, just so Seamus and Eddie could have a life again.

Jack called from time to time to see how the work was going.

"I'm afraid to say 'hello' to those lads for fear they'd try to recruit me." he said. "Do you know all the neighbours are going round by the back road, so as not to have to pass them?"

"Oh God, Jack, tell me you're joking!" she said, mortified, and he laughed and got back on his bike, leaving her none the wiser.

But they got it finished.

Ruth and Conor came down the weekend before Easter bringing Clare's brother Dermot and his friend Steve with them, and they painted the walls and finished the little kitchens, and built a wonderful playground behind the courtyard in a safe grassy spot away from the road.

They painted the doors and windows of each of the buildings in different colours which glowed against the fresh whitewash, and discussed names for them, and then Kate turned up with beautiful painted nameplates, *Ocean* for Donal's apartment with its rich blue paint-work, and *Saffron* for the deep yellow of the hostel, and *Wildwood* for the forge with its little stand of trees behind. And that was settled.

On Tuesday night they held Ruth's birthday party, only a day late, all of them exhausted but delighted with themselves. Clare took a few moments to wander around outside, examining the little courtyard with its tubs overflowing with flowers, just as she had imagined, and the apartments surrounding it, bright in the moonlight.

It was beautiful, all of it, beyond anything she could have hoped for. She felt as if she'd never stop smiling.

"We got it right!" she thought. "Absolutely right!"

Niall arrived as she stood in the open doorway looking at the crowd of people inside.

"You did it!" he said, giving her a kiss on the cheek.

"No," she said. "They did."

They were all there, Eddie and Seamus and the whole football team, young Jody and Jim trying to sneak some beer when no-one was looking, Ruth and Conor and Dermot and Steve.

The chat was lively as they grouped around the fireplace or in the little kitchen, laughing and joking, enjoying the recounting of all the difficulties, now that they had overcome them.

The glow from the lamps threw soft light all around the walls and terracotta floors, while the scent of fresh wood mingled with the lasagne and garlic bread, and the wine and beer were flowing, and Ruth was encouraging Eddie to dance as Conor got the music going, and Clare couldn't remember when she had last felt so happy.

She moved inside with Niall, arms around each other, smiling at everyone, pausing to set down the champagne he had brought.

She glanced back at the doorway to see Kate standing there, a look of wonder on her face. "It's perfect, Clare, absolutely perfect."

She came across to hug Clare. "I can hardly wait for Easter!"

Niall popped a champagne cork quietly and poured the bubbling, golden liquid. He handed a glass to each of them.

"To Easter!" he toasted.

"To Easter," Kate responded. "And your first guest!"

"Yes," said Clare, smiling at them both as she sipped the champagne.

"To my first guest!"

Chapter Nine

"Careful, Kate! I didn't know it was so heavy!"

Kate stood up, brushing back the hair that had pulled loose from the band at the nape of her neck, looking accusingly at the big wooden bench and then at Clare.

"You're sure you wouldn't just leave it where it was? It's grand there!"

"No, it's in the shade!" Clare puffed, grappling with it again.

"Can I give you a hand?" The voice was male, a warm, gravelly voice that Clare didn't recognise.

"Thank God, reinforcements!" Kate said, as they both turned towards the gate.

"You timed it well, Donal," she added, going over to give him a hug. "We never even heard you coming – we were busy."

"So I see," he answered, smiling at them, looking from Kate with her loose hair and mud-stained skirt to

Clare who brushed at her filthy jeans, suddenly self-conscious. Kate introduced them.

"My nephew, Donal McCarthy. And Donal, this is Clare Delaney."

"You're very welcome, Donal. "You don't mind if I don't shake hands?"

He laughed as she indicated her grimy hands, reached out his own anyway.

"A bit of dirt never did any harm," he said, and she found her hand clasped in his and blushed slightly, something she hadn't done in years. Kate hadn't said how good-looking he was, she thought, taking in the broad smile, the dark hair and deep-set blue eyes.

She wished she had put on something decent, then told herself not to be ridiculous as he let go of her hand and looked around.

"It looks really great," he commented, looking around the courtyard. "Did you –"

"Daddy, let us out. Hi, Aunty Kate!"

They turned towards the red Sierra parked just outside the gate, its two little occupants calling and waving through the open back window.

"I have them child-locked in. I suppose I've no choice but to release them!"

Kate laughed.

"I'll do it," she said, waving to the boys. She walked towards the car and was back in a moment with a child on either side of her.

"Say 'hello' to Clare, boys!"

They stood, obviously dying to run and have a look around.

"Clare, this is Luke, and this is Michael. Or is it the other way round?" she teased.

They howled in protest, laughing at her, insisting she knew which was which. They were shy with Clare for a moment as she bent down to their level to talk to them.

Then Luke found his courage again.

"Is this your house?"

"It is, and you're going to stay here for a few days, and I hope you have a great time! My brother made a playground over there, especially for you!"

"Cool! Come on, Mike, let's go!"

They ran off, scampering over the little wall, racing each other, Kate following behind them more sedately.

Donal looked anxiously after them.

"They'll be fine, safe as houses!" Clare said. "Now, would you like to see the apartment?"

"In a minute. I'll move the bench first. Where would you like it to go?"

"Over there, I think, beside the Stag's Horn tree."

"Fine. It'll only take a minute."

They walked towards the bench and Clare bent to lift one end.

"No, it's okay, I'll do it on my own," Donal said. "It's a bit heavy."

Clare looked at him, still holding one end of it.

"You'd find it easier on you own than with my help?" She sounded cross.

119

"Sorry." He looked uncomfortable. "I suppose I'm used to . . ." His voice trailed away.

"No, I'm sorry," she said, awkward now. "I grew up fighting my corner with a younger brother who thought he could do anything and I could do nothing, just because he was male! He's better now," she added quickly, looking towards the play area where the twins were obviously enjoying themselves.

Donal smiled, and she thought for a moment how it transformed his face, made him look younger.

"At least you had someone to fight with!" he answered. "I used to have to do everything on my own. It probably made me too independent. Jenny used to say –"

He stopped, smiled. "Sorry. Let's get this moved."

She was right, he thought a few moments later when they had the bench in position. It was the perfect place for it, under the Stag's Horn tree, shaded from the sun, within sight of the play area.

The sat watching the children for ten minutes or so, chatting, until Clare stood up.

"I'd better show you the apartment, so you can settle in and have something to eat."

They crossed the courtyard and Donal paused for a moment to look at the lettered sign.

"*Ocean*? It's a beautiful name for it."

Clare smiled. "Kate did the signs. She said she really didn't care what we called it, as long as we knew it was 'Donal's Place'. She had us all calling it that until last week!"

He laughed, following her through the blue door,

finding himself in a big, cosy room with soft white walls, a terracotta floor with rugs here and there, and a stone fireplace where there was already a fire lighting. He moved towards one of several seascapes on the walls, attracted by the bright splash of red against a blue sky.

"One of Kate's?" he asked, checking for the signature, admiring the powerful image of the red-sailed hookers on a choppy sea.

"They're all Kate's," Clare said, bending to put more turf on the fire. "Aren't they beautiful?"

"They are indeed. The whole place is beautiful. When Kate told me I'd be staying in a cow-shed, I must admit I was a bit worried –"

He broke off, laughing at Clare's expression.

"You'll be all right here, won't you?" she asked anxiously.

"I'm teasing, Clare. Of course I'll be all right – better than all right. It's perfect."

He found himself relaxing as he looked around. He would be comfortable here, he thought. In some ways – probably because of Kate's paintings – it felt like home.

"I'll go and get the bags," he said, but before he had a chance the boys burst through the door demanding food. Kate was just behind them.

"These fellas are always hungry!" Donal laughed.

"I expected that," said Kate, going down to the small kitchen area. "We've a stew ready for you, it only has to be heated up."

"I'll leave you to it, then," said Clare. "I'm just across in the cottage there if you need anything."

121

"Fine. I'll see you. And thanks."

"See you."

She left, not asking what he was thanking her for, knowing that it was to do, somehow, with feeling welcome here.

He was an attractive man, she thought. An interesting man. But there was a sadness about him. When they were sitting on the bench she had found herself wanting to touch his face, ease away those lines etched into it.

"Stop it!" she told herself firmly.

Men were definitely not on her agenda right now, and certainly not a man who, from what Kate had told her, was still in mourning for his wife.

She crossed to the old forge, the little building they now called *Wildwood*, with its lettered sign outside and its deep green paint-work mirroring the small grove of trees behind.

Going inside she had to admit that Ruth had been right – it was perfect as a little romantic hide-away.

She switched on the two lamps in the deep recesses of the windows and bent to put a match to the fire. Ruth and Conor were due in about an hour and, although the weather was warm for Easter, she wanted the little place to feel really cosy for them.

She climbed the steep stairs up to the loft bedroom and stood looking down over the banister to the fire that was taking hold in the big old fireplace.

The room looked perfect with its two deep armchairs beside the fireplace and the rug in shades of red and soft blues and greens lying on the wooden floor in front of it.

The scent of *YlangYlang* from the burners over the light-bulbs began to fill the air as she looked towards the bed, its red Mexican bedspread a warm splash of colour against the rough white wall.

This was her favourite apartment, and most of it had been Kate's doing. The *piece de resistance* was one of her paintings called *Longing*, very different in style from her usual land and seascapes. It showed a man and woman looking towards each other, their faces in shadow, fingertips barely touching.

It was, thought Clare, the most beautiful painting Kate had ever done, and she had been overwhelmed when Kate brought it to her as a housewarming gift for *Wildwood*. It hung in pride of place over the fire, and Clare felt she could stand all day in the little bedroom, just gazing down at it.

Instead, conscious of the time, she came downstairs again and went into the bathroom just behind the fireplace, where the store-room used to be, to check that everything was ready.

"You got it right!" A voice echoed her thoughts and she jumped. Ruth stood in the doorway.

"You brat," said Clare. "You frightened the life out of me!" She laughed, clutching her heart for effect.

"You never even heard me come in, you were so engrossed!" Ruth said. "Now, let me see everything!"

She exclaimed in delight over the white bathroom suite with the brass taps, the tiled terracotta floor half-covered by a deep green rug, the fluffy towels sitting on the little wicker stand.

"What's that for?" she asked, indicating the tall beeswax candle standing in a verdigris holder in the window recess.

"In case the overhead light is too bright," Clare said, grinning at her. "And there are some aromatherapy oils," she added, pointing to the tiny bottles on the ledge that was cut into the whitewashed wall two feet or so above the bath. "They were Kate's idea."

"Oh? And whose idea was this?" Ruth picked up the bottle of Armagnac that Clare had left sitting on the ledge along with two brandy snifters.

"Well, in case you couldn't find anything better to do!"

" Conor will love it," Ruth said, replacing the bottle.

"And you won't?" Clare asked, laughing.

"Okay," Ruth agreed. "Just for you, I'll force myself!"

Conor arrived in with the bags and Clare left them to it, saying she was going to have a bath herself, and an early night.

"Sure you won't come to Clifden with us? We're going to check out Kingfisher. I talked to Niall this morning, he said he has it up and running just in time!"

"Think I'll give it a miss, Ruth. I'm really shattered. Tell him I'll call in for lunch tomorrow, okay?"

She really was exhausted, Clare thought, as she ran the bath and added some lavender oil. The past few weeks had been exhilarating, but a huge strain.

She climbed into the bath, lying back in the scented water, closing her eyes. The lavender would have a calming effect, help her to relax. She'd had an uneasy feeling for the past hour or so, an anxiety she couldn't name.

"Stop being so stupid!" she told herself, shaking her head, dismissing the butterfly-feeling in her stomach.

A good night's sleep was all she needed.

She was sitting in her dressing-gown in front of the fire, a towel wrapped around her wet hair, when the phone rang.

"Are you all right, Clare?" Niall asked, his voice concerned. "I expected you in with the others."

"I'm fine, Niall. Just a bit tired. Old age catching up with me!"

"Must be running fast! But you're missing the craic – it's rocking in here!"

She could hear the noise in the background. "Sounds like a great night!"

"Could be. Sure you're okay?" He still seemed reluctant to finish the conversation.

"Certain," she answered. "It's just – "

"Just what?" he asked, quickly.

"Oh, just a weird feeling I have. I'm sort of on edge. I think an early night would be the best thing."

"Sure you won't come in, Clare? I'd go and get you, only I'm up to my eyes. But – "

"I'm fine – honestly. I'll be in tomorrow for lunch."

"If you're sure – " he said doubtfully.

"Absolutely!"

She forced herself to sound more positive than she felt. Maybe a milky drink would help, and then bed, definitely.

She was coming out of the kitchen when the front door opened. She glanced over, remembering she had left it on the latch, expecting to see Kate. She nearly dropped the mug with fright as Tony came in, closing the door against the darkness behind him.

"Hello, Clare."

He spoke softly but her heart began to pound.

He glanced around. "You're alone?"

She didn't answer. There was something strained about him, an impatience in the way he flipped back the blond hair out of his eyes. He needed a haircut, she thought, almost laughing at the absurdity of noticing that. She realised that she was fighting to keep the terror at bay.

He stood watching her from just inside the door. He was wearing his grey suit, the one she had helped him choose last October. A lifetime ago.

"What are you doing here, Tony?" she asked, trying to keep her voice calm, hoping he wouldn't notice the slight shake.

"I came to see you, Clare, what else? You wouldn't talk to me on the phone, wouldn't answer my letters. You gave me no choice. And it's a long bloody drive. The least you could do is spare me a few minutes – if it's not too much trouble."

He slurred the words slightly, and she realised, in panic, that he'd been drinking as well.

"Get out of here, Tony," she said, moving backwards, conscious of how vulnerable she felt in her dressing-gown, her wet hair wrapped loosely in the towel.

"Do you hear me?" she repeated. "I said get out, Tony. I don't want you here!"

She realised that he was between her and the front door, that the back door was locked and bolted.

"It won't take long, Clare, we just need to talk. Sit down."

She looked wildly back towards the kitchen. No escape there.

"I said, sit down!" His voice was quiet, menacing.

She stood, clutching her dressing-gown to her, her face drained of colour. The horror of their last night together was as vivid as a scar. She was afraid to go near him.

"Sit down, Clare," he repeated.

Still she hesitated, and he spoke again, his voice soft and cajoling now.

"Just for a few minutes. Come on, I promise I won't touch you."

He sat down in the nearest chair as she walked towards the table slowly, calculating her chances.

Okay," she said finally. "But only for a few minutes. And then I'll make coffee, if you want some."

She was moving casually as she spoke, down along the side of the table towards the chair opposite him, the one next to the door. She reached slowly for the chair, holding her breath. He sat watching as she positioned it and sat down, careful not to go too close to the table.

For a minute or two he said nothing while she sat across from him, holding his gaze as steadily as she could.

"I miss you, Clare," he said at last. "I want you to come back."

She flinched, quickly trying to hide her reaction.

"Well? Say something, for Christ's sake!"

She took a deep breath. "What can I say? It's over, Tony. You know that. It's finished."

"You don't mean that. I know you. I know what you want."

A spark of anger rushed through her, giving her courage. "What I want, Tony, is for you to get back into your car and get out of my life."

She was standing now, eyes blazing, edging towards the door. He moved fast, but she was faster, and the table blocked him as he reached for her.

"Stupid bitch!"

She ran through the doorway and into the darkness in a blind panic, heading towards the courtyard, stumbling as she rounded the gable wall of the cottage. Someone caught her as she fell, steadying her, holding on to her. Her heart was racing, she was afraid to look up until she heard Donal's voice.

"Clare?"

She couldn't answer for a moment, glancing back to where Tony had stopped a few yards away, his face an ugly mask of rage in the light from the window.

"What's going on, Clare?" Donal asked.

He moved slightly to stand between herself and Tony, never taking his eyes from him. Clare put up her hand, still trembling, to brush her hair back where it had come loose from the towel.

"I – nothing. Everything's fine now. Tony is just leaving."

He glared in her direction, muttered "Bitch!" again and headed for the car, looking back for a long moment before getting into it and driving away.

Clare couldn't stop trembling even when she was back inside, sitting at the fire, dressed in jeans now, cradling some brandy in a small glass.

"You're sure you don't want me to call the police?" Donal asked.

"No. No, there's no need. Really."

Donal looked doubtful. "He seemed dangerous."

"He . . . he's an ex-boyfriend."

"And that means he's not dangerous?"

Clare sighed, put down her glass, sat hunched into the chair with her arms wrapped tight around her.

"Not *very* dangerous."

"You can't know that!" Donal sounded sharper than he intended. "And you can't stay here on your own to-night. I'll get Kate to come across when I go back to the boys."

"No, I'll be fine."

"You're still shaking."

"I'll be fine, Donal," she repeated Her voice was louder now, as much for her own benefit as his. "I'll lock the door, he won't get in again. Anyway, I really don't think he'll be back tonight."

"What about your sister – she came today, didn't she? Has she gone out?"

"She'll be back later. But I don't want to worry her. I'll tell her in the morning."

"Are you sure – I'm sorry, it's none of my business, is it?"

"I didn't say that."

"You don't have to, I know it. Just promise you'll lock the door the minute I go."

She did and was immediately sorry she'd refused to let Kate come over. But this was something she had to get through on her own.

She put out most of the lights, leaving just a small lamp burning by the fireplace, and went to bed where she lay tossing and turning through the long night, unable to sleep for fear of the nightmares that were sure to come.

Chapter Ten

The pounding on the door dragged her from a fitful sleep. It was barely light, and she struggled out of the bed, her head heavy. She dressed quickly and went downstairs, hesitating as she reached the front door. She paused in the act of opening it and went to the window first to see if she could make out who it was in the dim morning light.

"Clare, answer me!"

Relief flooded through her as she recognised Niall's voice. She hurried to undo the bolt, finding that her hand was still shaky. "God, Niall, you frightened me."

"Sounds like I'm not the only one!" he said, coming in and standing just a few feet from her. "Why didn't you ring me last night? I'd have dealt with him!" His face was dark with anger.

"How did you know?"

"Kate rang me first thing this morning."

"She shouldn't have!"

"Come off it, Clare! They were worried about you!"

He crossed over to her, put his arms around her. "Do you know they stayed up half the night, watching to make sure he didn't come back?"

Clare moved back slightly so that she was looking up at him.

"They really shouldn't have – there was no need."

She moved over to one of the armchairs and Niall, with an exasperated sigh, sat down facing her.

"Clare, a man comes threatening you, chases you out of the house, calls you names, and you won't let them ring the police, or anyone else. What else were they to do? The way I see it, you were damn lucky they were here."

She sat looking at him, saying nothing, twisting a strand of hair round and round on her finger.

"They were worried," he repeated gently. "And they didn't want to tell Ruth, in case she'd be afraid to leave you on your own, so they rang me instead."

Clare gave a soft laugh. "She'll know something is up now, with all the banging!"

"I'll just tell her I was badly in need of a cup of coffee," he laughed. "Which I am. I don't suppose you've had breakfast?"

"You look exhausted," he said a few minutes later, as they sat at the table having something to eat.

"It wasn't a great night," she admitted. She got up, moved to the window where she stood, arms folded protectively around her. Her back was to him as she spoke.

"I didn't mean to drag anyone else into this, Niall.

It's something I have to do on my own. I didn't think he'd follow me down here, though."

"You told me you were finished with him." He was watching her carefully.

Clare nodded, still not looking at him.

"But there's more to it, isn't there?" His voice was gentle, but she turned around quickly, startled. "How did you – "

"You told me so yourself, remember? The night in Kingfisher when Jim got burned? You started to tell me something."

"I . . . yes." She looked across at him, her face vulnerable, frightened. Her voice shook when she spoke.

"I have to do this myself, Niall."

There were tears in her eyes and he went over and put his arms around her. She was shaking, her face in against his shoulder

"I'm afraid for you, Clare. If that bastard is threatening you, and if you won't let anyone help – "

"I just feel I have to do it on my own. Can you understand that?" She pulled away and sat down again.

"No, actually, I can't." He moved to sit opposite her. "I'm sorry, Clare. I've seen you do a lot of things, and I've seen you wanting to do them on your own. And I could understand most of them – but not this, Clare. This is something different. Something dangerous. Why did he come after you?"

"I'm not really sure. He said he wants me back."

"Funny way of showing it."

"I know. But there's something more to it, something he's not telling me."

"You're not going back to him."

"God, no."

"So why wouldn't you let them call the police last night?"

"It's a bit complicated. And I don't think he'd hurt me, not really. Besides . . ."

"Why take the risk?" he interrupted.

"I need to prove something to myself, Niall." She was twisting her hair again, round and round on her finger. "I need to prove to myself that I'm stronger than him. That I'm – well, not afraid of him. And I need to know I can have a life that has nothing at all to do with him."

"But you can do that anyway, can't you? What's stopping you?"

"I wish it was that simple, Niall." She sighed. "Make some more coffee, would you?"

"You won't drink it."

"I know. But it'll give me time to think."

He brought it back, filled another cup and set it in front of her.

"I really loved him, Niall." She sipped the coffee this time, looking away from him, talking almost to herself.

"He was different from anyone else I'd known, so sure of himself, sure of what he wanted. I fell for him, big-time. And we went out all the time – parties, Leeson Street – I never did any of that before."

"You never wanted to." His voice was soft.

She shook her head, impatiently. "I wanted to with him. And it was great, for a year or so, but then he started to change."

She looked at Niall, paused.

"What happened, Clare?" His voice was still soft, he held her hand, sat looking at her as she took a deep breath.

"A lot of things. Things I haven't talked about before. Even Ruth doesn't know the full story."

She took another deep breath.

"He started acting strangely. Nothing I could put my finger on. But all the signs were there. I suppose I just didn't want to see them. Tony loved excitement, lived for it. He got a real buzz out of everything. But nothing was ever enough for him – he always wanted more. He'd work all day, come home and two hours later he was ready to go out again. He never had enough."

She folded her arms tightly around her again, protecting herself.

"Damn him!" Her face was white, closed.

"What happened?" Niall prompted.

"He started using cocaine. God, I was such a fool! I didn't even notice at first, can you believe that? I just thought it was the buzz from work. He loved his job – he'd come home high as a kite sometimes, talking about deals he'd landed. But it got worse. He was high nearly all the time, edgy, tense, and finally I knew it wasn't just work, there was something else going on."

She hesitated, lifted a teaspoon, began tapping it idly on the table. Niall sat waiting, not saying anything. She took a deep breath and started again. "One night I came home early. He was already there, in the bedroom, and I wasn't sure for a minute what he was doing – he had a mirror lying flat on top of the bed, and there were little rows of white powder on it. And finally I realised what he was at. And he said it was nothing, everyone he knew snorted coke, I was boring."

Her voice was quiet, seeming to come from far away. Still she played with the teaspoon, and Niall sat, not saying a word.

"So I tried to ignore it. I still wanted him that much." She made a sound that might have been a laugh, shook her head. "But eventually I couldn't stand it, he was using it nearly all the time. We had a blazing row. And a few days later I found him with someone else, a woman who worked with him. He told me it meant nothing. I wanted to believe him. He promised it wouldn't happen again, promised he'd stop doing cocaine, promised the sun, moon and stars. And I believed him. Fool that I was."

"You had no reason not to. People can change – "

"You're right. I had no reason not to – for a while, anyway. Things settled down a bit, but then he started getting jumpy again. Getting at me for no reason. I suggested a holiday and he really freaked, asked me where the hell I thought he'd get the money."

"But he has a good job, hasn't he? I thought money wasn't a problem?"

"That's what I thought, too. But it was – a huge problem. Because a lot of it wasn't his – it belonged to his company."

"How did you find out?"

"It took a while. I was still living in cloud-cuckoo land then, thinking everything would be all right."

"But it wasn't?"

She shook her head, sighed. "He told me he was spending Christmas with his family, and I believed him. no reason not to. And he went abroad two days later – for work, he said – and the day before he was due back I went round to the apartment with some champagne. A sort of welcome home present."

"And he was with someone else."

She looked up, startled. "How do you know?"

"You told me, remember? The night in Kingfisher?"

"Yes, I'd forgotten. But what I *didn't* say – there was wine on the table, and glasses. And then I heard voices from the bedroom – the door was open. I should have gone. But no, like a fool I had to push open the door – otherwise I wouldn't have believed it."

She hesitated, bit her lip, looking so upset that Niall wanted to get up and hold her, but didn't dare move, didn't want to interrupt whatever she was about to tell him.

"I just stood there. I was stunned, I couldn't say anything, didn't know what to say. Because – " Again she paused, as if she found it impossible to go on.

"It was a man, Niall. He was in bed with a man. And when he saw me he wasn't even embarrassed, or sorry – he was *going* to introduce me . . ."

"I know." His voice was gentle. "You told me, though I didn't realise it was a man he was with."

"I turned and ran," Clare continued after a moment. "I can't even remember getting home."

"You didn't know he was gay,"

"No. No, not at all. And that's the worst of it, that I didn't realise . . . I feel so used, so very – used, and – well, stupid, I suppose. Why the *hell* couldn't he have told me?"

"I don't suppose he would."

"No. No, I suppose not. I don't even know how long it had been going on. Whether it was a one-night stand. Anything. You'd think I'd have known, wouldn't you? You'd think I'd have bloody-well known."

"Clare, I'm not sure how to put this, but . . . you already knew he'd been with someone else, right?"

"Right," she said cautiously.

"So you knew he could be unfaithful – "

"But with a *man!* Don't you see what that means? That he was capable of hiding so much from me. We never had a real relationship at all. I never knew him – I only thought I did."

She stopped, tears running down her cheeks now. She fumbled for a tissue, took the one Niall offered her.

"He came after me that night," she continued after a while. "About two hours later. I was in the apartment, crying my eyes out. Feeling like a complete fool. And like a fool I answered the door and he pushed his way in. He was like a lunatic. He'd been drinking, and I think he was on something, too. And he was ranting about how it was my fault, the whole mess, everything was my fault. I still didn't know what he was talking about,

I thought he meant – the guy. But then he said if I hadn't wanted so much, holidays and things, if I hadn't been on at him all the time . . ."

She paused, looked at Niall, pushed her hair back with both hands, sighed.

"Can you *believe* that?" she said again.

Niall was shaking his head. "Doesn't sound like you."

"Am I making sense?" she asked.

"Yes, but . . ."

"There's more – I'm coming to it. He was stealing money from his company."

"Fool. He didn't need to, did he? He was probably well paid. Not that that makes a difference."

"He was very well paid – but it seems it wasn't enough for him. And I never wanted any of those things, I never put pressure on him. I loved the excitement of it, weekends away, all of that – but I usually paid my way. And I certainly didn't ask for anything!"

"I know that, Clare."

"And if I'd known what he was up to – my God . . ."

She sat, staring at the table, rearranging cups and bread and cutlery, lost in her thoughts. A minute or two passed in silence.

"What happened, Clare?" he asked gently.

She didn't answer for a moment, and he thought she hadn't heard. Then she looked up at him, and her eyes were wide and filled with fear again. He reached across to take her hand, and found it was trembling.

"He hit me."

Niall swore.

"It doesn't sound much, does it, when you put it like that? He slapped me across the face, and I was terrified, I backed away, only it was towards the bedroom, and he came after me, and he pushed me, I was still backing away, I fell against the bed, and he looked so *different*, angry, but different, somehow – he was a stranger. And I was afraid – I was terrified that – "

She started to sob, taking big gulps of air, half-choking on the sobs, and Niall fumbled for another tissue and dabbed at her cheeks with great tenderness, until she took the tissue herself and blew her nose, and rubbed her eyes on the back of her hands, and took a deep breath.

"And then the phone rang in the living-room, it seemed to startle him as if someone had come in. And he called me a filthy name and just . . . *left*. As if nothing at all had happened. As if he hadn't terrified me."

She paused, exhausted, then suddenly laughed, a strange sound after what she had been saying.

"It was you phoning, you know. Just as he came at me. I found out from the machine next day. I never thanked you properly, did I?"

"Can I take it you'll never complain again about my midnight calls?" he asked lightly.

He smiled at her and she smiled back, feeling the tension drain away.

"No guarantees," she said. "How about a walk on the beach? I need to get out."

"I should be getting back, but – okay, what the hell. Let's go."

They walked along the water's edge for a while, not talking, Niall bending every now and then to skim stones across the rolling waves. Clare watched, her hair blowing in the soft breeze, feeling as if she had finally let go of a huge burden.

She turned and began jogging along the shoreline, loving the feel of the firm sand beneath her feet, hearing nothing but the lapping of the waves and the screech of the gulls until Niall ran up beside her.

"Race you!" he said.

They ran until they reached the nets and lobster-pots beside the upturned curraghs at the far end of the beach. Then they threw themselves down on the grassy bank, laughing and panting for breath, looking out at the horizon. Finally he broke the calm silence.

"Clare?"

"Mmm?" She plucked a piece of grass, began to chew it absently as she turned to look at him.

"There's more, isn't there?" he asked. "I get the feeling you haven't told me everything."

"God, Niall, I don't even want to think about this any more."

They sat watching a hooker in the far distance, black sails straining in the effort to get free of the waves.

"That's how I feel," she said suddenly. He turned towards her.

"Like that boat," she added. "I'm fine on the surface, getting along, going places, but underneath I'm being pulled back, pulled down."

"By what happened?"

"By my fear of what might happen." She sighed, kept watching the horizon as she spoke. "He wants me back. I know why. The company will be doing their end-of-year accounts – they'll find out the money is missing. He's covered his tracks well – I'm the only one who knows exactly what he's done."

"You'll have to tell them, Clare."

"No!" Her voice was sharp. She continued more softly after a few minutes, looking at him this time. "They'll find out eventually, Niall. But I can't tell them." Her voice was almost a whisper now. "I'm still afraid of him. And . . . another thing – "

She glanced down and when she looked at him again there was fear in her eyes.

"He phoned in February, just after I got here. He said I needed to take a HIV test."

Niall breathed in sharply. "And did you?"

"It was too soon. I went to the hospital, they said I'd have to wait three months before a test result would be accurate."

"So when can you go back?"

"This week. I'm dreading it."

"Would it help if I went with you? Or is this something else you want to do on your own?"

She bit her lip, then smiled up at him. "It would be a great help."

"You'll be fine. Clare."

"I can't be sure of that, Niall. But yes, probably. I hope."

Chapter Eleven

"This is what life is for!" Clare announced. She raised her glass towards the others as they smiled back at her.

"I'll drink to that!" Ruth said, raising her own glass and giving Conor a dirty look as he muttered that she'd drink to anything. "You know that's not true, so don't be showing me up in front of the visitors!"

"So who are the visitors, Ruth?" Kevin asked, laughing at her. "I've lived here since I was six years old!"

"But you hadn't the sense to stay!" she said.

"I had the sense to come back, hadn't I?" Kevin answered.

They laughed and joked as Kate sat beaming at them all. It was a long time since she'd felt so relaxed and happy, and Kingfisher was the perfect place to bring her family and friends together. They were all in great form, in holiday mood, although Ruth and Conor would have to return to Dublin tomorrow and Donal was going back on Thursday with the twins.

The big, round table at the back of the room was lively with conversation when Niall joined them.

"Everything okay?" he asked, sitting down at the chair they had left for him and loosening his tie slightly. "I thought I'd be out sooner, but it was crazy tonight!"

"Be grateful!" Donal said, smiling across at him. The two men had met several times over the Easter weekend and got on well together.

"Oh, I am. Believe me." Niall was delighted to see Donal having a night away from the twins. Kate had intended asking Nan Kinsella, Jody's eldest sister, to mind them for the evening. It must have worked out, Niall thought, as he turned to talk to Kevin.

"So, have you had a chance to settle in? Or are you still jet-lagged?"

"Getting over it, but Rick still doesn't know what hit him!"

"Oh, I'm starting to get used to it!" Rick laughed.

As he began an anecdote about their plane journey, managing to make a near-emergency sound funny, Clare found herself warming to him in spite of the way he looked. He can't help it, she thought, and anyway it was nothing to do with her. She'd never fall for that kind of man again – blond, very attractive, far too confident for his own good . . .

Her day-dreaming was interrupted by Ruth's whisper.

"Stop it, Clare. You're drooling!"

Clare shot her a look, and Ruth realised she was sailing close to the wind.

"Sorry," she said, turning her attention to Kevin as

Clare asked him how long he and Rick would be staying in Rossdarra.

"Or have you decided?" Kate, she noticed, seemed eager for the reply.

"I think my travelling is over for a while," Kevin said. "It was great while it lasted, but I'm glad to be back now. This place beats the socks off Manhattan. I'll be staying here a while, if Mam will let me . . ."

He smiled as Kate placed her hand on his. "Then I'll probably try for a job in Galway," he said. "Or even go back to college. I'm not too old . . ."

"You're never too old," Niall agreed. "And I'm sure I could find a job for you at weekends and holidays, if you want one. You worked in a restaurant in the States, didn't you?"

Kevin nodded. "Flaherty's. That's how I met Rick, he has shares in it."

Rick turned. "*Had* shares. They're on the market at the moment. Dentistry's enough to keep me going!"

"You're a dentist as well as running a restaurant?" Niall asked, surprised. "God bless your energy!"

"Oh, I wasn't really serious about it," Rick replied. "I was kind of a sleeping partner, just put up the stake and let them get on with it. I had two good guys running it. Shame one of them left!"

He grinned in Kevin's direction, and Clare found herself wondering briefly about them.

"Stop it!" she told herself silently. She couldn't be speculating about everyone she met. And it was nothing to do with her, anyway.

"You gave it an Irish name," she commented.

"My own name. My great-grandfather came from Connemara."

"Didn't everyone's?" asked Barry as he sat down to join them.

Niall grinned at Barry. "What do you want, anyway, Murtagh? Did you come out to see if I'd managed to poison anyone?"

"Actually, I came to ask if you enjoyed the meal, the atmosphere, the company – and to see if there was any drink going."

They laughed as Niall passed the bottle. "God, the things I have to do to keep good help these days!"

"And lucky you are to have me, Boss," said Barry as he helped himself to some wine.

"Go on," Niall said, laughing. "That last place you were in paid me large sums of money to take you away!"

"And you'd never have managed without me since. Not that I wouldn't leave like a shot, if I got a better offer!" He laughed, enjoying Niall's reaction

"Two chances, Barry. No-one else would have you!"

"What would you do, anyway, Barry?" Ruth asked. "If you had the chance?"

Barry hesitated, sipped the wine, seemed to take the question seriously.

"I love it here, you all know that. But sometimes – I don't know, I feel there's a big wide world out there that I haven't even started to see. And if I'm ever to do it, it'll have to be soon. I'll be thirty next year – "

"Oh yes, God forbid that you should wait 'til then! You can't *ever* do anything new once you turn thirty, can you, Clare?" Ruth said, laughing. "I'm for the high jump myself next year, I'd better start making plans . . ."

She laughed louder when she saw that Conor, as well as Niall, was now looking a bit alarmed.

"Oh, come on, we're only joking, aren't we, Barry? People talk about doing things all the time, without ever meaning it."

"No, I'm serious, Ruth, since you asked. Oh, don't worry, Niall, it's the long-range forecast I'm talking about here, and I wouldn't have said anything only Ruth brought it up – I don't intend to do anything at all for a year or two."

"And what then?" Niall asked quietly.

"Oh, I don't know, something mad, probably. I've always had the notion of going off on a cruise ship, something like that. Think of all the places you'd see, and you'd be travelling in style."

"You'd be stuck in the bowels of a ship working your back off, that's what you'd be doing," Kevin said. "You should go to Manhattan instead, that's where you'd really see the world!"

"I thought you hated it?" Conor said.

"Not at all. I loved it at the beginning, I just found it all a bit too much after a while. But at least I saw it!"

"That's what life is for," Ruth declared, her eyes shining as she took another sip of wine. "Seeing places, meeting people. Excitement, doing different things. I'd love to go travelling again . . ."

She sounded wistful now, and Clare, seeing Conor's horrified expression, jumped in quickly.

"Well, my travelling days are definitely over. I'm not planning on anything except holidays from now on!"

"I think that's what Ruth means, Clare," Kevin laughed. "You lose all your zest for life once you go past thirty!"

She could see he was joking, but wondered for a fleeting moment if it might be true.

"That's rubbish, and well you know it!" Kate broke in robustly. "It's only as you get older that you begin to get sense!"

"And then you haven't the energy to do anything with it!"

Suddenly they were all joining in the argument, laughing, shouting each other down. All except Donal and Rick, Clare noticed. Rick was smiling at them, amused by it all, but Donal was sitting quietly, looking pensive. Before she could say anything to him, Rick tapped his glass with a silver teaspoon, making a ringing sound that brought them all to order.

"Enough!" he said, laughing in Kevin's direction. "You thought Manhattan was noisy? I'm getting the next plane home for some peace and quiet!"

"We're not always like this!" Kate protested.

"No," Conor muttered quietly so Ruth wouldn't hear. "Usually they're much worse!"

"Well, you obviously enjoy travelling, Rick, or you wouldn't be here. Kevin tells me you're going on to London after a week or two."

"That's the plan. I've been meaning to do this for a long time – I never got the chance since I went back."

"Went back?" Clare asked.

"I came to England after I graduated College. I was supposed to go to France after a month or two, but I never got that far. I loved London, stayed nearly a year, would have stayed longer but Dad got ill and Mom needed me back home – there's only me, no brothers or sisters. I planned on coming back, but it didn't work out."

"Did you get a chance to see Ireland then?" Niall asked.

"No, I intended to, but I never got round to it."

He was lost in thought, seemed to forget he was speaking aloud. "There was a girl, you see . . ."

"Isn't there always?" Niall said.

Rick looked across, smiled.

"Yeah, I guess you're right. And now I'm here with a little time on my hands and some idea of looking her up – but I don't even know where to start. Or even if I should do it. She never answered my letters, probably came home to Ireland soon after I left, she was due back in College. And I don't even have a Dublin address for her, I just know that her folks used to live somewhere near that big park . . ." He paused, tapped his fingertips against the table. "Crazy, isn't it? Fifteen years is a long time – she's probably married by now, with a couple of kids."

"So how will you find her?" Conor asked. "I mean, there's phone books, electoral registers, but – "

"I tried the phone books for years – no luck. I got a

friend to send on the new ones every year, then he moved back to the States and I let it go. She's probably changed her name anyway, if she married."

He looked around the table, seeing the sympathetic expressions.

"So I guess my chances aren't good. But while I'm in London I'll maybe look up some of her old friends. Another long shot. It just seemed like a good idea to come over when Kevin said he was coming back home. And at least I'll finally get to see Ireland."

He had a warm smile, Clare noticed, that included all of them as he looked around the table.

"Well, you're starting in the best possible place," she said. "There's nowhere in the world like Connemara."

"True enough," Kevin said. "But you don't intend to stay here, do you, Clare? I mean, you've your life in Dublin."

Niall and Donal glanced at each other, noticing the look that passed across her face, both wishing that Kevin would leave it at that.

She gave a tight little laugh. "That's what I'm trying to get away from! Anyway, we'll see. There are worse places than this to live your life!"

"And better ones!" Ruth said. "I fancy somewhere in Provence myself!"

Conor's exclamation was interrupted by the scraping of a chair as Donal stood up abruptly. Clare was taken aback by his expression as he said he'd better get back to the twins, it wasn't fair on Nan. Kate started to say that Nan was a great girl and would manage them no bother.

Then she, too, saw Donal's face and hastily agreed that it was late and she'd go back with him.

"You stay on here," Kate said to Kevin, as he stood up. "I'm sure Clare will give you a lift, won't you, Clare?" she added, glancing across at her.

"No, it's fine, Mam," Kevin answered. "Rick is just about hanging in there as it is."

Not true, Niall thought, as he busied himself getting coats and undoing the bolt on the door. Rick, like all of them, had been enjoying himself until Donal got upset, whatever caused it. You only had to look at him, standing tensely just inside the door, to know that the man was just about holding himself together.

After a flurry of goodbyes Ruth sat back at the table, looking upset.

"So what did I say?" she asked them.

Clare put her arm lightly on her shoulder.

"Nothing you shouldn't have. But I think you touched a raw nerve, somehow."

Conor, sitting on her other side, took her hand.

"Maybe something to do with his wife? You weren't to know, Ruth, whatever it was."

Ruth sat biting her lip, not entirely convinced.

"I still wish I hadn't said it, whatever it was."

"Come on, Ruth," Barry said, trying to cajole her. "It's not the end of the world. How about another drink? Or a coffee?"

She smiled at him.

"Thanks, Barry, but actually I wouldn't mind getting home too. It was a great night – until I ruined it."

"Okay, Ruth, that's it," Clare said. "You're beginning to wallow a bit. Don't mind her, Niall, she loves being dramatic. And it *was* a great night. We'd better settle up and go home."

"You *are* joking," he said.

"No, there's a lot of us here, it's not fair – "

"To insist on paying, when I invited you," he laughed. "Now, go home, Clare Delaney, and no more of this nonsense. I've never had to throw anyone out yet, but . . ."

"No," Barry added. "He leaves the rough stuff to me, as well as nearly everything else."

"I'd be happy to throw you out too, Murtagh, if you don't shut up!"

Clare knew that the bantering was intended to lift their mood, bring back some of the good humour they had been in until Donal's departure. She was grateful to them, especially for Ruth's sake, and it worked. They were all laughing as they went out into the crisp night air and Niall closed the door behind them.

Clare woke early the next morning, anxious to make the most of Ruth and Conor's last day with her. They had planned a trip over to the National Park at Letterfrack, where they could have a walk and a picnic lunch before it was time for the two of them to set off for Dublin.

She drank some coffee and wandered outside into the courtyard, wondering if they were up yet, sure that they would be, but there was no sound as she neared the old forge. She decided not to disturb them, crossing instead to the little orchard at the back of the forge, to check if there were buds yet on her apple and plum-trees.

She knew nothing at all about fruit-trees, but Kate had assured her that they should do well in that spot, sheltered from the sea breezes.

She stood by the trees, lifting her head to feel the warm breeze that had begun to stir. She was warm enough in her jeans and sweater, with no need of the light denim jacket she was wearing.

That's the best of a late Easter, she thought. The weather is great, I can feel summer coming already.

She left the orchard and climbed the few steps to the big field, drawn by the sound of voices in the play area there. She sat on the stone wall, unwilling to intrude on Donal and the twins as they played. Then she realised it wasn't Donal at all, but Kevin.

The dark hair had misled her for a moment, but Kevin was slighter than Donal and not nearly as tall. As she watched he chased the twins towards the mock fortress and astonished them by climbing up the outside of it in a quick, easy scramble.

"Good on you, Uncle Kev!" one of them shouted.

"He's not our uncle, silly, he's our cousin."

That had to be Luke, Clare thought, smiling as Michael defended himself stoutly.

"Doesn't matter. He climbs better than you, anyway. And so do I."

"Do not!"

"Do too!"

And they were off, two little dark-haired figures in jeans and bright sweatshirts, scaling the side of the fortress, spurred on by the friendly rivalry Clare had noticed when she minded them on Saturday night.

She was just thinking about the abrupt end to last night's outing when Kevin saw her, waved, and jumped down to join her after declaring that the race to the top of the fort had ended in a draw.

"How's the head?" he asked. He seemed remarkably cheerful, she thought. Close up he couldn't be mistaken for Donal. The only feature they really had in common was the dark hair – they were entirely different in build. And Kevin was probably a bit better-looking than Donal, in a conventional way, she decided. Donal definitely looked more interesting – but if anyone felt like being interested, they'd have their work cut out for them, she thought.

"Oh, the head is grand, thanks, Kevin," she answered him. "I didn't drink that much. You're up early," she added.

"Jet-lag. My body doesn't seem to know what time it is! I thought I'd take the young fellas out, give Donal a bit of a chance to lie on."

He really is nice, Clare thought. It was obvious that, along with the curly dark hair and high cheekbones, he had inherited Kate's warm nature.

"How's Donal this morning?" she ventured.

Kevin grimaced. "God, he was a bit of a pain last night, wasn't he? Still, you can't blame him. I hope he didn't spoil things for everyone, though."

"Not at all, it was time we were going anyway. Ruth was feeling guilty, though. She knows she upset him somehow."

Kevin started to say something, then stopped, giving her a direct look. His eyes were a lovely shade of blue, she noticed. Lighter than Kate's, but just as compelling.

"Donal is on edge a lot of the time," he said. "It took an awful lot out of him when Jenny died. She was only twenty-nine – it happened two weeks before her birthday."

"Oh, God. And all that stupid talk last night about life ending at thirty."

"You weren't to know. Sure, I forgot myself. I only remembered when Ruth mentioned Provence, and he got up and left."

"Why did he – "

"That's where she died. An accident, while they were on their holidays." His voice was quiet as he glanced across at the twins.

Clare was spared any attempt at an answer as Donal himself came towards the play area from the other direction.

"Look, don't tell him I said anything, will you? It's not something he talks about. Maybe I shouldn't have told you, but . . ."

"It's all right, not a word."

Donal stopped for a moment with the twins before coming towards Clare and Kevin

He was wearing a black sweater over a pair of jeans and walked with an easy stride, looking relaxed. That colour suits him, Clare thought. And he looks in better form than last night.

His cheerful greeting confirmed that.

"I thought I'd take the boys riding today. Do you know of anywhere we can go?"

He walked with her to the cottage, where she had a list of local riding-stables. He stopped just inside the door, gazing around the room.

"It's beautiful, really lovely. You have very good taste."

"Thanks. It works, doesn't it? And Kate's paintings help a lot. I really love this place."

She was rummaging in the old roll-top desk in the corner as she spoke, and drew out the leaflet she was looking for.

"Do you want to ring a few places from here? I haven't got around to putting phones in the apartments yet."

"Thank God for that, I've been enjoying the peace and quiet!" He smiled as he took the leaflet from her.

"Would you like some coffee," she asked him on a sudden impulse. "I was just about to make some more, while I'm waiting for Ruth and Conor. And the boys will be fine with Kevin for another while, won't they?"

He paused, glanced down at the leaflet, looked back at her.

"Actually, I'd love some. If you don't mind."

"No bother. Make yourself comfortable while I put on the kettle. The phone's just there beside the armchair."

She could hear the sound of his voice as she busied herself making the coffee. A nice voice, she thought, deep and confident. A musical voice. She found herself wondering if he liked singing. It was something she really loved, something else she had let go since she met Tony, who used to find it irritating. Forget him, she told herself quickly, going back into the sitting-room with the tray.

Donal was sitting in the armchair, flicking through a magazine, looking relaxed, and she thought fleetingly that, in spite of last night, being here had done him good.

"Did you find anywhere?" she asked, as he stood up to take the tray from her and carry it to the table.

"All set up," he smiled. "They can take us in an hour, and they promised me two quiet little ponies for the boys and a decent horse for myself. Not that I'll get much chance at some real riding with the lads in tow!"

"You like horse-riding?"

"Love it. Or used to. I haven't done any in years, Jenny didn't – "

He broke off. "Sorry. There I go again. Do you ride yourself?"

"Not as much as I used to. My boyfriend hated horses. *Ex*-boyfriend," she added emphatically.

He nodded in sympathy. "Him?"

"Him. I never thanked you properly."

"No need. I'm just glad I was there."

"Not as glad as I was!"

They drank their coffee in silence for a few moments.

"You don't think he'll cause you any more hassle, Clare? I mean, you're out here on your own . . ."

"I'll be fine. Kate and Jack are great neighbours. And I'm going to get a dog."

He smiled at her across the table. "I suggest a Rottweiler."

She laughed. "I was thinking of a little collie, but maybe you're right!"

She poured some more coffee and they drank in companionable silence for a minute or two before Donal put down his cup, looked towards the window, ran his hand through his hair. He turned to look at her again.

"Clare, about last night . . ." He hesitated, seeming unsure of what to say next. "I over-reacted. I didn't mean to spoil the evening."

It was Clare's turn to hesitate. She was about to pass it off as she had done with Kevin, say something meaningless about how they were all set to leave anyway. And then he looked at her, and she found she couldn't be anything but honest in that direct gaze.

"I'm sure there was a good reason, Donal."

It was a gentle invitation, and he was about to respond, started to say something when the door opened.

"Whoops, sorry!" Ruth said, standing in the doorway, trying hard not to look surprised at the sight of them sitting across from each other, heads bowed slightly towards each other.

"I'll come back," she said quickly.

"It's okay, Ruth," Clare said as Donal got up and moved towards the door, but Ruth had already gone, crossing the little courtyard to disappear through the door of the old forge.

"Time I was going anyway, I'll be late for the horse-riding."

Clare returned his smile, wishing Ruth hadn't interrupted.

"Enjoy it," she said. "Wouldn't I love to be doing that!"

"Well, why don't you?"

"Laziness, I suppose. I'm out of practice."

He smiled again and began to leave, pausing when he was halfway through the door. He turned back to look at her, his hand on the doorknob.

"I was thinking of going for a ride on the beach early in the morning. I don't have to leave for Dublin 'til after lunch."

"Sounds lovely."

"Why not come along? If you'd like to . . ." He waited.

Her heart jumped a little, taking her by surprise.

"I'd love to! I haven't done anything like that for years! But – you're sure you wouldn't prefer to go on your own?"

"I'm sure. Would eight be too early?"

"It'd be perfect." She was smiling as she closed the door, ran upstairs to see if by any chance she had brought her riding-boots.

"You're in great form!" Conor commented as they walked along the trail at the National Park. The day was perfect, warm and bright with just a few clouds here and there.

"Why wouldn't I be?" Clare asked. "I'm in the best place in the whole world, and the company is great if you don't count Ruth . . ."

"Always the bitter word," Ruth said, smiling as she linked her arm through Conor's.

"Oh, I can be much worse than that!" Clare grinned. "But seriously, you know I really think I'm going to make a go of this holiday-home thing."

"Hmm. They won't all be like Donal," Conor said.

"No. But with any luck most of them will be okay."

"Speaking of Donal," Ruth said, looking sideways at her. "You two looked very cosy when I burst in on you."

"Now stop it, Ruth. We were just talking!"

"Did he say anything about last night?"

"He didn't get a chance, did he?"

"Point taken."

They walked in silence for a few minutes, following the path where it led between the trees, being careful not to slip on the moss beneath them.

"He *is* lovely, though, isn't he?" Ruth continued. "I mean, he tells great stories, and he's got a great sense of humour, once he gets going. Pity he's so moody."

"Leave it, Ruth, will you?"

"Okay." She managed to stay silent for half a minute. "But d'you think you'll be seeing him again? Has he said anything about coming back?"

She was impossible, Clare thought. She'd have her married off to him before she could blink. She decided not to answer, then changed her mind, grinning in devilment.

"Actually, we're going riding on the beach first thing tomorrow."

Laughing, she sprinted off up the path with Ruth in her wake, while Conor trailed behind with the picnic bags.

"Food always tastes better outside," he said later, as they finished off the last of the cheese and began packing what was left of the picnic.

"I know. Wish we didn't have to go back," Ruth said. "Imagine Dublin after all this!"

"You'll be itching to get there by the time you hit Kinnegad," Clare said. "I know you!"

"I might, if there wasn't work to face into tomorrow!" Ruth leaned back, head back, resting her arms on the ground behind her, taking deep breaths. "I love the air here. The smell of the trees. And that mountain – what's it called again?"

"Diamond Hill. I climbed it once with Niall," Clare answered.

"Maybe we'll do that next time. What d'you think, Conor? We'll need to come back soon to keep an eye on her."

Clare laughed. "Come on. We'd better go if you want to get on the road."

Reluctantly they stood up, packed the remains of the picnic into the two bags and went back to where they had left the car.

She'd miss them, Clare thought, as she bolted the cottage door late that night. The little forge, its lights quenched, was invisible in the greater darkness of the orchard beyond. She looked towards Donal's place and found comfort in the glow from the lamps burning there. She went to bed early but found it hard to sleep, as excited as a child at the thought of the morning.

Chapter Twelve

All she could hear was the pounding of hooves on firm sand, louder than the crash of the waves and the cry of the gulls. She could smell the salt air, the sweat rising from the horses, the rich tang of leather, turf-smoke on the wind from an early fire in one of the small cottages near Rossdarra Strand.

She had forgotten the sheer joy of it, the exhilaration of galloping, the feel of the wind in her hair and on her face as she sped along the beach, reins firm in her hand, loving the power and motion of the horse beneath her.

Donal, two lengths ahead, slowed to a canter, finally reining in as he reached the rocks near the far end of the beach. She drew up beside him and they sat looking out at the sea, not talking. The horses snorted quietly, still breathing hard but anxious to go again. The big bay tossed his head and Clare reached forward to stroke his neck, quieting him.

"You're good," said Donal. "Very good."

"Thanks," she answered. "You too, I thought I'd never keep up with you!"

"I've had a lot of practice. I used to go to Phoenix Park every week, and out around Enniskerry in the summer. And I worked in some stables for a while just before I went to college."

He reached forward, stroking his horse's neck, then turned to her. "What about you? Where did you learn?"

"I stayed with my Aunt Ginnie often, in the summers. She has a little place in Wicklow, and her friend has horses near there. And you won't believe it, I went to Enniskerry too." She laughed. "But only once, the first time I ever went riding. The blasted animal had a mind of his own and he tore off in gallop with me hanging on for dear life. I hadn't a hope of stopping him. We led the field, even the instructor couldn't keep up with us. And of course I fell off."

"You must have been terrified." He looked at her sympathetically.

"Actually, I wasn't. I loved it. I know, it sounds mad, doesn't it? But I can still feel the thrill of it, the excitement. It didn't matter that I was going to fall off, I didn't care. It was worth it for the thrill of it, the speed, and the sun on my back and the mountains all around me. I didn't have time to worry. I felt so . . . so *alive*." She laughed again. "For a minute or two, anyway. That's when I fell off. I was seeing double by the time they scraped me up off the ground and put me back on the horse."

He was laughing with her now. "They say that's the best thing to do."

"Of course they do, they've a business to run! Where

would they be if everyone was turned off on the first go? Anyway, you're in such a state when you fall off, you'll believe anything they tell you – you can't even think of blaming them!"

"It didn't put you off horses, anyway."

"No, the opposite, I was hooked. And then Aunt Ginnie arranged lessons for me, though I didn't tell her about that little episode for a long time!" She turned the horse, facing back up the beach. "Race you?"

"You're on." He touched his heels to his horse as he spoke and shot past her. She bent low in the saddle, kicking with her heels, encouraging her own horse, and caught up with him as they neared the old boat-house and the slip leading down to the water's edge.

They slowed to a trot, then a walk as they guided the horses towards the narrow track that would take them onto the road back to the stables. They didn't talk as they rode single file along the side of the road, keeping well out of the way of the occasional car.

There were some French and German number-plates around, she noticed. The tourist season had definitely started, and she reminded herself that she needed to advertise in the next week or two, now that she had the place up and running.

They rounded the bend in the road, turning to look at the sweep of the bay stretching out to their left. The water was glistening in the light of the early sun, and the mountains, still half in shadow, rose steeply on both sides, green and gold where the sun touched them, purple in the hidden spots.

Donal pulled his horse into a small grassy patch at the side of the road and Clare followed. They sat, perfectly content for the moment, watching the gulls wheeling in the clear sky, as the horses bent their heads to graze the long acre.

"I could sit looking at that all day," he said. "No wonder Kate wants to paint everything in sight!"

"I know. It's perfect, isn't it? I love this place. There's nowhere like it in Dublin, or anywhere else." She moved her head slightly as she spoke, watching the progress of a small boat out towards the horizon.

"What about Howth?" He asked, turning to look at her. "Or Killiney?"

"They're lovely – but not the same. It's – I don't know, there's a kind of wildness about it here. A freedom. Nothing at all in front of you for five thousand miles. The edge of the world."

"The edge of the world can be a very frightening place." He said it quietly, almost to himself. Then, before she could reply, he said, "Come on, we'd better be getting back."

He clicked to the horse, guiding him back onto the roadway and up the hill to the stable-yard. He dismounted in silence, came over to offer her a hand down and walked to the car while she was still talking to the stable owner.

He was quiet on the way back in the car, and Clare found herself thinking that Ruth's view of him was accurate. He was an interesting man all right, but moody as hell. She found herself wishing for the end of the short journey, babbling to fill the silence that was no longer companionable, but oppressive.

"Clare?"

"Yes?" She glanced sideways to look at him. He was staring ahead, intent on watching the road as he drove.

"I'm sorry I'm so distracted. I found myself thinking . . . well, things I'd prefer not to think about."

"It happens. We all do it sometimes."

"I know. But it makes for lousy company." They pulled into the round gravel yard in front of the cottage as he spoke.

"Are you anxious to get back to Dublin?" she asked, for something to say.

She was sorry the moment it was out, but he answered fairly readily.

"Yes and no. I want to see how my mother is, and get a few things organised before term starts. Other than that, I'd stay here forever."

"Do you mean that?"

"Oh, yes." His voice was quiet. "I've always loved it here."

"Kate said you used to spend all your summers here when you were young."

"Yes – I was about five when we started coming. My father liked nothing better than to rent a house near the sea and spend his days reading. Mam and I used to walk on the beach in the mornings looking for shells. I still remember the feel of them in my hands, the smooth ones that were white and brown and gold, and those crusty, cone-shaped ones that I always threw back because I thought there were things living in them. Mam loved the ones she said looked like pleated skirts, all dressed up for a dance. We collected lots of those, she used to make things from them." He paused. "Just what you needed, isn't it? A lecture on shells!"

They met each others eyes and began to laugh.

"I remember a flowerpot I made once," she said, when she could control the laughing. "It was covered with shells – the most ugly thing imaginable. It didn't last long, I think my mother broke it on purpose!"

"Where did you collect the shells?" he asked. "Where used you go, when you were young?"

"Galway, sometimes," she said. "But mainly Kilkee. My mother's from Limerick. The whole of Limerick goes down there for the summer. I was eighteen when I discovered Connemara and I can't get enough of it ever since."

"I was still coming when I was eighteen, by then Kate was back here a few years and I used to stay with herself and Kevin. And then later, I used to come with Jen. She really loved it, she wanted to live here."

He turned his head slightly, looking through the windscreen towards the orchard, where the sun was dappling the little trees.

"It's what we thought we'd do, what we planned."

Clare was unsure if she should say anything. Then, as the silence lasted, she couldn't keep quiet any longer.

"It must be very hard for you."

He turned to look at her, the pain sharp in his eyes. "My mother is a great help. And Nuala, our housekeeper. We'd be lost without her."

He seemed lost anyway, she thought suddenly. Just for a moment, he had a vulnerability she hadn't seen in him before, even at those times he lapsed into silence or seemed moody. What could she say? There was nothing, she realised. Nothing at all that might help.

"Do you think you'll come back again?" she asked, hoping it wasn't the wrong thing to say.

It wasn't. His smile was quick and seemed to come from deep inside him.

"Try and stop me," he said as she returned the smile and opened the car door.

"Clare?"

She turned.

"Thank you," he said softly.

He was out of the car before she could ask what he was thanking her for.

She saw him once more before he left, when he came with the twins to say goodbye. "I'll miss you two," she told them.

It was true. She had got used to the noise and the laughter. Luke darted forward and gave her an impulsive hug, then raced Michael to the car as Kate arrived on her bicycle for the final farewells. She waved to Clare and Donal before reaching down to hug the two boys.

"They'll miss her," Clare said to Donal as they stood watching.

"I know. But I hope we'll be back before too long. It would make a big difference if we could stay here – I hate landing in on Kate, though she never seems to mind."

"Just ring her when you decide to come, she'll let me know. Or, you have the number here, haven't you? When do you think it might be? Not that it matters, I'd just want to be sure I had the apartment for you."

"I'm not sure exactly. I've a lot of things to work out. But the end of June, probably, when they finish school."

"See you then," she said lightly, smiling at him.

"See you," he replied, smiling back at her.

His eyes were warm, with no trace now of the earlier sadness. He seemed relaxed again, and she found herself, for a moment, wanting to reach out and touch him. But shaking hands was too formal, and she could hardly give him a hug, however casual.

Then he turned and called the boys, and Clare waved again to Kate and the boys and went back into the cottage, closing the door behind her.

She heard the car starting up just as the telephone rang.

"Clare?" It was Niall. "I'm going to Galway this afternoon."

She took a deep breath, trying to stifle the sudden butterflies in her stomach.

"Clare? Are you there?"

"Sorry, Niall. Yes, I am."

"Well?" he asked quietly.

She played for time. "I thought you usually went in on Friday?"

"Yes, but I'm free this afternoon, if you are. The sooner you get it over with, the better."

"I'd have to think about it."

"Why? No time like the present."

"You're a bully, do you know that?" She smiled in spite of her anxiety.

"Only in a good cause," he said.

"I don't have an appointment."

"It's okay, you don't need one. I checked."

"You're determined to get me there, aren't you?"

"I'm determined to help, if it'll make it easier."

She hesitated for only a moment longer.

"It'll make it easier. And Niall?"

"Mmm?"

"Thanks."

"Pick you up at about two o'clock?"

"Fine. Great," she said.

Not great at all, she thought, hanging up. But she had to do it, and he was right, the sooner the better. Damn Tony, damn him! She'd never forgive him for this.

She went to the kitchen to prepare something to eat. She hadn't eaten since last night, but she wasn't hungry – her stomach was in knots. Still, she'd better have something, she thought – it could be a long wait in Galway.

The kettle was coming to the boil when there was a tap on the window. It was Kate.

"Are you all right, Clare?" she asked, coming in.

"Fine, just a bit distracted."

"I won't keep you, I just wanted to let you know I stripped off the beds. Will I put the sheets on to wash in the apartment, or do you want to do them here?"

"God, Kate, you didn't need to worry about that!"

"No bother," Kate said. "It only took a few minutes,

and it will save you doing it. What should I do with them?"

"I'll wash them here, it's handiest. Would you like some coffee?"

"Sit down, I'll make it, you look tired. You were up a bit early this morning." She was smiling as she said it.

"It was worth it. We had a great time – did Donal tell you?"

"He did indeed. He said he'd forgotten how much he enjoyed horse-riding, and that the company made it even better. You know, he hasn't stopped talking about you for the past three days."

"Kate!" Clare smiled at her from where she had curled up in the armchair.

"I'm only saying he enjoyed himself here. God knows, he needed the break."

She moved out to the kitchen, was busy there for a few minutes.

"Now," she said, coming back with a mug of coffee and a scone, handing them to Clare. "I won't stay, I just wanted to tell you Kevin is cooking dinner for myself and Rick tonight. He said to ask you if you'd like to come."

"I'd love to, Kate, but I can't tonight. Niall is taking me into Galway – I might be back very late."

"That's all right, if you change your mind let us know. And if not, we can always do it another time."

"Tell him I said thanks for the invite."

"I'll do that. Now mind yourself," Kate said, bending to kiss Clare on the cheek. "You look washed out."

"I'll be fine. And thanks, Kate."

Kate touched her briefly on the shoulder, moved to

the door and was gone. Clare finished the coffee, glad of
the comfort it gave her. Then she went across to collect the
sheets. The apartment didn't need cleaning – Kate had
seen to that, too – so she came straight back to the cottage
to put on a wash and tidy up, anything at all to keep her
occupied and take her mind off what was facing her.

Niall arrived bang on two, and by twenty-five past three
they were turning in the gates of the hospital. The big
cream building terrified her.

"Do you know where to go?" he asked gently as he
parked the car and turned to look at her.

"Over there," she said.

"I'll walk across with you."

"No." She shook her head, seemed to hunch down
into the seat.

"It's okay," he said. "I won't actually come in with
you – unless you want me to."

"No. I don't know. God, Niall, I'm scared."

That bastard, Niall thought. She really doesn't need
this.

He put his forefinger under her chin, gently tilting it
upwards.

"You can do it. I'll be waiting here."

"I thought you had things to do. That's the reason
you came in, isn't it?"

"This is the reason. A very good one." He was
talking quietly, his hand against her cheek.

She bit her lip and he could see the tears starting in
her eyes.

"You're a dote," she said. "Okay, this is it. I'll go in myself, but wait for me, okay?" She took a deep breath, got out of the car and started walking.

It was a long two hours. Niall walked around for a while, then got back into the car and turned on the radio. He didn't want to go too far in case Clare came back – he had no idea how long she'd be in there.

He wished he had brought something to read, took out the menus for the following week but found he couldn't concentrate on them. He was wondering if he had time to walk as far as the river when she appeared at the side of the car and got in quickly.

"You okay?" he asked.

She nodded, let out a long sigh.

"At least that bit's over. I'll know the result in a week."

"God, it'll be a long bloody week." He started the engine. "What do you want to do? Head back? Or go for a drink?"

"A drink." They turned towards the city centre.

"The Quays?" he asked.

"I don't mind." She rubbed the misted-up window, looked out at the weir as they crossed the bridge.

"Actually, I'd like something to eat," she said. "I had nothing much today."

"Fine, there's a new place I've been wanting to try out. See what the competition's like."

"Fifty miles away?" She was smiling now. "I think you're probably safe enough."

"True," he grinned. "But you know me, any excuse!" He pulled into a parking space, switched off the engine.

"Have you time for this?" she asked. "I mean, I could eat at home. Or at Kate's, Kevin invited me. Only . . ."

"I know." They got out of the car and he put his arm around her as they crossed the road to the restaurant.

Clare began to relax a little once she had some roast chicken and a glass of wine in front of her. She sipped at the wine, began to pick at the food. Niall ate his steak in silence for a few minutes.

"Want some chips?"

She nodded, took one, dipped it in Niall's pepper sauce.

Niall was nearly finished eating when he broke the silence again.

"Was it awful, Clare? Or would you prefer not to talk about it?"

She shook her head and he waited, not certain if she wanted to talk or not.

"It was okay. Not as bad as I expected. They were lovely. Only I felt awful about the whole thing. I hated having to go there."

"Do you have to go back in next week? Could you just phone?"

"No. They said I'd have to see someone. A counsellor."

"Why?"

She took a deep breath.

"In case it's positive." She said it very quietly, speared one of his remaining chips, concentrated on dipping it in the sauce.

He found it hard to read her expression. Bastard, he thought again.

"Clare . . ."

She looked up.

"I'm sorry you have to go through this. And you know that if – well, if . . ."

She reached across and touched his hand.

"I know. I'd be lost without you, you know that?"

He smiled, squeezed her hand lightly, and then the coffee arrived and they drank it in silence.

"What do you want to do now?" he asked. "Go for a walk? Or head home?"

"What I want to do now, most of all, is put this whole bloody thing out of my mind as much as I can. I'll keep myself busy every minute for the next week."

"That's the spirit."

She meant what she said. As soon as she got home she rang Kate to say she wouldn't be over, but that she'd make lunch for them all next day if they were free.

"I have to go and work in the shop," Kate said. "But Kevin is taking Rick to see Ashleigh Falls. Why don't you go with them?"

"I couldn't do that," Clare said.

"You don't want to?" Kate asked.

"No, it's not that. Kate, I don't even know them, not really – I can't just butt in."

"Rubbish – bring a picnic and they'll be glad to have you! I don't think they meant to spend every minute together anyway, but Kevin wants Rick to see as much of Connemara as he can before he heads for Dublin."

"When is he going?"

"Monday or Tuesday, for a couple of days before he goes across to England. Kevin will come back here while he's away, and try to decide what to do with himself."

"Tell you what, Kate, check with them, and if they're happy to have me tagging along, I'll be glad to go."

It had been a lovely day, Clare decided as she cooked herself an omelette late that evening. They had walked for nearly two hours at Ashleigh Falls, and she was feeling the pleasant tiredness that comes from exercising in the fresh air.

Kevin and Rick had been very good company. Kevin proved knowledgeable about the area and Rick was the best kind of visitor – interested in everything, eager to see more, clearly enjoying himself. She found herself warming to him in spite of his passing similarity to Tony.

"What about joining us for dinner?" Kevin asked later as they were on their way back. "We were thinking of going to Niall's – or we could try somewhere else, if you like, and I promise not to tell!"

"Thanks, Kevin, but I'm going up to Dublin tomorrow for a few days and I need to do some packing. Ruth was telling me on the phone this morning that my parents have nearly given me up for lost!"

"Pity," Kevin had said. "I was hoping you might help me show Rick a bit more of Connemara. And we're going across to Inishmore tomorrow or the next day. You're sure you won't stay and come with us?"

It was a compliment. They had obviously enjoyed

her company. "Tell you what," she had added on the spur of the moment. "Why don't you ring me when you get to Dublin? We could meet up, I'd show you around a bit."

"Now *there's* a great idea," Rick had answered. "If you're sure you'll have the time. Kevin tells me he only knows the pubs!"

"Sure, what more do you want to see?" Kevin asked as he took Clare's phone number, promising to ring when they got there.

"Everything else. As *well* as the pubs." Rick winked at Clare as he spoke, and she laughed.

"I'll do my best. Now, here's the phone number, ring me when you get the chance . . ."

Chapter Thirteen

They rang on Monday afternoon, just as she got back from a run in Bushy Park.

"Where are you staying?" she asked. She was still slightly breathless, hot from the run. She sat on the chair in the hall and pulled off her sneakers as she talked.

"Temple Bar," Kevin answered. "Donal offered us a bed, but it didn't seem fair, with the kids. Are you free this evening?"

"Well, I'm going out with some friends. But we could all meet up, if you like."

"They won't mind?"

"Not when they see that American hunk you have in tow!" she said, laughing.

"Oh, I see. He's a hunk, is he?"

She felt herself reddening and was glad he couldn't see her.

"Shut up, Kevin," she laughed.

"Charming. I thought my mother said you were a nice girl."

She laughed. "She doesn't know the half of it! So, are you on?"

"I'm on. Where'll we meet?"

"Do you know O'Neill's in Suffolk St? We'll start off there. I'm meeting Mary and Deirdre in Neary's later."

"I know it, all right. What time?"

"Is six okay, or too early?"

"It's grand. See you then."

They were sitting with pints when she arrived just a few minutes late.

"Traffic," she explained. "I swear it gets worse every week. Thank God I'm out of it."

"For the time being, anyway," Kevin answered. "What'll you have?"

They chatted for a while about Clare's plans, and about what Rick would like to do while he was in Dublin.

"If you wanted to try and trace that girl, Rick – what was her name?"

"Beth. Elizabeth."

"Elizabeth. Well, if you wanted, I'd help you find electoral lists and stuff."

"It's good of you to offer, Clare. The thing is . . ."

He paused and took a sip of the pint.

" . . . Kevin and I were talking about it just now, and I don't know, I guess I'm not sure it's the right thing to do. Maybe after all this time it's better just to let it go." He looked pensive as he spoke, his gaze on something in the far distance.

"But would you not always be wondering what might have happened, if you found her?" Clare asked.

"I've been wondering that already, on and off. But I'm not sure where to start. And when it comes right down to it, I'm not sure it's what I really want to do."

"Why not take a chance?"

"Because if I did find her, I could spoil whatever she might have going now, and I wouldn't want to do that. I guess we had our time. And now it's gone."

Pity, thought Clare. But it was his decision. She left it at that.

Her friends' faces were a picture when she arrived in Neary's with Kevin and Rick.

"God, I finally see what the attraction *is* in Connemara," Deirdre said, when the two men went up to the bar to order.

"Which of them is it, Clare?" Mary asked. "Because I want the other one!"

"You can have the two of them! I'm off men, I told you. They're just friends."

"You've been off men for two months now," said Mary. "That's long enough!"

"No, it's not," Clare answered. "It's nowhere near long enough."

Deirdre laughed, and Mary started again. "But . . ."

And then she noticed Clare's expression, and decided she'd better change the subject.

The rest of the evening was light-hearted and great fun. They enjoyed taking Kevin and Rick on a tour of all their favourite haunts, and Clare was as happy as any of them to join in, balking only when Kevin mentioned Leeson Street.

"What is it?" Rick asked.

"There are night-clubs there," Kevin explained.

"It'd be very quiet tonight," Clare objected. "And besides, we're not really dressed for it. They probably wouldn't let us in . . ."

"You look great to me," said Rick. "I don't see why – "

"Not great enough," Mary said firmly before he could finish. She knew well why Clare didn't want to try Leeson Street. The chances of meeting Tony were slight, but why risk it?

"You'd need to be dolled up to the nines to get in," she continued. "And even then you wouldn't be sure."

"Let's try Break For The Border," Deirdre said, copping on. "It's a great place, and we can get something to eat. I'm starving!"

Clare woke next morning feeling the effects of her night on the town. I'm getting too old for this, she thought, as she hurried to have a shower before heading into Bewley's to meet the lads. At least, she thought, today would be less frenetic – although Rick was still insisting that he wanted to see "just about everything" in Dublin.

The phone rang just as she was about to leave. She answered, hardly recognising the voice at the other end.

"God, Kevin," she laughed as he identified himself. "You're sounding the worse for wear!"

"It was all that cigarette smoke," he said. His voice had a sorry note to it.

"Oh right," Clare agreed. "It was never the drink!"

"I hardly touched a drop," he protested.

"I know you didn't touch it, you were knocking it back too fast! Are you still on for today?"

There was a pause.

"Actually, that's why I'm ringing." He sounded embarrassed. "I'm not really on for all this museum lark. Boring as hell I find it. And there's someone I'd like to look up. I don't suppose you'd . . ."

"Take Rick off on my own?" Clare finished for him.

"That's it." He sounded relieved.

"No problem. Only you owe me," she teased.

He laughed, a rasping sound. "Okay. I owe you," he agreed.

She met Rick in Bewley's and took him off to see the city. They didn't quite manage to see everything, but she did her best. Trinity, the National Museum and the Art Gallery, a quick break for lunch before trekking across town to the Hugh Lane Gallery, then back down O'Connell Street.

"That's the cultural bit done," she said, as they crossed the bridge over the Liffey. "Now, if I had the energy, I'd show you the *real* Dublin."

"Not yet," he begged, laughing. "I could use a coffee."

"Me, too. We'll go back to Bewley's. Or what about the Winding Stair?" She paused as she spoke, ready to turn right along the Quays.

"Depends how far it is!"

"Not far," she said. "Just down there" – she indicated – "over the Ha'penny Bridge."

"It's a pretty bridge," he said as he followed her up

183

the steps and over the curved pedestrian bridge leading back to the North side of the river.

"In ye olden days it was a toll bridge," she said.

"Looks like it still is," he commented, eyeing the young woman sitting begging on the far side, a shawl wrapped around her and a young baby folded securely into it.

Clare paused to drop a coin into the outstretched hand, returning the woman's smile.

Rick was shaking his head as they crossed the street and entered the Winding Stair bookshop. "That's crazy. You didn't need to do that. I mean, you have a welfare system here, right?"

"Yes, but . . ."

She led the way up the dark, winding stairway to the coffee shop. They took a table by the window overlooking the river and sat facing each other while a waitress cleaned off some used coffee-mugs. Two or three of the other tables were full, and the room was warm and bright, with soft music playing and books lining the far walls.

"Great place," Rick said. "What do you recommend?"

"Definitely the carrot cake."

"I'll go get it. Coffee or tea?"

He went to the little counter and Clare sat looking out the window while she waited. She could see the bridge easily from here. The woman with the child was still there, ignored by most of the passers-by.

"You have a soft heart," Rick said, following her gaze as he set down the coffee and plates. She didn't know if he meant it as a compliment or not.

"It's not that, it's just – well, she wouldn't do it unless she had to. And I realise how lucky I am when I pass somebody like her."

"Middle-class guilt. And just a mite smug, if you don't mind my saying so."

She stared at him, her cheeks beginning to flush red.

"I do mind, actually! Who exactly made *you* judge and jury?"

"I didn't mean it the way it sounded . . ."

"Good. Because it sounded rotten!" She was sitting with the palms of her hands on the table, her eyes furious.

He brushed a hand through his hair.

"I'm sorry, Clare. Really. It just sort of slipped out. I guess my mouth's too big sometimes."

"It's all right," Clare said, taking a deep breath. "But would you really not give her anything?"

"Well, it's just – I suppose I'm surprised that there are so many panhandlers about?"

"And there aren't in New York?"

"It's different. Maybe it's not quite so obvious. And from what Kevin said, your system's better here. But still there are lots of people trying to rip it off."

"Probably," Clare agreed. "But you couldn't blame them – it's not a fair system."

"No system's fair, Clare. People just do the best they can to make it work. Or try to change it. And you don't do that by encouraging people to beg."

He began to eat the carrot cake. Clare sat thinking for a minute or two, still looking out the window.

"I know. Well, in my head I know it. But how can you walk past someone? I mean, I do it sometimes, most times probably, but I hate it. I wish there was something I could do."

"There is. Stop giving them money. After a while they won't be there."

"Rick!" She sounded horrified, fiddled with the spoon that was on the table beside her untouched coffee. "It's not that simple, Rick," she added more quietly. "It's no solution."

"I suppose nothing ever is that simple," he agreed. "Do you want more coffee? That's got to be cold."

"No, it's okay," she said, drinking it quickly, barely tasting the cake. She felt uncomfortable with him now, slightly thrown by the conversation.

They left the Winding Stair and turned left and left again, with Clare giving just the briefest of glances at the young woman across the road on the bridge.

"Look at that!" Rick was laughing as he examined the bronze statue of the two women sitting chatting on a bench, their heavy bronze bags beside them.

"The Hags with the Bags."

"The what?" he asked, still laughing.

"Hags with the Bags. Lots of the Dublin statues have names. You remember we passed one near Trinity? The Tart with the Cart."

"The Molly Malone statue? Sure, I remember. Not very complimentary!"

Their mood was lighter now as they headed in the direction of Henry Street.

"I'm taking you to see Moore Street."

"Could we do some shopping there? I'd really like to buy something for Kate."

"Not in Moore Street – it's a sort of outdoor fruit market. But there are plenty of shops near there."

She walked ahead of him for a moment, negotiating her way through the crowds. The pedestrianised streets were busy even on a Tuesday afternoon.

"We're almost there," she said, as he caught up with her again.

"And you're sure that's what you want to do?" he asked. "Go shopping?" He was walking along beside her now on the crowded footpath, and she glanced up at him as they crossed the road and turned into Moore Street.

"The truth!" he added.

He had a really nice smile, she noticed, as they stood for a moment looking at each other. His eyes crinkled at the corners when he was amused. She grinned back, stood facing him as the scents of fish and vegetables rose around them. The stall-holders were calling out to passers-by, and he had to lean closer to hear Clare's reply.

"The truth?" she said, still smiling. She felt at ease with him again, their brief difference of opinion past.

"The truth is that on a lovely day like this I don't want to be in the city at all, I'd much prefer to be out by the sea or in the mountains."

"So, why don't we do that?" he asked. "Can we get there?"

"Easily," she answered. Then she stopped. "God, *I'm* sorry, Rick – I didn't mean – I mean, I'm supposed to be showing you Dublin – and we'd better get to the shops, so you'll have time – "

He was smiling at her. "To tell the truth, I'd be happier on a mountain-top right now. Or by the sea. The museums and stuff were great – but shopping isn't really my thing."

She laughed. "Great! So what are we doing here?" she asked. "I'll tell you the best places to shop tomorrow, okay?"

He nodded, still smiling. "So let's go!"

"Where to?" she asked. They were still standing facing each other in the middle of the pavement, with people eddying around them. "Mountains, or the sea? We can get to both of them quickly, that's one of the great things about Dublin!"

"The sea, then. If it's not too far."

"Twenty minutes, about!" she said, going to one of the stalls to buy some fruit.

They turned back up the street, careful not to slip on the occasional piece of fruit or cabbage leaf that had fallen underfoot. They reached the station quickly and were lucky to catch the DART straight away.

"We're going to Howth," she informed him as the train pulled out. "It's an old fishing village. We can walk up to the Summit from the station – it's a bit of a distance but it'll be worth it."

"Doesn't look much like a fishing village," Rick commented when they came out of the station and stood taking deep breaths of the tangy air.

"You expected currachs?" she laughed.

"Well, something a bit less affluent, I guess. Those are yachts, not fishing boats . . ."

"The trawlers are just over there," she said. "And you can buy fresh fish in those little shops on the pier. Come on!" She ran off suddenly towards a bus that had just pulled into the station yard.

"I thought you said we were walking?" Rick called as he followed her.

"This is quicker," she said as they got on the bus. "But don't worry, we'll walk, all right!"

The bus turned right at the end of the village, going uphill, and a minute later the driver was calling "The Summit – last stop."

The air was bracing as they stepped down from the bus along with two other passengers and turned to walk the remaining few yards to the top of Howth Head. They stood for a moment by the small wall surrounding the carpark at the top, looking out over the broad sweep of Dublin Bay to the Wicklow Mountains beyond.

"We can walk down there," Clare said, indicating the promontory with the Baily lighthouse at the far end. "Or we can go left along there, on that track heading along the cliff. You can see as far as the Cooley Mountains in the North, if the weather's right."

"Is the cliff dangerous?"

"I don't think so. There isn't a steep drop."

They turned left, going through the gap in the wall that led onto the track. The sea was far below to their right, blue-grey and sparkling. There were small boats, some with red sails, some white, dotted here and there on the water.

"I love watching them," Clare said. "Don't they look wonderful?"

They walked along at a steady pace, not too quickly, enjoying the feel of the place. They passed a few people, mostly heading back at this stage of the late afternoon. All of them nodded to Clare and Rick as they passed.

"Do you know *everybody* around here?" he asked, surprised.

"I don't know any of them," she laughed. "They're just being friendly."

They continued on, rounding a curve in the track, the mountains of the North coming dimly into view ahead of them. They could see a man in the far distance, walking along the track towards them.

"Now, there's someone you *do* know!" Rick said.

"Who is it? I can hardly see him at this distance. You must have good eyesight!"

She looked again, and saw, to her surprise, that it was Donal.

"You never know who you'd meet up here!" she greeted him as he drew near.

He was wearing a pair of dark green cords and a cream-coloured woollen jumper, and looked relaxed and comfortable as he stood there with the wind blowing in his hair.

"You're the last people I expected to see," he answered, smiling. "Kevin told me you were up for a few days, but I didn't expect to see you around here! What do you think of it, Rick?"

"It's wonderful. I can't understand why Clare would want to leave Dublin!"

"And you told me you didn't like Howth," Donal said.

She laughed. "I just said I prefer the Atlantic, if I remember rightly. And I do."

"Are you going much further?" Donal asked. "It's getting a bit chilly."

"We were nearly ready to turn back."

"How are you travelling?" he asked.

"DART," she said, brushing back the hair that was now beginning to whip around her face. "We got the bus up here from the station."

"I'll drop you back down, if you like." Donal said. "My car's just over there. And you're welcome to come back to my place for coffee – unless you've other plans?"

Clare glanced at Rick.

"Lovely – if you're sure," she said to Donal. "I don't fancy rush hour on the DART!"

They were back at his house in Clontarf in a few minutes, to the great delight of the twins, and Nuala, the house-keeper, who looked at Clare with interest and said that Donal and the boys hadn't stopped talking about her since they got back.

"Enough of that, Nuala," Donal laughed, taking a plate of scones from her. "You'll be giving away all our secrets!"

He drove them back into town afterwards, in spite of Clare's insistence that they could easily get the bus.

"Will I see you before you go back, Clare?" he asked as he dropped them in D'Olier Street.

"I have to go back tomorrow afternoon," she said. "Do you think you'll be down again? Have you decided yet?"

"The end of June, for definite. I promised the lads – they're counting the days!"

"If you ring with the dates I'll book you in."

"I'll do that." His smile was warm as she closed the car door behind her. He was still sitting there, watching them, when she turned to wave from the far side of the street.

Chapter Fourteen

"Would you like to have dinner with me tonight?" Rick said as they walked along Westmoreland Street.

"You don't have to . . ."

"I'd like to. Or is that a 'no'?" he asked, glancing at her as they walked. "Maybe you've other plans . . . ?"

She smiled. "None. It's just that I can't go anywhere looking like this!" She indicated her jeans and well-worn jacket. "Unless it's a pizza place, or something."

"Or McDonald's?" he laughed. "Tell you the truth, I had something fancier in mind."

They had arrived outside his hotel while they were talking, and he stopped near the door, looking thoughtful for a moment.

"Tell you what. I'll get you a taxi to get you home. You get some glad-rags on and meet me back here. I'll make a reservation meanwhile. What do you say? It wouldn't be too late?"

"I could be back by quarter past eight," she said, glancing at her watch and doing a quick calculation.

"Eight fifteen?" he confirmed. "Fine. I'll make the reservation. It'll be just the two of us, probably, I don't suppose Kevin is back."

Clare arrived back a minute or two early, to find Rick already waiting at his hotel door. He hopped into the taxi as it pulled in at the kerb.

"The Shelbourne, please," he told the driver. "Is that okay?" he asked, turning to Clare. "I've heard it's good."

"Fine. But it's not far, we could have walked."

"Not if you're exhausted like I am. And I bet you're wearing heels!"

"They're not *that* high," she said, grinning at him. He looked really great in a dark dinner jacket, his blond hair gleaming, and she was glad she'd made the effort to dress up. The burgundy sheath dress was simple, but she knew it looked lovely with her dark hair. The only jewellery she wore was a gold chain, but it was enough, and the velvet cape she had borrowed from her mother fitted her perfectly.

The meal was excellent, and she enjoyed herself far more than she had expected. Rick was surprisingly good company, and the tension of earlier that day, in the Winding Stair, had completely disappeared. By the time dessert arrived they were both feeling mellow, and she laughed as Rick sneaked a taste of her ice cream.

"Wonderful," he pronounced. "In fact, my whole visit has been wonderful. Mostly thanks to you, Clare."

"A bit unfair on Kevin, isn't it?"

He laughed easily. "So don't tell him! No, really, it's just that this is a kind of unexpected bonus. I didn't expect to be having such a good time. I thought I'd be . . ."

"Searching for Elizabeth?" she asked, when he didn't continue.

"I guess. But I'm beginning to feel that maybe that was just a dream, finding her. As if it's not going to happen. It's too late, and maybe I should just leave it at that. I mean, even if I found her now, it wouldn't be the same. Couldn't be, because the Beth I knew just doesn't exist any more – she's a different person now, and so am I."

"But if you don't at least *try* to find her, do you think you'll regret it?"

He shook his head, toyed with the spoon on the empty dessert dish in front of him.

"I don't know. I simply don't know, at this point. I'm sorry already that I let her go in the first place. But maybe I need to accept that she's gone. It just seemed like a good idea, when Kevin said he was coming home – you know, an opportunity to give it one last shot, even if nothing came of it. Then maybe I could move on . . ."

She nodded. "I know what you mean."

He looked directly at her. "Do you? Have you ever had a feeling that you're at some kind of cross-road? That you can't go back, but there's something you must do before you can go forward? That's how I feel right now. I just haven't figured out what's the best thing to do, exactly."

The waiter brought coffee and a little salver of *petits fours*, wonderful little confections of glacéed fruits and chocolate-dipped shortcake.

"They're wasted on me," Clare admitted. "I absolutely couldn't eat another thing."

Rick smiled across at her as he stirred his coffee. "I'm not really making much sense, am I?"

"Yes, you are. More than you know. I'm at a sort of cross-road myself, I needed to take time out. It's why I went to Connemara."

She stopped suddenly, annoyed with herself. She hadn't meant to get into anything personal with this man, she hardly knew him. And yet, the atmosphere, the wine, the attention were all having an effect, and she found herself opening up, saying more than she had intended. She took a deep breath.

"I've just finished a relationship with someone, and I need time and some space to sort out where I'm going."

Rick nodded.

"And what about you?" Clare continued. "Are you – sorry, I shouldn't really ask."

"No, that's okay. I'm not in a relationship, if that's what you're asking. Haven't been for quite a while. I guess no-one ever really matched up . . . not even my wife."

He paused, picked up one of the glacéed fruits, sat looking at it for a moment before raising his eyes to look across at Clare again.

"I got married when I was twenty-eight. A big mistake – for both of us."

"And how long – ?"

"Did it last? Not more than a year or so, barely that. I knew Connie from High School, we dated for a short while when we were about fifteen. Should have left it at that. But I guess we were feeling pressured – you know, family, friends, all that stuff. And we got on really well together. We just shouldn't ever have got married."

"So you're divorced now?"

"A long time ago. No children, so that made it easier. I guess."

"It must have. I mean, it would be terrible if you'd had children and had to decide who they'd stay with, and work out all kinds of arrangements and things."

"Would it?" His voice was quiet. "Maybe you're right. I suppose I thought they would have been with me. That was part of the problem – Connie didn't want kids. And I did – a whole tribe of them, if I could. Funny, when I'm an only child. Or maybe *because* . . . anyway, that's part of the reason it didn't work out. I love kids, wanted lots of them. I really would have liked that."

Clare was struck by the sadness in his voice, his wistful expression. She looked for words to reassure him.

"It might happen yet, Rick. You never know . . ."

"That's right – you never know. Except that, since Connie, I haven't had a single relationship that lasted more than six months. It's as if I've been searching for something I just can't find. And there's nothing in my life that satisfies me right now – even my job. I'd give it up tomorrow, but I just couldn't do that to my Uncle Joe – he runs the practice with me, he and Dad worked hard building it up . . ."

He laughed. "Crazy, isn't it? You'd think at thirty

eight I'd know what I wanted from my life, and go for it? And all I've got is the feeling that I left the most important part of it behind, fifteen years ago. So, when Kevin invited me over, it seemed like the best deal on offer – even if I was just chasing a dream, a fantasy of what might have been."

"It could work. You might just find her, it might all work out . . ."

He shook his head, almost impatiently. "Not now. No, I don't think so. Because, in a way, this isn't really about her any more – it's about me, and what I want from my life. And what I want right now is to wrap up the past somehow, and move on."

"Easier said than done, sometimes."

"True. But I should start by lightening up a little. Here I am, having dinner with a beautiful woman, and all I can do is give you a sad story. You're too easy to talk to, Clare!"

She laughed, relieved that the conversation was moving to a lighter note.

"What about more coffee?" he asked. "And maybe some brandy?"

"Not brandy, I've no head for it. But I'd love a Bailey's."

They sat sipping coffee and their drinks, chatting about what Rick would do in London, what gift Clare might help him choose for Kate tomorrow, before she had to catch the afternoon train back to Galway.

He really was a very attractive man, she thought, and nothing at all like Tony except for the same blond hair and blue eyes. He was taller, sturdier, but also, it seemed, far more sensitive than Tony could ever be.

She concentrated now on what he was saying.

"So tomorrow's going to be busy. But there's still tonight, and it's not too late. Tell me where you'd like to go next."

"Bed," she said. Oh God, she thought. "I mean, I'm absolutely exhausted, I really should get home soon."

Rick sat there smiling at her.

"Sure, if that's what you want. But I kind of thought we might check out the night life, go dancing or something."

She finished the Bailey's, took a sip of coffee. "I really don't think I could, Rick. I'm dropping as it is, I'm really sorry."

"No problem. Just an idea. Would you like another drink?"

"Not after all the wine!"

He raised his eyebrows a little, grinning across at her, and she gave in.

"Well, maybe just one," she said. "Wait," she added, as he was about to signal the waiter. "We could go to La Cave for a while, have a drink there. It's a great place, I wouldn't mind going there for half an hour or so."

"A night-club?"

"A wine bar, just around the corner. I think you'd like it."

La Cave wasn't too crowded yet, and they found two stools at the end of the tiny bar and sat there chatting for a while as the place filled up and the noise level rose. She had to move closer to hear him.

"You're right, I like it. I'm glad we came here."

"Good. I think it's . . ."

"Clare!" a voice interrupted, and she turned to see Deirdre with four or five people Clare thought she recognised.

"And Rick! I didn't expect to see you two here!" Deirdre was grinning, a knowing look in her eyes. Clare could see that she was adding two and two together and getting sixty-four. Please God, let her not say anything embarrassing, she thought. But Deirdre was too busy introducing everyone to comment on anything just yet.

"So we decided at work that since Brian is finally taking the plunge, we'd better take him out on the town while we could! We'll be shattered tomorrow, but his stag party's on Thursday so we're running out of time."

"Stag party?" Rick asked, moving closer as he strained to hear her above the noise.

"Bachelor party," Clare translated.

Rick nodded, smiling at her. "Like some more wine?" he asked, indicating her almost-empty glass.

"None for me, thanks!" Clare said. "I'd better just have a Ballygowan, otherwise I'll be totally out of it."

"So what do you want to do now?" he asked a few moments later, handing her the glass of mineral water. "Sure I can't persuade you to go dancing?"

"Well, I'm beginning to get a second wind, but it's not really my scene . . ."

Deirdre had been talking to Brian, and she turned back to Clare just at that moment.

"We're all going to Reynard's, Clare, what about you two?"

"You know I'm not into night-clubs," she began, but Deirdre cut her short.

"Well, *I'm* into Tom there – "

Clare looked discreetly towards the guy with curly dark hair and a beard, who stood talking to Brian and the others.

"And I'm going to need help persuading him to come, and moral support when I get him there," Deirdre said. "Come on, you know I'd do it for you!"

"Only because you love dancing!" Clare laughed.

"So do you, remember? Come on!"

The battle was lost. With Rick on one side and Deirdre on the other, Clare found herself cajoled into agreeing to go to Reynard's, 'for a short while, anyway'.

She was glad she went. The music seemed to give her energy, and she was immediately up on the floor, dancing with Rick. He was good, she noticed. Really good. The eight of them danced for an hour or so, in groups or in couples, changing partners as the mood took them until the music slowed right down, and Rick moved towards Clare. She moved easily into his arms, noticing as she did that Deirdre was now dancing with Tom. Good for her.

Rick danced well, and she found herself relaxing against him, enjoying the music, enjoying the feel of him holding her. She hadn't noticed his scent before, masculine, warm, subtle. His breath was on her cheek as she closed her eyes and rested her head against his shoulder, all the time moving with him to the gentle rhythm of the music. She felt warm, mellow. She hadn't been held by a man since . . . what matter. She was being held by one now, and it felt wonderful. She found herself wondering what it would be like to . . .

"Clare, we're going now. I'll ring you, okay?"

Thanks, Dee. Lousy sense of timing, she thought, moving back slightly from Rick

Deirdre leaned over to whisper to her. "I know. Purely platonic." Grinning, she left with Tom in tow before Clare could strangle her. Rick smiled, and she wondered if he'd heard.

"Do you want to stay, Clare?" he asked, putting his hands on her shoulders and drawing her back to him. "Or go? Whatever you want."

He folded his arms around her and moved closer, swaying gently with her to the slow rhythm. She really was enjoying this, the music, the soft lights, the feel of him holding her. She gave herself up to the music, closing her eyes, relaxing against him. And then, with a start, she recognised the song that was playing – 'The Power Of Love' – the song she had danced to with Tony, had thought of as their song. She stiffened, pulled away slightly, and Rick was quick to react.

"You okay?" His face was full of concern, and for a moment she wanted to go back into his arms, but she couldn't do it. The memories were crowding in, too much to bear.

"Do you mind if we go, Rick? I'm sorry. It's just that – I'm sorry."

He nodded, seeming to understand.

They walked towards Stephen's Green, heading for a

taxi rank. She pulled the velvet cape tighter against the chill air. He noticed, and put his arm lightly around her, drawing her towards him.

"You okay?" he asked again.

"Fine, I think I'm just tired. I need to get home."

"Clare?" She stopped, turning to face him. "I know something happened back there, I don't know what. But I don't think it was really to do with me, was it?"

He paused as she slowly shook her head.

"I'd like to see you again, Clare. If you want to, I'd really like that."

His hand was touching her arm lightly as she stood, clutching the velvet cape around her, not responding but not pulling away, either.

She gave a little laugh. "You'll be seeing me again tomorrow, remember? We're going shopping for something for Kate."

"You know that's not what I meant, Clare."

His voice was soft, her response softer.

"I know. But I need a bit more time, Rick. We both do."

"Maybe you're right. It's just that . . ."

She nodded. She had felt it too, the sense that there could be something between them. It just wasn't the right time.

"I know," she repeated. "But I'm just not ready, Rick."

"Okay, I won't push it. Do you still want to go shopping tomorrow? Kevin would probably come instead."

She laughed, a proper laugh this time.

"Kevin would make you grab the first thing you saw. I can't let him do that to Kate, I'll *have* to come."

They laughed, hugged each other briefly, and walked quickly to the taxi rank as a taxi drew up. He held the door open for her, touched her lightly on the cheek before closing it, and was gone.

She sat in silence all the way home, so lost in her thoughts that the driver didn't even attempt to engage her in conversation. She had a lot to think about, starting with her unexpected response to Rick.

She had thought she was finished with men. And she still had a lot of things to sort out. But maybe, just maybe, she might be able to begin again. With the right man.

Chapter Fifteen

The journey to Galway seemed long the following afternoon, and Clare spent most of it deep in thought. She liked the relaxed rhythm of the train, the smooth motion lulling her half to sleep. She was tired after another morning in Dublin, more tired still at the thought of what was facing her tomorrow in Galway. At least they had done what they had intended and found a lamp for Kate, a beautiful piece of work with red and green and blue glass. Kate would love it.

"You should really give it to her yourself," she had said to Rick when he asked if she could give it to Kate for him. "I'd be happy to do it, if you want me to – but you should be there to see her reaction. She'll be thrilled."

"I hope. But I don't have time to come down right now. I have to get to London by Friday – I'm already a couple of days late."

His tone was light, as it had been all morning. Clare was grateful to him, and very relieved. She had begun the morning on edge, sure that there would be tension between them, but thanks to him there hadn't been.

"Will you be coming back to Rossdarra?" she had asked, her tone matching his.

"Probably. For a short time, anyway. And maybe you're right – I'll wait and give her the lamp myself. And if I can't do that, if I find I can't get down, then I'll give it to Kevin. He's decided to stay in Dublin for another week."

"So much for coming home to Connemara," she said, and they both laughed as they walked along the quays towards the station. They passed the traveller woman begging at the Ha'penny Bridge, and Clare paused to give her some coins. To her relief, Rick said nothing this time.

She was still thinking about him as the train pulled into Galway, glad to have had something to occupy her thoughts and take her mind off tomorrow.

She stepped off onto the platform, glanced quickly around and was surprised to hear her name being called.

"Niall!" she said, as she turned towards him. "What are you doing here?"

"Meeting you." He leaned forward to kiss her on the cheek.

"But how . . ."

"I rang your parents – you don't mind?"

"No. Of course not. But . . ."

He took her bag. "Come on, I have the car outside," he said, leading her towards the exit.

"Niall, I'm not sure . . ."

"You think you might stay in town for the night?"

She nodded. "But since you've come all the way in . . ."

"No matter, I wanted to meet you anyway. I'll stay here to-night, if that's what you want."

She linked her arm through his. "What would I do without you?" she said. There were tears in her eyes. "I'm not sure what I want, isn't that mad?"

"What about a drink, would you want that? Or something to eat?"

Her smile was a bit shaky. "You're always giving people something to eat or drink, no wonder you run a restaurant!"

"The offer stands." He was smiling back at her, encouraging. "You'd better decide – we can't stay out here all night."

"You're right. I don't know what I want, though. Just for tomorrow to come, and be over."

"I still think you need to eat. When did you have lunch? Four or five hours ago? Had you anything on the train?"

He was steering her towards a nearby restaurant as he spoke, and she went gratefully, glad that he was taking charge. She felt she really couldn't think straight at the moment.

"I want to stay in Galway," she decided as they finished eating. "There's no-one expecting me back but you, and if I go home and happen to meet Kate, she'll think it's very strange that I'm coming back in here again so soon."

"She won't. You know Kate – she minds her own business."

"Yes, but – I don't know. I think I'd find it very hard to get home and have to drag myself back in again, for this."

He nodded. "In that case, you're staying here. The question is, do you want me to stay with you? Or come back in tomorrow to meet you?"

"You're very good, Niall – you've no idea – would you really stay?"

"Of course. I told Barry I probably would. He doesn't know I'm meeting you," he added quickly, to reassure her. "Now, we just have to find somewhere to settle in, then we can go for a jar, or stay in and talk, whatever you want."

As they approached the door of a nearby hotel he pulled her aside for a moment.

"Clare?" He hesitated. "If you want me to stay with you, in the same room – I mean, no strings, just to keep the demons away . . ."

She laughed. "And who'll keep you away?"

"Oh, that day is gone." He said it lightly, and she smiled gratefully at him.

"I'll be fine, Niall. Just as long as I know you're somewhere close."

He could see by her at breakfast next morning that, like him, she hadn't slept much. Her eyes looked sunken, lacking their usual brightness, with traces of shadows beneath them. She moved slowly, as if reluctant to meet the day.

"You have to have something," he said, as she came to sit opposite him with just a cup of coffee from the buffet. "Some cereal, or a bit of toast, at least."

"There you go again, feeding people," she said. She was attempting to joke, but he could see her heart wasn't in it. Better to talk about what they *had* to talk about, he decided.

"What time will they be open?"

"I thought I'd go in about ten."

"You're up early, in that case. It's not even eight yet "

"I couldn't stay in bed any longer. And it's fine out, I thought I might go for a walk by the river. You know, clear the head, whatever."

"Clare?" He reached across the table for her hand. She waited.

"We're friends, right?" he continued. "You've been the best friend I've had, over the years."

She nodded, wondering, half-knowing what was coming.

"If it's positive – no, wait, I have to say this." He talked quietly, urgently, catching hold of her other hand as well, pressing them gently as he spoke.

"Clare, if it happens that you have this – thing, this virus – well, you know I'll be there for you. We'll face it together."

She shook her head quickly, started to pull her hands away.

"Well, why not?" he asked, never taking his eyes from her.

"Don't promise something you can't deliver, Niall." Her voice was sharp, angry.

"I *can* deliver. I wouldn't say so otherwise. You know that by now."

She bit her lip. There were tears in her eyes, and her voice, when she spoke again, was softer.

"Oh, Niall, I'm sorry. Look at me. You're doing everything you can, and I'm acting like a bitch. It's just that I'm terrified."

"I know that."

"And if . . . if this bloody thing is positive, I'll have to live with it for the rest of my life. Whatever that means. But I won't have you living with it too. I couldn't do that to you. You don't need it."

"And you do?"

"Need it or not, I mightn't have the choice."

"Maybe we should go for that walk. Clear the head, like you said. Or do you want to go on your own?"

"No. I want to go with you, and talk about anything and everything but this bloody result. Until I have to."

They left their bags in the car and walked briskly through the town, heading for the river. Galway was well awake and traffic crowded the narrow little streets as they joined the rush-hour crowds in Shop Street.

"Let's go to the Claddagh," she decided suddenly. "We've plenty of time."

They turned down towards Quay Street and out into the open space of the old fishing village, with the scent of the sea and the calling of gulls all around them. They meandered around for a while, their hands dug into the pockets of their jackets, collars turned up against the stiff breeze coming in off the Atlantic.

"What now?" he asked, when it was nearly twenty to ten.

"Right now I'd give anything to be out there," she said, nodding in the direction of the Aran Islands.

"You can be, if that's what you want, later on. First you have to get this thing over and done with."

Her gaze swept along the houses, stopping when she saw the church. "Not yet. There's something else I have to do first."

He followed her, a bit puzzled. Clare wasn't religious. At least, not this kind of religious. Then he remembered her absolute awe when they visited the churches in Venice the year they first met there, her insistence that "Even if there's nothing, there's something. Don't you feel it, Niall?"

She went into the church and stood watching as the sun danced through the stained glass windows, touching the mural on the back wall behind the altar. Her gaze moved after a moment to the red sanctuary lamp, the rows of little lights in front of the statues, and she went to kneel in front of the statue of the Virgin, groping in her pocket for coins before reaching to press the switch for one of the lights. She regretted that there were no longer real candles to light, needing the ritual, the sense of placing her petition there with all the others in the flickering candle-flames.

She knelt like that for a few minutes while Niall waited quietly in a pew at the back of the church.

"Laugh if you want," she said defiantly, digging her hands into her pockets as they walked quickly in the direction of the hospital.

"I'm not laughing."

"But you want to."

"I don't," he insisted. "It's just that . . ."

She glanced at him as he frowned, looking for the words. "Just that you don't believe in any of that."

"Right now, Niall, I don't know what I believe in. I believed in Tony, and that didn't work, did it?"

"That's different."

"I know."

They had reached the hospital.

"Same story?" he asked. "I'm to wait outside?"

"I could be a while."

"That doesn't matter. What would you like me to do?"

She bit her lip, looked towards the doorway. Made up her mind.

"Come with me, Niall. Will you?"

He looked at her, standing close, reassuring her. "Of course."

He found the waiting almost unbearable, sitting with the two or three others who were there, lifting leaflets he had no interest in and flicking through them, just for something to do.

Finally, when he felt he must start pacing up and down just to rid himself of the tension, the door opened and she came out. She looked pale and shaky, biting her lip again, fragile. He didn't ask anything, just put his arm around her and led her to the door and out into the bright morning. He could feel her trembling against him. He looked around urgently, seeking a quiet place, but there was none. And then suddenly she was crying, racking sobs she could no longer contain, while he held her and soothed her as he might a child. He stroked her back and waited.

Finally she lifted her head and wiped her eyes, and smiled at him.

"God knows what I'd be like if it was positive!"

"You mean . . . ?"

"I'm okay!" She sniffed, took out a tissue, smiled shakily at him before blowing her nose. "Sorry about the performance. I think it's just the relief."

He smiled, hugged her. They laughed and couldn't stop, letting go the last of the tension, holding each other now at arm's length, laughing more at the expressions of one or two people coming through the gate who stared at the mad couple and gave them a wide berth.

"What next?" Niall asked, when at last they were able to stop.

"Next, I get on with the rest of my life," said Clare, linking her arm loosely through his as they went back out through the gate and headed towards the city centre again.

"There's just one thing I have to do first. And I have to go back to Dublin to do it."

Chapter Sixteen

"You bitch! You bloody bitch! I'll kill you first!"

She could almost believe he meant it, Clare thought, as she sat looking at Tony. She wasn't afraid, didn't react as his face grew dark with rage and he stood up, palms flat on the table, and shouted across at her. She knew she would never be afraid of him again.

Niall had been appalled when she told him what she planned to do.

"Have sense, Clare. You can't go there on your own, you know what he's like. And as for this idea of yours – couldn't you just tell the police or something, or else go straight to his company? I mean, why warn him? And why put yourself at risk?"

"It's just something I have to do, Niall. I know I should probably see him in a hotel or something, somewhere public. But this way, meeting him on his own ground – I have to prove to myself that I'm a match for him. And this is the best way to do it."

"You're mad, Clare."

"Yes, I am. Mad with anger, Niall. Raging that I had to go through all this. Raging at myself for being such a fool."

"At least give yourself a few days to think about it. There's no need to go tearing back up there right away."

"I don't want to put it off any longer. It's something I should have done long ago."

Niall had sighed, staring down at the river. They had stopped on their way back into town to lean on the bridge over the Corrib. Clare love the rushing water of the weir, loved the noise of it. It was there that she told Niall her plan.

"You probably won't let me come with you."

She had smiled at him. "No, Niall, but thanks for the offer. I'm a big girl now. I got myself into this, I can get myself out."

"In one piece?" He had looked very worried.

"I'll do my best," she had said, still smiling, still not reassuring him.

"You know, Clare, that you could walk away from this. Put it all behind you."

"I couldn't do that, it would be letting him get away with everything."

Niall was silent for a minute or two before turning to her. "Well, why not? Just walk away. Let him get on with his lousy life, and you get on with yours. You're free of him now."

"No, Niall. I'm not free of him. I thought I would be, once I had the test. But I'm not, and I won't be until I do this."

"What about forgive and forget?"

"I never forget, Niall. And I very rarely forgive. It's why I'm a bad enemy."

"This *is* Clare we're talking about? Come on, you haven't an enemy in the world, you never bitch about people or do the dirty on them, you're the most easy-going person I know. You let people away with murder, you're the one who always makes excuses and only sees the good in everyone!"

"Thanks, Niall, that's just what I needed to remind me why I'm doing this. That's how Tony saw me too, a wimp who wouldn't say boo to him, someone he could treat like dirt."

"You know I didn't mean it like that," Niall interrupted.

"I know. But I know as well that I might let people get away with a lot, but there's a line they can't cross. And Tony did, and he'll regret it."

"You weren't this angry before."

"I wasn't letting myself be. I had too much to do worrying about the other thing. Now that's out of the way, I can concentrate on dealing with Tony."

"You'll destroy him, you know."

He said it quietly, but she rounded on him, her eyes flashing. "Why shouldn't I? He nearly destroyed me."

"He didn't manage it. But he might try, if you go ahead with this."

"I'm not afraid of him any more, Niall. I know I'm not. But I still have to prove it to myself. And anyway, there's a more important reason."

"If there is, I'd like to hear it, because I still think you're crazy to do this."

"I'm doing it for someone else as well."

"Oh?" He turned to look at her, leaning one elbow on the river wall. Clare was looking down into the water, arms on the wall in front of her, hands clasped.

"I think I told you, did I? Way back?" she said. "When Tony stole that money from his firm, he covered his tracks well. So well he couldn't resist boasting about it. And now they'll have discovered it's missing, and the blame will land on his boss Gary. That's how Tony set it up. He was delighted with himself, said Gary deserved it if he was too stupid to see what was happening under his nose."

"Maybe he has a point."

"Niall! You don't mean that, do you?"

"Well, why should you take risks, when Gary should have seen it himself? You don't even know the guy, do you?"

"Actually, I *do* know him, and I know how Tony got away with it. Tony would be smooth and charming, and say "Don't worry about that, I have it all under control," and Gary would believe him because Gary is the decentest man you could meet. He wouldn't suspect him for a minute."

"He wasn't doing his job properly, you mean."

"You're being very hard, Niall. It's not like you."

"I see the situation it's left you in. Gary should've been watching his own back."

"Maybe. Instead he was watching his wife dying."

217

"God, I – "

"And Tony knew that, and took advantage of it."

"And – Clare? Did you know what he was up to?"

"Not at the time, no. But afterwards. When it was too late, and Tony had set him up."

"You could still go to the police – and the company. They'd believe you, you can explain what he did. And you should warn Gary. Though he'll probably get a hammering anyway, for not keeping an eye on Tony, if that's what he should've been doing."

"He might have some explaining to do. I don't know. But he'll have a lot more if I don't tell them what was going on. I have to do it."

"You don't have to do it this way." He looked at her, willing her to agree with him.

She turned, leaning her back against the bridge, palms flat against the stone.

"Yes, Niall, I do. Because I want to see his face. I want to see his expression when he knows it's all over, that he hasn't won. That he can't treat people like dirt, and get away with it."

"You're taking a huge risk."

"It'll be worth it. And I'll be very careful."

She was careful. The first thing she told him, once she arrived at his flat, was that the police knew exactly where she was, and exactly what time she should be back at the police station, and exactly who to blame if she didn't arrive back there. The second thing was that Gary Andrews was on his way over even now with the company's managing director and accountant, to hear at first hand the details of what Tony had done. And then they, too, would be contacting the police.

She could almost feel sorry for him, sitting with the untouched dinner in front of him, a dinner he had prepared for Clare's return. She didn't feel at all guilty that she had implied she was coming back to him. She had wanted the satisfaction of catching him off guard, making a fool of him. It was what he deserved, what he had done to her. She wanted him to suffer. Then, maybe, she could let go of this rage she felt.

Tony tried a different tack.

"We were good together, Clare. You know we were. We could have all that again. I've given up the stuff, I swear it. And I've plenty of cash put by. We could start again, somewhere else." He was beginning to sound desperate now.

"You just don't get it, do you, Tony? You have nothing. You don't have me, or a job, or whatever money you think you have. They'll freeze your bank accounts."

"Not the ones in the Isle of Man – they won't know about them." He was sorry the minute he said it.

"Fool," she thought, smiling at him. "They'll know now," she said.

It was then that he threatened to kill her and she sat unmoving, unafraid, wondering how in God's name she had ever thought she loved this man. The charm and sophistication, the confidence that was really arrogance, were gone. Instead she saw a frightened boy trying to get his own way with threats.

She didn't even find him attractive any more. He had lost weight, and his face looked sharper, sly, almost vicious. The blond hair still gleamed, but that was almost all she recognised of the old Tony. She could walk away from this man very easily indeed.

He was still in a rage. "I did it all for you, you know that. You didn't say no to the holidays, the presents, any of that!"

"You're starting to repeat yourself, Tony. You know I never asked for any of that. Which reminds me . . ."

She reached into her bag, withdrew a large black velvet-covered jewellery box.

"These are yours. They're all there. I have no use for them."

She stood up, placed the box on the table, watching as he glanced down in distaste. "What would I want them for? I only bought them so you'd look half-decent when we went out."

She was about to reply, stung at the injustice of it, when he continued. "And besides, you needn't worry, I bought them with my own money, they're not 'tainted'." He was sneering now. "And besides, *darling*, believe me, you earned them. Not that you didn't enjoy doing it!"

I won't let myself cry, she thought. I will *not* give him the satisfaction.

"You really are a bastard, Tony." Her voice was tight, controlled. "You deserve everything that's coming to you."

They were standing like that, facing each other, furious, when the doorbell rang. "Don't think I'll ever forget this!" he said, giving her a filthy look as he crossed to the door.

"I'm hoping you won't be able to," she answered. She was determined not to let him see how rattled she was.

He opened the door, still angry, to face the three men who were standing there.

"You can refuse to let us in, Tony," the grey-haired man was saying. "But it might be better in the long run if you didn't."

Tony moved back wordlessly, opening the door wider to allow them through. Gary nodded almost imperceptibly to Clare as he followed the others towards the big black leather couch under the window. All three of them remained standing just in front of it.

Gary looked miserable, Clare thought. Anxious and miserable. He didn't need this so soon after his wife's death – or at any other time, for that matter.

The grey-haired man, still standing in front of the couch, turned to address her.

"This can't be easy for you, Miss Delaney. I assure you it's not easy for any of us. I'm James McPartland, by the way. We spoke this afternoon. And you may remember we met at the office party last Christmas."

Clare nodded. She had recognised the Managing Director, and assumed that the dark-haired man standing next to him was Paul Feeney, the accountant.

"Now, how do you want to do this?" James McPartland continued, turning to Tony.

Tony decided to try to bluff if out.

"I'm not really sure what this is about, Mr McPartland," he said with a quick, calculated smile. "But perhaps I could offer you all a drink while you tell me why you're here?"

The response was cold. "I suggest you do the decent thing at this stage, Tony, rather than adding to the trouble you've caused. I presume Miss Delaney has already told you that she telephoned me this afternoon. Although why she wanted to do it this way, God knows, but that's her business. She's saved us all a lot of trouble – not least Gary, here," he finished, looking towards the man on his left.

Gary spoke for the first time. Clare felt sorry for him. He looked wretched.

"Why, Tony?" he said. "Or is there any point in asking?"

Tony had the grace to look slightly ashamed, but didn't reply.

"They've been investigating me for the past week," Gary continued. "Did you know that? Or did you give a damn? You planned it well, I'll hand you that." The man looked on the point of breaking down. "You landed me rightly in the shit, and only for Clare . . ." he stopped and drew a deep breath.

"You can imagine how the rest of us feel, Tony." It was James McPartland who was speaking now. "Gary should never have been under suspicion, his loyalty was never in question before. It's been a rough week for all of us. And it will get rougher."

"I don't see why you're blaming me. You can't prove

anything, since there's nothing to prove." Tony's voice was calm, reasonable, ice-cold at the edges. "Gary was the only one with access to those bogus accounts . . ."

Too late, he realised his mistake as James McPartland raised an eyebrow.

"And how would you have known that there were bogus accounts, if you weren't involved?" His voice was equally chilly as he stared across at Tony. "And please, spare us any suggestion that it was Gary who instigated it – we know better than that now, based on what Miss Delaney has told us. And she has told us a great deal. You really shouldn't have given her so much detail, Tony. That wasn't clever."

"You only have *her* word for it!" Tony said, nodding his head curtly in Clare's direction. "And believe me, that's worth nothing – I should know!"

James McPartland sighed. "I expected better from you, Tony. But then, I've been wrong all along the line, haven't I? You're a convincing man. And an intelligent one. A pity you didn't use those talents more wisely."

"Oh, I was doing fine," Tony said, dropping the pretence at politeness. "I'd still be doing fine, if it wasn't for *her!*" He almost spat the word.

Clare stood calmly, looking at him. He can't hurt me any more, she thought, surprised. It really is finished.

"I had hoped to do this differently, Tony," James McPartland said. "It would have been easier all round if you had volunteered the information. As it is, you leave me no option. May I use the telephone?"

Without waiting for a reply he crossed to the desk in

the corner and lifted the receiver. They waited in a tense circle as he dialled the number of the fraud squad.

"I can't thank you enough for your assistance, Miss Delaney," James McPartland said. It was the following afternoon, and they were sitting in his plush fifth-floor office in the Financial Services Centre. "And I know Gary is most grateful to you."

Gary nodded in response. He looked very different from the man she had met yesterday, the haggard look almost gone.

"We all have questions to answer," McPartland continued, "and we need to re-examine our procedures thoroughly. But at least the blame is now being placed where it belongs – thanks to you. Now . . ."

James McPartland paused as the phone rang. "That's excellent," he said, in response to the caller. "I have some people with me who will be very glad indeed to hear that."

He allowed himself a slight smile as he hung up the phone and turned again towards where Clare, Gary and Paul Feeney, the accountant, were sitting.

"It seems that an evening with the gentlemen of the Fraud Squad has had the desired effect. Tony is apparently willing to make a full statement."

Clare wasn't alone in heaving a sigh of relief.

"Now," he continued, "I do hope you will allow us to show our gratitude." He picked up a brown envelope. "The amount is not so big as to embarrass you, but you may find it useful and I hope it brings you pleasure."

"No!" Clare's voice was louder than she had intended. "I mean, I'm sorry, but I don't want it. That wasn't why – "

"I fully appreciate that."

"I still can't take it. I just wanted to do the right thing. I couldn't let Gary take the blame. I'm only sorry I didn't do this sooner. And I've got everything I need from this. Believe me."

"Well, if you're quite sure . . ."

He seemed undecided whether he should try to persuade her further.

"There is one final thing. " He reached into a drawer in his desk and removed a black velvet jewellery case. "Tony asked me last night if I would ensure that you got this. He said it belonged to you, and he was quite emphatic that none of it was purchased with this firm's money. I hope I did the right thing?" he asked, suddenly uncertain as he saw her expression. "He gave it to me before he went with the police, just after you'd left. He said you wouldn't take it from him, but that it is definitely yours."

Clare hesitated a moment longer before reaching for the box, hating Tony and the message he was sending her. She could still hear him sneering 'You earned it'. But she was unwilling to embarrass this man further by refusing his attempted kindness.

She took the jewellery case, tucking it firmly into the side-pocket of her hold-all as she stood up. The three men stood also, and Mr McPartland extended his hand.

"Don't forget, if there's anything at all we can do for you, we should be very glad to help."

She smiled her thanks, said goodbye to them and left.

The early afternoon sun was bright as she walked along Burgh Quay. She wasn't sure of the train times but she could be at the station in twenty minutes or so and she was happy to wait. She had finished her business in Dublin.

Well, almost. The weight of her hold-all as it bumped against her hip reminded her of the jewellery. Nearly four thousand pounds worth of it, she remembered from the insurance valuation. How in God's name had she ever thought it was okay to accept those kinds of presents from Tony?

Except that she had thought – what? That they would be together for good, that's what she had thought. And now she had to decide what to do with it. He obviously didn't want it, and she certainly had no intention of keeping it. It had no meaning for her now, it would mock her every time she looked at it.

She was deep in thought as she passed the Ha'penny Bridge.

"Spare a few pence, Ma'am? For the child?"

The traveller woman was there again, sitting on the steps leading to the bridge, holding her baby against her and looking up at Clare with a smile.

"You must get cold, sitting here all day," Clare said.

"You do get used to it, Ma'am. And I need the money. I want to go to England, myself an the child. I have a sister there."

She was little more than a child herself, Clare thought, as she rummaged in her pocket for some coins. She hefted the hold-all back out of her way, and as she did so the hard edge of the jewellery case banged against her side.

She paused, leaving the young woman looking at her quizzically. She thought quickly. She couldn't – but why not? They were hers, she had *earned* them, he said, and she certainly didn't want them. She just hoped she wouldn't embarrass the woman, but she'd have to chance it.

"Wait a minute," she said, reaching into her bag and pulling out a notebook. "What's your name?" She started to scribble in the book.

"It's all right, Ma'am, you keep your money," the woman said, turning her head away.

"No, please, it's okay, I have something for you, I just have to write a note saying it's yours, that's all."

The woman turned to look at her again, still suspicious.

"Bridie Connors, Ma'am," she said finally.

"I'm Clare Delaney, and I have some jewellery here that I want you to have. It's mine, you won't get into any trouble. I just don't want it any more. And if anyone asks you about it get them to ring this man, Mr McPartland. He'll tell them it's okay."

She passed over the note and the jewellery box, and Bridie Connors folded them quickly into her shawl beside the baby. "Ma'am . . ."

"It's real gold. Make sure you get a good price for it. And I hope things go well for you in England."

"God be good to you, Ma'am."

Clare smiled at her and walked quickly off along the quays, leaving Bridie Connors staring after the madwoman who had just given her the chance of a new life.

Chapter Seventeen

Clare sat in the little courtyard, relaxing with a cup of coffee while she planned her day. The bright May sunshine, slanting through the trees at the back of the old forge, lit up the whole place and seemed to bring it to life. It would be a lovely day, and a great start to the holiday season. Her guests were due to arrive this afternoon.

She got up, leaving the empty cup on the wooden bench, and walked towards the gap in the wall that led to the paddock. She could smell the faint tang of the sea as she headed for the little hill with its stand of trees from where she could look out over the ocean. A walk on the beach would be perfect on a morning like this, but she had too much to do. She'd have to settle for just the sight of it for the time being.

She was standing there, leaning against the big mountain ash, when she saw Kate arriving on her big rainbow-bright bicycle. She waved, coming back down through the big field and opening the green iron gate that led back into the courtyard just as Kate began examining the flowers that tumbled from every possible container, making a blaze of colour in front of the apartments.

"Hi, Kate!"

"Morning, Clare! I see where they got the saying 'as welcome as the flowers in May'! Aren't they gorgeous. I must come and paint them while they're at their best. Would you mind?"

"Are you mad? I'd love it! Wish I could paint. I've been taking pictures of them instead."

"Well, photos can be lovely, too," Kate said.

She bent to examine some plants trailing from the big wooden wheelbarrow, then turned to look at Clare.

"Are you busy? I'm not coming at a bad time, or anything?"

"Not at all. You know I'm always delighted to see you. And I'm not busy 'til later. I've guests coming this afternoon." She was smiling as she said it.

"Have you now! Isn't that great! And who are they?"

"A couple, and a family. Two separate lots. It never rains but it pours!"

"How did they find you?"

"I put ads in the papers. Niall's idea. The phone hasn't stopped hopping."

As if on cue, the ringing sounded loud and clear through the open window.

"Back in a minute."

Clare lifted the phone, expecting it to be Niall, and was surprised to hear Rick's voice. She had thought that by now he'd be back in the States.

"I'm in Galway," he was saying. "Things took a while longer than I expected in England, and then I was in Dublin for a couple of days and I was going to fly home from there. But I've still got Kate's lamp. And I'd really like to see you again."

"Where are you staying in Galway?" she asked.

"I've checked out of the place I stayed last night. I already called Kate and she said I could stay with her tonight. I was hoping we might get together, maybe go for dinner at Niall's if you're free?"

"Well . . ." She hesitated, remembering the unsettling effect he had had on her the night in Reynard's. But she liked him, it would be good to see him again. Except that she had all these guests arriving . . .

"I can't. Sorry, Rick, but I've people booked in for to-night. I won't be able to get out."

"I see." He sounded disappointed. "Maybe another time?"

"When do you go back?"

"Sometime after I've seen you. Can I call you from Kate's?"

"Of course."

She went back outside, deep in thought. Kate, busy with a big green watering-can, glanced over at her.

"Are you all right?"

"Fine."

"You're sure? You look a bit distracted."

Clare brushed her hair back from her face with a sweeping gesture.

"Really, I'm fine. A bit surprised, that's all. That was Rick."

"Oh?" Kate's attempt to look innocent wouldn't fool anybody.

Clare laughed. "You know well he's around. He's staying with you tonight, isn't he?"

"Okay, so I know. Now, can I have a cup of tea? Or do you need to get things organised?"

"No, I've plenty of time. I only *feel* busy, as if there's loads I should be doing."

"Nonsense, the place looks grand," Kate said, following Clare into the cottage. "And I'll give you a hand checking the apartments in a few minutes, so you can relax until they come. I'm dying for a chat. How long is it since I've seen you?"

"Two weeks?" Clare said, filling the kettle.

She came to sit opposite Kate at the pine table. "When I came back from Dublin you weren't around. I rang you a few times, then Niall told me you were up in Dublin yourself."

"That's right. Molly's not too well."

"I'm sorry to hear that, Kate." She knew Kate and Molly were very close. "Is it anything serious?" She regretted asking the minute she saw Kate's expression.

"I'm afraid it might be. Molly's desperate really, she keeps things to herself, you nearly have to drag them out of her. She'd never admit to being sick."

"So why do you think it's serious? How does she seem?"

Kate looked anxious. She sat with her elbows on the table, her hands joined and her chin resting on them. She was gazing into the distance, through the window, and she didn't answer for a minute or two.

"She's lost weight," she said finally. "And she's

exhausted all the time. She's the same build as me, she's always been very thin but now she's skin and bone. And she hasn't a scrap of energy."

"Did she tell you what's wrong?" Clare asked, filling a cup from the little blue china teapot and pushing it across the table towards Kate. Kate didn't seem to notice.

"She refused to talk about it. She kept saying she was okay, that I shouldn't be worrying about her. I felt she didn't want me there and that's not like her, either."

"What made you go to see her? Did she ask you to?"

"No. No, she didn't. There was something I needed to talk to her about. Only I never got the chance – she kept changing the subject, and I hadn't the heart to press her when I could see how she was."

"Does Donal know what's wrong?"

"I don't think so. He'd tell me if he did. He knows she's got thinner, and slowed down a lot, but he's putting it down to her age. But she's still only in her sixties. Whatever is wrong, it's not because of her age."

"Maybe he'll talk to her, if he knows how worried you are. Would you think of asking him again?"

"No," said Kate. "He has enough on his plate. And besides, he'd never leave her if he thought she was sick."

"Leave her?"

"I forgot you didn't know – sure I haven't seen you since. Yes, he's talking about getting out of Dublin."

"Where would he go? Has he decided?"

Kate laughed. "Would you believe, he's thinking of

coming back down here. His housekeeper is leaving to go home to Sligo, so he thought this was as good a time as any to look for a year off. He's been thinking about it for a while. And he always loved it here, you know. Himself and Jenny used to talk about moving down."

"I know," Clare said. "He told me."

"Did he, now?" Kate looked surprised, but the anxious look was gone, replaced by her obvious pleasure at the thought of Donal being nearby. "He doesn't often talk about her."

"He talked to me, a bit."

Kate glanced at her cold, untouched tea, stood up to empty it along with what was left in the teapot, switched on the kettle again.

"He likes you a lot," she called to Clare from the kitchen, after a minute or two.

"And I like him. He's an interesting man." Clare smiled as she sat at the table, turning to watch Kate as she came back into the room. "But don't go getting any ideas, Kate," she added. "I'm past all that!"

"Oh, I'm not the one getting ideas. As well you know!"

"What do you mean?" Clare asked, reaching for the cup Kate was handing her.

"You know what I mean. Our friend Mr Flaherty!"

"That's all he is, Kate. A friend," Clare said. She was annoyed as she felt herself blushing.

"Of course he is. And that's the reason he's coming traipsing back down here, because you're friends!"

"Kate . . ."

"I know, I'm only teasing you, and maybe I shouldn't be. But, Clare . . ." She paused, choosing her words. "How long has it been now since you went out with anyone? You're a young girl, Clare. Make the most of your chances!"

"It's not that simple, Kate. I'm really not looking for another man. Not for a long while, anyway. Not until I feel ready again."

"Just don't leave it too long, Clare." The older woman looked wistful as she said it.

"Kate?"

"Yes?"

"Tell me to mind my own business if you like . . ."

"I might."

"Well, you didn't look for anyone either, did you? I mean, you must have had loads of chances after you came back here with Kevin."

"It's not easy for a woman with a small child. Anyway, I wasn't free to go looking. Even if I'd wanted to, which I didn't."

"Why weren't you free? I mean, I thought . . ." She paused. "Sorry, Kate. I shouldn't be asking all these questions."

"You thought I was widowed?"

Clare nodded.

"People just assumed that," Kate said. "I was known as Mrs Kavanagh, and I still was Mrs Kavanagh. And it was true that he died working on a building-site, but that wasn't until a good bit later."

"Does Kevin know you left him?"

"He does now. It took him a long, long time to forgive me for that – he felt I should have stayed, if only for his sake. And maybe he was right. I don't know. I thought I was doing the right thing at the time."

"That's all you can do," Clare said. "What you think is the right thing at the time."

"No, Clare. That's too easy, it's a cop-out. What you can do is think a bit harder before you do the *wrong* thing."

"But how could you do that, Kate?" Clare asked, surprised at her tone. "Sometimes you don't know what's the right or the wrong thing until much later, when you see how it all turns out."

Kate sighed. "I know, you're right. That's what makes it all so complicated."

She got up and brought the cups to the sink.

"Now, enough talking. I thought you told me you had guests coming?"

"I nearly wish they weren't, now. I'm a bit worried about how it'll go."

"Why is that? You've done it before, for Donal and the boys."

"A trial run," Clare said. "It didn't seem real, it was like having friends here. It'll be different with strangers – I'm not sure now how I'll feel."

"Well, get ready to find out, because here they come!"

Clare turned, surprised, to look through the window, and was nearly petrified to see four tanned, athletic-looking women with huge rucksacks strapped to their backs coming through the red gate that led in from the main road at the front of the cottage.

"Oh God!" she said. "Let me out of here! These aren't even the people I booked in – it's supposed to be a family and a couple, not – "

Kate stood there laughing at her. "Well, you wanted guests, and that's what you have! Be careful what you wish for, you might get it! Who was it said that?"

"Oscar Wilde," Clare answered absent-mindedly. She was waiting for the knock on the door.

When she opened it she was greeted with big, wide smiles and cheerful Australian accents.

"Hi there! We're looking for a place to stay, and we met a guy called Jack who said you could maybe help?"

The girl who spoke had cropped black hair and, though she was much shorter than the others, she carried the big rucksack easily. She looked about eighteen or nineteen.

"Well, I'm not really sure," Clare started. "I've two groups of people coming later. But there are some really good places in Clifden."

Groans all round from the girls, one of whom dropped her rucksack in the doorway and leaned against the door frame.

"That's six or seven miles away, right? I don't think we'll make it!"

"Are you hitching? Clare asked.

"Yeah," responded one of the others. "But it's really hard to get a lift for all four of us together, and we don't want to split up again, that gets kind of messy."

"I suppose I could drop you into Clifden . . ."

The girls looked at each other.

"No chance at all we can stay here?" the dark-haired girl asked.

"Of course you can!" Kate said briskly, coming forward to the door. "Clare, the other apartment is free to-night, isn't it? *Saffron?*"

"Well, yes, but I haven't got the beds made up or anything . . ."

"No worries! We've got sleeping bags!" The blond girl who spoke looked relieved. "See, we've kind of had it with hostels for a while. And we can't afford B and B all the time. So we were hoping to find a quiet place, settle in for a few days . . ."

"You found it!" Kate said, smiling at them. "Will I show them around, Clare, or do you want to do it?"

"I'll do it," Clare said, lifting the key from its hook behind the back door and leading the way.

"You'll like it!" Kate called after them.

They loved it.

"It's cool! Glad your Mom talked you into this. What do you charge, anyway?"

"Twelve-fifty each, per night," Clare said, not bothering to correct her. "The kitchen and bathroom are down there" – she gestured towards the far end of the living-room – "and there's just one big bedroom, through here. It's a dormitory really, there are six beds in it."

They filed past her into the big, bright room.

"Don't worry, I won't put anyone else in here," she

added quickly, seeing their horrified expressions. "And I'll do a good deal if you stay more than one night," she added, getting into her stride. "Say, ten pounds a head after tonight."

She was beginning to enjoy this. Her initial panic at being confronted by four unexpected guests had nearly subsided.

"This is really great," the dark-haired girl said as they came back into the big living-room. "I'm Carly, by the way. You sure it's okay for us to stay here?" She had settled on the couch, and didn't look as if she was about to go anywhere.

"It's fine. You're very welcome. I was just a bit thrown when I saw you all, because this is really my first weekend to have people here. I don't even have a sign outside yet."

"We promise to behave ourselves, then!" one of the blond girls said. "I'm Stacy, and that's Megan and Kelly."

"I'm Clare. I'll leave you to have a look around – call in if you need anything."

"There's a beach near here?"

"Just down the laneway."

"Safe for swimming?"

"Very safe. You'll find it freezing, though."

"No worries, we're used to it by now. Well, almost!"

She left them to it, going back in to Kate.

"Thanks. I would have sent them packing."

"You'd have done more than that. You'd have given them a taxi service into Clifden and deposited them in the willing arms of the competition. What kind of businesswoman are you, at all?"

"A better one than I was five minutes ago, thanks to you!"

"What in God's name were you thinking of?"

"I panicked. I remember staying in the hostel in Glendalough years ago, and four Australian women arrived and took over the whole place, we couldn't get near the showers or the fire, and they played their transistor morning, noon and night . . ."

"So let them," Kate said. "You won't even hear them. And this is business, remember? Speaking of which, you'd better get ready for your other guests!"

Clare was about to have a well-earned shower at ten that evening when the phone rang.

"Just checking," Niall said when she answered. "How goes it?"

"Great, but I'm wrecked. A full house, Niall! Ten people!"

"That's what you want! Managing all right?"

"No problem. Kate stayed around to give me moral support. The O'Learys got here at about four. They're from Cork and they've two small kids and a baby – actually, that's *eleven* people – and there's a young couple down from Dublin, they only look about twenty and they're very nervous. I think it's their first weekend away together . . ."

Niall laughed. "Well, just give them plenty of space, Clare. At least they're well away from bawling babies."

"And bawling Australians."

"What?" he laughed.

"The other guests. Four Australian girls. They're great. But very loud. But great . . ."

"You're trying to convince yourself?"

"Not really. No, I like them. It's just that . . . well, you'd know they're there!"

"It'd be worse if they weren't. Customers, Clare. Paying customers. Give them the red carpet treatment and everyone will be happy!"

"I'll keep reminding myself! See you Monday?"

"Great. Come in about half twelve if you can."

She had only hung up the phone when it rang again. She lifted it, thinking Niall was calling back.

"Is this a good time? It's not too late?"

"Hi, Rick. No, it's not late at all."

She was surprised to hear him, had forgotten he'd said he would ring.

"Kate told me you'd had a heavy day, I wasn't sure you'd be still up. What about lunch tomorrow? Or maybe dinner, if you don't have plans?"

"The guests will still be here tomorrow. I'll be up to my eyes."

"Is that a definite 'no'? I mean, if you really don't want to, I'd rather you just said so and I'll back off. But if you'd like to, then maybe we can figure something out?"

Clare thought for a moment. She really had enjoyed being with him in Dublin. So why not? Anyway, he was going back shortly, it couldn't lead to anything she didn't want.

"Yes, I'd like to. And maybe Kate can baby-sit the place here for me. I'll ask her, anyway."

"I've already done that, she said 'yes'."

Her silence answered him. "Sorry. I shouldn't have done that, right?"

She could have told a white lie just to be polite, but she had kept quiet for too long when she was with Tony. She wasn't about to do it again.

"Right. I would have preferred to ask myself. But it's okay. What about dinner tomorrow night?"

"Great. Kingfisher? I really liked it last time. Or Niall's other place, what's it called?"

"Albatross. But Kingfisher is quieter," she said, and was sorry as soon as she said it. She wasn't sure she wanted Niall to see her out with Rick, but couldn't have said why.

"I can pick you up at eight, would that be good?"

"Fine. You have a car?"

"I hired one in Galway."

"I'll be ready. "

He arrived promptly at eight the following evening, dressed stylishly in black and looking every bit as good as she remembered. Twenty minutes later they were sitting in a secluded corner of Kingfisher, studying their gold-embossed menus. Niall, after a brief stop at their table to welcome them, had left them alone after raising his eyebrows to Clare, with a slight smile, while Rick was studying the wine list.

"It's not like that," she had wanted to protest, but how could she? She'd have to await her chance to tell Niall he was jumping to conclusions.

"You look really lovely, Clare. Green suits those beautiful eyes of yours."

She smiled her thanks across the candle-lit table. She liked Rick, but that was all there was to it. Still, it was lovely to be complimented. She had become too used to hearing only criticism from Tony.

"I really wish I didn't have to go so soon. I'd like to get to know you better, Clare. A lot better."

"When do you have to go?" she asked, neatly side-stepping his other comment.

"End of the week. No choice, really – I've left Uncle Joe on his own for too long. And I really don't have any reason for staying longer. Do I?"

His voice was soft, and his expression, in the candlelight, seemed wistful.

"You've definitely given up trying to find Beth?" she asked, deliberately misunderstanding.

"Yes. " His voice was firmer now. "And maybe now I can let go of this feeling that it was really important that I come to Ireland right now. My dad used to get those sort of feelings, too. Mom always put it down to what she called the Irish in us. It was her explanation for anything she didn't really understand."

"Like what?"

"Oh, I don't know. Sometimes we'd get crazy ideas like putting money on a no-hope baseball team, knowing they didn't stand a chance. We'd just have a hunch, a strong feeling, and follow through on it. That kind of thing."

"Did it ever work out?"

"Never – but that didn't stop us!"

They were laughing, heads close together, when Niall passed by and kept on going, winking at Clare. She was distracted for a moment, forcing her attention back to Rick.

"And maybe this hunch about coming to Ireland really was the right thing to do. Because I can let go of Beth, finally, and start getting on with my life."

"And you really can let go now?"

He paused before answering, lifting the bottle to pour the last of the wine into their glasses.

"Have to. I've done just about everything I can. It wasn't meant to be and I can finally believe that."

"How come? I mean, what made you believe it?"

He sipped the wine before answering. "I thought about what you said, that night in the Shelbourne, and I decided you were right – I might regret not giving one last shot at finding her. So while I was in London I called to see an old friend. Well, she was more Beth's friend, Beth used to room with her. She was still at the same address, it was her parent's house."

"And . . . ?"

"She told me Beth had gone away without even saying where she was going, right after I left. And then she heard she'd gone back home to Ireland, back to her family – to start College, I guess. And Debbie, her friend, had the address there, so she passed on all the letters I sent after I went back to the States."

"But you never got a reply?"

"I never got a reply. Neither did Debbie."

"So . . ."

"So she didn't want to hear from me. Or Debbie. She never heard from her again either."

"So that's the end of it? You're fairly sure she got the letters and just didn't answer?"

"I know Debbie *sent* the letters. That's all I know for sure. So I decided to go to the address."

"Debbie still had it?"

"In an old college diary. This lady keeps everything! She's still ticked off at Beth for losing touch, but she looked up the address for me"

Niall passed again, saw the intent expressions on their faces and kept going.

"So I went there. A big old red-brick house in a place called Phibsboro. You know it?"

Clare nodded. "And?"

"An old lady answered. Said she'd lived there for ten years, never heard of anyone called Elizabeth and didn't know where the previous occupiers went. Said she wouldn't tell me even if she did."

He stopped, a puzzled expression on his face.

"Did you believe her?" Clare asked.

"No reason not to. But I still can't figure why she was so hostile. Told me she'd call the cops if I came bothering her again. So that's that, I guess."

"It seems an awful way to have to leave it. I mean, if you could have seen Beth, or if you'd heard she was married or whatever, at least you'd know . . ."

"I know now, because I've done all I can. If she didn't know Beth, that's it, and if she *did* know her, well, the only explanation is that Beth didn't want me to contact her. Otherwise, she wouldn't have blocked me with that witch. So that's my answer. It really is time to leave it and move on."

"And you feel you can do that now?"

"I know it's possible. Especially if I've got someone to help me," he said, smiling across at her.

She decided to be direct.

"This really isn't a good idea, Rick. I'm just getting over someone. And so are you, when it comes to it."

"You're right. And I'm not pushing. But we can be friends, can't we? I'd really like that."

"You're on. I need all the friends I can get!"

It was still early when they arrived back at the cottage. He gladly accepted the offer of coffee, ignoring the fact that he had just drunk two cups at Kingfisher.

"I'll just drop Kate home, I can be back in five minutes."

He was really a nice guy, she thought as she measured coffee into the filter. Good-looking, too. Tony's colouring, but that was all they had in common. Rick was every bit as sophisticated as Tony, but there was something else – a sense that he was *genuine*, something Tony had never been.

She opened the door in response to his gentle tap and they sat drinking coffee and talking for another hour or so.

"I probably won't get to see you again before I go back, Clare. But I'll call you, okay?"

He stood there, seeming reluctant to go.

"Fine. But Rick . . ."

"Mmm?"

"You know that . . ."

"I know. But I also know I want to keep in touch. It's been great meeting you, Clare. Really great."

He moved closer to her, and she wondered if he was going to kiss her and how she'd react if he did.

She wasn't about to find out. The door opened after a brief knock, and Stacey was standing there.

"You'd better come quickly. Looks like there's a fire in the little apartment."

Rick was already running across the courtyard while Clare grabbed the extinguisher from the wall. She could see smoke pouring through the open window as she ran, but there was no sign of flames yet.

The door opened and the young man came through, dragging a blackened duvet behind him. He dropped it on the ground and began stamping on it while Rick grabbed the extinguisher from Clare and helped him to put out the last of the smouldering flames.

"Where's Orla?" Clare asked frantically.

She ran through the door and into the bedroom, lifting another extinguisher from the wall just inside the door.

She found Orla sitting on the bed, her head in her hands, a dressing-gown wrapped around her, sobbing. She seemed okay, and there was no sign of any damage in the room.

"Are you all right?" Clare asked. "What happened?"

The young girl looked up miserably, wiping away tears.

"I'm sorry. I'm really, really sorry. I'll buy you a new one."

"But you're okay?" Clare repeated.

"It just caught fire," Orla said, as if that was an answer. She was crying again.

"How . . . ?" Clare asked, and then she saw how as she lifted the remains of a bottle of sparkling wine from the floor beside the bed and bent to blow out the three candles flickering romantically on the bedside locker.

"Don't worry about it," Clare said. "No damage done. And the main thing is that you're both all right."

Orla started to cry all over again. They'll never try *that* again, Clare thought. She reached to touch Orla on the shoulder, reassuring her.

"Really, it's fine. Honest. It could happen to anyone." She wondered if lies counted in this kind of situation.

"Cool," said Stacey, leaning against the doorway of the bedroom. "I can't *wait* until it happens to me!"

Chapter Eighteen

Donal phoned the evening before the June bank holiday.

"I thought I'd take advantage of the long weekend rather than wait for the summer. But you're probably booked out – Kate said you're doing very well."

"I had a cancellation just half an hour ago, would you believe! You must be meant to come – it's the apartment you were in last time."

"Great. The boys will be thrilled. We would have stayed with Kate otherwise but they regard your playground as theirs! We'll get there early, all right? And I promise not to set fire to the place."

She laughed. "Kate told you?"

"She did. I'm surprised it hasn't put you off."

"It would take more than that. But I've a new rule now, no candles!"

"Spoilsport! It could have been very nasty, though," he added, sounding more serious.

"I know, Donal. Even though I can laugh about it, it terrified me really."

She was out in the garden just after lunch the next day, enjoying the sunshine, when Jody arrived.

"Clare! You'll never guess," he said, face alight with excitement.

She smiled. "So what is it this time?"

It seemed he was there almost every day recently, bringing something new for the little pet farm she was beginning to put together. The paddock was filling gradually with assorted hutches and kennels and little roped-off areas. She had her hands full at this stage with the two pups he had brought over from Jack, the kittens from Kate – God knows why she'd agreed to take two more, Mishka's two were half-grown by now. There were some rabbits as well, that Jody had got from a friend of his. And the *piece de resistance* was the donkey he brought last week.

"You have to take him, Clare," he had insisted. "They're going to have him killed if you don't!"

She had muttered to herself that it wasn't a donkey sanctuary, but Jody had been right. She couldn't resist Neidin's coal-black coat and big soulful eyes. He seemed healthy, maybe just a little past his best. She couldn't possibly let him be put down. Still, it had made her a bit wary about Jody's unexpected presents, and she wondered, as she went over to him, what it was this time.

There was nothing in sight except Jody himself. She hoped he hadn't anything creepy-crawly in his pockets.

"So where is it?" she asked, smiling a bit tentatively.

"Kevin is bringing it over now. He got a lend of a horse." He stopped abruptly. "How do you know?"

"Know what?"

"What's coming."

"I don't. I wish I did!"

"But you said . . ."

He was interrupted by Kate arriving on her bicycle, flushed from hurrying. Her long dark hair, flecked with silver, was streaming behind her, escaping from the purple scarf she had tied hastily around it.

"Isn't it great?" she asked, almost out of breath. "I can't wait . . ."

"You wouldn't like to tell me what's going on?" Clare asked, amused.

"But I told you," Jody said. "There, look!"

There was the sound of hooves, and then she saw it cresting the brow of the hill. Her gypsy caravan. And Kevin, fitting her image of a Romany with his black curls and slight tan, sitting lazily on the little seat at the front and flicking the reins as if he was born to it, grinning at her as he came to a stop just outside the gate.

"Kate, you remembered! God, it's wonderful!" she said, coming to have a closer look. "I love it, it's perfect!"

"I wouldn't exactly say that," said Kate, a bit doubtfully. "But it could be very good once we finish with it!"

It had definitely seen better days, Clare agreed. But it was still exactly what she had in mind.

"Where did you find it? I haven't seen one of these in ages, the travellers all have mobile homes now . . ."

"My friend Phelim found it," Jody explained. "He got it from a fella that used to rent them out for horse-drawn caravan holidays. He has two more if you want them, he'll let you have them cheap."

It was the kind of caravan the travellers used to have before mobile homes took over, made of wood, with a curving roof so they looked a bit like the old covered wagons in the wild west films, but brightly painted, with a little door at the front and two windows, and two little seats for the driver and whoever was keeping him company.

"Can I try it?" Clare asked, hopping up beside Kevin as she spoke.

"Here you go. Mind you don't set him galloping, now!"

She glanced sideways at him as she took the reins, biting back a reply when she saw him grinning, and concentrated on getting a response from the pony. They set off slowly, Jody running alongside, and went about three hundred yards down the road before she made use of a big lay-by to turn him and set him back towards the slight incline again.

"You know what you're at!" Kevin said, admiringly.

"I've done it before." Just as she was wondering whether the hill was a bit steep for the pony, Jody materialised beside the caravan and, catching hold of the harness, encouraged him up the final few yards until they were settled again on the grass verge just outside the paddock.

"So far so good, but how do you get it inside?" Kate asked.

"Nothing for it but to take down the wall," Kevin

said. He was still sitting at the front of the caravan, leaning back lazily in the little seat, looking totally unperturbed.

"Are you able to do that, Kevin?" Clare asked doubtfully.

"It's easy enough if you know how," he answered. "You know these stone walls have no cement, or anything? It's just stone on top of stone, and you can take it down easily, and put it back."

"So do you know how to do it right?"

"Well, I could give it a go . . ."

"Or you could get Jack."

They all turned to look at Jody as he spoke. "Jack'd know what he was at – he'd do it for you no bother. Will I go across and ask him?"

They were all busy when Donal and the twins arrived. Jack, Kevin and Jody were dismantling the wall, and Clare and Kate were standing by to give moral support and keep an eye on the pony nibbling the grass on the verge outside.

"The man himself!" Kevin called over to him as he got out of the car. "Just in time for a bit of honest work!"

Donal came towards them smiling, shepherding the twins ahead of him along the grassy margin.

"God bless the work! It makes a change to see Kevin doing something useful."

He was laughing as he turned to kiss Kate on the cheek.

"You'll be kept busy too, Kate," he added. "Didn't you promise Clare you'd paint it for her if she got it?"

"I did, and I will. You're looking great, love!"

It was true, Clare thought. He looked much more relaxed than last time he arrived. "Can we pet the pony, Daddy? Can we climb up?"

The boys were like puppies straining on a leash in their eagerness to get over to the caravan.

"If you wait a few minutes, lads, we'll have it inside," Clare said. "Then you can do whatever you want."

"Okay, Clare," Luke agreed, while Michael just smiled across at her.

Donal walked over to stand close to her.

"So what are you going to do with it?"

"Clean it," she said, wrinkling her nose. "It's fairly grotty inside. And after that we'll paint it, and then . . . I don't know. I just have a notion that it would look great at the back of the paddock, over near the trees, and the kids can use it for playing in, and we might even use it as extra accommodation if things get a bit crowded."

"I suppose it's crowded enough this weekend?"

"There's a French couple staying in *Wildwood*, and the Dillons got here last night and they're staying in *Saffron*, and *Ocean* is all set up for yourself and the boys."

"You're keeping the names?"

"I am, it's easier than saying the forge and the hostel and Donal's Place all the time!"

"Right, Donal, we'll let you do the easy bit and lead in the pony. Put the lads up there!" Kevin said. He was grinning across at them, well satisfied. The wall had been completely dismantled across a gap of about eight feet, the stones stacked carefully to one side of the opening.

"Come on, lads," Donal said, helping his sons up onto the little seats. "Hold on tight there."

He caught the harness on one side, and with Jody walking at the opposite side of the horse's head, they led the animal into the paddock and on up to the place Clare indicated, sheltered by the stand of trees at the top of the small hill.

"Perfect. Near the *lios*, but not too close," Clare said.

"What's a *lios?*"

"A fairy fort, Luke. A magic circle," Kate answered him, coming up beside them. "Isn't it wonderful? I can't wait to get started!"

They were interrupted by a whooping and hollering from the far end of the paddock.

"The Dillons," Clare explained. "They're a bit boisterous."

"How many of them are there?" Donal asked, looking slightly concerned as he saw the little gang racing towards them.

"Five boys, and one girl. All aged between five and twelve. *Saffron* is bursting at the seams – I had to put in two camp beds. They'll be company for the twins," she added brightly, trying to look as if she believed it

"Time I was off, anyway," Kevin said, beginning to unharness the horse, and Donal looked as if he'd like to join him.

"I'll come with you, Kevin," Jody said. "Unless Jack needs a hand putting back the wall . . ."

"Don't worry, I'll do that," Donal offered. "You'd better make your escape while you can!"

Further conversation was impossible for the moment as the Dillon clan arrived, trying to grab hold of the horse, swarming all over the caravan. Jody took one look at them and headed off down the road, followed by Kevin. Clare wasn't sure if she was imagining the sympathy on Kevin's face as he said goodbye.

"Do you want them doing that?" Donal asked her, nodding towards the caravan with the children in it. One of the boys was doing his best to climb up onto the roof.

"Well, no, not really, not until I have a chance to examine it. But how do I stop them? They'll never hear me. And they wouldn't listen anyway."

They were making an almighty racket, but Clare gave it a go, trying in vain to be heard above their excited yells. She might as well have saved her breath. One of the boys, aged eight or nine, heard her, stopped for a moment, made a rude gesture and continued trying to push his older brother off the front seat. The girl, who seemed to be about seven, was balancing precariously as she walked up along one of the shafts of the caravan, now angled downwards unto the ground. Dear God, Clare thought, there have to be easier ways of making money. Like selling insurance, or something.

"Will I get them to stop?" Donal asked, close to her ear.

She nodded. "I wish you luck."

He hardly needed it, and he didn't even have to raise

his voice much. So *that's* what all that training is for, she thought as, one by one, the children stopped what they were doing to listen to him.

"Clare would like you to get off. *Now,* please. She might let you have a look later. Right now, she'd like you to go down to the playground."

Some of the older boys looked mutinous but climbed down anyway, glaring at Clare. They trailed off in a little group, muttering under their breath, darting her venomous looks now and then over their shoulders.

"So that's how it's done," she said, a trace of wonder in her voice. "I'd never have managed it."

He laughed. "Long years of practice."

"Worth every minute, obviously. Come on, boys, let's go to the playground while your Dad is fixing the wall. You're sure you don't mind?" she asked him.

"Not at all, we'll be finished in no time," he said, heading over to Jack who was bent over the work.

"Well, *I* mind!" This was Luke, who was doing his own share of glaring now.

"Daddy sent those big boys down to our playground. How're *we* supposed to play there now? You *said* your brother made it for *us!*"

"Well . . ." Clare looked helplessly in the direction of Donal's back, and Kate, laughing, came to her rescue.

"Tell them that, then!" Kate said to the two boys. "Tell them it's your playground, and if they don't behave themselves, your daddy will come and put manners on them!"

"I don't think . . ." Clare began.

"Don't worry, Clare, kids understand that kind of language. At least, Donal says they do. Go on down, I'll follow you in a minute."

Kate moved towards the caravan, stroking its sides as if it were a living thing, smiling to herself as she imagined the bright colours she would paint it in the following day. When Clare looked back she was leaning back against the caravan, hands behind her to support her, her hair blowing in the slight breeze, looking across to where Donal and Jack were bending, moving steadily and easily, working together to put the wall back in place.

"How long are those people staying?" Kate asked, coming into the kitchen a few minutes later.

Clare had the twins sitting at the table with buns and milk, looking sorry for themselves. They had given up the unequal fight for space in the playground, and even Clare hadn't been able to help much since the Dillons seemed determined to ignore her completely.

"Too flipping long! Oh, I know . . ." she added as she saw Kate's expression. "They *are* guests, and I should be doing my best for them, and I *am*, it's just that their parents don't seem to give a damn. They think babysitting's all part of the service, and they've been out there sunning themselves on the patio since early morning without taking a blind bit of notice of what the kids are doing. I caught the eldest fella up on top of the shed and d'you know what his father said? He said isn't it great to see he has a head for heights. Honest to God, I don't know how they don't get killed, because I found two of the younger ones half-way up that tree over there, not able to get up nor down, and the parents ignored them completely though they were screaming the place down."

"It won't be for too long more, will it?"

"They're leaving tomorrow," Clare said. "Only they don't know it yet."

"Do you know the little girl is out there picking flowers?" Donal asked, coming into the kitchen.

"Well, at least that's better than – where's she picking them from?" Clare's voice rose several decibels as realisation dawned and she ran for the courtyard. Too late. The girl had a lovely collection of red-and-yellow tulips, held together in a straggly pile, and was taking the petals off them, one by one. Clare turned around and walked slowly and carefully back into the cottage, closing the door softly behind her.

"You didn't say anything to her?"

Clare turned to look at Kate, her face grim. "I couldn't. What I wanted to say wasn't fit for a child's ears. I was going to kill her instead but I stopped myself just in time."

"You could say something to the parents."

She turned to him.

"I could, Donal, but I'd have to say it very slowly and in words of one syllable. And even then they probably wouldn't get the message. Look at them."

He looked, standing back a bit from the window. They were still sitting on the garden chairs from which they hadn't stirred since he arrived, and they were looking across at their daughter, smiling approvingly as she continued to decapitate the flowers.

"Will I say something?" asked Donal. "Or should I keep out of it?"

"Thanks, but I'll go. Only I'll probably kill them instead of their daughter."

"In that case, let me go," he said, smiling at her. "The guards have enough to do on the Bank Holiday without a murder on their hands."

He went out to the patio and was about to cross to where the couple were sitting when he heard shouts from behind the barn, over beyond the barbecue area, and went across to investigate. He glanced over at the playground as he passed. Empty. He hoped they weren't up to devilment.

It took only a moment to see that they were. Two of them were up on Neidin, the donkey, while the two small boys held sticks in their hands and the eldest dragged on a rope he had knotted roughly round the donkey's neck. It was a wonder the poor animal hadn't tried to kick or bite them.

Donal debated whether to roar at them, but instead came up quietly so as not to startle Neidin.

"Let go of him."

Five pairs of eyes turned to glare at him.

"I said, let go. Get down off the donkey and leave him alone."

Though he spoke quietly his voice had a steely quality. The eldest boy, brave now within shouting distance of his father, had no intention of obeying this time.

"It's none of your bleedin' business, anyway. We were here first."

"Let go. *Now*."

"*Eff off*," the boy said, staring back at him.

Donal considered for a moment. He could lift the children bodily off, though he'd probably get kicked or worse in the process. Or he could call their father, but that mightn't help much. And he'd make a fool of himself in front of them, and he didn't want to do that.

He looked around for inspiration, and it came as he looked towards the little shed. He wondered if that's where Clare kept the pups. Jack had told him he sent them over a week or two ago, and Donal hadn't seen them around the place.

He whistled.

"Masher! Here, boy, come get them! Come on, boy!"

He looked expectantly past the boys towards the shed.

"There isn't any . . ." the eldest Dillon boy began, then realised he was on his own. Abandoning the rope, he followed his fleeing brothers.

"You'll be bleedin' sorry," he shouted back to Donal, who smiled as he went to lift up the two little pups who had struggled from their basket in response to the whistle.

"Thanks, fellas. Wait 'til the twins see you two!"

He put them carefully back in their bed, bending to tickle them before going back to check that Neidin was okay.

Clare was in the courtyard, facing the Dillons, when he came back, and he realised she had seen what had happened with Neidin. She was very angry and so were they. The eight Dillons stood in a tight semi-circle, ready to back each other up. Clare was on her own, opposite them, and Kate was standing in the doorway, trying to keep the twins back while they tried to peep out to see why there were raised voices. He crossed the courtyard quickly to stand beside Clare.

She was well into her stride, giving vent finally to the list of everything the Dillons had done, and shouldn't have.

"Now wait a minute!" Mr Dillon said when she paused for breath. "It's not fair to put the blame on the kids, there's nothing for them to do! You should have activities and things!"

"I never said there were activities," Clare responded, totally exasperated. "I said there was a playground, and there is!"

"Not much of a bleedin' playground, if you ask me."

"And you said there were animals," his wife added. "And what's the point of having animals, if you won't let the kids play with them?"

"Play with them, yes. Chase them round the field throwing stones at them, no."

"We didn't . . ."

"*He* did, yesterday," Clare said, pointing to the culprit, who had the grace to look guilty. "He was running after the lambs up there in the paddock. He nearly frightened the life out of them."

"There should be something for them to do," Mr Dillon repeated.

"Activities," Mrs Dillon chimed in, nodding vigorously.

"That's a very good idea."

They all turned to look at Donal.

"You're quite right," he continued. "Kids need something to do besides mistreating the animals and nearly breaking their necks climbing trees. Or destroying the flowerbeds."

"So what are you saying?" Mr Dillon asked. He was standing, arms folded, still ready for an argument.

"I'm saying they need to be kept occupied. And since this isn't a holiday camp, and we're not being paid to mind your kids, it's up to you to do it. But we'll help," he finished easily, as Mr Dillon's jaw dropped.

"Now, look here . . ."

"No, *you* look here. It's very simple. They're your children. You're staying here until . . . ?

"We haven't decided yet."

"Midday tomorrow." Clare's voice was crisp.

"We never said . . ."

"You said you weren't sure, but that you definitely wanted to book for last night and tonight. So that's how long you're staying. And you're welcome to stay that long, *provided* you keep the children under control."

"We can't afford anywhere else, not with all these kids, nowhere else will take them so cheap on the Bank Holiday weekend."

"We'll have to take them back home," Mrs Dillon added, looking furious.

"Then I suggest you make the most of your time here," Donal said. "We'll help, if you want. But we're certainly not going to keep them occupied all the time. That's up to you."

Mr and Mrs Dillon looked at each other and decided, silently, that they were beaten.

"So what are you suggesting?" Mr Dillon sounded, if not friendly, at least less hostile.

"Activities, as you said. Games. The lads play football, don't they?"

Mr Dillon nodded. "Sure. Annie too. She's good," he added, winking at her.

"Fine. So we'll have five-a-side, we've enough players. And then we'll make an obstacle course through the playground. And after that . . ." He smiled at the children. "After that I bet you'll be starved, so we'll get your Mam and Kate to bake some cakes, and maybe you can help them."

"Sorry, Donal, but I mightn't be back in time. I've to go into Clifden for a while."

"And don't expect me to do it," Mrs Dillon announced. "What d'you think shops are for?"

"Well, maybe we could . . ."

"I can do it," Clare said.

"Great. So that's it, lads – and Annie. Everyone agreed? Let's go!"

They hardly had time to disagree before Donal had them all, twins included, up in a flat part of the paddock with a ball he had taken from the car, and Clare and Kate retreated to the kitchen, closing the door on the roaring and shouting, and on Mrs Dillon, still sitting sunning herself in the courtyard.

"Thank God that French couple seem to be out for the day. They'd probably pack up on the spot with the racket!" Clare said, moving to put on the kettle. "Have you time for a quick cup?"

"I'd love some, but it'll have to be *very* quick. I'm meeting Niall at four."

Clare didn't comment, busying herself with cups and milk, knowing Kate would tell her what she wanted to, when she wanted. And she did, as soon as Clare was sitting down across from her.

"He said he has a proposition for me."

"Any idea what? Or should I ask?"

Kate sipped the tea, thinking for a moment. She looks happy, Clare thought.

"It's something to do with painting, that's all I know – but I'm very excited! I've a feeling it will be something good."

"It wouldn't be anything else, knowing Niall!"

"I know that. But I mean, really good. I'll let you know when I get back."

She rang just after seven. Clare was relaxing, having spent the best part of the afternoon baking for the children, and helping them cut out shortbread figures, and feeding them, before their parents finally took them back to their own apartment. She felt as if she could do without seeing any children for quite a while. The rest of her life, if possible.

"You'll never guess, Clare!" Kate sounded breathless. "Niall wants me to do some paintings for him, lots of them! All seascapes, he knows I love doing them. He'll hang them on the walls in Kingfisher, with little stickers saying they're for sale. And some in Albatross as well, that would be a bit cheaper. I'm really excited, I can't believe it! It's a great chance to show my work."

"That's brilliant, Kate! When will you do it? Have you anything ready, that you could use?"

"A few. But I'd want to get cracking, I'll start tomorrow. Don't worry, I'll get your caravan done too, but I might have to call on a bit of help!"

"Maybe we'll let the Dillons do it? It would keep them occupied."

Kate's response was short but not sweet.

"Kate," Clare answered, laughing. "I didn't think you even *knew* words like that!"

They were examining the caravan the following morning when they heard loud voices down below in the courtyard. The French couple were there, the woman talking very loudly, the man saying nothing but his body language as angry as her tone. Donal was standing talking to them, the twins at his side.

"I'd better see what's up," Clare said, and she and Kate went down to join them.

As they got nearer the Frenchwoman was speaking even more loudly, in rapid-fire French. Donal seemed to have little difficulty understanding her, but Clare hadn't a clue.

"What's wrong?"

"It seems she lost her purse."

"Sto-len," her partner corrected. "It 'ave been sto-len."

"When did she miss it?" Clare asked.

"Sometime after breakfast," Donal said. "She remembers having it on the picnic table while she was eating, and then they went for a walk on the beach, and she missed it when they got back."

"Could she have lost it at the beach?"

"She doesn't think so. And the real problem is, the Dillon kids were playing around here at the time, and she's convinced they had something to do with it."

"Oh, hell. That's all we need," Clare said, as the Dillons, all eight of them, appeared at the little gateway to the lane, all with wet hair and towels and in great form. They greeted the others cheerfully.

"I'd better figure out how to handle this, and quickly," Clare muttered, as the Frenchman advanced towards the Dillons.

"Attendez! Monsieur!" Donal called, then walked quickly over as the man turned, and spoke quietly to him before turning back to face Mr Dillon.

"We seem to have a problem, and we're hoping you can help."

"What's up?" The man was smiling, in better form than either Clare or Donal had seen him.

"This lady has lost her purse, and she's offering a reward to whoever finds it."

He had their attention. "How much?" Mrs Dillon asked.

Donal quickly asked, in French, how much was in it. A considerable amount, came the answer. Mostly in French francs, with some travellers' cheques.

"Twenty pounds," he told the Dillons.

Mr Dillon whistled softly. "Must be a hell of a lot of dough in it."

"Mostly travellers' cheques, no use to anyone else – they just don't want the hassle of waiting for a refund. They'd rather get the purse back."

"And what makes you think *we* can help?" Mr Dillon asked. He was back to being hostile, his eyes narrowed as he looked at Donal.

"Because they're bright kids. I bet they're really good at finding things!"

"Only if they want to," their mother said.

"We do want to, Ma! Twenty whole quid!"

The eldest boy was obviously willing to give it a go.

"C'mon, Da, why not?" he pleaded.

"Well, all right," Mr Dillon agreed reluctantly. "But be quick. You can do it while we're packing, we've to go soon."

He shot a look in Clare's direction, his good humour gone, annoyed again as he remembered that she was still holding them to the deadline. He followed his wife into *Saffron*, leaving the children in the courtyard. The biggest boy went into action immediately, directing the others to fan out and cover every inch of the place.

"Where else were you, Missus?" he asked, and Donal, amused, translated.

"Jasus, lads," the boy said when he heard the answer, "We'll never cover the whole bloody beach!"

They were well into their search when Clare realised that the little girl was sitting by herself in a quiet corner of the courtyard, scrabbling with a small stick in the earth of one of the flowerbeds. She went over to her.

"Not helping them search, Annie? You'd never know, you could be the lucky one!"

"Don't want to," the child muttered. "I'm too tired."

"That's a pity," Donal said, coming over to join them and crouching down so he was on Annie's level. "Because you see this shiny pound? I'm going to give this to whoever finds the purse, and they could keep it for themselves, and not have to share it with anyone! You could put it in your little bag there, and use it for sweets when you get home."

The child clutched the bag to her, but she was definitely interested now.

"What do you think, Annie?"

"I'm tired," she repeated, a bit more loudly this time.

"I know that." His voice was patient. "You've been swimming, and we had a great time yesterday, hadn't we? You must be *very* tired."

She nodded.

"So, if you want to help us searching, maybe you should just look around in this little corner here, where nobody else will think of looking. And Clare and I will go away over there to search and you can call us if you find anything, okay?"

Clare stood up when he did, and he glanced down at the little girl.

"Okay, Annie?" he smiled at her.

She nodded again, looking tiny as she sat there hunched over the bag.

It took less than a minute. She came up behind where they were sitting on the bench and tapped him on the shoulder, wordlessly holding out the purse to him and waiting while he produced the pound coin, which she quickly put into her empty little bag.

"How did you know she had it?" Clare asked later as they sat in the cottage drinking coffee after having lunch with Kate and the twins, who were now gone to the beach. There was perfect quiet. The French couple, asking no questions, had gone out again, and the Dillons had departed happily enough, pleased with their little windfall.

"Just a feeling," Donal replied.

"Do you think . . . ?"

"Who knows? She's only a kid, she probably 'found' it and was afraid to own up. Anyway, they're all happy now. Except you. I shouldn't have been so rash with your money. I suppose I thought the Frenchwoman would pay. I should have checked."

"It was better not to ask her. She was still very suspicious. At least it's sorted now, thanks to you."

She was smiling as she poured more coffee. "You wouldn't like a job, would you? I could do with you around here!"

He smiled back. "Be careful, I might take you up on that. Did Kate tell you I'm moving down?"

And they sat talking, not noticing the hours that passed, until Kate finally knocked at the door to say that the twins were having their supper, and Nan Kinsella was with them and would put them to bed and stay until Donal came back, because she had to go home to paint.

They went to the kitchen to cook omelettes while Kate, smiling to herself, set off on her bicycle. And then they sat and ate and talked for a while longer. And by the time Jody arrived to walk his sister home, and Donal went back over to the twins, Clare felt that she knew him a lot better. And wanted to get to know him even more.

Chapter Nineteen

July was shaping up to be hectic. Clare had been run off her feet for most of June, but this month looked set to be even busier, with solid bookings right through to the third week. It was thanks to Niall mainly, who had put up a discreet notice in the foyer of Albatross and suggested that she advertise in the national papers as well as locally. The phone had hardly stopped ringing since, and every day there were one or two bookings in the post as well.

"It's a good complaint," Niall had said when she met him briefly for lunch and told him she was exhausted. "You're enjoying it, aren't you? Although you'll never make a fortune. You're not charging enough, that's why you've so many takers!"

"I'm charging enough," she had reassured him. "I'll have enough to meet my monthly repayment to you, and to keep myself. That's all I need."

"Clare. " He looked a bit uncomfortable. "You know you don't need to pay me back. Not for a long time, anyway. Until you're back at work, maybe. Maybe not even then."

"I wouldn't dream of it, Niall, and you know it. I couldn't do it – and I wouldn't want to. But thanks a million!"

"But this was meant to be a bit of fun, wasn't it? Part of a year off? I don't want to see you killing yourself, and scrimping as well, just to pay me back. The restaurants are doing fine, I don't need it."

"You're a great friend, Niall. But business is business. And anyway I don't feel I'm scrimping. I haven't the time or the energy to go anywhere at the minute."

"Have you time to come in here Friday night, do you think? There's someone I'd like you to meet."

"It's not Nicole, is it? Kate said she was coming over."

"Wait and see. And bring a friend, if you like."

"Great. Kate might come with me."

"It was her nephew I had in mind. I hear he's around a good bit."

"We're only friends, Niall!" She laughed at him, brushing her hair back from her face as she spoke.

"Right." He looked maddeningly innocent. "That's what I said, isn't it, to bring a friend?"

"Mmm. Good job you and I are friends, otherwise I'd thump you."

"For what?" He was still the picture of innocence.

"For making all kinds of assumptions that are . . . well – "

"Too close to the bone?" he finished for her.

"No. Definitely not. Even if I was interested – which I'm not – *he* isn't, because he's still not over his wife. He still talks about her a lot."

"So you're seeing a good bit of him?"

"He's staying with Kate for a few days. He's talking about moving down here and wants to get things sorted out."

Niall raised his eyebrows.

"Forget it, Niall," she said. "I'm really not interested in him."

"So who *are* you interested in?" he asked, switching the topic neatly. "Our American friend?"

"Rick?" She concentrated on her salad.

"Oh, there's more than one?"

"Niall! Drop it! Bad enough that Kate keeps on at me."

"Does she?" He paused for a moment, signalling to Maura to bring some more mineral water.

Clare nodded. "She feels it's time I came out of hiding, as she puts it. She'd like to see me with Donal, I think, but she doesn't really care who. Just as long as it's someone. She's afraid if I stay on my own too long, I might get to like it."

"Maybe she's right – thanks, Maura," he added, turning to the waitress who gave Clare a quick smile and left them to it.

"Niall, you know how I feel," Clare continued once Maura had moved away. "I don't need a man in my life."

"True, you don't. Not even me . . ."

"Friends are different."

"They are. They're the ones who tell you the truth."

He paused for a moment.

"You gave that bastard enough of your life, Clare," he said quietly. "Don't give him any more, by letting him put you off all the decent men who are out there."

She just sat there, not answering, not meeting his gaze.

"Promise me, Clare?" he asked softly. "It'd be a waste, a pure waste. Don't let him do that to you."

"You're right, Niall," she said finally, looking up and smiling at him. "It's just – I suppose I'm not ready yet."

"But you will be."

"Probably. Yes. I'm not sure when. But you're right. I will be."

The post had arrived by the time Clare got home, and she picked it up, scanning the envelopes idly for handwriting she might recognise. The phone rang while she was still glancing through them. She picked it up, accepting a reversed charges call from Ruth.

"You don't mind, sis? Only I was dying to talk to you, and we've hardly a bean left at this stage, I can't afford to get a callcard."

"Do you need some money? And where are you? The last we heard was that card Mam got from Skiathos, four or five weeks ago."

"It was gorgeous. We left there a while back, though – we're in Amsterdam now, on the way home. And thanks, but I don't need anything, we've enough to get us back home. We just need to be a bit careful."

"How's Conor?"

"Bearing up well. He started getting into it once we hit Italy. I knew it was a great idea to have a last fling, before we have to really get serious about houses and wedding plans and things."

"But you'll have to postpone all that, won't you? I mean, you have to be broke after taking all that extended leave from work again."

"We still have the money we got after Conor's gran died – we put that away to buy a site, we're not touching it for anything else. We'll worry about the money for building when the time comes. And Dad will be paying for the wedding."

"You can't let him do that, Ruth! He's retiring next summer, remember? He'll need to hang on to whatever he has . . ."

"That's what I told him, but he said he'd be only too delighted to pay for his daughter's wedding, and since I'm the only one showing any signs . . ." She stopped. "Whoops, sorry, Clare. Me and my bloody big mouth . . ."

There was silence at the other end.

"Clare, come on!" Ruth's voice was apologetic now. "You know I didn't mean it. The best thing you ever did was get rid of that sleaze-ball, even if you *never* get married."

"This *isn't* why you're ringing me from Amsterdam?" Clare asked tightly. "To discuss what I should be doing with my life?"

"God, have *I* touched a raw nerve!" Ruth was beginning to sound a bit impatient. "Look, Clare, I'm sorry if you're upset, you know I am, but I didn't say anything out of line. Really I didn't. You're overreacting."

"You're right. Sorry," Clare said finally. "I know I'm a bit touchy at the minute. Niall was just telling me I should be out looking for another man. And so is Kate . . ."

"Looking for another man?" Ruth sounded surprised.

"No, idiot!" Clare said quickly. "Telling me *I* should be . . ."

"Well, you could do worse . . ."

"For *God's* sake will people stop telling me what to do!"

"Oh God, here we go again. What's the *matter* with you, Clare? You got rid of that creep, you've everything going for you, you should be in *great* form, not snapping people's heads off."

"I know. You're right. But I think I'm just getting a bit fed up of everyone assuming I need a man in my life. I don't. You were right when you said I'm better off on my own than with Tony, or anyone like him. But I suppose, once bitten, twice shy. I'm just not too keen on getting into all that again."

"It doesn't have to be the same, you know. There's a lot of the good guys still around."

"That's what Niall said."

"He's right. And you don't have to get serious. You could just, you know, go out with a few guys, have some fun. No big deal. You used to *like* going out!"

"Mmm. I'll see. I'm nearly too busy, anyway. I fall into bed most nights before eleven."

Ruth laughed. "That's no problem. The problem is . . ."

"If you say it's that I'm there on my own, I'll kill you. *I swear!*"

"So I won't say it. But think about it . . ."

"Ruth!" Clare laughed. There was no winning with her. "So why did you ring, anyway? Besides reminding me how empty my life is!"

"To tell you we're still in one piece. And to see if you'd put us up, the week after next. We'll be back in Dublin the end of next week, we were going to come down after that if there was any chance of a bed. Or have I blown it?" She was laughing as she said it.

"Close, but not quite. Put a zip on your lip when you get here, and I'll let you stay with me in the cottage. We're packed to the gills otherwise."

"So no romantic hidey-hole? We christened that little apartment for you, remember?"

"Afraid not, unless you want to share with the couple who've booked in. Might make for an interesting weekend."

Ruth laughed again. "I'll break it *very* gently to Conor . . ."

"Or you could tell him I have camp beds in the loft. Unless you want the caravan?"

"What caravan?"

"My gypsy caravan. It's wonderful, Kate painted it for me. Wait 'til you see it, you'll love it."

"Brilliant. Can't wait. And Clare . . . I love you. That's the only reason I was going on at you, I want things to be right for you. I worry about you a bit."

"Well, don't. There's no need. Things are fine, Ruth, really. You'll see when you get here."

"Okay. See you in two weeks!"

"Great. Love you. Say hi to Conor."

Clare put down the phone, deciding not to even think about how much that had cost her. It was worth it just to hear Ruth, whatever it cost, and no matter what she was saying. And maybe there *was* something in what she said, maybe it was time to lighten up and have a bit of fun. As soon as she had the time.

She rang her mother to report that Ruth was alive and well and on the way back to Dublin, and chatted for twenty minutes or so, deciding again to ignore the phone bill as well as the note of concern in Mrs Delaney's voice.

"You're sure you're not working too hard, love? It sounds like an awful lot of people to have around the place, and a lot of cleaning and other work to be doing . . ."

"I love it, Mam. I really do. It's a bit tiring from time to time, but it's fun. I'm meeting lots of interesting people from all over the place. And Kate is a great help."

"But are you getting any chance to go out and enjoy yourself? Are you, well, are you making any friends down there?"

"Great friends, they're lovely people here. And I see Niall all the time."

"But . . ."

Don't ask about men, Clare said silently to herself. Just don't.

"As long as you're happy," her mother finished a bit

lamely, into the silence. She knew about Tony. Well, the parts Clare had chosen to tell her, which was a carefully edited version. She also knew when to let a subject drop.

"I'm happy, Mam. So stop worrying, okay? I'll ring again next week."

"Do that. Bye, now, love. Mind yourself."

Clare made some coffee and sat down to go through the letters. Booking deposits, mainly, and one or two bills. Details from Bord Failte that she had requested about registering with them, and a letter from Deirdre that she had missed first time round.

And then she saw it. The heavy white envelope with the American stamps and the sender's address sticker placed carefully in one corner. She put it to one side and opened Deirdre's letter first, delaying for a few minutes the pleasure of reading the one from Rick. He had never written to her before, preferring to phone her. She'd had at least one call a week since he went back, just to see how she was getting on. He always kept the tone light, amusing her with anecdotes about his patients, listening with obvious enjoyment as she told him what was happening in Rossdarra, never bringing the conversation to a more personal level, though she occasionally felt he might want to. She looked forward to these calls more and more as the weeks went on, never telling anyone about them, hugging them to herself like a delicious secret.

Deirdre's letter was newsy and funny, and full of 'Tom this' and 'Tom that'. They had obviously been getting on very well indeed since the night in La Cave.

She read on a bit more, absently sipping her coffee. They were planning on a weekend away, apparently, and thought July in Connemara might be a great idea. Could they come and stay with Clare? Well, why not, she thought. Everybody else in the world was coming.

She got up and walked to the sink, pouring away the remains of the cold coffee, rinsing the mug and automatically putting on the kettle again.

The little window over the sink gave her a view across the courtyard to the play area, and beyond that to the paddock. She could see Jody there, patiently showing two small children round the little pens where the chickens and the rabbits were, while their parents watched happily from the bench in the shade of the Stag's Horn tree, where they sat feeding the baby.

Jack was at the far end of the paddock, where he seemed to be checking the stone wall. Two of the five people who were staying in *Saffron* came into view, walking along the verge of the road and stopping to chat to Jack for a few minutes as they passed.

Funny, thought Clare as she stood watching. Jack was always friendly to her guests, and he seemed to be around whenever she needed him, even without her asking, but in some ways he still kept very much to himself. He had never again referred to the conversation they had just after she arrived, when he had advised her to go after what she wanted, in case she mightn't get the chance again. Since then he had avoided any situation where they might have any sort of personal conversation. And yet he was there whenever she needed him, doing bits and pieces around the place, and she knew that there was no way of thanking him that wouldn't be an embarrassment to the man.

She made another cup of coffee, bringing it back to the table with her, and sat down to savour the letter from Rick. It was fairly long, three pages, and the tone was as light as in the phone calls. Until she got to the last paragraph. She read that twice, feeling her heart begin to flutter, not knowing if it was in panic or anticipation.

'I'd really like to see you again, Clare,' he had written in clear, flowing script. *'I enjoy our calls, and I think you do too, and I feel I'm getting to know you better all the time. And I'm greedy, it's not enough for me. I want to see you again, soon. I want to see the way your eyes light up when you laugh, I want to watch your hair blowing in the breeze . . . but enough of that. I promised myself I wouldn't go over the top, scare you off. And I promise you I'll keep in line if you let me visit. We can be friends, if that's what you want. Or – well, whatever you want, I'll go for it, I won't try to turn it into something you don't want. I'd just like to give us this chance, see where it takes us. What do you say? I'll ring Saturday, that gives you a couple of days to think about it. Either way, it's your call, and I'll go with it.'*

He had signed it simply, *'Rick'*.

Clare put the letter down with the others, beside the untouched coffee, and stood up, stretching. She had to get out, go for a walk, think about this. She went out, pulling the door behind her, not bothering with even a light jacket. The weather was glorious, and had been for about three weeks now. She thought nobody would ever bother going abroad for holidays, if only they could depend on weather like this.

She was walking down the laneway to the beach when she passed Jack, who was now busy examining the paddock wall that bounded the lane.

"Afternoon," he said, straightening up as she came closer.

"Hi, Jack. I was just thinking I don't know what I'd do without you."

He looked a bit embarrassed, as she expected, but pleased at the same time.

"You'd manage away, I suppose," he said, smiling. "I'm not doing it all on my own, anyway. Young Jody's a great help, a good worker and not a bit of bother."

"He's brilliant," Clare agreed. "He won't let me pay him properly, though. He takes the odd tenner, but nothing on a regular basis."

"I think he's happy enough to be up here, to have an excuse to get away from that misbegotten blackguard he has for a father."

"I don't know his father at all," Clare said.

"You're better off," Jack answered, pushing back his cap and scratching his head idly as he looked over to where Jody was showing the children how to throw sticks for the two pups.

"Kinsella was always a fool, but it's worse he's getting, ever since . . ."

He paused, pulling his cap back down over his eyes and bending to rearrange a stone at the top of the wall.

"The man can't see when he's well off. If I had a son, or a grandson, like Jody . . ."

His head was down as he bent to lift a stone from the ground and place it into a small round gap in the wall, and Clare stood there uncertainly, not sure if he was going to say anything else, not sure that he even realised, in his concentration on the work, that she was still there.

"I'll head on, Jack," she said, after a while. "I might see you later. Go in and make yourself tea if you want to – the door's on the latch."

He looked up when she said this, his blue eyes light against the weathered tan of his face.

"Are you sure that's wise? There's an awful lot of strangers around."

"I'll take my chances. It's probably foolish of me, but I'd rather trust people and be wrong, than not trust them at all."

She went on down the lane, thinking about what she had said. If she meant it – and she really believed she did – then maybe she should think about applying it to a lot more than the things she had in the cottage, important as they were to her.

There were a good few people on the beach, but it was still possible to find a quiet spot to walk on her own once she went past the headland. She needed to think about things, including how she would manage for July, because from the look of it she'd be inundated with visitors. Where would she put them all?

She bent to pick up a stone and turned to lash it into the waves, putting all her impatient energy behind it.

She stood for several minutes looking at the bright sea with the foamy, splashing waves before continuing her walk down the beach, head slightly bent, hands dug into the pockets of her jeans.

She was annoyed with herself that she was beginning to see her friends in terms of where she could find space for them instead of being delighted that they were choosing to come. And she really did want to see Dee, and Tom if he was part of the package. It was just that she'd feel awkward if her friends started staying in the apartments, because she could hardly charge them, so it would be much better if they'd wait until September or October. And the place was full for most of July anyway, so it would mean Dee and Tom staying in the cottage with her, but that would be a bit crowded if they planned on coming at the same time as Ruth. And where on earth was she going to put Rick, if he came at the same time?

"Penny for them?"

She glanced up to find Donal standing there, leaning back against a stone wall that bounded the beach, smiling at her. The twins, in swimming togs and tee-shirts, were building a big sandcastle nearby.

"I was just thinking about you," he continued.

"Don't tell me. You were wondering if you could come and stay for the rest of July."

It was out before she could stop herself, and she was sorry the minute she saw his face.

"God, that sounded awful, didn't it? You know I didn't mean it. I'm just feeling a bit, well – "

"Swamped?"

She looked at him. "How do you know?"

"Because Kate told me how busy you are, and that she thinks you're exhausted. And anyway, I can see it for myself. How long is it since you had a day off?" he asked.

She opened her mouth to protest, but gave in instead. "I don't remember."

"Which means it's too long."

"I'm taking a night off this Friday," she said. "I'm having dinner at Niall's."

"Good."

"And he suggested I bring a friend, and I was going to ask Kate but I need her to keep an eye on the apartments, if she doesn't mind. So . . ."

"So?" He was grinning at her, arms folded, still leaning back against the wall.

"So I was wondering would you like to come with me?"

"You could still bring Kate, and I'll keep an eye on the place for you."

"I couldn't ask you to do that."

"I don't see why not – you're asking Kate."

"That's different, she's a friend."

"I see."

"God almighty, you're impossible, Donal McCarthy. Do you or do you not want to come to dinner with me?"

"Well, since you're asking so nicely . . ."

She laughed, her anger gone as quickly as it had flared up, and they agreed a time to meet on the Friday. She found, as she turned to walk back down the beach, that she was looking forward to it already.

Chapter Twenty

Niall was in great form on Friday evening, greeting them at the door and ushering them to a secluded table in Kingfisher.

"I can find you a space in Albatross if you prefer, but it's fairly crowded – it's 'Beginner's Luck' tonight. You'll have a better choice in here, and you can go in later for the music if you want. And I'll join you for dessert, is that okay?"

And he was gone, leaving Clare to explain to Donal, as they settled themselves at the table, about the tradition of the 'Beginner's Luck' meals that she had helped invent soon after the restaurant opened.

"So, it's a sort of cheap and cheerful night, with only a few dishes on, and live music?" he clarified.

"That's right. It's usually packed to the gills, people seem to like sampling something a bit different. And the music can be very good. Well, sometimes!" she said, wrinkling her nose.

"But not always?" he asked.

"I'm probably not being fair, they've had some great sessions in there. But Niall believes in giving everyone a chance, so it might be their first time playing for an audience. Unfortunately, it doesn't always come off."

"But most of the time it does?"

"Right. And then it can be brilliant."

As Clare finished speaking a gold-embossed menu was thrust under her nose. She looked up to see the waiter smiling at her.

"Kevin!"

"The very man, at your service!"

He bowed low, his right hand in front of his waist, the gesture fitting well with the elegant dress suit.

"So what are you doing here? I mean, why aren't you in Galway? And why are you all dressed up?"

"I've been back two weeks," he said, nodding to Donal. He pulled out a chair and sat beside them.

"Did Donal not tell you?" he asked, glancing at him. "Or Kate?"

"I've hardly seen them, I'm so busy."

"Good complaint. I'm going to be up to my eyes myself, I'll be working here at week-ends as well as on the building with Seamus and Eddie during the week."

"What brought this on, a rush of blood to the head?"

"It makes a change, all right," Donal agreed, smiling at them across the table.

"Will you listen to them!" Kevin said. "As if the pair of you knew what work was! Let me tell you, I worked my back off when I was in Rick's place. Good money, but the work was fairly killing!"

"So now all the money's gone, and you're back to having to earn a crust?" Clare said.

He laughed. "Not exactly. I've a good bit put by, but I've plans for it."

"Well, is it a secret?" Clare asked, when he said no more.

"Not really. I've decided I'm going back to college. Hotel management. Tourism is looking up all the time. I'm getting in there with some training, so I'll know what I'm at when the time comes."

"The time for what?" Donal asked.

"The time when I have my own place."

He sat watching them, letting it sink in.

"You're serious?" Donal asked finally.

"Of course. Well, why not? If Niall can do it – no disrespect to him – then so can I. And I will. I intend to have my own hotel by the time I'm forty."

"Fair play to you, if you can do it."

"I don't see why not, Donal. It'll take hard work, and a lot of saving, but I'm only twenty-seven, I've time on my side. And Rick said he'll finance me. Only I want to do most of it on my own."

"It's a brilliant idea," Clare said. "No reason why you shouldn't do it."

"It'll mean a change of lifestyle," Donal said. "You're used to having money to spend, and time for yourself, to do what you want."

"It'll be worth it. And this *is* what I want. And Kate is delighted. "

"Did you always call her by her first name?" Clare asked, as the thought struck her.

"For as long as I can remember. Now," he said, smiling at them, "I'll leave you in peace to look at the menu – I don't want to get the sack until I'm here at least a week."

"He seems very determined about it," Clare said later as they began eating.

"Not before time. He's been pulling out of Kate for far too long."

"In what way?"

"Financially, as well as emotionally. Kate doesn't have that much money, but whatever bit she has, she gives to him. At this stage he should be well able to support himself."

"But he was, surely, in the States. And he is now, from the look of things."

"Maybe. But Kevin has big ideas and expensive tastes. Whatever he earned in the States, Kate saw none of it, because I know from one or two comments she let drop that it was she who was sending him money from time to time, not the other way round, as you'd expect. And now it seems he managed to save while he was over there, while she was doing without here."

"She must have been getting a bit fed up with that, I don't think she has much to spare."

"She never complained. It's not in her. She's very protective of him, won't hear a word against him. But mollycoddling won't do him any good."

"Did you ever say anything to her?"

"Once or twice, but it's not up to me, I'm only her nephew. I just hate to see him taking advantage of her."

"And you think he is."

"Yes. Though in fairness to him I don't think he asks for anything, he just doesn't refuse it when it's offered, and never thinks about where it comes from."

"So she's doing it because she wants to, not because he's putting pressure on her?"

"I suppose you're right. She let slip once about never being able to make it up to him."

"Make what up to him?"

"She didn't say. Growing up without a father, I suppose."

"You're very close to her, aren't you?"

He nodded. "I'm very fond of Kate. I always got on well with her, nearly better than with my own Mam when I was younger. She's always encouraged me, no matter what I wanted to do. Molly's the opposite, in some ways. A bit fearful of things, always worrying about what might go wrong. But she's the best in the world, they both are."

They stopped talking for a few moments as the main course arrived, pausing to sample it before continuing the conversation. Kevin returned briefly to pour some wine, winked at Clare, and went to look after another table.

"You know, Kevin seems fine to me." Clare said. "I mean, he seems to get on really well with Kate, he's very affectionate to her and always praising her. And it was his idea, apparently, that she should show her paintings here, and he put it to Niall, and Niall thought it would be great. But it was Kevin who set it up for her."

"Maybe he's changing. He does seem a bit different, more mature. Maybe the year in the States did him some good. And I probably shouldn't be so critical of him, I just think she hasn't had it easy and she needs all the support she can get."

"Kate is doing fine, you know, Donal. She has Kevin back, and she's thrilled that you're going to be living down here, and she has her painting, she tells me she's been selling a lot to Niall's customers. She's in her element."

"You're absolutely right, Clare," he said after thinking about it for a moment. "I think I just need to see past that image of her, coming back here to nothing much, with a little six-year-old boy in tow, trying to make a fresh start. "

Clare concentrated on her salmon steak for a minute or two, before deciding to take the risk.

"Is that why you've come down, Donal? To make a fresh start?"

The food on his plate seemed suddenly fascinating, and he spent a few moments examining it before looking up at her.

"I'm not sure there's ever really such a thing as a fresh start, Clare," he said finally. "I know, I said that's what Kate did, and it's a way of putting it. But it's hard to start afresh, as if nothing happened before, as if you can meet the world, oh, I don't know, in the same way you did at seventeen or eighteen. That's when you have your fresh start, and you can't do it again twenty years on, or even ten years. It's just not the same. You're a different person. You know too much, maybe you've been hurt too much. And you bring all that along with you, when you try to make your fresh start."

"In that case, people might as well not bother trying, Donal. If you're right."

"If I'm right. And maybe I'm just playing with words, and what I mean is a *different* start. And you need energy for that, and the hope that it might work out. Otherwise, you're right, nobody would even bother trying."

"Used you feel like that?"

"I *still* feel like that sometimes, Clare. As if it's all too much. But it's getting better now. There used to be times when I didn't know how I'd get up and face the day. Or why."

She took a sip of the wine.

"Do you still feel like that?" she asked, taking the risk.

"Only the odd time now. The twins kept me going. And Kate and Molly, and my friend David. He said to me once that I had two choices. I could give up on life, and just go through the motions. Or I could try and rebuild something real for myself, and for the kids."

"So that's what you're doing."

"That's it. And I didn't want to do it here at first, because that was the dream Jen and I had, and I just didn't want it without her, when it wouldn't be the same. But now it feels like the right thing to do, better than staying in Dublin, better than anything else I can think of."

"Kate said you have a job lined up."

He brightened, smiling across at her.

"I have. Though it's a bit further away than I would have liked, even if I can rent a house over in that direction. But it'll be worth it. And the time off is good, as people keep reminding us teachers. As if we didn't earn it!"

"No comment. What'll you do about the boys?"

"I've enrolled them in the national school at Carrigrua, I heard it's good, and that's where I'm looking for a house. And I'm hoping that Molly might think of moving down and helping to look after them. She often says she'd love to be back living in Connemara."

"And is she well enough to be minding small children?"

"She's grand, as far as I know. A bit tired, but she seems okay. Not that she'd ever tell you."

He paused to take another sip of wine.

"You're a very good listener, Clare. I haven't talked so much in a long time. What about you, though? Are things going as you hoped they would, down here?"

She had barely begun to answer when Niall arrived at their table with Nicole.

Clare stood up, delighted, kissing the Frenchwoman on both cheeks in greeting.

She had changed, Clare noticed while she was being introduced to Donal. The straight black hair was cut very short, and she had filled out slightly, which suited her. But there was something else – a certain air of confidence that hadn't been there before. This was a woman who, now that she was almost thirty, was coming into her own.

"I'm going to have to leave you three for a few minutes," Niall said. "My so-called musicians have let me down, after promising they'd do anything for a crack at a real audience. So now I've to scour the countryside to find some kind of replacements in the next half hour or so."

Clare made a sympathetic face while Nicole smiled at him.

"*Bonne chance*, Niall," she said.

"No dessert, Clare?" she smiled, as Clare turned down Kevin's offer of the menu. "I remember how much you like cheesecake!"

"No chance, Nicole. I want to look like you do!"

"Oh thank you! But you look really lovely as you are!"

"Oh, no, I need to –"

"You need to do absolutely nothing," said Donal, surprising her. "Nicole is right, you look lovely as you are."

"Thanks, Donal," she said, slightly flustered. "But still no cheesecake!"

"Maybe I'll try some myself, just to let you know what you're missing."

Donal had finished the cheesecake and they were having their coffee, laughing at something Nicole had said, when Niall returned to the table, shaking his head.

"No go, not a musician to be had this side of Galway.

I'll have to break it gently to the people out there – the music is part of what they come for."

"Maybe some of them can play? I mean, that was the original idea, wasn't it, that people could just get up and borrow the instruments, and play something if they felt like it?"

He shook his head again, looking glum. "I've already tried that, no takers. Unless – ?

He was looking at her hopefully now.

"Oh, no, Niall. I know that look. Forget it!"

"How much have you had to drink?" he asked, smiling.

"Half a bottle of wine. Not nearly enough for what you have in mind!"

Donal and Nicole looked from one to the other, mystified.

"Perfect for what I have in mind," Niall continued. "Just enough to make you relaxed, but not so much that you can't do it."

"Do you two want to be alone together?" Donal asked, grinning at them, while Nicole continued to look bewildered.

"It's not alone he wants me," Clare said as Niall burst out laughing.

"No, I want herself and her mandolin out there in Albatross, playing sweet music for my late-night diners."

"Pity I didn't bring my mandolin."

"Good job we've got one out there."

"Two chances, Niall."

"Please, Clare."

When he looked at her like that she was sunk, but she gave it one more try.

"It wouldn't sound right on its own, Niall. I can only do all the slow airs and stuff if I'm playing on my own, and people would soon get fed up of that."

"But you could sing, too, couldn't you? You've a gorgeous voice."

"I can't sing and play at the same time, I never got the hang of it, and it wouldn't sound right anyway, not if I'm playing slow airs, and . . ." she trailed off helplessly, hating to let him down.

"Just one or two, then? You play beautifully, Clare, you know that."

"Flattery will get you lots of things, Niall, but I'm still not going to – "

"Would it help if I back you up on the guitar, Clare, if Niall has one handy?" Donal broke in. " I can sing a bit, too."

"Would it help if – God Almighty, man, why didn't you say so?" Niall demanded, turning to grin at Donal.

"What d'you think, Clare? Will we give him a go?"

"Not on my own," Donal said. "I'm a bit out of practice."

"We'll soon cure that, after a few hours in there you won't know yourself."

"I never said – "

"Save your breath, Donal, you'll need it for singing!" Niall said as he led them to a small back room and handed them the instruments, and left them to tune up for a few minutes. And before they could come to their senses they were out on the little stage in the corner of Albatross, in front of the eager audience.

They started off a bit tentatively, getting used to the instruments and to each other's style of playing, and then they started into 'Raglan Road', with Donal singing in a melodic, gravelly voice and both of them accompanying him softly. And suddenly it all came together, and it was magic, and their audience felt it too and wouldn't let them stop for the next two hours, calling for all the old favourites until they finally had to plead exhaustion and make their escape from the stage.

Niall offered them coffee and – only half joking – a regular spot on Fridays and Saturdays if they wanted it. They refused both, laughing together as they went out to Donal's car, delighted with themselves. As he dropped Clare home Donal promised to call over with the twins in a day or two.

So this is what it's like, she thought later as she lay in bed, still wide awake. I just have to say 'yes', and get out there and get on with my life. I can still enjoy myself the way I used to. It's all there waiting for me.

And she drifted off to sleep and was still on a high when she woke early next morning, so that when Rick rang just after breakfast, she didn't hesitate for even a moment before telling him that, yes, he was very welcome to come and visit, she was looking forward to it.

Chapter Twenty-one

"I don't know what you're on, Clare, but you should bottle it and sell it. You're in brilliant form."

Ruth smiled at Clare who was just coming down the stairs. Then she clapped her hand to her mouth, remembering Tony and what *he* had been on. "Oh, God," she added, "I didn't mean – well, it's just that you look great, I haven't seen you like this for ages . . . I'll shut up," she finished as Conor shot her a look and Clare came over to hug her.

"You're looking pretty terrific yourself," she said, admiring her sister's light tan. "And it's okay, Ruthie, you can even say his name now without me screaming. It's finally over."

"Really? I mean, it's really finished, and you can forget what a bastard he was, and stop thinking every other man is the same?"

"That sums it up," Clare said, and was rewarded by a huge grin.

"And what about the next step in the process? I

mean, just to be completely sure, you should really . . ."

"Don't even say it," Clare said, but she was laughing. "Just trust me. Things are looking up."

"Tell me!" Ruth caught her by the arm, smiling at her.

"Nosy! Nothing to tell, really. Well, not 'til after dinner, anyway. You must be starved. Or did you stop on the way down?"

"No, we kept going, we knew you'd feed us!"

"Throw your bags up there in the gallery while I put out the dinner. Dee and Tom are in the spare bedroom, but they're leaving tomorrow morning, you can move in there then if you want. Or stay in the gallery – whichever."

"We'll probably stay there, I like it."

She and Conor went upstairs with the bags, going through the door into the gallery bedroom, with its four-foot-high timbered rails at one side, so that the occupants could look down over the living-room. It was gorgeously cosy on winter nights with the fire blazing, and still wonderful, Ruth decided, in the middle of July with a big Mexican blanket draped over the rails to give privacy from below, and the mottled red and green and blue glass squares inserted in the gable wall, which were the only source of light apart from what came up from the living-room.

"This room is quite satisfactory, thank you. We'll take it," she called down to Clare who placed a steaming dish of vegetables on the table and turned to give Ruth a mock bow.

"Okay, *now* tell me," said Ruth, as they finished the

last of their meal and Conor topped up their wine glasses again.

"I've told you everything you wanted to know about our travels. Your turn now."

"Not much to tell, really," Clare said. "I'm up to my eyes, and the place is going great, I haven't an empty bed for the whole of July. I've had a brilliant weekend with Dee and Tom, and they liked Niall's place so much they're in there again tonight. And Niall's French girlfriend, Nicole, is staying for the summer to help him manage the restaurants . . ."

"Do you mind?" Ruth asked.

"Of course not, why would I mind?"

"Because – "

"I don't mind," Clare repeated, firmly. "And Kate is having a brilliant time, she can hardly paint fast enough to replace what Niall is selling for her. Kevin is working flat out, between the restaurant and building three new holiday homes near Roundstone with Eddie and Seamus. And Donal is staying here next week with his niece and the twins, because he's coming to work in Connemara for a year and the house he's renting won't be ready for another little while. And that's about it, I think. Oh, except that . . ." She paused to take a sip of wine, smiling at Ruth who was nearly out of her chair with impatience

". . . except that Rick is coming over on Friday to stay for two weeks."

"Rick the *American?*"

"He's the only Rick I know."

"And he's coming *here?* This Friday?"

"That's the plan."

"To see you?"

"No, to look for leprechauns! Of course, to see me. Why not?" she added, enjoying her sister's expression.

"Correct me if I'm wrong." Ruth was talking very slowly, and very carefully. "It's two weeks since I was in Amsterdam. Not *even* two weeks. And you told me, you *definitely* told me, less than two weeks ago, that you weren't going to get into all that again. That's exactly what you said, that you weren't ready to get into all that again."

"And you told me to lighten up, and have some fun, remember? You told me that there were still decent men around, not just creeps like Tony. So that's what I'm doing, just what you said. I'm going to have some fun!"

"That's the first time you've ever listened to me, I suppose I should be grateful! And the worst that can happen is that you'll go off men all over again and join the nuns, and leave me the cottage and the apartment when you take your vows of poverty. Can't be bad!"

"I wouldn't hold your breath," Clare said, laughing at her. "You might be waiting a while."

Clare was up early next morning to say goodbye to Dee and Tom, and to be around in case any of the guests came looking for her.

"You're really lucky, you know, Clare. This place is gorgeous now."

"Yes, I know. Very lucky. And you are too, look at that man of yours, he's mad about you!"

"Long may it last!" Deirdre laughed quietly as Tom came back in from the car, telling her the bags were in and they were all set. They left, promising to come back before the end of the summer, and Clare lingered in the courtyard for a few minutes, enjoying the early morning sun, wondering would it work if Rick had the spare room in the cottage, or whether it would be awkward with Ruth and Conor there. She could hardly see what else to do, unless she persuaded them to take the caravan, which was great now that it had been fixed up. The weather was lovely, they'd be perfectly comfortable there and would probably enjoy it, and they'd have some privacy . . .

Which would leave herself and Rick in the cottage, which wasn't exactly what she had in mind, so maybe she should take the caravan herself . . .

The ringing of the phone interrupted her, and she ran quickly to answer it before it could disturb Ruth and Conor who were still in bed.

"I'm really very sorry," the woman on the other end told her, "But I have to cancel my booking for next week. Things didn't work out quite as planned."

"I'm sorry to hear it," Clare said automatically, leafing through her bookings diary to note the cancellation.

"Don't be," the woman answered, laughing. "We've been at each other's throats for the past month, we wouldn't have been able to appreciate a romantic week away, and you wouldn't have wanted us screaming at each other all the time!"

"Well, maybe you could come again sometime."

"Maybe, but not with my husband – I've someone else in mind, which was part of the problem in the first place – Peter was never very understanding about these things . . ."

I wonder why, Clare thought as she hung up the phone, glad that she had received a sizeable deposit, happier still when she realised that it freed up *Wildwood* for the first week of Rick's stay. She'd worry about the other week later. For now, she just needed to concentrate on where she'd fit Donal, and the twins, *and* their cousin, when they all descended on her next week.

"So, who's around?" Ruth asked, coming down in time to join Clare for coffee and croissants. "I want to see what a real live guest looks like."

"Oh, they're very civilised, this lot. Not one of them with two heads, or cloven hooves!"

"Boring! But I hope there are no babies, either."

"You're out of luck. The Byrnes are over in *Ocean* with a six-month-old and two other small kids. But they're great, you won't hear a peep out of them – the kids spend all their time playing with the animals, and you wouldn't even know the baby was there."

"Who's in *Saffron?*"

"A group of hikers, six of them. And two women in *Wildwood.*"

"But that's for couples, isn't it? There's only the one double bed." She helped herself to another croissant.

"That's right. They're a late booking, the original couple cancelled. But they're still a couple."

Light dawned and Ruth paused with the croissant halfway to her mouth, staring at her sister.

"You mean they're . . ."

"Lovely women," Clare said. "Very interesting, you'll like them."

Ruth leaned back in her chair, chewing slowly on the croissant.

"Are you enjoying this, Clare? I mean, really? It seems like a lot of hard work, and now you're stuck with it for the summer."

"I love it. And, yes, it's a lot of hard work. But I like it much better than what I was doing. I'm my own boss. I'm here in this gorgeous place. And I'm meeting all kinds of people."

"Who was the worst?" Ruth asked, pouring herself more coffee.

"God, the Dillons, definitely," Clare said. "They were impossible, until Donal took them in hand."

She gave Ruth a brief run-down as she buttered another croissant.

"But at least I had no problem knowing how many beds *they* needed."

"What do you mean?" Ruth asked, laughing, as Conor came to join them at the table.

"Well, there was an elderly couple – Mr and Mrs McEldowney – who had booked in for a weekend and when I showed them *Wildwood*, the woman turned to me and said it was excellent, she'd be very comfortable there, and where would her brother be sleeping?"

"Whoops!" Ruth said, laughing. "So what did you do?"

"You mean after I panicked? The place was full, so all I could do was leave the brother in *Wildwood* and offer her the spare room in the cottage – she wouldn't hear of *him* being in the cottage with, as she put it, 'a woman alone'. They refused to let me book them in somewhere else, so she slept in the cottage for the three nights. And I was worn out apologising all weekend for my 'inefficiency', as she put it, in taking the booking in the first place. They were *not* happy campers."

"Wonderful," Conor said, "How had it happened, anyway?"

"She made a booking for two in the name of Marjorie McEldowney, and she just said that she and Edward would be arriving late. It never occurred to me to ask who he was – he could have been the dog for all I knew."

"We live and learn!" Ruth said.

"It took me a while," Clare said, laughing. "There was another woman who rang about three weeks ago, and said she was coming with Daddy, and I told her I only had *Wildwood* free, and there was only a double bed in it. And she said that would be fine, and I was a bit confused, I asked if it would suit her father and would she mind using a camp bed herself. And she got very frosty, and said he wasn't her *father*. And when I apologised – I'm getting good at that – and said I hadn't realised he was her husband, she began to get a bit ratty and said she never *said* he was her *husband*, she just called him Daddy because the children did . . . she never showed up in the end."

"I wonder why!" Ruth said, when she and Conor

could control their laughter. "There *has* to be an easier way of doing this, Clare!"

"There is. Niall suggested I tell them there's only a double bed, and ask if that would suit. So that's what I do now, and it works like a dream, no more worries about whether I've insulted anyone or accidentally enquired into their marital status, when really I don't care a jot."

"You don't see yourself as keeper of the nation's morals?"

"What do you think? But if you like, I could arrange separate rooms for you and Conor, now that Dee and Tom have left."

"Thanks, you're very good. But I think we'll stay where we are."

"I would, if I were you. It's going to be like musical beds around here for the rest of the month."

"Because Rick Flaherty is coming?"

"He's the least of my worries," Clare said, deliberately misunderstanding as she started to clear off the table. "The world and his wife are coming, and I've no idea where I'm going to put them all!"

Rick was the easiest of all to sort out, because he was prepared to be pleased by absolutely everything from the moment Clare and Ruth collected him at Shannon on Friday morning.

"That is one gorgeous man," Ruth whispered to Clare as they spotted his tall, blond figure emerging from customs. He was dressed in jeans and a light blue polo neck, and carried a white linen jacket over his right arm, casually steering the trolley with his left hand.

Ruth was right, he looked wonderful. Relaxed, and confident, and – wonderful.

Clare gave a brief wave and saw his eyes light up as he caught sight of her. She moved forward to meet him, leaving Ruth where she was, and he dropped the jacket onto the trolley and abandoned it and crossed over to her in a few easy strides.

"Clare." He stood smiling at her, holding her shoulders lightly, and bent to kiss her cheek. "You look wonderful."

"So do you."

"Oh? Do men look wonderful?"

"You do!"

They were laughing as they walked back together to get the trolley, and went to join Ruth who had been watching every move. The three of them chatted easily on the journey back, resisting the temptation to take the scenic route because Clare wanted to get Rick settled in before exhaustion hit him.

She brought him across to *Wildwood* while Ruth began preparing lunch.

"Wow, this is really something! Who designed it?"

"I did."

"But who helped? You had an advisor, an interior designer – I don't know what you call them here?"

"Nobody but myself and Kate," she said, enjoying his response. "And the lads who converted it, of course. Think you'll be okay here?"

"Better than okay! A bit lonely, maybe, with all this space just for me . . ." He was smiling at her.

"I'll loan you one of the kittens, they're six weeks old now, and beautiful. Very good company."

"But not exactly what I had in mind."

"Make the most of it, I'll probably have to squash Donal and his gang in here with you – they're arriving next Tuesday and the place is already full. I don't know where I'm going to put them."

He gave her a slow smile.

"A lot could happen by Tuesday."

"You're right, it could. Starting with the two families I've booked in for the next two weeks, and from the sound of things they've arrived."

Ruth's frantic knock at the door confirmed it.

"Duty calls, sis. Looks like there's about twenty of them, anything I can do to help?"

"God. Count them again, for a start. I've only twelve booked in . . ."

"No problem," Rick said, winking at Ruth. "Ruth and Conor and I will just go and find a nice quiet hotel, that'll leave you plenty of space, and you can join us for dinner when you get through – say, in about ten days?"

"You're a great help, the pair of you! Go and have lunch, I'll shout if I need you."

There were only twelve after all, it just seemed like a lot more. Clare got them organised quickly, hoping they wouldn't be too noisy, reminding herself that they were on holiday and were entitled to be as noisy as they liked. It wasn't as if there was anyone else around who'd be bothered by them, just as long as they didn't do a repeat performance of the Dillons.

They didn't. They settled in very easily, delighted with the play area for the five children, and the barbecue that two of the men were already getting started, and the shady bench where the two older women sat while one of the younger ones brought them tea.

They were, Clare remembered, all belonging to one big family, with three sisters, and their mother and aunt, and the husbands of two of them, and assorted children. From the sound of things they were all set to enjoy themselves, and barring emergencies, Clare could relax and enjoy herself too, starting with a trip to Dog's Bay tomorrow and dinner tomorrow night at Albatross.

"This has got to be the greatest beach on this part of the coast."

Rick stood looking around him, a light shirt open over a pair of navy swimming shorts. He looked relaxed and rested, having gone to bed straight after lunch on Friday and not surfacing again until eleven on Saturday, just in time to head for the beach with the others.

"I really don't understand you guys," he had said. "It's the hottest part of the day, you'll fry!"

"And love every minute of it!" Clare had answered. "Don't worry, we'll use sun block. It's just that we get so little sun here, we have to make the most of it."

"See," he said when they got there. "There's hardly anyone out in this heat."

"That's the way it usually is here," Clare told him. "It'd be the best place in the world, if only the weather was always like this!"

The four of them played in the waves like children, tossing around a ball Ruth had brought, splashing in the occasional big breaker. Rick was a powerful swimmer, Clare noticed as he struck out after the ball when Ruth threw it wide. She dived into the waves and headed in his direction, reaching him just as he caught the ball and threw it back to Conor.

"You're a good swimmer," he said.

She smiled at him, pleased that he had noticed, treading water while they talked.

"You, too, you're great. I love swimming, ever since I learned when I was five or six."

"Want to race?" he asked.

When she nodded, he pointed to a large, flat rock a reasonable distance away.

"I'll give you a head start."

"No need," she said. "Go!"

It took a huge effort. He really was very good. But she managed to do it, touching the rock with her fingertips just before he did.

They were both laughing as they climbed onto the rock and sat watching the other swimmers and Ruth and Conor in the distance, and two men carrying a currach, its shiny black coating glinting in the sun, down to the water's edge.

"It's paradise, Clare. I feel I could spend a lifetime here."

"You'd miss New York."

"Maybe, maybe not. Not if I found somewhere better."

"This isn't better. Different, maybe, but not better. It can't be."

"You've been there? I thought . . ."

"No, I haven't. I've only seen it in films, and read about it, but I'd love to go. We were supposed to, the summer before last, but Dee got appendicitis and we had to cancel. I know I'll get there sometime, though."

He sat looking at her, his eyes very blue against his tan.

"You could come visit, if you wanted. At the end of the summer, when all your guests have gone."

"I didn't mean – "

"I know. But why not? It'd be fun. And you're right, you'd love it!"

"I'll see. Thanks for the offer. Let's not make plans yet, okay?"

"Okay. But – "

"Come on, race you!" she said as she dived cleanly into the water, leaving him to follow her back to the beach.

She hardly saw him alone for the rest of the weekend.

Ruth had appointed herself activities organiser and wouldn't take 'no' for an answer, even when Clare pleaded absolute exhaustion. There was a trip round the bay on a hooker on Saturday afternoon, and dinner at Albatross that night, and a tour of the Burren on the Sunday.

"Is she always like this?" Rick asked when they finally got a moment together on Sunday evening before going to a local pub for a music session that Ruth was convinced Rick would love. "Don't get me wrong," he added. "She's really good fun, it's just – well, not exactly what I had in mind."

"Me neither," Clare admitted, thinking that at least it gave her time to be around Rick without any pressure. "But I think she's just trying to make sure you feel welcome, and that you enjoy yourself!"

"I can think of all kinds of ways of enjoying myself, without even leaving here."

They were sitting outside in the half-dark courtyard as he spoke.

"Unless – did you ask her to do this, Clare? Play chaperone? Fine if you did, it's just . . ."

Clare laughed aloud at the idea.

"Not at all, and she'd be disgusted if she thought that's what she was doing. I think she has great hopes for us."

It was out before she stopped to think, and she could have kicked herself.

"I see. And what about you, Clare? Do you have hopes for us?"

His voice was soft, close. She could feel his breath warm against her cheek.

"Rick, I . . ."

She broke off as Ruth and Conor came into the courtyard.

"Ready to go, you two? It's nearly nine."

Well done, Ruth, she thought, as Rick gave a soft sigh and stood up with her. Charge in feet first as usual. Except you saved me from answering, when I don't know yet what the answer is.

"Coming."

Rick put his hand on her arm, holding her back for a moment as Ruth led the way to the car.

"I go back in two weeks. Think maybe we can grab just five minutes together before then?"

He was smiling at her in the soft light pouring through the windows that faced onto the courtyard.

"You're in luck. She's going home next Saturday. So the coming week will be busy, especially with Donal and the others arriving, but after that it'll be different. Promise."

"Good. I'll hold you to that."

Donal and the twins were delighted to be staying at Clare's. His niece, Tish O'Brien, was clearly not. She wore black clothes, clumpy shoes and a scowl that stopped Clare in her tracks when she went to over to say 'hello'.

She was really beautiful, Clare thought, slim and very tall for her fourteen years. Her eyes were a startling blue against ghost-pale make-up, and her hair, short and spiky, would probably look wonderful if she let it grow a bit and had it all one colour instead of a patchwork of burnished copper and orange.

I'm getting old, Clare thought. It's probably *meant* to look like that. One way or the other, it's a very definite statement.

She smiled at the girl, not expecting or receiving a response, and turned her attention to Donal who had already sent the twins off to the play area.

"Great to see you. You know we're a little bit stuck for space at the minute, but I thought if you and the boys took the spare room in the cottage, Tish could sleep in the gallery. Ruth and Conor are moving up to the caravan . . ."

She was interrupted by a sound that was not pleasant.

"I have to stay in this crappy place and I don't even get a *room?* I have to stay in a *gallery*, whatever the hell that is. Great."

"That's enough, Tish," Donal interrupted. "You can share the room with the boys if you like, and I'll take the gallery."

"So why can't they have the gallery with you?"

"Not enough room," he answered. "Besides, it's not safe for them – they could climb on the railings and fall over."

Tish's expression said that this would only be a very little tragedy.

"Let's go inside," Clare said. "You can have a look and see what you think."

Tish seemed ready to refuse, but instead turned and followed Clare reluctantly.

"You *are* joking," was Tish's response when she saw the gallery. "Think again."

"No, *you* think again," Donal said, angrier than Clare had seen him before. "I've just about had it, Tish. You've been like this since you arrived at Kate's on Saturday. And you know we can't really stay there, she needs all the space she has for her paintings. So this is it, and it's great of Clare to fit us in. So if you're staying, make the most of it. And if you want to go home, just say so right now."

Tish turned on him, her blue eyes filled with venom.

"Home. Sure. Where's *that* supposed to be? With my grandmother, who's about ninety and has all these stupid rules, and doesn't care a damn about me?"

"She – "

"Or that school you sent me to? Only, unfortunately for you, they have to close *sometimes*, when normal people go home to their families!"

"Tish, we – "

"Don't say it! *Don't* say it, because you are not my family. You're not my father!"

The two of them stood in the gallery, facing each other angrily. Clare decided that she could do nothing useful by staying there and wandered outside, silently wishing Donal luck.

She was passing by *Wildwood* on her way to the paddock when the door opened.

"Hi! Everything okay?" Rick asked.

"Hi, Rick. Yeah, fine, more-or-less."

"Could you use a coffee?"

"I'd murder my granny this minute for one!"

He was smiling as he made the coffee. Clare was sitting on the sofa in front of the fireplace, beginning to relax.

"It'll be like living in a battlefield for the next week if they both stay in the cottage. I need to figure out a better option."

"There's at least *one* better option."

She waited.

"You could escape from the battlefield and leave them to it. Stay here."

"Here? But where would – Ah."

"It's an option."

"You're right, it is an option. Except I think I should look for a different one, just at the moment."

Donal had it sorted out by the time she returned to the cottage.

"The boys and I will take the caravan, if that's okay, and if Conor and Ruth don't mind staying on in the gallery. That would leave Tish the spare room. What do you think?"

Great, Clare thought. So it'll only be *half* a battlefield.

"Well, if you're sure . . ."

"I've already put my bag in there," Tish said, as if that settled the matter.

"Right. Fine," Clare said, wondering how on earth she'd survive a week with this little madam. She decided to leave her to it for a while. Maybe her mood would improve. She didn't hold out much hope.

"Okay if I take the bags up to the caravan, Clare?" Donal asked.

"Sure. I'll give you a hand. It's all set up, there's a fridge and cooker and everything, but you can eat down here if you prefer."

"I'm vegetarian," Tish announced. She made it sound like a challenge.

"Fine, I do a mean aubergine *tian.*"

"For every meal?" The sarcasm was heavy.

"Only if you want me to," Clare replied, determined not to let Tish get to her.

It got better as the week went on. Slightly better.

Ruth went to great lengths to get on with Tish, and even managed occasionally to get a response that was a bit less than hostile.

Donal spent most of his time on the beach or in the playground with the twins, having given up asking if Tish would like to join them.

And Clare hung in there, counting the days until the following Monday, when Tish would be leaving, and wondering how she'd get through the weekend sharing the cottage with her after Ruth and Conor left, and escaping occasionally to join Donal or Rick for coffee and much-needed time out.

She was relieved that the family who were staying in *Ocean* and *Saffron* seemed to be having a great time and were making no demands on her at all. Tish was demanding enough for all twelve of them.

"I'm really sorry, Clare," Donal said when he finally managed a quiet moment alone with her. "I didn't mean to land her on you. She's not usually this bad – and I'm trying to make allowances. But she has no idea how close I've come to packing her off back to her grandmother."

"And could you do that?" Clare asked, hardly daring to hope.

He shook his head. "No. Not really. Bad enough that she has to live with Madge at all. She has a rough time of it there."

"And what about her – ?"

"Her mother's dead," Donal cut in quickly. "I'll go and check on the boys," he added, before Clare could say anything more.

She stood watching Donal as he walked back to the playground. It explained a lot, she thought. She resolved to try even harder now to get on with the girl.

But to everyone's surprise it was Rick who managed to do that, with no apparent effort.

"Pick your jaw up off the floor, Clare," Ruth said when they saw the two coming back from the direction of the beach on Friday afternoon. "At least I won't feel guilty leaving you tomorrow, now. Looks like our American friend has worked some kind of miracle."

"Thank God for that, we needed one! I was thinking of leaving with you . . ."

"And abandon Donal and Rick? You can't, it wouldn't be fair!"

"Just watch me."

"Sorry, sis, you're nabbed," Ruth laughed. "Try to see it as a lesson in parenthood."

"I will. It'll remind me never to have kids."

"Unless it's with someone like Rick," Ruth said, grinning. "He seems to know what he's at."

Clare ignored the comment. "I feel a bit sorry for him," she said. "I don't think this is what he had in mind for his holiday."

"Oh?" Ruth grinned. "What did he have in mind, do you think?"

"I'm not sure, exactly," Clare teased. "But I've all of next week to find out, haven't I?"

And she went out to examine the garden before Ruth could say another word.

Chapter Twenty-two

"The silence is incredible," Rick said as he stood in the sunlit courtyard, taking deep breaths of the salty air. Clare was sitting on the bench, her head back and eyes closed, enjoying the warm July afternoon.

She nodded agreement. "Takes a bit of getting used to, doesn't it? I keep expecting to hear children yelling. We'd better make the most of it."

He sat down beside her, looking at the flowers, the gleaming paintwork, the caravan away over on the little hill.

"You've really created something special here, Clare."

"I had a lot of help. I don't know how I'd manage without Jack and Jody, now Kate's so busy with her painting."

"I've seen Jody around a lot. Nice kid."

He looked sideways at her.

"You know he has something going with Tish?"

"What?" She sat bolt upright, turning to look at him. "He can't have! She's only fourteen."

He laughed. "So what were you up to when you were fourteen? Playing with Barbie dolls?"

"I certainly wasn't getting up to anything with boys – my father would have murdered me!"

"Not for this. It was harmless, kid's stuff. I caught them behind the barn once or twice, when I went out for a breath of air at night."

"She was in bed every single night at ten. I said goodnight to her myself."

He laughed again. "Sure," he said, looking towards the flat roofed-shed near the gable wall of the cottage. Just within reach for a determined and agile teenager.

"God, Donal will kill her when he finds out."

"Does he really have to know? They weren't up to much, truly."

"Yes, but . . . yes, I think he does have to know. He's responsible for her while she's here."

"Guess you're right. I'll tell him tomorrow. Better yet, maybe I'll make her come clean. You really think he'll be angry?"

"Well, he probably won't be pleased. Not if she's sneaking out the window to meet him. How did they react?" she asked, as the thought struck her.

"Jody seemed embarrassed. Tish was defiant, said I had no business spying on them and she'd report me."

Clare laughed. She couldn't help herself. "What for?"

"Infringing her right to privacy, she said." He laughed again at the thought of it.

"God, she's something else, isn't she!" Clare said. "Poor old Donal has his hands full."

"She's not a bad kid, you know," Rick said. "When you get to know her. I thought I'd take her swimming tomorrow, if she wants. It might take the pressure off."

Clare shook her head. "Nice offer, but I don't think so. She's absolutely terrified of water. Won't go anywhere near it."

"Really? That's a shame, I thought she might go for it."

"You really took to her, didn't you? How come you know how to get through to her?"

"I don't, I kind of make it up as I go along. And she seems to respond. She's really a vulnerable little kid, in behind all that barbed wire."

"Maybe," Clare said, remembering what Donal had told her. "But I'm still counting the minutes until she's gone!"

"Then you've got it wrong. She's a decent kid."

"But very hard work," Clare said. "I've tried to get to know her a bit, but no go."

"At least you tried," Rick said. "That's got to be good, even if she can't appreciate it." He sat for a moment in silence before deciding to change the subject. "Do you have plans for today?"

"What I'd love is to do absolutely nothing, just enjoy the peace and quiet until they all come back."

"And then?"

"Escape to dinner somewhere."

"You don't have to go far. I do a mean chilli. You told me you like Mexican food, right?"

"Right. Not that I know much about it – I've tried it once or twice in Niall's. You're able to cook?"

"Try me."

She turned and gave him a big smile.

"I thought you'd never ask."

He laughed and stood up. "Then I guess I'd better hit the supermarkets in Clifden. Wonder if they've heard of enchiladas?"

She laughed as she stood up and stretched.

"I'd say they've heard of everything at this stage!"

She left him to it, deciding on a walk on the beach and a long leisurely bath before it was time to go across to *Wildwood*.

She knocked on the door just after eight, and as he opened it she heard the soft, unfamiliar music that filled the room behind him. She followed him into the living area, enthralled. *Wildwood* looked and felt just the way she had imagined it, with lamps casting soft pools of light here and there, and music, and the scent of sandalwood mingled with exotic cooking smells. And a man and a woman, alone together.

She sat down where Rick indicated at the little pine table and watched as he moved easily between the kitchen and the little dining area, bringing in food and wine. He was, as he had said, a very good cook. The spicy smells were tantalising, and she could hardly wait to try it. "Anything I can do?" she offered.

"No need. You're the guest tonight, Just relax, enjoy."

He looked relaxed himself in a black tee-shirt, faded black denim jeans and sneakers. In fact, he looked great, and she wondered for a moment whether to tell him that.

"You look great," he said, and she laughed.

"That's funny?" He smiled as he opened the wine and poured it into two glasses, handing her one.

"I was thinking the same about you," she smiled, sipping the wine, beginning to feel the tension of the past week seeping from her.

"Thank you." His gaze searched hers for a moment. Then, "Come on, let's eat," he said, and he removed lids from various dishes, encouraging her to try the contents, laughing as the chilli caught her and she spluttered, reaching for more wine, gulping it down, laughing.

They spent a lot of the evening laughing. He was very good company, witty, attentive. Enjoying her stories, telling his own – and all the time he never took his eyes from her, so that she felt attractive, interesting. And exhilarated. Wondering what would happen. What she might want to happen.

"You really love it here, don't you, Clare?" he asked later as they sat on the sofa in front of the fireplace. The meal was finished, the last of the wine was in their glasses and there was music playing gently in the background.

He had switched off two of the lamps, leaving only the one in the far corner. He had lit candles on the mantelpiece and hearth, and shadows danced on the walls as the scent of sandalwood rose from the burner and filled the room with heady fragrance. She felt completely relaxed.

"It feels like home," she said simply, after thinking about it for a few moments. "It feels like my place, as if I'm exactly where I should be."

"More than Dublin?"

She thought for a moment. "Actually, yes. Much more than Dublin. And I never thought I'd say that."

"So you don't miss it? No regrets?"

"No," she said, surprised that it was true. "None at all, except that it took me so long to get here."

"You mean, to finishing the apartments and everything? Or to the cottage itself?"

"To where I am right now," she answered.

Her gaze was on the fire and she played with the wine-glass in her hand. He sat half-turned towards her, unwilling to break her silence, watching as the firelight lit up her face, her hair.

"You're very beautiful, Clare," he said, finally. His voice was soft as the soft candlelight.

She didn't answer, just turned to him smiling and very carefully put down her glass on the little table in front of them. He sat for a moment longer, watching her face in the flickering light, and then he moved slowly, very slowly, to touch her cheek, to trace the curve of her neck, lifting her hair where it curled against her shoulder. And then, not knowing who moved first, they were in each other's arms, his cheek against hers, mouth seeking her mouth, softness and firmness and warm moistness melded together so that they were gasping for breath when they finally broke away.

"You've been practising," he said, laughing gently, his breathing still ragged.

"Not for a long time," she answered.

Her voice was shaky, her breathing still fast as he

reached for her again, and for long, long moments they were lost in the feel and the scent of each other, and she didn't want him to stop, didn't want to stop and finally he stood, drawing her to her feet, moving towards the foot of the stairs . . .

"No, Rick," she said suddenly, as he began to lead her upwards.

She felt as if she was waking, still slightly dazed.

"I'm sorry." She broke away from him, drawing a hand back through her hair, moving towards the table to put some distance between them.

"I'm sorry," she repeated, pouring some water, gulping it down. "I can't. I didn't mean . . . oh, God." She was afraid to meet his eyes, afraid of the hurt, anger, whatever she might find there.

"But why?" he asked, taking a step towards her, stopping as he saw her expression. "I thought – "

"I just can't, Rick. I shouldn't have . . ."

She looked at him, seeing the hurt, the bewilderment.

"I wasn't exactly forcing you, you know. I thought you wanted – "

"I did . . ."

"So where's the problem?" He folded his arms, looking as if he was holding in the hurt. "We're all grown up now, Clare. We can do what we want."

"I can't," she repeated. "It would have to mean something."

"God damn it, Clare, it *would* mean something! I thought it would mean something for you, too!"

She poured some more water and went to sit on the

armchair. He moved slowly, sitting down on the couch, at a distance from her, the air between them bristling.

"It's too soon," she said, finally. "I panicked, I didn't . . . I'd need to know you better . . ."

"You know me." He said it quietly. "But you don't trust me, is that it? Or maybe . . ."

"It's not you, Rick. Really, it's nothing to do with you. It's me," she said, taking a deep breath.

He waited, giving her a chance to continue.

"Clare," he said finally, when she didn't. She turned to look at him and he saw the glint of tears in her eyes. He forced himself to stay where he was, not to move towards her.

"I promised you, no pressure." He spoke quietly. "And I meant it. I think we're missing something good. But like I promised, it's your call."

She sighed softly, realised she had been holding her breath.

"I'd better go," she said.

"No." His voice was gentle. "Why would you go? Stay, have coffee, talk to me. Will you do that?"

She nodded, biting her lip slightly, finding the taste of him still there. He stood up, moving to the kitchen area, making the coffee, coming back with the two mugs and handing one to her. She took it, concentrating on it, still finding it hard to meet his eyes.

"Do you want to talk about it?" he asked, after a while. "Or we could pretend it didn't happen, go back to where we were, and you can tell me how you'll spend the rest of the summer."

She laughed, uncertainly. "We can't do that, can we?"

"Talk about summer?" He was smiling now, gently, as he sat on the sofa taking a sip of his coffee.

"Go back to where we were," she said.

"We can do whatever we want, Clare."

She shook her head.

"It's not that simple, Rick. I wish it were, but it's not. Life isn't like some tape, where you can rewind it to edit out bits you don't like."

"You didn't like it?"

"I didn't say that. I didn't *mean* that. It's just . . ."

And almost without realising, she began to tell him about Tony, watching the feelings flit across his face as he sat, saying nothing, just listening to every word until finally there were no more words, just the soft sound of her breathing in the stillness.

"Sounds like you had a rotten deal, Clare. You were unlucky. But not all guys are like that. Truly. And I'm not just making a pitch for myself. If you walked out of here right now and I never saw you again, I'd want you to remember that, that not all guys are selfish bastards. You were just plain unlucky."

She gave a half-nod. "Except I can't see it like that. It wasn't just bad luck, it was me being stupid. My friends never liked him, but I didn't listen, I defended him. I got taken in. And now I'm afraid to try again."

"Clare?"

"Mmm?"

"How long were you with Tony? Couple of years?"

She nodded.

"And you're, what, thirty?"

"Thirty-two."

"So there must have been other guys, right?"

Another nod.

"So some of them must have been okay, even the ones that didn't work out. They can't *all* . . ."

"They weren't. But he was different."

"You loved him."

She sighed. "And trusted him."

"And for that, you're giving yourself a hard time?"

She put down the mug and looked directly at him.

"I got it wrong, Rick. I hadn't ever . . ." She broke off, gazing into the fire for a moment, turning to look back at him.

"I never slept with anyone else. He was the first. He was important to me, I trusted him enough for that – and I got it wrong."

"No, Clare." He was emphatic. "You didn't get it wrong. *He* did. The only thing you'll get wrong is if you stop trusting everyone else, just because of him. Don't let him do that to you, Clare."

"Ruth says that. And Kate. They say I should get out, meet people. Forget about him."

"They're right."

"Maybe." She looked down for a moment before meeting his gaze again. "So you see, it's not really to do with you. I really like you, Rick. It's just that . . ."

"I rushed things a bit?"

"It didn't feel like that, not until – I think I just need time."

"We've got plenty of that."

"You're going back on Sunday."

"It doesn't have to end right there, Clare. You know that. Not unless we want it to."

"Rick?"

"Mmm?"

"Thank you."

He got up, watching her reaction, and crossed to give her a light kiss on the cheek, taking her hands as she stood up to face him.

"We have all the time in the world, Clare. No pressure. And we have all this week, just two friends, having fun, if that's what you want."

"I haven't blown it?"

He shook his head slowly as he opened the door.

"No way. I promised, your call. I think we could have something special, Clare. Really, I do. But if I have to, I'll settle for being friends."

She smiled for the first time.

"Okay, friends. And we'll see how it goes."

Chapter Twenty-three

They had a great time. The guests were booked into the two apartments until Friday, and did their own thing anyway, not needing Clare for anything at all, so it was almost like a holiday for her. Donal and the twins had moved to the house he rented, along with Tish who, to Donal's surprise, had refused to return to Dublin on the Monday as planned, insisting she would stay another week "whether or not she was wanted."

"I don't know what to make of her," Kate said when she called to the cottage that evening with an answering machine Niall had sent over for Clare. She glanced at Rick, stretched out on an armchair in front of the fire, gave Clare a huge smile and declined the offer of coffee, saying she should get back to her painting.

"Kate," Rick began, guiltily aware that he should have said something to Donal about Tish and Jody. But Kate was already halfway out the door, closing it behind her, blocking Rick's view of her as she winked at Clare.

"I'll ring Donal," Rick said, standing up, but there

was no reply, and there never seemed to be a moment over the next few days as he and Clare tried to make the most of their time before he had to go back.

The days passed quickly. They had set up the answering machine, leaving a message saying that there were no vacancies until the second week in August – the truth, she assured Rick – and spent hours driving through the countryside as she showed him all her favourite places.

"Kinvara has to be the best," he said, as they got back from an afternoon in the little village, and a tour of the south coast of Connemara. "I love the harbour, and the old castle. Some day, I'd like to live in a place just like that."

"The castle?" she teased. "Wait 'til you see Bunratty."

He laughed. "The village. In one of those little cottages. And I'd paint it bright yellow, and keep a lamp shining in the window to welcome me when I sailed back into the harbour . . ."

"You'd have a boat?"

"Of course. A hooker, maybe, with those big black sails, except I definitely couldn't tell anyone in the States I had my own hooker, they'd get the wrong idea . . ."

They were back in the cottage, beginning to prepare a late dinner, laughing and chatting as they worked together. He really was easy to get on with, Clare thought, and great fun, and, as he had promised, there was no pressure, he was letting her take things at her own pace.

And yet, at the same time, there was an awareness

between them, so that the ease became charged sometimes with a pleasurable kind of tension that left her alive, and tingling, and afraid to be anywhere within touching distance of him, because she didn't trust herself not to reach out, knowing that, this time, there would be no turning back. And as the days passed and she got to know him better, she found she didn't want to think of Sunday, when he would have to leave.

She turned to him now where he was preparing vegetables at the sink, and was about to ask if she would open a bottle of wine when the phone rang.

"Clare? Donal. Sorry to bother you, but I don't suppose Tish is there, by any chance? She hasn't come home for dinner. I've tried everywhere else I can think of, I thought maybe . . ."

He broke off, sounding distracted.

"Sorry, Donal. I don't think Rick has seen her since he dropped her back to your place, the day before yesterday. You remember, they went walking on the beach? But hang on, I'll check . . ."

She turned to Rick, who had picked up the gist of the conversation and was looking concerned. He shook his head.

"When did they see her last?" he asked, waiting as she repeated the question to Donal.

"At breakfast," Donal answered. "She went out straight afterwards, and no mention of what her plans were – I assumed she was going for a walk, and I'm still hoping that she'll just turn up. But it will be dark soon . . ."

"She's with Jody," Rick said, suddenly certain. "Tell him to come on over."

"My fault," he added, looking worried as Clare hung up. "I really should have told him. But I guess I didn't want to cause trouble. And it really wasn't any of my business . . ."

Donal arrived within ten minutes. He must have hit the road in spots, Clare thought as she opened the door and went to get into the car, followed by Rick.

"Kate is waiting for us as well," Donal said as he pulled away from the gate.

"Who's with the boys?" Clare asked from the back seat.

"Molly."

Clare nodded. She had forgotten his mother was down for a few days.

"I'm not sure where to start," he said, as he drove quickly towards Kate's house.

Rick explained briefly about Jody, and Clare, from the back seat, caught Donal's expression in the rear view mirror.

"I'm sorry."

"It doesn't matter." His voice was terse. It did matter, of course. Clare knew he would have kept a tighter rein on Tish if he had realised that she was spending time with Jody. No doubt she had used Rick as an unwitting alibi whenever Donal asked any questions.

Kate was already at her gate, waiting anxiously since the phone-call from Donal.

"Well, that makes it much easier," she said when they were sitting in her kitchen, telling her about Tish and

Jody. "No, think about it, Donal," she added as he started to object. "At least she's not on her own, and Jody is a sensible lad, and he knows every inch of the place for ten miles around. He won't let her come to any harm."

"But what if – "

"Stop worrying, and let's see can we figure out where they might be."

"Nowhere public," Clare added. "They'd be afraid of word getting back to Donal." She bit her lip as she caught Rick's expression.

No-one said anything for a minute or two as they considered the possibilities.

"They probably just want a bit of privacy," Kate said. "And they won't have gone far. They hardly have much money, have they?"

"I don't think so," Donal answered. "And it narrows things down, all right. But where do we start?"

Rick grinned as he spoke for the first time since arriving at Kate's.

"Well, I don't know about you guys, but I remember when I was a kid, about fourteen or fifteen, on holidays in Vermont – there were a couple of places all the kids used. The back of a car, if maybe an uncle or a cousin or someone had left one out of sight. Or in the woods, because it was summer and warm enough. Or in a hayloft, that was always best, because . . ."

He paused as the other three of them, light dawning, began to smile.

"That's it!" Kate said, following Donal who was already sprinting down the pathway to the car.

If Jack was surprised he didn't show it, when he opened the door to the light tap and found Clare standing on the doorstep with Rick and Donal. Kate had waited in the car, saying they didn't want to be crowding him, and Clare remembered how uneasy she often seemed when Jack was around.

"Is it the guards are after you?" he asked, a smile on his face as he led the way into the kitchen, where a turf fire was burning in the big black stove in spite of the warm weather. The room looked much as it had been when Clare was last there, shortly after she came down in February.

Jack sat down at the table, inviting them to do the same. He had obviously been in the middle of his supper. There was a blue and white striped mug in front of him, half full of tea. A loaf of soda bread and some butter on a plain white dish sat in the middle of the table.

"Sit down there," he said, taking his place again at the table. "Will ye have a cup?"

He half-turned in the chair to reach back to the big aluminium teapot sitting on top of the stove. "I always make gallons of the stuff."

"Thanks, Jack, but we haven't much time," Donal said. "We're looking for Tish, and we think she might be with Jody. Have you seen either of them?"

"Jody was here for a while, doing a bit for me," Jack answered, pausing to take a mouthful of tea. "But I haven't seen your niece since the other day, over at Clare's."

"When did Jody leave?" Donal asked.

"I wouldn't know for sure. Round about five, I think. Paddy Ryan passed on the road in his van, heading out your way. Jody took a lift from him."

"So he didn't go home?"

"No, now you mention it. He went the opposite way. But I didn't pay much heed, he's always going places. Anywhere sooner than go home."

"Is there any chance they might be in your barn? Up in the hayloft?" Donal asked.

Jack's face was a picture, torn between embarrassment, and amusement, and sheer disbelief.

"Is that what you think? Shouldn't you go and have a look, so?"

"We need to do it quietly – we don't want to frighten them off if they're there."

"There's only the one way out of it," Jack said, standing up. "So you can frighten them all you like as soon as you're at the door. Come on, I'll go with you."

"No!" They all looked at Donal, startled by his tone.

"Sorry," he said. "It's just that I'd better go on my own, just in case . . ."

Jack nodded, understanding.

"Why don't I come with you?" Clare asked.

Donal thought for a moment, then agreed. He moved to the back door, Clare following, leaving Jack and Rick in the kitchen. Quietly they crossed the darkening yard, picking their steps carefully towards the big barn.

It was dark inside, pungent with hay and the scent of animals. They stood for a moment listening, their eyes getting accustomed to the dimness. In the faint light through the murky windows they could pick out a wooden ladder leading to the loft above their heads, and almost at the same instant they heard the sound of voices coming quietly from up there.

Donal moved quickly towards the ladder and was beginning to climb when Clare reached out a hand to stop him. He came back down the two steps, nodded, and instead called out to them. There was absolute quiet in response.

"Come down *now*, please, Tish, or we'll have to come up. You too, Jody."

There was still silence for a moment, followed by Jody's voice.

"We're coming, Mr McCarthy."

He was first down, looking shame-faced.

"We weren't doing anything, honest. Just talking."

He turned to stretch his hand up to Tish and she took it, jumping lightly off the second-last rung of the ladder and moving to stand beside him. Clare could sense, rather than see, her scowling at them in the dim light.

"She's a real handful," Clare said later when she and Rick had gone back to their belated meal. "It's tough on Donal."

"Tough on her, too, don't forget."

"Yes, but she makes it harder. She keeps reminding him he's not her father, when he doesn't try to be or even want to be. What he *does* want to do is the best he can for her. But she doesn't make it easy."

"Kids are like that. Goes with the territory."

"How come you're such an expert?"

"Oh, I've got lots of friends with kids. I'm godfather to a couple of them. I see what it's like all the time, but at least I can walk away from it."

"But you like them."

He nodded. "Always have. Especially the ones like Tish. Independent. A bit wild. But soft on the inside, once you get to know them. She's really something special, you know. We've talked a bit, walking on the beach. Under that cold steel shell, she's pure gold."

He caught Clare's sceptical look as she took their empty plates from the table, coming back with the coffee percolator.

"Really," he said, as she sat down again opposite him. "If I had a kid, I'd want her to be something like Tish. Maybe just a bit less prickly. But not much."

He reached and pressed down the plunger on the percolator, and she passed him the two mugs.

"What about you, Clare?" he asked, concentrating carefully on the coffee, not meeting her eyes. "Do you ever think about having kids?"

"Not now. I used to, when I was younger. And when I see my godchild Niamh – my brother's little girl, she's four, all blond hair and big blue eyes – sometimes I think I'd love to have a child like her. Or like those twins of Donal's, they're great kids. I love them at that age – it's the baby stage I'm not so sure about."

He laughed. "It passes."

"So I've heard," she agreed. "And for about ten or twelve years you have wonderful, marvellous children, and you think you've got it right. And then one night the fairies come and spirit them away, and leave you with monsters who *look* like your kids, but act like nothing on earth – "

He laughed. "And because you're their parents, and part of you still thinks they're wonderful because they look just like your kids, you somehow put up with them and get through all the years until they become people again . . ."

She laughed now, interrupting him. "And all the time they think their parents are the monsters, who don't even try to understand . . ."

"Unless you're like Tish," he said, suddenly serious. "If you've never known your father, it's too easy to imagine him as some kind of cross between Superman and Santa Claus, which is where Tish is at. She really thinks that some day he'll come riding by on a white horse, looking for her."

"She told you that?"

"She told me a lot of things. Like that Donal and her grandmother won't tell her anything at all about him. And she hates them for it."

"Kate told me they didn't know anything. Tish's mother refused to tell them."

"Makes no difference, she has to blame somebody. So she's blaming them."

"That's hardly fair, is it?"

"No. It's not fair at all. But that's how it is."

Chapter Twenty-four

They only saw Tish once more before Rick left, when they all went to Kate's on Saturday for lunch. She was frosty with Donal and Clare, still blaming them for "embarrassing her for no reason" in front of Jody and the others. She was pleasant enough to Kate and the twins, and to Rick she was sweetness itself, listening to every word he said and agreeing with most of them.

They had a lovely lunch, in spite of her, and the only regret was that Molly hadn't felt able to join them because she was feeling exhausted.

"I'm worried about her. Would you talk to her for me, Kate?" Donal asked as they worked together in her small kitchen, handing food and dishes to Clare who ferried them back and forth to the table set up in the sitting-room.

"I'll do what I can, love, but you know Molly."

She picked up a wooden bowl filled with salad, turning to hand it to Clare, reaching round Donal as she did so. "I can't wait until I have more space here. Did I tell you, Clare? Kevin is extending the house for me, building a conservatory at the back and a little studio. I won't know myself!"

"Kate! That's wonderful! You'll be able to see out over the whole bay. It'll cost a fortune, though, won't it?"

Kate looked embarrassed for a moment. "He's paying for it himself., every last penny. He tells me he can afford it, and I'm not to worry about a thing!"

"Looks like he finally *has* grown up," Donal said quietly to Clare as they went in, ahead of Kate, to rejoin the others.

"Don't knock it, it's a lovely thing to do. You can see she's thrilled."

They all left together just after four o'clock, Rick driving Tish and Clare in her car, Donal following behind with the twins. They were going to call into the cottage for a while so the twins could work off a bit of steam in the play area, and Rick and Tish were going for a final walk together on the beach. She was taking it very hard that he was leaving for home the next morning.

"We'll have to leave at about seven in the morning to make sure . . ." Clare began, then gasped as Rick swerved hard to the right to avoid the coach that had skidded across the road and was hanging, nose first, over the four-foot drop at the ditch on their side. From the look of things it had just happened, and already two cars had stopped.

She turned in her seat, watching as Donal came into

view and pulled into the side of the road, well beyond the coach.

"Stop, Rick," she said, surprised that he kept going.

"It's okay," he replied. "Somebody has stopped."

"Donal has. We have to go back to him."

"But – "

"Rick, turn around. Now."

He pulled in, reversing into a gateway to turn, making no comment on her tone. Clare ignored Tish's murmur of 'bossy bitch' from the back seat. She had the door open almost before Rick had brought the car to a stop facing Donal's.

"Come on, let's go!"

"We don't need – "

"Are you mad? Come *on*, they might need help!"

"I'm sure the cops are on the way. Somebody's sure to have telephoned."

"Who, exactly? Rick, if you're not going to help, at least drive back to that house we passed and get them to phone the guards. Tish, could you go round that corner and get the traffic coming to slow down? Please?"

The girl looked frightened, and paler than ever, but she nodded and got out, hurrying towards the bend as Rick turned the car again and Clare ran to the coach.

"Daddy's in the bus!" the twins called through the open window of one of the cars as she ran past. The other occupants, an elderly couple, were obviously very shaken and said nothing, just sat watching as, in ones and twos, schoolchildren of about fourteen or fifteen began to climb out of the coach.

Some of them had grazes, one boy was holding his side, a girl who looked about twelve had blood streaming from a gash on her cheek while her friend tried to stop the flow with tissues and hankies. Several of them were crying or holding on to each other, but for the most part they seemed unhurt.

"Okay, everybody, listen!" Clare said as loudly as she could.

They all turned to look at her, reassured by the adult presence.

"We need to get in off the road, okay? There's help on the way. I want you all to walk over there to those cars, and stay there, well in. And nobody move, okay? The guards will be here in a few minutes."

Once satisfied that they were doing exactly as she told them, she climbed into the coach, steeling herself for what she might find inside. It was a bad sign that Donal was still in there.

Her first impression was of noise. Noise, and people slumped in their seats. There was the sound of crying, and a young girl screaming, and near her a woman sat, head back, eyes closed, moaning.

Clare was about to move to her when the woman opened her eyes, and in the same moment Clare realised that she couldn't reach her because there was a man – the driver, she thought – lying in the aisle, his head near the doorway. A woman was bent over him, her hands in a fist pressing on his chest, moving awkwardly in the cramped space to get to his mouth, breathing slowly, one-two, then back again, hampered by the seats.

"I'll come to you as soon as I can," Clare called to the woman passenger, getting a faint nod in response. She turned and bent down beside the man on the floor.

"I'll do the breathing," she said, moving into position, and the woman kneeling there glanced at her gratefully, moving a bit to make room for her, and Clare barely had time to register that it was Nicole Gautier. They slipped into a steady pattern, working together fluidly.

Finally she paused, signalling to Nicole to wait. As she bent her ear to the man's mouth she could hear the faintest of breaths. The faintest, but it was there. And then she heard voices outside, and footsteps, and she climbed onto one of the seats to make space for the ambulance men to lift the man out of the coach.

She glanced around again, looking for Donal. It took her a moment to locate him, down near the back of the coach, barely visible above one of the seats. She was about to call to him when the woman near her moaned again. One of their teachers, Clare presumed, stretching out a hand to reassure her, looking around for the others.

A young man with a beard was talking to the six or eight teenagers remaining on the coach, calming them, reassuring them, so that they waited quietly as the ambulance men brought the driver out on a stretcher.

Once the aisle was clear the children were carried or led to the waiting ambulances, until finally the only people left on the coach were Donal and the girl he was tending, who refused to let go of his hand until her stretcher was placed in the last ambulance and he smoothed her hair, promising that they would take good care of her.

As the ambulance moved off he walked over to where Clare was standing with Nicole.

"You were brilliant," he said, hugging her. "Both of you."

He smiled at Nicole who was leaning against one of the cars, exhausted.

"Team effort," Clare said.

He nodded, turning to look towards the group of children who still waited by the side of the road, where she had sent them. "Back in a minute."

He was gone, running towards them. There were several other adults there now, talking to them and comforting them. The teacher began moving from group to group, and gradually everyone else started to drift back towards their cars as they saw that the situation was under control.

"There's another coach on the way," Donal said when he came back. "But there's only one teacher with them now, and he thinks they'll be terrified getting onto a coach again. It might be difficult to keep them all calm. I've offered to go in with him. Do you think . . . ?"

"I'll take the twins," Clare said.

"No, I will do it," Nicole offered quickly. "I will take them to Kate's and I will look after them there, until you can come back, Donal. Would that be a good idea?" She turned to Clare. "And then you can go with him on the coach, if you want."

Rick and Tish had joined them in time to hear the end of the conversation.

"I'll come with you on the coach," Tish offered suddenly. "Maybe I can help."

They looked at her, surprised.

"Good idea, Tish," Donal said, and she ran to join the other teenagers as they began boarding the replacement coach that had just pulled up.

"And I'll follow in Clare's car," Rick said. "You'll need a ride home from Galway."

"It's ninety miles, there and back," Donal reminded him.

"No problem. I'm all packed for tomorrow anyway."

"Thanks. I'd better tell the twins what's happening."

"You could have done without this," Donal said to Clare as the coach neared Galway. They were sitting together near the front, talking quietly, while the youngsters sang at the top of their voices behind them as they had done all the way since Maam Cross, thanks mainly to Tish. She had been amazing, going from one group to another, laughing and joking, encouraging them.

"They could all have done without this," Clare answered. "It's a hell of a way to finish a summer camp."

"You're right. Of course. I just meant that – well, it's Rick's last night. You were probably planning to go out."

"It doesn't matter."

They lapsed into silence as the bus pulled into the parking area of a hotel just outside the city.

The teacher came over to them as the bus slowed to a halt.

"This is it, end of the road. Now I just have to face thirty sets of parents with the bad news. Though they'll know anyway, the guards will have told them about the accident and got some of them to the hospital. There's bound to be panic. Wish me luck!"

"Will we go in with you?" Donal asked.

"No, it'll be fine. But thanks. Thanks a million."

And he was gone, opening the coach door, running lightly down the steps ahead of the youngsters to address the parents already gathered at the coach door.

"You were great, Rick."

Tish was sitting in the front seat beside him on the way back to the cottage. "Nobody else thought of ringing the guards."

Clare could feel Donal tense slightly in the seat beside her.

"Clare's idea," Rick answered.

"But *you* did it," Tish persisted.

There was silence for a minute or two.

"You were pretty great yourself," Rick said, finally. "I'll bet you were a real help to all those kids. I could see you moving round on the coach, all the way into Galway."

They were all quiet for the rest of the journey, and Clare found herself drifting off to sleep, her head bending to rest on Donal's shoulder.

She woke abruptly when they came to a stop at his car, still parked beside the coach on the roadway. They got out, stretching their legs, Clare and Donal cramped from the small back seat.

"Guess it's time to say goodbye!" Rick said, holding out his hand to Donal.

"We'll see you again, maybe?" Donal asked.

"I hope!" Rick answered, turning to offer his hand to Tish who instead gave him a quick hug and fled towards Donal's car where she stood with her back to them, shoulders shaking, beside the locked door. Donal nodded to Rick and Clare before moving quickly across to open it for her.

"She'll really miss you," Clare said later to Rick as they sat in the cottage later having tea and sandwiches.

He put down the cup and looked at her.

"And what about you, Clare?" he asked softly. "Will *you* miss me?"

She stood up, moved to the sink and began rinsing her cup.

"We had a good time, Rick." Her back was to him.

"Sure," he said. "But that doesn't answer my question."

She reached for a towel to dry her hands, playing for time.

"Clare?"

This time she looked at him.

"You're pissed at me, right? Because I didn't get into that coach?"

"You weren't even going to stop, Rick! That's what I can't understand!"

"They didn't need me."

"You couldn't know that!" Her eyes were flashing with anger.

He got up, walked to the window, stretched, clasping his hands behind his head. Then he stood for a moment resting his hands on the deep sill, looking out into the dark night, before turning to face her again.

"It's hard to explain, Clare. But I really didn't want to get involved."

"But they were kids! How can you not – "

"My grandfather was a doctor," he interrupted. "A good one, I'm told. And as far back as I can remember, until he died when I was about fourteen, he told me not to get involved in things like that. He even said that's why he persuaded Dad to become a dentist, instead of following him into medicine. Because nobody needed emergency dental treatment at the side of the road. He said it as a joke – but he meant it."

"But that's ridiculous! I mean, I'm sorry, he was your grandfather, but surely you know that, don't you? You have to get involved if people need you."

"Maybe it was ridiculous. I don't know. But in his case, it was understandable. He was about fifty years old when he stopped to help a man who had a heart attack on the sidewalk. He did his best, but the man died. His widow sued. And the judgement went against my grandfather. It shouldn't have, but it did, and it all but destroyed him. It left him a bitter man. He never practised medicine again."

Clare bit her lip, put down the towel. "Rick, I – well, what I said – " She paused. "It must have been desperately hard on him."

"It was. And on my dad, growing up in the shadow of it."

"So that explains why your grandfather felt like that." Her voice was softer now. "But not you, Rick. You're not like that!"

He sighed. "Maybe I am. I never really thought about it before. But I guess it had an effect, hearing that story all the time I was growing up. It was a strong lesson. If you don't get involved, you can't get hurt!"

"If you really believed that, you'd never have got involved with anyone. Not your wife, not Beth, not . . ." She broke off. "You *weren't* involved with Beth, were you? I mean, not really. Because if you were, you wouldn't have lost touch . . ."

"That's not true! I told you, I had to go back quickly, there wasn't time – "

"To get an address? A phone number?" she asked gently.

"It wasn't like that!" he said, his voice hard, angry.

She moved to sit at the table, still watching him, and took a deep breath.

"I'm sorry, Rick. I shouldn't have gone on like that, it's none of my business. I didn't really mean that, about Beth. It's just that, I think I'm still a bit shaken. And I found it hard to take, that you didn't want to stop."

He came across slowly, pulled out a chair to sit opposite her.

"Would an apology help? And a promise to think about what you've said?"

"You don't . . ."

"No, wait." His eyes never left hers. "Maybe you're right. Maybe I have been scared of getting involved."

He reached across, touched her hand. "But maybe it's about time I changed. I still believe we could have something going for us, Clare. I still want to give us that chance."

She thought of how she had felt that first night in *Wildwood*, thought about the buzz between them and how much they had laughed together in the past few days. And by the time they said goodnight shortly afterwards and he went to try and get some sleep before the early start in the morning, she had agreed to give them time.

No promises, no pressure. But she would go and visit him in September.

Chapter Twenty-five

"Well, I hear you lot were the heroes of the hour!"

They were sitting in Albatross, about to have lunch, and Kevin had come across to them, putting on his best performance as a waiter.

"I wouldn't exactly say that, now, Kevin!" Clare laughed.

"Don't see why not, Clare, everyone else is saying it. And the good news is, the driver is out of danger. You two saved his life, from what I'm told," he said, nodding in Nicole's direction to include her.

"And a girl called Michelle sent a message for you, Donal," Kevin continued, smiling at him. "She said she's doing fine, she had two broken ribs but she'll be grand. And she says she'll never forget you."

"Where did you hear all this?" Donal asked, looking slightly embarrassed.

"Local guards. The lads in Galway have been keeping them posted."

He turned to Nicole.

"And as for yourself, Mademoiselle Gautier! You've been keeping very quiet about your talents. I never knew you were a nurse. I thought – "

"That I am a restaurant manager."

"Sure, that's what you are."

"And this means I cannot also be a nurse? Like you are a builder. So where is the problem?"

He laughed.

"You're right, no problem at all! I'd say you could be anything in the world you wanted, if you put your mind to it!"

"You flatter me so I will tell Niall that he would be lost without you here!"

"She has me sussed!" he smiled, winking to Donal and Clare.

"Well, isn't it the truth, Nicole?" he said, turning back to her. "Tell him he's lucky to have me, and a pay rise would do very nicely, thank you!"

She smiled up at him, brown eyes sparkling under the black fringe. "You are, what is this expression, pushing your luck!"

"No harm in trying!" He laughed as he went to get the lunch menus, and Nicole went back to their previous conversation.

"And you are absolutely sure that every Friday and Saturday evening for the rest of August, you will be available to sing for us? I cannot believe it is so difficult to get musicians for this month, but it seems that every single person has gone on their holidays right now. Like in France!"

"They're all over here!" Clare said. "Maybe you should have a French night, and put a poster outside asking for French musicians. I love Breton music."

"It is an idea. But – does that mean that you would prefer perhaps not to be doing this? I know that you will be very busy, especially at the weekends."

"No, just joking. Except – well, I do think it would be a good idea to have a few Continental nights during August, everyone's in a holiday mood and they'd be willing to try something a bit different. And we're happy to be the star attraction, if that's what you want . . . well, I am anyway," she said, glancing at Donal, who smiled.

"Count me in. If only for moral support!"

"We will count on you for much more than that, Donal," Nicole said. "We know now that you are a man who can be counted on!"

He was prevented from replying by Kate's arrival.

"I'm absolutely famished! Hope there's something I like on the menu, Nicole."

"And what do you like, Kate? Niall has told me I am to look after you very well, because he had to go to Galway on business today. So if you will tell me what you would like, I will try to arrange it."

Kate laughed. "I like nearly everything, so I'm safe enough. And it'll be great just to sit here and have it handed to me – I've been flying around the place all morning!"

"I will go and ask the chef to prepare something truly wonderful. What is it that you would really like?"

"What I'd love is a Spanish omelette and salad. I don't suppose that's on the menu?"

"It will be. I will be back in a moment," she said, standing up. "And I will bring back menus for the two of you, since Kevin seems to have completely forgotten. At least he is looking after *some* of our customers."

All four of them looked towards where Kevin was busy talking to two young women, obviously advising them on the menu.

Nicole was still smiling when she returned with their menus.

"He will remember by the time you are drinking your coffee. He is often like this. But the customers love him! Now, I will go to the kitchen for a moment."

She was back before the waitress had finished taking their order.

"The chef has promised that he will make the perfect omelette for you, Kate." She chatted for a few minutes more until their food arrived.

"Now, I will leave you to enjoy it!" and she moved to check on some of the other tables.

"You know, I hardly see you these days, Kate," Clare said as soon as Nicole had gone. "I hear you're up to your eyes. Donal tells me you've sold nearly thirty of your paintings already."

"Not counting the ones Niall bought for Kingfisher," Kate smiled, looking delighted with herself. "I loved doing those. I love them all really, I can't believe I'm actually enjoying myself *and* making so much money." She paused, taking a bite of the omelette. "God, this is lovely, I should come here every day!"

"You could be making a lot more money, you know,

according to Niall," Donal said. "He thinks you're not charging half enough."

"I don't know how he can think that, I was mortified with the amount he paid me, they're never worth that but he insisted they were."

"Niall is a great friend," Clare said. "But a good businessman, too. He knows an investment when he sees it."

"That sounds a bit hard, Clare. Niall is doing me a huge favour, displaying my paintings for me. I'd never have sold more than one or two but for him."

"That's probably true, because you'd have no real outlet without him. And I don't mean to be hard, I think it's a great chance for you. I just think you should give yourself a bit more credit. And maybe up the prices a bit."

"I couldn't charge any more than I do, Clare."

"You could, if you saw what they're charging inside in Galway, or up in Dublin. Did you ever go round Merrion Square on a Saturday, and see what people sell there? Some of them are brilliant, but they're still not a patch on yours!"

"Maybe I'll have a look next time I'm up. I was thinking of going soon, anyway, to see Molly."

"I need to see her as well," Donal said. "I've to go up with Tish on Monday week, so I thought I'd call in then. I'll only be there for the day – that probably wouldn't suit you, would it, Kate? But I can bring you back down if you like."

"Who'll mind the children?" Clare asked.

"Nan Kinsella."

"I'd be happy to – " Clare began.

He smiled. "Thanks – but you've enough on your plate. You're booked up now for the rest of August, aren't you?"

She nodded, reaching across for some garlic bread.

"Can't say I'll be sorry to see the end of it!" she said.

"That sounds bad," Kate said. "Seeing there's nearly three weeks still to go!"

"Not that bad, really, I suppose. But it's exhausting, trying to make sure everyone is happy. I mean, value for money is one thing, but some of them seem to expect wall-to-wall free babysitting, or an evening meal that was never part of the deal, and one of my latest guests came looking to 'borrow' some whiskey the other night – he said it was ridiculous that there was no pub nearer than Clifden, and he seemed to think it was somehow my fault."

"What did you do with him?" Kate asked.

"Sent him packing back to his apartment and told him I didn't keep spirits on the premises as a matter of principle."

"And he believed you?" Kate brought the napkin to her mouth to stifle a fit of coughing at the thought.

"Seems so. He doesn't know me! So now he's staying in Clifden, leaving his wife outside in the apartment with three young kids. She told me the other day it's the best holiday she ever had."

"God, the poor woman," Kate said. "She must be codding herself completely."

"No, I think it's the opposite. She's having a great time on the beach with the kids every day. If you ask me, she's had time to think and she's *stopped* codding herself. I think your man is going to get his comeuppance when they get back home!"

"Sooner you than me, Clare. I wouldn't be able for it."

"You most certainly would, Kate, if you wanted to do it."

"Which, thanks be to God, I don't. I've more than enough to keep me busy and happy with the painting. And when I've my little gallery set up . . ."

"Gallery?" Donal asked.

"That was Niall's idea too," she said, turning to him. "You know Kevin is started on the conservatory – that's part of the reason I'm going to Dublin, to get away from the noise and the commotion. Well, Niall suggested that if he made it a bit bigger, brought it out to the side as well and brought it along by the studio, once that's finished, then it would be big enough to hang some paintings in it and people could come in and buy them from there. He said if I put up a sign I might get a lot of people stopping on the road, tourists are always looking for something a bit different to bring back home with them."

"Sounds great. And you'll still sell them from here?" Donal asked.

She nodded in reply.

"It'll be a lot of work. If you're putting that much into it, you'd really better work out a proper price," Donal said.

"Maybe you're right. I'll have a look around when I'm in Dublin – I should have a bit of time to spare."

"Does Molly know you're going up?" Donal asked. He was frowning slightly, and Clare realised that he was anxious, though he tried to hide it.

"I haven't told her yet, in case she might try to put me off. But I'm going anyway. I'm worried about her – I'm not sure she's well in herself."

Donal nodded. "I feel the same, though she says she's fine." He paused. "Sometimes I wish I hadn't come down at all."

"Now that's mad, love – you know it is. The last thing Molly would want is you to go regretting that you're here, when she's probably right as rain!"

Maura came to take the plates, handing the menus to them again, and Kate took advantage of the pause to change the subject. She didn't want him dwelling too much on Molly, Clare thought. Or maybe she wanted to put her own worry out of her mind.

"What's this I hear about Nan?" Kate said once they had ordered dessert. "Kevin tells me she's looking after the boys full-time?"

"That's right. Jody happened to mention to Kevin that she was looking for work, so Kevin suggested asking her. I'll need someone to mind them in September anyway, and I've a lot of preparation to do before that – "

"You did well to get her," Kate said. "She'll be great with them. But I'm surprised her father agreed – she has a brood of sisters and brothers to mind."

"He agreed readily enough. Jody told Jack he was a bit worried about how his father would react, and Jack went over there and talked him into it."

"Jack Staunton is the only man I know who can talk Kinsella into anything," Kate said. "I'm sure Nan was glad of the chance to get away from him and earn a few bob. And she knows the boys well enough by now. Is she settling in all right?"

"She seems to be, Kate. She sleeps in her cousin's place, near us, and the cousin told Jack that Nan is delighted. She hardly opens her mouth to me, she looks terrified if I ask her anything – so I don't. But she's good with the twins, and they like her, that's the important thing."

"How old is she?" Clare asked.

"Hard to say," he answered. "She looks about twenty but she seems younger. Because she's so unsure of herself, probably."

"And will she manage the twins okay, if she's that unsure? Minding children full-time could be a lot harder than the odd night's babysitting."

"Nan has had to manage a lot worse than two small boys, let me tell you," Kate said. "She's twenty-two now, and she's been mother to that family since she was fifteen. I suppose the next girl is old enough now to take over the minding. The twins could do an awful lot worse than Nan Kinsella."

"And what happened to Mrs Kinsella, Kate, do you know?"

"Everyone knows, Clare. And nobody knows. It's

not something that's talked about much. For the children's sake, mainly."

"But if everyone knows . . ."

"They know she drowned. What they don't know is whether she meant to."

"How did it happen?" Clare asked softly.

Kate took a sip of coffee. She sat looking into the distance for a moment or two before taking a deep breath.

"She was a strange woman, Sadie Kinsella. A strange, sad sort of woman. You got the feeling that there was a lot more to her than you knew about, sometimes she'd smile at you or come out with something so witty you'd nearly stand looking at her, wondering could it be Sadie Kinsella who said that. But mainly she kept to herself, her and the children. And that brute of a husband of hers. He gave her a desperate time. He has the name of farming, but most of his time is spent in the pub, and when they put him out of one he moves on to another, and tries to get in there. Sadie and the children learned to keep away from him as much as they could."

"Why did she stay with him, if he's that bad?" Clare asked.

Kate gave her a sharp look.

"What choice had she, with all those children? And even supposing she wanted to leave, the place was hers. Her father's, and his father's before him. It didn't come easy to them, and she wouldn't let it go easily. She wanted it for her children."

"Couldn't she have got him out?" Clare said.

"Maybe she could – but she didn't try. Instead she took to walking on the strand on her own for hours at a time, and she'd collect shells and bits of driftwood. And she'd smile in a dreamy sort of way at anyone who passed, and I remember once she said to me, 'Sadie. Sadie. It's the right name for me, it sounds a bit like sad, doesn't it? I was born to be sad.'"

Kate was lost for a moment in the memory of it.

"I didn't know what to say to her. The poor woman was losing herself altogether, and Kinsella wouldn't listen to anyone who suggested she see a doctor, and Nan had to take over more and more with the younger ones, while Sadie walked on the beach and sometimes danced there, barefoot, even in the cold weather, and she had a big bright scarf she used to drape around her, and sometimes she'd dance with that, like a little girl with a big rainbow-coloured kite. The breeze would catch it, and she'd hold onto it, running with it, laughing as she ran."

"And was there nobody at all who could help?" Clare asked, unwilling to believe that the woman could have been so alone.

"She had no family left around here," Kate said, "and she wasn't a woman to make friends. And when the doctor finally came to see her, I don't know what Kinsella said to her, or to him, but nothing came of the visit. She had good days from time to time, and I suppose that's when Kinsella sent for him."

"But why wouldn't he have wanted her to get help?"

"He wouldn't have wanted anything that would upset things for him, or that might point the finger back at him in some way. And then we heard she was expecting again, from a neighbour who saw her out in the field one day. And she stopped going to the beach, no-one saw her for a long time.

We wondered how she'd manage, she was finding it hard enough to look after the little ones she had already. And we took it in turns calling the odd time, but Kinsella would never let us in, he always told us she was fine. And then one night he came looking for Jack to drive them to the doctor, he couldn't drive himself with the amount he was after drinking. The child was coming early, much too early, and any sane man would have left her there in the bed and stayed with her and sent for the doctor. But I suppose he got into a panic. Anyway, Jack got them there as quickly as he could. But it was too late. And Sadie seemed to be her old self for just a few minutes, and she said to Kinsella that she would never forgive him. Never, as long as she lived."

"What did Kinsella say? Did Jack tell you?"

"Jack didn't tell me any of it. He'd never repeat what someone said in private. But Peg Moloney was there with them, a neighbour he picked up on the way because he felt Sadie might need a woman with her. Peg is a great neighbour, if you don't mind the world knowing your business."

"And how did . . ." Clare hesitated.

"How did she drown? Like I said, no-one knows for sure. But she took to walking on the beach again, and running and dancing with her scarf. And one morning she went out early, it was a desperate day with a high wind and the waves lashing in on the beach. The children were worried, and after a while young Jody went out, he was only about eight at the time but he has more spunk than his older brother, and he wouldn't let the girls go. And when he got to the beach she was nowhere to be seen, there was only the scarf flapping in the wind, tangled on some barbed wire. It took three days for her body to be washed up. And the hardest part of all was not knowing if she meant to do it."

"The hardest part of all is that she drowned." Donal had been quiet for so long they had almost forgotten he was there. Now, as he spoke, his voice was distant, and his face, when Clare turned to him, seemed set in stone.

"Drowning is drowning, whether you mean it or not. The end is the same."

"Donal, love," Kate said, her face soft with concern. "Oh, Donal, I wasn't thinking . . . but it's not the same at all, you know that."

"How is it different, Kate? Jenny died, she drowned. Liz, too. On a day that should have been perfect. And I'm no better than Kinsella, when it comes to it. Because it was my fault she died. I let her drown."

Clare and Kate both started to say something, just as Nicole arrived back at their table.

"I wonder if you two would do me a huge favour? There is a man here for lunch, with all his family, and he heard you singing last Saturday and would love to hear you again, but he returns to Holland tomorrow, he will not have . . . oh, I am sorry." She looked from one face to the other. "I have interrupted at a bad time. How stupid of me, I am sorry, I will tell him . . ."

"Tell him I'll do it."

"You are sure, Donal?" Nicole looked anxiously from Kate to Clare, then back at Donal. "You do not have to . . ."

"I'll do it. Just one song."

He glanced across at Clare, who nodded.

"We'll do it." His voice was tight, controlled. Clare looked at him as they collected the instruments, but he didn't seem to see her. He led the way to the little stage in the corner and began to play, and she concentrated on picking up the tune since he didn't tell her what it was going to be. And then she joined in softly on the mandolin, her throat aching as she watched him sitting there, his eyes closed, singing the haunting, beautiful ballad, changing it a little bit, his voice mellow and gravelly at the same time, full of the same unshed tears she could feel, full of infinite pain and loss.

Little by little the room quietened down until finally there was no clatter of dishes and knives and forks, no doors opening or closing, no voice but his in the yearning silence.

> *"Black was the colour of my true love's hair*
> *Her lips were like red roses fair,*
> *And now my love, she has gone for good,*
> *And I love the ground whereon she stood.*
> *Black was the colour . . .*
> *Of my true love's hair . . ."*

Chapter Twenty-six

Clare was dreading Friday evening. She was beginning to regret ever agreeing to sing in Albatross with Donal, but she didn't want to let Nicole down.

She spent the day outside as much as possible, feeding the animals, doing some gardening, enjoying the warmth and the sensual feel of the slight breeze on her skin. The courtyard looked lovely, blazing with flowers, and the paddock beyond was like a little wonderland with the animals roaming in large pens and the trees in full leaf, and the gypsy caravan bright in the near distance. As she went from pen to pen with the two pups scrambling along behind her, she began to relax, enjoying the freedom of it. She loved having no-one to answer to but herself.

The answering machine was blinking when she arrived back in, and she checked it to find a brief message from Donal, saying he would pick her up at eight if she wanted. He'd be out for the afternoon, but she could ring after seven and let him know.

She ran upstairs quickly and got into the shower. As the soothing water poured over her she thought about the evening ahead. She could handle it, she decided. She hoped Donal could.

It would be awkward, though. Straight after he finished the song on Wednesday he put back the guitar, went to say goodbye to Kate, said 'See you, Clare' and was gone before she could answer. To her relief, because she had no idea what to say in the face of such grief.

"My God, how could I be so stupid?" Kate had said, half to herself, as Clare sat down again opposite her. They talked for about an hour, Kate telling her about the accident that had happened while Donal, Jenny and Liz were on holiday in France with Tish and the twins, three years ago.

"I don't know much about it," Kate had said. "Just that they were out rowing on a lake, and the weather was lovely, everything should have been all right. But somehow, they drowned. Both of them – Liz as well as Jenny. Donal never talked about it much. I remember his face, those first few days after it happened. A terrible, terrible time. Coming home from France with the bodies. Standing in Glasnevin on a day when the sun was splitting the stones, a day to be out on the beach, not burying people. Molly and I thought he'd never talk again. We knew he'd never get over it. But never once did we think he was blaming himself."

"Has he talked to anyone at all about it, do you think?" Clare asked. She could feel the tears in her eyes, thinking of what it must have been like for him.

"I don't know, Clare. I suppose he wouldn't want to talk to myself or Molly, he wouldn't want to worry us. I know he has good friends in Dublin, he might have talked to some of them. But in ways he's a very private man. Like his father."

"Is his father dead long?" Clare asked.

Kate looked startled, and Clare realised she had interrupted her train of thought.

"Oh, Brendan is dead about eight years now, since just after Donal and Jenny got married."

"That must have been very hard on Donal."

"Well, yes, but he was never really that close to Brendan, they were very different in a lot of ways. He was much closer to Molly, and it was hard for her when he left, and then Brendan died soon after. Just like it's hard for her now, with Donal down here. But she wouldn't want him back in Dublin. She knows it's time for him to make a new life for himself."

"She must love him a lot," Clare had said.

"She does," was Kate's answer. "And the best of it is, he knows it."

Clare was still thinking about the conversation as she came downstairs and began preparing a snack. She'd accept the lift, she decided. If she was going to feel a bit awkward with him, far better to get it over with on the way in rather than when they got there.

After she had eaten she checked the apartments again for the guests who were arriving that night. She had *Saffron* ready and was just putting fresh flowers in *Wildwood* when the first couple arrived. She settled them in quickly, just as the family arrived to take over *Saffron*, and left them happily drawing up rotas for use of the barbecue. Back in the cottage she smiled to herself, thinking that maybe this week, at least, would be easy. She felt more lighthearted as she rang Donal, just after seven, and arranged that he would pick her up in half an hour.

"How are the twins?" she asked as she settled into the car.

"Fine, Kate is with them."

They didn't talk again until they were in Clifden and Donal had manoeuvred into a space just in front of Albatross. Then they both began talking at once and Clare stopped and waited.

"I'm not in great form, as you can see," Donal said. "And if I had my way I'd be at home with the twins, drinking a beer and listening to some music. But I didn't want to let Nicole down."

She hesitated a moment. "Donal, do you think you'll be okay? I mean, there's no point putting yourself through this . . ."

He smiled for the first time that evening.

"I'll be fine. I intend to sing nothing but happy songs, even if it's 'The Wild Rover' twenty times over."

"Wonderful. I can hardly wait."

She said it deadpan, and this time, when he smiled, he touched her briefly on the shoulder.

"Wednesday was a one-off. An aberration. I suppose because of what we were talking about. Normally I manage to keep it all under control. Tonight will be fine."

"Okay," she said, after a moment. "If you're sure. Come on, let's give them a great night."

And they did, that night and the next. And though Donal was very quiet on the way home both nights, at least there was no awkwardness and Clare found it easy to be with him, both of them alone with their thoughts.

"Would you like coffee?" she asked as they drew up outside the cottage on Saturday night.

"Thanks, but I'd better keep going, it's nearly two."

"Okay, see you." She reached for the door handle.

"Clare – "

She turned in the darkness.

"Are you free on Tuesday? We're going for a picnic. I'm trying to find things to keep Tish occupied before she goes back."

"How is she?"

"What can I say? She's Tish. If anything, she's worse than before. But I've relented a bit. I told her Jody can come on Tuesday. It's the only reason she agreed, I think."

"You've got over finding them in Jack's?"

"Yes and no. My only problem with it really is her age, and the fact that I'm responsible for her. I don't think they were up to much."

"No, I'm sure you're right."

"Can you come, do you think? It would lighten the atmosphere a bit, if you could."

She laughed. "I'll bring the sambos!"

"Great! Cheese, if you can manage it, the twins have decided to go vegetarian too, only they won't eat vegetables. It's a nightmare!"

"Don't envy you! What time Tuesday?"

"Two o'clock okay?"

"Fine – see you!"

She ran towards the cottage, taking her key from her pocket as she went, and he sat watching her in the brightness of the yard light until she was safely inside and had turned it off, her signal that she was okay.

The car was packed when they arrived on Tuesday, but she would have sat on the roof in her eagerness to get away for a few hours.

"Hard time?" Donal asked, smiling at her sympathetically as she plopped herself into the front seat and let out a sigh. Jody had happily vacated it to squash in beside Tish and the twins in the back.

"Not exactly," she said after a moment, smiling at him. "They're very nice people, just, well, lots of them! And I think I took on a bit too much, between chickens, and pups, and donkeys and sheep, and now we've four new kittens as well . . ."

He laughed. "Can't say I didn't warn you! And anyway, it's only one donkey." He glanced at her for a moment, alarmed. "Isn't it?"

"Well, yes." She giggled. "Don't mind me," she said. "Hysteria! I've some lambs that are growing so fast I don't know *what* to do with them!"

"Mint sauce?" he suggested.

"You are *so* gross!" Tish said from the back seat, but at least she didn't threaten to get out and walk. That had to be progress, Clare thought.

The picnic was a good idea. Jody had picked the spot, a secluded inlet near Little Killary, with some woodland and hills, and a grassy, open space where they stretched out a blanket within view of the water, but at a little distance from it. And while they ate he kept them going with stories and jokes.

"I'm glad now I let him come," Donal said to Clare. He was sitting with his back against a tree, looking relaxed, chewing a blade of grass. Tish and Jody had taken the twins for a walk through the woods, having promised to stay in sight and keep a careful eye on the boys.

"Do you think I was a bit over the top?" he asked, as he scanned the trees to see if he could spot them.

"No. Not now."

"You did before?"

"Well, you were a bit protective of them. But I could see why."

"Did Kate tell you?"

"About Jenny?"

He nodded in response.

"Not much more than you had already told me," she said. "I knew that – that she had died, three years ago, and . . ."

"Next week."

"What?"

"Three years next week. It'll be three years."

She sat, not knowing what to say.

"And every bloody year it gets harder. Not easier. Harder."

"Donal?"

She had to repeat his name softly before he turned to look at her.

"Mmm?"

"What you said the other day, with Kate, about it being your fault?"

"It was my fault."

He was looking into the distance now, watching the little group who had circled through the woodland and were now working their way along the path towards the jetty, just fifty yards away down the slight slope, separated from them by trees and bushes.

He stood up, not taking his eyes off them, and she followed his gaze.

"They shouldn't . . ." and he started to run, forging his way through the thick bushes, and Clare was on her feet too and beginning to run by the time they heard the scream, and she couldn't see what was happening, just focused on running, fast as she could, through bushes that tore at her legs, and then she stumbled on a root, feeling the sharp pain in her ankle as she steadied herself, forcing herself on as she reached the start of the pier, seeing in a single moment the twin, one twin, screaming, and Tish screaming as Jody held her, pulling her back, and Donal running for the water, tearing off his tee-shirt, bending to grab at sneakers, and she did the same, wincing at the throb in her right ankle, forcing herself on, ignoring it, calling to Donal as he reached the end of the jetty.

"Wait!" she called. Could he swim? She didn't think . . .

"No!" he shouted, the word lost as he dived, and she wasn't sure if it was a response to her, or something else. She ran and dived a moment later, wincing again at the cold and the pain, striking out to where she could see Donal breaking the surface.

There was no sign of the child.

And then he went down again, and she did, and again, and when she broke the surface at a distance from him she could see that he had the boy, he was holding his head, supporting him with one arm while with the other he flailed the water, kicking strongly, bringing them towards the jetty and the steps at the side where Jody was already poised, life-belt ready, the end of the rope secured.

Clare struck out towards them, gasping at the pain in her ankle, suddenly hardly able to catch her breath, gulping water as a wave caught her unaware, pain exploding now as she tried to pull herself towards the jetty, kicking as hard as she could with her left leg. She could see Donal climbing the steps, the child in his arms, and then disappearing from view. She was still struggling but the jetty seemed so far away, and then a wave struck her again and she realised the tide was going out, and she pushed as hard as she could, forcing herself through the water.

Then she saw Jody at the top of the steps, crouching, calling to her, and a moment later Donal was there beside him, tall against the sun as he came to the edge and dived again.

She closed her eyes for a moment, exhausted from

the effort, and then he was there, almost beside her, there, reaching for her as a wave broke and she went under for a moment until she felt his arms around her, clutching her against him. And then panic for a moment, as he let go.

"Come on, Clare!" His breath was coming in gasps.

It was all right. His voice was behind her, his hand under her chin. She could feel him kicking strongly below her.

"Come on," he said again. "I need you to help – can you kick?"

She couldn't answer, just tried to kick with her good leg, tried to make herself light in the water, imagining herself floating, safe.

And they were nearly there, she could see the wall now, the steps, the red and white of the life-belt as he reached for it, clung to it, and there were hands reaching, and arms lifting, carrying her and then she was lying on the cold stone of the jetty, and then –

"Clare? Can you hear me, Clare? Clare!"

Donal. She could feel him beside her. She concentrated, opened her eyes, closed them again, the sun too bright, the world spinning. Pain. Pain in her ankle, in her chest . . .

"You'll be fine, Clare, I promise. You'll be fine. There's help on the way."

She struggled to speak.

"Luke? Michael?"

He grimaced. "Luke. Who else? He's fine. Except . . . he's fine."

She could hear voices, and then the sound of an engine, doors slamming, more voices. She felt a touch on her hand, a man's voice.

"Are you all right?" She nodded, concentrating on taking deep breaths. "Fine," she said after a moment. "My ankle . . ."

"Don't worry, we'll look after you," the man said. He helped her up into the ambulance and put her lying on the stretcher along one side of it.

Luke sat across from her, huddling into Donal, his pale little face paler against the blood-red of the blanket he was wrapped in. There wasn't a sound from him. Michael, on Donal's other side, cried until well past Clifden, looking at Luke, then Donal, then Clare across from them on the stretcher, then back again to Donal.

The ambulance man sitting in the back with them did his best to keep Michael amused, finally getting him to laugh just as they came to a stop outside Galway Regional.

They were still waiting for the results of Clare's x-ray when Kate and Jack arrived.

"Tell me," Kate said, rushing to Donal, grasping him by the arm, her worried expression matching his own.

"They're fine," he said. "We're all fine. Except for Clare's ankle. We're waiting to see if it's broken."

"At least they've given me something for the pain. God, I feel like such a wimp! Talk about a liability!"

"Don't," he said.

"Don't what?" she asked him.

"Call yourself that, you're anything but."

"Sure. Even though you had to get back into the water again. You could've – "

She caught Kate's warning glance just in time.

"I was wet anyway," Donal said, managing a smile. He reached out and squeezed her hand. "And at least I can swim properly now." His expression was tinged with sadness for a moment.

Just then the doctor arrived back.

"No breaks," she assured Clare.

"I suppose you're sure?" Clare asked. "It's killing me, I thought I'd made bits of it."

"We're sure. But you wrenched it badly. The ligaments will take a while to settle and you'll have to stay off it for the next couple of weeks. No walking, no anything. You'll need to use ice-packs and keep it elevated."

"I can't just – "

"You'll have to," the doctor said firmly. "You're going to be on crutches for three weeks or so."

"Oh, God," Clare said. "But – "

"She'll do it," Kate said firmly, turning to the doctor. "We'll make sure of it. Would you be able to lend us some crutches?"

"I'm sure we can sort something out," the doctor said, above Clare's protests that she wasn't an invalid.

"We'll do everything for you," Kate said, "except carry you. So take the blessed crutches."

It was nearly half past ten by the time they got back home. Luke, wrapped in a dry blanket now, over pyjamas, was carried into Clare's kitchen, and though he looked exhausted he was still wide-eyed. He hadn't spoken a single word since he was taken from the water.

They were all going to stay the night. Donal refused to let Clare stay on her own, so the cottage, with its spare room, made most sense.

"I'll stop here too, if that's okay, Clare," Kate said. "I can sleep in the loft with Tish. Will you go over and get her, Donal, while I make a bit to eat?"

Donal hesitated, and Jack, sensing his reluctance to leave Luke, offered to go instead. "Let you ring her and tell her I'm on the way, I'll be there in ten minutes."

Donal rang, and rang again. He was ringing for the third time when there was a knock at the door. He opened it to Jody.

"I was watching for the light, so I'd know when you got back."

"Where were you watching from?" Clare asked. She knew her cottage couldn't be seen from Kinsella's.

"Jack's barn," Jody answered. He seemed distracted, looking around him in an agitated way.

"Is everyone all right?" he asked finally, focusing on Clare and then the twins, curled up on the couch, wrapped in blankets, Michael sound asleep, Luke still staring wide-eyed.

"We're fine, I'm just stuck with this for a while." She indicated the bandaged ankle. "And Luke's still a bit shaky, but he's all right."

Kate began setting the table.

"Here they are," she said as a car pulled into the yard, "Just in time."

Donal crossed to open the door. Jack came in, taking his cap off. He was alone.

"No sign of anyone there at all."

"Sorry, Jack, you had a wasted journey. She was with Jody, over in your place."

They turned to Jody who looked from one to the other.

"No, she wasn't, Mr McCarthy."

He looked terrified, a shadow of the boy who had been on the picnic. "She ran off on me, just after you left in the ambulance. I couldn't find her at all. And then that couple who came down to help us, when you got Luke out, they were still there and they gave me a lift back to Kate's. We thought Tish must have gone back to your house, but when I went over I got no answer, so I thought . . ." He lapsed into silence, looking at the little circle of faces. "I don't know what I thought, that she followed you into Galway, maybe. But she's not with me. I haven't a clue where she is."

Chapter Twenty-seven

It was Jody who found her, just before two in the morning, in a place no-one else would think of looking. She was curled up against the wall of an old church, in a disused graveyard he had shown her, her small white face the only thing visible in the light of his torch.

His shout brought the others running, and then he was bending, half afraid to touch her, calling her name urgently, and she stirred just as Donal got to them. He lifted her as easily and as gently as if she were one of the twins, hugging her into him as Jack came up beside them with Martin, Jody's older brother.

Donal carried her down to his car on the roadway, past the grey stone wall of the cemetery, and settled her into the back seat, wrapping blankets around her thin, shivering body. He stroked her hair, brushing it back from her forehead. Her eyes were open now, dark against the stark white of her face.

"Are you all right, Tish?"

She nodded.

"You're sure?"

Another nod, slighter this time.

"Right, let's get you home."

"I'm coming with you." Jody opened the other door, began to get in beside her.

Martin put a hand on his arm. "You'd better come home, Jody. Da'll go mad."

"Let him."

"But – "

"He can't blame you, Martin, he doesn't know you were out tonight."

His brother still looked reluctant.

"Go on," Jody said, firmly. "I'll be well back before he's up. And if he asks you, say nothing. Right?"

"Maybe you should go on home, Jody," Donal suggested.

"I'll go when I know she's all right."

It was the first time any of them had seen him look defiant.

Jack took charge.

"You go on, Martin, and don't worry about him. Donal, I'll get hold of the others and let them know we have her."

"Will you manage it on your own?"

"No bother. Here's one of the lads now, he'll spread the word. "

Kate had a fire lighting and some soup on the stove when they arrived back.

"Thanks be to God. Where did you find her? Are you all right, Tish? Come over here to the fire."

Kate was talking non-stop, from sheer relief. She led

Tish over to the big armchair, Jody following her like a shadow.

"You must be exhausted, all of you," Kate continued. "Come on, have something to eat and then we can all get to bed. Clare is staying down here on the couch, for tonight anyway. Tish, you and I are sharing Clare's bedroom, is that okay? Or you can have it to yourself and I'll take the loft."

"No." Her voice sounded small, frightened.

"Okay, Clare's room then. And Donal, the twins are already asleep in the spare room, we put the camp bed in there for you – and Jody, you could have the loft if you want to stay . . ."

She turned to Clare.

"Will you listen to me, taking over the place . . ."

Clare smiled at her.

"You're minding us, that's what you're doing. I think it's what we all need right now."

She moved further back into the armchair, feeling herself begin to relax finally.

"You're looking better," Kate commented. "Don't move from there, I'll get you some soup."

"I'll do it." Donal was on his feet in a moment, though he looked exhausted. He put a small side-table in position beside the armchair, then brought a bowl of soup and some bread.

"Can you manage?" His voice was gentle.

"Fine. Thanks."

She began eating the soup as he went upstairs to check the boys before sitting down himself.

"Do you want a lift, Jody?" he asked later, after they had eaten. "It'll only take a minute to drop you across, and Tish is fine, as you can see. You can come back tomorrow, or stay the night, if you want."

Jody decided to go, after one last anxious glance at Tish. Donal went out with him and was back in no time.

"He wouldn't let me bring him as far as the house," he explained. "He was afraid his father would hear the car."

Kate nodded, understanding. She knew how difficult Kinsella could be.

"Try and get some sleep, now, love. Tish is sound already – I looked in on her a minute ago."

"I don't think I could sleep," he said, sitting down at the kitchen table. "Not yet, anyway."

"Please yourself, love. But I think you should try. I'm going on up myself, I can barely stay standing. Will you be all right, Clare? You have everything you need there beside the couch, haven't you?"

"I'll be fine. I won't sleep either, not for a good while. I'm too wound up."

"I'll make you some coffee," Donal offered, "with a drop of whiskey. I think we've earned it."

There wasn't a sound in the house by the time Donal returned to the living-room with the coffee and the bottle of Black Bush, and two glasses.

"Whiskey or coffee?" he asked. "Or both?"

"Both," she said. "But separately."

He nodded, poured the coffee, then took a glass and poured in a measure of whiskey. He began to bring it across to her but she stopped him.

"Could you help me over to the table?" she asked. "I'm beginning to feel trapped here in the armchair!"

He left down the mug and glass and crossed to her, supporting her with an arm round her waist as she hopped as far as the table.

"Why do you think she ran away?" she asked, when they were settled at the table with the coffee and whiskey in front of them.

"I'm not sure," he said. "But I suppose she thought I might blame her for Luke falling in."

"You don't, do you?"

"How could I? It was my fault."

"Donal, that's ridiculous – it was an accident!"

He didn't answer. They sat drinking their coffee in silence, and then he put down the mug and took a sip of the whiskey. He still hadn't spoken by the time Clare finished the coffee. She reached for the whiskey, rolling it round in the glass, watching the deep golden colour of it against the light. She sipped it, then sat thinking for a while as Donal took up the bottle and poured another small measure into his own glass.

Finally she broke the silence.

"I don't know if you want to talk about today, Donal. And I won't press you. But I think it would be a good idea."

He sat staring down into the glass, then took a deep breath and looked across at her.

"What would you like me to say, Clare? That I nearly got the three of us killed? That I can't believe how stupid I was, to let it . . ."

He stopped, turning away from her.

"Happen again? Is that what you were going to say? Is that what you think?"

"What else could I think?" His eyes looked haunted, she thought. Haunted, not seeing her, seeing something else, in a different, pain-filled time.

"You could think that he fell in, by accident, a simple accident, and you saved his life. And mine, don't forget. You could think that, but you don't. You think it was your fault, just like you think it was your fault that . . ."

"That Jenny died? It was."

"But even if – "

"If what?" His voice had a raw edge to it. "You weren't bloody well there, how can you know whose fault it was?" He was angry as well as sad, she realised. Angry, and devastated, from the look of him.

He reached for the bottle again, started to unscrew the cap, made an impatient noise and moved it back, almost out of reach. He sat, elbows on the table, running his hands through his hair. And suddenly he was crying, huge, wracking sobs, and she felt awkward and a bit embarrassed. She reached out a tentative hand to touch him, not sure whether or not he would want that.

She felt so helpless in the face of his pain that she almost wished she could just slip quietly away. Instead she waited, her hand lightly on his arm, and finally, after what seemed like a long, long time, the sobbing stopped and he sat there, not looking at her, saying nothing.

She thought she might suggest they should get some rest, wasn't sure how he might react.

And then he started to speak, and in the soft light of the lamps his face was etched in shadow, and in pain.

"It was a perfect day. That's how it started, a perfect day. We were staying in Provence, on a campsite near a lake. You could hire boats at the far side of the lake. We cycled round there, through the vineyards. I can still remember the smell of them, I suppose it was whatever they put on the fields, but to me it was the smell of summer in France. We had great fun on the way over, Jenny and I with the boys on carriers, Liz and Tish going on ahead, teasing us, calling us slowcoaches.

They didn't want to go on the lake. Jenny, Liz, Tish, none of them. They were enjoying the bikes, wanted to keep going, up into the forest. But I talked them into it. The boys wanted to go out in the boat, we could go to the forest the next day, I promised. The next day."

There were tears running down his cheeks, but he didn't seem to notice.

"And then we were out rowing on the lake, on this perfect day. It was late afternoon, the other boats had gone in. I wanted to stay just a bit longer. It was like something you'd dream up, the lake, the sunshine, the kids at the back of the boat, laughing. Jenny and Liz sitting across from me because they wanted to take turns rowing. The kids were safe, we'd put lifejackets on them.

It was my turn to row, and it was easy. Not a ripple. I was keeping an eye on the children, looking past Jenny and Liz, and I had to turn sometimes to see where I was going – the girls were teasing me, they were supposed to be keeping watch. And they were laughing too, Jenny had said something and Liz was laughing, and I looked at her and I thought how beautiful she was, they both were. And I turned away, to watch where I was going, and Tish screamed . . ."

He fell silent, and Clare waited, not daring to move, not daring to speak. When he began again his voice was raw. He reached for the water jug, poured some into the almost-empty whiskey glass, swirling it around.

"Luke was in the water. Jenny said 'stay there' and I did, because they were better swimmers, and besides, someone had to stay with the other children. So she dived in, and so did Liz, but they couldn't find him. It seemed to take hours. Tish was screaming, Michael crying. I tried to calm them, tried to keep the boat steady, in the one place. Watching for help, watching for the girls. Seeing Luke's little lifejacket, abandoned in the bottom of the boat, near where he had been sitting.

Then Tish stood up, she was still screaming – I let go the oar to grab her, and it fell into the water before I could catch it.

And when I looked for the girls again, they had him. The two of them were holding him and then Liz let go, she seemed to be in trouble. I wasn't even sure it was Liz until Jenny swam back with him. We lifted him over the side between us, I remember the water splashing from his mouth as I hauled him into the boat. Liz was still out there. I wanted to go, but I knew I wouldn't get to her. Even exhausted, Jenny was better than me. We both knew it. It had to be her.

And still I was looking around for help, but there was no sign of anyone, either on the lake or on the shore, not even the man looking after the boats. Jenny swam over to Liz – she had her, they were coming back. I bent over Luke, trying to make sure all the water was out. Checking if he was conscious. Trying to make sure the others didn't move and fall in too."

His voice trailed off. He looked as if he was carved in stone.

"When I looked again I couldn't see them." He said it quietly, she had to strain to hear. "There was only a boat in the distance, setting out from the shore. Nothing else. No sign of them. Only that bloody boat, coming too slow and too late. And me sitting there helpless, with the children, and only one oar. There was nothing at all I could do then. Nothing."

"They trawled the lake for four hours that evening. And all the time I sat there, next to the bikes, watching and waiting. Someone was looking after the kids, people had come across from the campsite and some of the local people were out. And all the time I sat beside the bikes, holding Jenny's sweater that she had left there. And among all the footprints in the sand at the edge of the lake I noticed hers. It was quite distinct, I knew the pattern well. I had seen it so often – she wore those sandals all that summer. And there it was, leading to the lake.

And still I sat and waited, until finally, late that evening, they carried them out. Liz first. And then Jenny. My beautiful Jenny."

He was crying now, tears pouring unheeded down his face.

"I remember touching her cheek. And then they put them into the ambulance, and I wanted to go, but the word had gone out that they had been found and people came running, and the kids were there, and I didn't want them to see Jenny and Liz, not like that, so I ran over to them and when I turned again the ambulance had gone. Jenny and Liz had gone."

His voice was almost a whisper through the tears. Clare had to strain to hear, and she wanted to move her leg, it was getting cramped. But she didn't dare, didn't want to interrupt because it was as if he had forgotten she was there.

And then he remembered, and looked at her.

"I hardly know what happened over the next few days, it was like being in a nightmare, where you just get on with things but you can't let yourself think about what's happening. You don't dare. I only remember snatches here and there. I must have phoned Molly, because she was there, with Kate, with my friend David.

Mrs O'Brien didn't come, Liz and Jenny's mother. She met us at Dublin Airport instead. She took Tish from me. I'll never forget how Madge O'Brien looked. Never. And then the funeral. And later, the inquest, in France. David came with me. I couldn't have gone back alone."

"What did they say, Donal?" she asked, when he was silent for a few minutes.

"What they said doesn't really matter. It was still my fault. I brought them out on the lake that day, when they didn't want to go, when they wanted to cycle in the forest instead. I brought them there."

"What was the verdict?"

"Death by misadventure. Or whatever phrase they used, but that's what it came down to. Nobody's fault. An unfortunate accident occasioned by the child slipping out of his lifejacket. Unfortunate. And two people dead."

They both turned at the sound, a half-cry, stifled, coming from the direction of the stairs. It took Clare a second to pick out Tish, in the long dark tee-shirt she wore to bed. In the same moment Donal had crossed to the stairs and had caught her by the hand, leading her towards the table.

"It wasn't a good idea to sit there listening, Tish. It really wasn't."

"But that wasn't how it happened!"

They thought she was answering him, until suddenly she was crying, looking about twelve years old as she sat hunched at the table in the thin, dark tee-shirt, her face buried in her hands, trying to hide or hold back the tears.

"That's not what happened, Donal!" she managed to say.

He reached for her. "Tish, what . . ."

She took her hands away now, turning to look at him, the tears running onto her jaw as she hastily wiped them away. Her eyes looked huge in her pale face.

"It was all my fault! My fault! I took off the lifejacket, Luke was too hot, he wanted it off and I helped him. I didn't know. And then he thought he saw a fish, he went to grab it and he fell in. I was meant to be minding him, and he fell in. And then Mammy and Aunt Jenny tried to get him, and . . . It's all my fault."

Her voice sounded like a little girl's again, the little eleven-year-old who had been in the boat. She was sobbing her heart out, and Donal took her by the hand and led her to the couch, cradling her there as he would a small child, while she sobbed as if her heart was breaking. Or had broken already.

She cried for a long time while Clare sat there helpless, feeling like an intruder on their shared grief, wishing she could leave without their noticing, knowing that she couldn't.

Finally the crying subsided, and Donal sat wiping Tish's face tenderly with his hand, smiling at her as the make-up smeared. She wasn't able to smile back, there was something she had to ask him first.

"If you don't blame me, Donal," and now the voice was Tish's again, the fourteen- year-old ready for battle, "then why do you hate me?"

"Is that what you think?" he asked gently, looking towards Clare for help, but there was nothing she could say.

"That's what I know. You act like you hate me."

He turned back to her, speaking carefully.

"I love you, Tish. I always have. I could never hate you – I've never had reason to, but I couldn't anyway."

"But if it was all my fault?"

"It wasn't. Trust me. And even if it was, I wouldn't

hate you. What did you mean, when you said I act as if I do?"

"You know." Her expression was mutinous now. She was back to herself, Clare was relieved, and suspected Donal was, too. He sat there, trying to find the right things to say, looking completely exhausted.

"All those rules and things," Tish continued, when he said nothing. "And you're never happy to see me, you just put up with me. And you try to stop me doing everything."

He sighed, smiling at her.

"That's what growing up is like, Tish. Sometimes you think all adults hate you, that they don't know you at all, and wouldn't like the real you anyway."

"You wouldn't."

"I probably would, you know."

They were talking quietly now, and she moved to lean her head against his shoulder. It was the first time Clare had ever seen her make a move towards him.

"Granny says you hate me."

"Your granny is an old – a very sad woman, Tish. She lost both her daughters, don't forget. She only has you now."

"And I only have her."

"You have me and the boys, don't forget."

"But I have no-one of my own. I want my father. If I can't have my mother I want my father. And no-one will tell me who he is, or where to find him."

"We don't know Tish. I wish I did, then I'd tell you. But I don't. Really, I don't."

"He'd want me. I know he would. He'd love me."

"I'm sure he would, Tish. And he'd probably fight with you, too!"

"Like you?"

"Yes, like me. I'm your godfather, don't forget. I promised to look after you."

She sat up, turning on the couch to face him, challenging him again.

"Then why can't I live with you?"

He sighed.

"I wanted you to. I really did. But so did your granny. And she had no-one else. I had the boys. But she had no-one, so I gave in. I hadn't much choice, anyway. And at least she agreed you could stay during holidays."

"She doesn't really want me, you know. She hates me. She's always telling me I'm just like my mother!"

"Tish." Her voice had been rising, but the gentleness in his calmed her. "You're doing very well, Tish, if you're just like your mother. Believe me."

She was quiet for a moment, considering.

"Could I not come and live with you, Donal? I hate that boarding-school, and my grandmother's house. Could I come and live here, just until I find my father? Because I will, you know. And I promise . . ."

She broke off, and he laughed softly.

"No promises? You're right, maybe it's better like that. Tell you what. We'll give it a shot. I'll ask, and if she agrees, then maybe you can move down, if we can get you into a school in time. I'll ask when I go back up with you."

"Couldn't you phone her, then we wouldn't have to go back?"

"No. It's better to talk face-to-face. Fairer, too."

She nodded, accepting what he said now.

"Okay. But just until I find my father. As soon as I'm old enough I'm going to start looking for him."

She was waiting for his response.

"It's a good idea, Tish. And even if you don't manage to find him, at least you'll have tried."

She moved over again to curl up against him.

"I'll find him. I know I will."

"And I'll help you. I'll start by talking to your grandmother again."

They had forgotten she was there, Clare thought, as they sat there with Donal lying back in the couch and Tish leaning against him, her arm around him.

If she could, she would slink away up the stairs and not disturb them at all. But it just wasn't possible.

"Donal," she said finally, when she thought she would collapse sideways out of the chair with sheer exhaustion. "I'm really sorry, but . . ."

"God, I'm sorry, Clare," he said, as he saw her face. "Come on, Tish, we'd better move and let Clare have her bed!"

He stood up, stretching, and Tish got up with him and they fixed the pillows and spread the sleeping bag out on the couch. As he went to the table to help Clare up, Tish came around the other side of her and kissed her on the cheek. Before she could respond the girl had given Donal a quick hug and was running lightly up the stairs, closing the bedroom door softly behind her.

"I hardly believe it, either," Donal said, smiling at Clare's expression. "I feel as if I've just caught a glimpse of someone I haven't seen for a long time."

"Will her grandmother agree, do you think?" Clare asked as he supported her across towards the couch.

"I don't know. Our only hope is if she's feeling her age a bit, and doesn't want the responsibility any longer."

He eased her back onto the couch as he spoke.

"Can I get you anything?" His voice was still very soft, gentle.

"Maybe, if you could leave the crutches beside me, just in case . . ."

He brought them over, positioning them carefully within arm's reach.

She was wearing the green tracksuit Kate had brought her in the hospital. She'd leave it on, she decided. She'd be having a bath next morning anyway – as soon as she could figure out how.

As she bent to remove the sneaker from her left foot Donal reached down to help, fingers brushing against hers as he undid the laces.

"I can manage," she said, then winced as a dart of pain shot through her bandaged right foot.

He touched her arm gently.

"Very sore?"

"I'll live." She gave a shaky smile, then concentrated on drawing her legs up onto the couch, reaching for the patchwork quilt to cover her.

"Clare?" He was on his hunkers beside the couch, face close to hers in the soft light of the lamp beside it.

She smiled again, but this time she could hardly keep her eyes open.

"Mmm?"

"Thank you."

"What for?" She opened her closing eyes, looked at his face, just inches away from her.

"Oh, I don't know. Jumping in after Luke. Giving myself and Tish space tonight . . ."

"But – "

"Shhh." He was smiling at her. "Night."

He pulled the quilt up around her shoulders, making sure she was comfortable. Then he kissed the tips of his fingers and touched them to her cheek, and was gone. She switched off the lamp and lay there in the quiet dark, the sense of his warm presence still with her, until finally she drifted off to sleep.

Chapter Twenty-eight

She was woken next morning by a gentle touch on her shoulder and opened her eyes to find Kate standing beside her.

"I didn't want to wake you, but you'll get stiff lying there too long"

Clare struggled to sit upright, brushing the sleep from her eyes

"Thanks, Kate. What time is it?"

"Nearly half past ten. I'll make your breakfast now."

Clare smiled at her, glancing down at the crumpled track-suit.

"I could do with a shower first."

"No bother, I'll make some fresh tea when you're ready. You've the place to yourself – they've all gone to the beach."

Clare winced as she swung her foot to the floor and reached for the crutches

"Is it bad?" Kate asked.

"Not as bad as yesterday – the tablets seem to be

working. Could you get me some clean clothes, would you mind? There's a blue track-suit in the wardrobe, on one of the shelves, I think."

She struggled across to the bathroom while Kate went to get the track-suit, some towels and anything else she thought Clare might need.

"You're an angel!" Clare said, when Kate tapped on the open bathroom door.

"I'll leave them in here for you," Kate said, reaching in to place the things on the little stool by the bath. "You're sure you can manage?"

Clare laughed. "I'll soon see. If I need you, I'll shout!"

"Do that," Kate answered, pulling the bathroom door behind her and going back out to the kitchen.

Clare managed surprisingly well once she got the hang of it, carefully keeping her weight off the injured foot. She was out of the shower, dressed and having her breakfast just over twenty minutes later.

"God, I feel better now! Hot water is the one luxury I can't do without!"

"I know," Kate said. "When I was growing up we heated pots of water on the range and washed in a big tin bath. The thought of it now!"

She laughed as she poured tea for Clare and passed across some brown scones.

"They went to the beach early, didn't they?" Clare remarked, smothering the scone with Kate's marmalade as she spoke.

"They did. Donal thought the boys might enjoy having breakfast there. He didn't want to wake you –

and besides, poor Luke had a bad night. So did Donal, for that matter. He thought a picnic on the beach might cheer them up. Michael was thrilled, he thought it was a great adventure, sneaking out without waking you. But Luke hardly said a thing – he isn't himself at all."

"Did he have nightmares?"

"I'm sure he did. He woke up at about four, crying his heart out. I could hear Donal trying to settle him."

"It was terrifying for him."

"Terrifying for everyone. Donal must have got a desperate fright, though he looks better than I expected this morning – Tish, too. She was in good form – she went off holding Luke's hand. I never saw her doing that before."

"She came back down to us last night."

"Did she ?"

There was a knock at the door before Kate could continue. It was Jack, refusing an invitation to come in, saying he was just passing and wanted to make sure everyone was all right.

"We're fine, now, Jack," Clare called through the open doorway. "Thanks a million for last night. Are you coming in?"

He leaned forward a bit to see her where she sat at the table, but made no move to come inside. "I'm not stopping," he called to her. "But tell me, how's the young girl?"

"She's fine, Jack, thanks to you and the others," Clare answered.

"Devil the thanks – we were happy we found her.

And it was young Jody who did it, anyway. I'll be off, so. I'm looking for him and I had the idea I might find him here. I'm up to my eyes and I could do with a hand."

"Your best bet might be the beach," Kate said. "That's where Tish is, with Donal and the lads. She's like a magnet to him!"

Jack gave a slow smile, touched his cap and was gone, a tall man in an old navy suit and heavy boots, wheeling his black bicycle down the sandy laneway towards the beach.

"He's a lovely, isn't he?" Clare said. "But shy. How well do you know him, Kate?"

There was no answer for a moment or two.

"Well enough. There was a time when I knew him better. Or thought I did."

She stood up from the table, lifting the teapot.

"I'll empty this and make a fresh pot. It's gone stone cold."

"There's no need, this is fine," Clare said, taking a sip. But Kate was already on her way to the little kitchen, and Clare, as she sat waiting, remembered the strain she often sensed between Kate and Jack. Kate came back with the tea and fresh cups and Clare was wondering whether she would say anything further when the phone rang and Kate got up again to answer it.

"Rick! How are you?" A pause. "Yes, we're staying here for a few days. Yes. everything's fine, now." Another pause. "I'll let Clare explain to you herself – I'll get her for you now."

She passed the phone to Clare, stretching the cord to place it on the table beside her, and went out into the courtyard.

Rick's voice sounded very American, and very far away. Clare was suddenly aware of how much had happened since she had seen him last, or even spoken to him. He sounded cheerful, full of energy.

"I was out jogging and cut it short – I really wanted to talk to you! I'm fixing my schedule – I can take a week off mid-September." He hesitated. "You *are* still coming, aren't you?"

"Of course. I promised. Only, don't panic, but I'm on crutches . . ."

Quickly she filled him in on what had happened, hearing his genuine concern for Luke and Tish as well as for her.

"Why didn't you call me? I know, crazy question, I couldn't do much from here – but I'd have liked to talk to you."

"It was late, I didn't even think . . . it was chaos here, I would have phoned you later today."

That mightn't actually be true, she realised. She hadn't even thought of Rick since his last phone-call. "What time is it there, anyway? About six?"

"Six thirty. I wanted to grab an early start. You're sure you're okay? I could come over . . ."

"I'm fine, honestly. Hobbling around, but I should be okay in a few weeks."

"And – assuming you're okay – you'll come for sure?"

"For sure."

She hung up, feeling uncomfortable. Kate looked back in, questioningly.

"Come on in, I'm finished. Not that I would have minded you staying in here."

"No, you've little enough privacy, with us all here on top of you." She moved the phone, began to clear away the breakfast dishes. "Clare, you're sure, aren't you, that we're not in the way too much? Two weeks can be a long time . . ."

Clare laughed. "I've no choice – I can't even make myself a cup of tea. And anyway, you can hardly stay in your own place, with Kevin building all around you."

"True enough, but we'd sort out something He's promised he'll be finished by the end of the month, and that it will all be worth it."

"You could stay on here, you know, if he's not finished. I'll be away from the middle of September."

"You told me before that he asked you over. So you're definitely going?"

"Definitely. I'm sure I'll be off the crutches by then."

"You will. And it'll be a great holiday for you."

"Yes."

Kate sat down again at the far end of the table. "You don't sound too sure."

"It's not that. It's just – well, I'm not sure if I'm ready for another man in my life. Six months ago I was finished with them all, for good."

Kate gave a wry smile. "That was six months ago."

"I know, but . . ."

"Clare, you like him, don't you?"

"Yes. Although I was furious with him that last evening, the way he reacted to the coach crash. But there's something lovely about him. And we get on well together, he makes me laugh. I'm just not sure . . ."

"Getting on well is a good start. Give it a chance – you never know. And one way or the other, you'll have a good holiday."

"You're right. And I've been honest with him all the time, I've told him I'll make no promises – we'll just see how it goes. And when I let myself, I get excited about it – I'm dying to see New York, and I'd love to see it with him. I just don't want to hype it all up and get carried away."

Kate looked thoughtful. "It'll be interesting one way or the other, seeing him on his home ground."

Clare nodded, grinning. "That's what it'll be, all right. Interesting."

There were voices outside, a brief rap at the door and Donal came in, followed by Tish. He stood just inside the doorway, smiling across at her. "How are you this morning, Clare?"

She smiled back, remembering with a sudden, unexpected flutter how she had felt when he left her the previous night.

"Fine, thanks. Much better. A bit frustrated, otherwise fine. What about you? And Luke?"

"He's okay, I think. At least he's laughing again. He raced Michael over to the play area once he saw the Nolan kids there. I thought they were going to-day?"

"They are. There's a family due any minute now, and another on Saturday for a fortnight, and the couple in *Wildwood* are staying another week. And then, thank God, that's the end of it!"

"I thought you were enjoying it?"

"I love it. But it's a lot of work, and now I can't do a thing."

"Don't worry about that," Donal began, then paused as a car pulled into the yard. He glanced back through the open door. "There's someone coming now – I'll go out to them."

"I'll do it," Kate said. "You sit and relax for a while."

She went out to welcome the family of three adults and four children who were staying in *Saffron*. To Clare and Donal's surprise, Tish followed her and was soon leading the children in the direction of the play area.

"Amazing, isn't it?" Clare said, watching her through the window.

Donal nodded. "She's like a totally different girl. I wish to God I'd known what she was going through. I should have made more of an effort to see her these past years. It's just that . . ."

"You've had your hands full."

"Well, yes, but that's not it. I wasn't exactly welcome there. The grandmother was never the easiest to get on with, but since the accident she really hates me. Can't stand seeing me. Not that I blame her but it makes it harder to spend time with Tish."

"And Tish herself hasn't been the easiest."

"No, but at least now I know why. She was

extraordinary this morning, like a different person. She's determined to come and live down here."

"Do you think her grandmother will agree?"

He sighed. "Who knows? I wouldn't bet on it but for Tish's sake I hope so. I'll talk to her on Monday, when I bring Tish home. Maybe I'll phone her first. I'll have to think about it. See what's best."

He moved back towards the door again. "I'd better see if Kate will keep an eye on the twins while I go and give Jack a hand. He could do with it."

"Isn't Jody there?"

"He is, but there's a lot to get done. See you at dinner-time?"

"See you."

He stood looking at her for a moment, then he was gone.

The day passed slowly for Clare. She was used to being in the thick of things, arranging, organising, and felt frustrated at the forced inactivity. Much as she loved reading, she couldn't settle because she wasn't doing it by choice, and she was grateful every time Kate, or Tish, or one of the twins, popped back to check and see how she was.

Even getting to the bathroom seemed like a major challenge but gradually she learned to master the crutches so that she was managing well by the time Donal returned, bringing Jack and Jody with him, for the dinner Kate had prepared with Tish's help.

"You don't mind, do you?" he asked Clare quietly, sitting beside her on the couch for a moment. Jack and

Jody were out inspecting the animals with Tish and the twins.

"It's Kate you should ask," Clare answered in a low voice, nodding towards the kitchen where Kate was busy putting the finishing touches to the meal. "She wasn't expecting them."

"It's all right, she always cooks loads. I'm sure she won't mind."

"I hope you're right, Donal," Clare answered in a low voice. "Sometimes I think she's a bit – I don't know, unsettled maybe – when Jack is around."

"I wouldn't worry about that. I know she likes him, has a lot of respect for him. I suppose she's just a bit shy with him. Rumour has it there was a romance there, a long time ago."

Clare nodded, remembering what Kate had said that morning, about knowing him, or thinking she did.

"What happened? Do you know?"

"Even Kevin doesn't know for sure. I think she left to go to England, and I suppose that was the end of it."

It was a great evening, once they had all begun to relax. Tish was the star of the show, amusing everyone, keeping the conversation going almost without help from the adults. She helped Donal clear the table, brought in tea and coffee and hot chocolate for the boys.

Finally Jack stood up. "I'd better be heading back. That was a better meal than I've had this long time." The look that passed between himself and Kate was brief, indirect, but had warmth in it. "Will you be all right for getting home, Jody?"

"I'll be fine, Jack. I'll be over to you by ten tomorrow."

"Right, so." He took his cap from the hook inside the door, nodded to them all, and left.

"God," Jody said, hitting his forehead with the heel of his hand. "I forgot I'll be at the pony show, I'd better tell him." He raced out after Jack as Donal, turning to Clare, saw her look of disappointment.

"I forgot about it, too. I meant to go this year, but I'll never manage with the crutches."

"You will, of course. Don't worry, we'll all help."

He was as good as his word, and Clare spent an exhausting but exhilarating day negotiating the streets of Clifden, stopping every now and then to lean on the crutches, or on Donal's arm, and take in the sights, the smells, the clamour and buzz of the pony show. Tish and the twins loved it, and Jody, in fairness to him, hid his boredom as much as possible.

"I'm not that interested in horses," he said quietly to Kate when she asked if he was all right. "Now, if it was motor-bikes . . ." He grinned wickedly at her.

"I don't even want to think about it," she said. "Why did you want to come, anyway, if you're not that fond of horses?"

"Because Tish was coming," he said quietly, glancing in Donal's direction.

"I see." She smiled. "I wouldn't worry about Donal – he won't make things hard for you. But you know she's going back on Monday."

He nodded. "I'll see her again, though."

"I'm sure you will. Come on, we'd better head for

Albatross or we'll never get a seat." She called to the others, who followed them down the street.

The restaurant was crowded, but Nicole had kept them a table at the back. Niall came out just as they got settled, greeting them all, kissing Clare on the cheek. "I only heard about your swim this morning, when I got back from Dublin. You're all right?"

"Fine. A bit sore, that's all."

"You were lucky." He glanced at Donal. "Someone was looking after you."

Clare felt Kate tense in the seat beside her, looked quickly across at Donal and was relieved to see his calm expression. "I know. We were very lucky indeed." The exchange passed over the heads of the twins, but Clare saw Jody move slightly to touch Tish's hand under the table. She wondered how much, if anything, Tish had told him of their conversation last night.

"Okay, lunch is on the house. Whatever you want."

"Whatever?" Jody asked, with a delighted grin.

"Yes, at the risk of saying goodbye to a week's profits! Whatever you want, and enjoy it!" Niall turned to Clare. "I take it you won't be here tomorrow night?"

"You're sacking us?" She grinned. "Are we that bad?"

"Yes, but I'm desperate," he said, grinning back at her. "I assumed you mightn't feel up to it."

"Try and stop me!"

He didn't, of course. Clare could hardly wait to get there on Friday, after a day spent around the cottage or garden, doing nothing much. Niall was waiting for them at Albatross and brought them to a little table near the back of the restaurant. "Great to see you. We've a few local lads in who are going to play, then you're on. Is that okay?"

"Fine," Clare said.

"Will you have something to eat later?"

Donal laughed. "Kate is nearly force-feeding us every time we turn around, but we just had sandwiches earlier. An omelette or something would be great, when we finish."

It was a wonderful evening, with everyone joining in – the three local musicians, young men who had been abroad for six months and had just arrived back, as well as two of the restaurant guests who were not only willing, but mercifully able, to play the borrowed instruments. And then Donal and Clare, easing into the performance, well used to each other's style by now, songs and music flowing seamlessly together in exhilarating harmony.

They were both in great form, relaxed and joking, all the way through the meal and on the way home.

"Wasn't it great?" Clare said. "I love the buzz, knowing they're enjoying it, and the sense that nothing matters but the music . . ." They had come to a stop outside the cottage, which was in darkness except for the outside light left on for them. "God, will you listen to me, talking non-stop. I'm just on a high from the music, and the wine – I shouldn't have had that second glass, you did well to stop at one."

He laughed. "No choice, I was driving. Maybe I'll have a brandy when we go in."

"Good idea. And some coffee. I'll need it."

She was smiling at him, her eyes sparkling, hair glowing in the half-light through the window. God, she was beautiful, he thought. It was as if he had never really seen her before. He knew how lovely she was, without realising, until now, how lovely she looked. He had reached for the door handle, meaning to go and help her out, but instead he closed the door again gently and turned towards her.

"Clare?"

"Yes?"

"You look really beautiful tonight." Before she could answer he was touching her face, his arms around her, leaning towards her as she half-turned in the seat. And then he kissed her, gently but insistently, and she responded, giving herself up to the sweetness of it, the feel of his lips, the melting, tugging sensation, the slight roughness of his cheek against hers as he bent to kiss her neck. She held him tighter against her, one hand moving to rest on his hip, and he made a slight sound, and it was as if she woke from a dream and pulled back from him, thinking, damn!

She leaned back against the headrest, looking sideways, seeing that he, too, was leaning against his seat, eyes closed, and when he opened them and looked at her she knew he was thinking the same thing as her – how did that happen? And what next?

"Clare – "

"Donal – "

They started talking at the same time, stopped at the same time, then he laughed.

"You go first," he said. "I don't know what to say! Except that I'm a bit embarrassed."

"Me, too. But there's no need, is there? We're friends, right?"

"Right. And I don't want to spoil that, complicate things . . . and besides, there's you and Rick."

Clare nodded. It wasn't Rick she had been thinking of just now.

Before she could reply he was out of the car and had opened her door, helping her out, going with her into the cottage as if nothing had happened. "It's late, I think I'll go straight to bed. Can you manage?" His voice was low.

"Sure. See you in the morning."

He nodded, touched her arm briefly and went upstairs in the soft light of the lamp. Clare got ready for bed, wondering if anything had changed between them. Hoping it hadn't. Hoping it had. Mostly hoping that it didn't "complicate" things.

If anything had changed for Donal, he showed no sign of it for the remainder of his stay at the cottage. He was in great form, spending his days helping with the guests, or playing with the boys, or doing bits and pieces round the garden and the apartments. He went across to Jack for a while most days, enjoying the physical work on the farm, returning in time to help with the guests or prepare the evening meal with Kate.

He and Clare were rarely alone together. When they were, he was relaxed and easy, touching her as he might one of the children, but nothing more. She wasn't sure how she felt about that, didn't want to think about it too much. She was relieved that the warmth between them hadn't changed. She felt no tension, only quiet pleasure in his presence.

She loved the late evenings, after Kate had gone to bed, when she and Donal occasionally sat in the living-room while he prepared his classes for the new term and she sat reading, with soft music playing in the background. It was at those times that she was most aware of him, of his physical presence, the way his dark hair curled at the nape of his neck as he bent his head, the shape of his hands, strong but with long, sensitive fingers, fiddling with a pen or drumming softly on the table as he concentrated on the books in front of him.

"Clare?"

"Mmm?" She looked up from the book she was reading.

He sat, half in shadow, sorting through textbooks in the light from the lamp beside him on the table. Neither of them wanted to put on the bright overhead light, preferring the soft intimacy of the lamps. "I'll miss being here, you know. I can't believe it's only been a week. In some ways it feels much longer."

She laughed. "That bad?"

"You know what I mean."

"I know," she said, putting the book down. "And I'll be lost without you all, I've got used to having everyone around."

"Your family will be here next week. And we'll be no distance away – six miles is nothing."

"It won't be the same."

"No," he agreed. "But I've promised the boys they can come back often, if that's all right. And Tish, if she comes down. They're missing her a lot. They're a bit apprehensive too about the new house and being away from you and Kate. Though having Nan around will help."

"And you think Tish will come?"

"Hard to say. At least her grandmother has said she'll think about it. I've suggested that Tish could go to Kylemore, since she'll be in boarding-school anyway, and at least she'd be with us for the weekends. But Madge – her grandmother – said she's happy where she is. Which isn't true, but maybe things will be different now. Tish has changed so much, it's incredible. She gave me a hug as I was leaving, made me promise to stay in touch. She never seemed bothered before, one way or the other. I told her I'll see her every two or three weeks, when I'm up with Molly."

"You'll be in Dublin that often?"

"I'll have to be. I'm worried about Molly. She's not well at all but she won't admit it. At least, not to me. She doesn't want me worrying."

"Which makes you worry all the more."

"Right. And she won't come down, so I'll have to keep going up."

"She definitely won't come here?"

"No, she says I don't need her in the way, I should be getting on with my own life. But Kate is talking about going up for a while. It's not fair on her, though, when she's up to her eyes with the painting, she really doesn't have the time to spare."

"If she's decided to go you won't talk her out of it, knowing Kate. And she'd be going because she wants to, not because she feels she should."

"You're right. She's very close to Molly. She says it'll be a chance to see the galleries again, and maybe try to sell a few things on a Sunday morning in Merrion Square. But really it's because she's worried too."

"Has Molly been to a doctor?"

"She says she has, and that there's nothing to worry about. But Molly is like Kate in lots of ways, she keeps things to herself, and she can be as determined as bedamned. If she doesn't want to tell you something, then she won't, especially if she thinks it would worry or upset you."

"Like most mothers."

He laughed. "I suppose so. She was always like that. The slightest trace of a cold when I was a kid, and I was whisked off to the doctor. But she'd always make light of it if it was herself, and she's still the same. She'd mother the whole world if you let her, but she's not the best at looking after herself."

"She sounds a bit like my own mother. She'll be all over me when she comes down next week, worrying about my ankle when I know myself it's getting better." She laughed. "And she's convinced she has to see me before I go to the States, in case I don't come back!"

"Is it likely?" Donal asked.

"Not a bit, but I suppose she's used to Ruth going

away for a weekend and staying a year. She's afraid there might be two of us in it!"

"Maybe you will stay. It's a great place."

"New York? Were you there?"

"A long time ago, way before Kevin's time. When I was a student. But I don't just mean New York – I could take or leave it – too noisy, too crowded for me. But I loved California, and New Mexico. All that space, and heat, and fabulous skies. I'd probably have stayed the year, if it hadn't been for Jenny. Maybe I'll go back when the boys are older. They'd love it there."

For the first time, Clare noticed, he said Jenny's name without hesitating.

"I'd love to do that, travel around a bit. But there just won't be time – not in ten days."

"You'll see a lot of New York in ten days. And you could stay longer, or go back again."

"Maybe. I'll see how it goes. There're a lot of other places I want to see first."

"Like?"

"Africa. And Paris, it's too long since I've been there."

"Paris is easy. An hour's journey."

"It's not just the place. It would have to be with the right person."

"Meaning?"

She laughed. "Meaning I'm not going just yet."

He laughed too, closing the book in front of him. "I hope it's worth waiting for."

"Oh, it will be. I'm sure of it."

"How about some French coffee in the meantime?"

"I'll settle for that. And Edith Piaf on the CD player."

He smiled at her. "That can be arranged." He paused on his way to the kitchen to put on the CD and the throaty voice filled the room as Clare lay back in her chair, eyes closed.

"Rien, je ne regrette rien . . ." – "I have no regrets . . ."

She wondered if it had been true for Piaf. Wished it were true for her.

Chapter Twenty-nine

It was a beautiful September day and Clare was enjoying the drive. Another ten minutes or so would get them to Shannon Airport. She relaxed in the leather seat, mentally running through her check-list – tickets, travellers' cheques . . .

"Great day for flying," Niall said. He was handling the big Jaguar expertly, pushing it to its limit. "Wish I was going with you."

"No, you don't!" Clare replied, laughing. "You can't bear to be away from that Frenchwoman of yours for more than a few hours!"

"Would you blame me?"

"No. She's really lovely, Niall. I hope your intentions are honourable!"

"Were they ever!" he said, grinning. "But this time's different. We're getting married in February."

"Niall! Brilliant! So why didn't you tell me?"

"I was going to, as soon as you got back. Nobody else knows except our parents."

"Lucky you. Lucky her."

"You really mean that? It could have been us, you know." He said it lightly, smiling across at her.

"That's right, it could. And we wouldn't have lasted two minutes before we were killing each other. Remember?"

"Could I forget! But we were a lot younger then."

"True. And at least we had the sense to stay friends and wait for the right person to come along."

He didn't reply for a moment, concentrating on changing lanes, before asking "And has he, Clare?"

"Has he what?"

"Mr. Right."

She shifted uncomfortably in her seat. "Whatever that means. How can you know? I thought Tony was right for me . . ."

"Any word of him?" he asked, after a minute.

""He's been convicted of fraud. My mother told me when she was down last week. He got five years."

Niall gave a low whistle. "Maybe there's a God in Heaven, after all."

"Seems so. But I was a complete eejit, wasn't I?"

"Maybe." He glanced at her. "But at least it's over now."

"That's what Mam said. I still feel really stupid, though. I showed lousy judgement, I wasted all that time on him. Well, I won't be caught again."

"Clare, if you believe that, you might as well not do anything at all, ever again."

"Mam says that, too. Says it's time to forget him, and move on." She sighed. "Wish it was that easy!"

"Isn't it?" He turned quickly to smile at her. "Come

on, Clare. Aren't you heading for the holiday of your life, with a man waiting at the far end for you! What more do you want?"

"You're beginning to sound just like my mother! When she heard I was going she nearly brought me to the plane there and then, a week ago, for fear he'd change his mind! And as for Donal – she made such a song and dance when he called, treating him like royalty, asking him a million questions. I was mortified, she doesn't seem to mind who I end up with, as long as I find *someone*. Well, anyone who's not Tony. You know what she's like."

He laughed. "Only too well. The best in the world, but I couldn't stand her looking at me again with that 'are you good enough for my daughter?' look. That's why I didn't call when she was down."

"Oh?"

"I was busy anyway," he added quickly.

She laughed. "You needn't have worried – she's long since given up on you."

"Now that she has two other men to concentrate on, you mean?"

"Donal doesn't count. We're just friends."

"Is that so? It's not what I heard from Kate."

"Kate is romancing. Seeing what she wants to see. We're just friends," she repeated. "And besides, he'll never get over his wife."

"No," Niall agreed. "How could he? But that doesn't mean that he won't move on in time, meet someone else."

"Well, it won't be me."

"Why not? I've seen the way you are together in Albatross."

"We enjoy the music."

"And that's all, is it?" He paused. "Or is it that you're serious about Rick?"

"Come on, Niall, what is this, Twenty Questions? I've just told you I'm not about to get involved again."

"So why are you going over?"

"Because I promised. And because it'll be fun."

"And because you fancy him?"

"You're getting away with murder, you know that?"

He laughed, seeing the slight blush, and left her alone as he turned off for the airport and began the search for a parking space.

"Promise me you'll have a great time," he said, kissing her cheek as he left her at the departure gate.

She hugged him. "I promise. Here," she said, handing him a slip of paper. "I forgot to give Kate the phone number, in case of emergencies."

"God forbid that we'll have any of those," he said, folding the paper and putting it in his pocket. "You know we'll keep a good eye on the place for you. Now go on. Enjoy every minute!"

"I will." She smiled, gave him quick hug and went swiftly through the security check and on into Duty Free. Then through U.S. Immigration, and she was on her way.

She walked easily, revelling in the freedom of moving without crutches, feeling that she would never take anything for granted again. In less than twenty minutes she was sitting on the plane, seat-belt fastened, relaxed as she waited for take-off.

She loved flying, loved the feel of the big aircraft as it lifted, tilting back, nose in the air. That brief moment of terror as it hung poised between earth and sky with nothing, it seemed, to hold it there but faith. And then the moment passed and she let out her breath, and began to relax for the seven-hour flight to New York.

It didn't seem to take that long. She read for a while, went through the little ritual of the airline meal, watched a movie and some old comedy sketches, read some more. And then the small screen in front of her filled with images of New York as they ran the information video, and suddenly her pulse was racing and she could hardly wait for the plane to land.

Rick was there waiting for her, tall and blond and every bit as gorgeous as she remembered. He shouldered his way through the crowd and swept her up into his arms.

"Welcome to America! You look really beautiful, Clare!" He kissed her briefly, then released her, touched her cheek with his fingers.

She laughed, loving his warmth, his openness. "I don't feel one bit beautiful, I can tell you, after all that travelling. I'm wrecked. But glad to be here."

"Ready for a bite of the Big Apple?"

"Ready to swallow it whole."

He laughed. "let's go – I've a car waiting outside."

It didn't look like a car – it looked like an apartment

on wheels. "This is *yours?*" she asked, unable to keep the astonishment from her voice as the chauffeur held the door open for her.

Rick laughed again, getting in beside her. "A limo service I use. I don't keep a car in the city – but I thought you might appreciate travelling in style."

She did. "I could live like this," she said, laughing, as Rick sat back in the seat, smiling, watching her as she peered through the window. "Where are we now?" she asked.

"Queen's – heard of it?" She nodded. "Shouldn't take long to get to Midtown – depends on traffic."

Traffic was light, and then they were over the Triborough Bridge and into Manhattan, where it was more chaotic – the streets seemed to be jammed with yellow taxi-cabs and traffic was hardly moving at all.

"Looks like I'll be spending my holiday here," Clare said.

He laughed. "Don't worry, that's Central Park, right there. Just a few more blocks and we're home."

"Wish we could walk," Clare said. "I can't wait to get out there, feel it, smell it!"

"You really want to do that?"

"Mmm! If it wasn't for my bags . . ."

He smiled. "Don't worry about those!"

He had a quick word with the driver, who managed to find a space to pull in. And then he was out on the pavement, holding the door open, taking her hand, and she emerged to take her first breath of New York air.

It smelled of horses, and she laughed, surprised, and

then looked over towards the Park with its carriages. Like Stephen's Green, she thought. But much more exotic.

"I'd love to go on one of those!" she said.

"If you'd like to, sure," he answered, taking her hand and crossing towards the Park. "But it's better after dark."

She looked horrified. "You're not telling me you'd go in there at night?"

He nodded. "Sure, it's not a problem, since Mayor Giuliani got going. It's a much safer city now."

"I'll take your word for it!" she said, head back as she looked up at the buildings bordering the East side of the Park. They were beautiful – not the stark, white towers she had imagined, but wonderful elaborate buildings in soft colours, soaring above her, exuding an air of wealth.

So that's what New York *really* smelled like, she thought. Horses – and money.

They began walking along the side of the Park, heading north, he told her. "We're on Fifth Avenue right now. My apartment's at 75th and Lex, not far." They crossed the street again. "And my office is close by, on Park, same as your Consulate."

They continued walking for a few minutes until they reached Lexington Avenue and turned left. It was a different kind of neighbourhood, lovely, more intimate. Less obviously prosperous than Park Avenue or the apartment buildings owned by the seriously rich that Rick had pointed out as they walked along by the Park. It still wouldn't come cheap, Clare thought, wondering how the prices compared with Dublin.

They passed one or two coffee shops and a little bookshop that looked interesting. And the streets were slightly quieter than those nearer the Park. A wonderful place – she could see why Rick would want to live here.

These buildings had an old feel to them, with their ornate windows and their mellow red or pink or brown stone. Looking up, she could see what seemed to be roof gardens dotted here and there. And they weren't particularly high, not here. They were like houses she had seen in Europe, she thought, as they passed one with shutters and over-flowing window boxes. Not at all what she had expected in New York.

"This is it, right here," Rick said as he stopped in front of a compact four-storey building. There were three windows at each level, surrounded by elaborate moulding. The top two floors were stepped back slightly. Clare looked up towards the top floor, with its wrought-iron balcony, and above that, fastened to the chimney pots, a little fence that spanned the width of the building.

"The garden," Rick said, following her gaze as he took out his keys.

They stepped into a small, bright lobby with two doors leading from it. He ushered her into an elevator in the corner and pressed the button for the fourth floor, laughing as they stepped out and he saw her bags stacked neatly by the door to his apartment.

"How long did you say you're staying?" he asked as he opened the door and reached to lift the bags.

She followed him into a bright hallway with five doors opening off it.

"Only ten days, don't worry! But I'm hopeless at packing – I've probably got every stitch I own in there."

"Maybe you'll stay longer, get a chance to wear everything."

She wasn't sure if he was serious until she saw the slight smile twitching at the corner of his mouth.

"You'll want me gone long before then."

"I doubt it." This time, he looked serious. "This is the living-room," he continued, pushing open the door, "and the bathroom's back over there, if you want to freshen up while I put these bags in the bedroom."

"Fine," she answered. "I'll just be a minute."

The bedroom? she thought as she crossed the hallway. *One* bedroom?

She went into the bathroom, locked the door, sat on the side of the bath. How come she hadn't thought of that? She had told him, no promises. Surely . . .

Relax, the little voice of reason told her. There's a sofa bed in the living room. There's bound to be. Isn't there?

She washed her face quickly, used the toilet and returned to the living-room to find Rick opening a bottle of champagne.

"Pink champagne! I love this stuff," she said, smiling as she took a glass from him. She glanced quickly round the room before she sat down. The furniture was wonderful, old burnished mahogany and rosewood, not what she would have associated with Rick. I hardly know him, she reminded herself. I don't really know what his taste in furniture might be. But it obviously didn't run to sofa beds.

She moved towards the big window and glanced out, wondering if she could catch a glimpse of the Park.

"This is a really lovely apartment, Rick – you were lucky to find it."

He laughed quietly and came over to stand behind her, glass in hand. "Luckier than that. My grandfather left it to me, about ten years ago. No way I could afford to buy the place now, in this location. Would you like to see the rest of it?"

"There's more?"

"Kitchen, bedroom, two bathrooms. Oh, and my study."

"Sure you have enough space?"

He smiled. "I manage. No dining-room, so I've got this big table over here. I used to have it downstairs until I converted the place into three apartments. And some offices on the first floor."

"You own the *whole building*?"

"Like I said, I was lucky – I'd never have had it without my grandfather."

He returned to the table for a moment, came back with the champagne bottle in its silver cooler, placing it on a side table near them and replenishing her glass.

"Are you hungry? We'll go out to eat soon – unless you'd prefer to stay here?"

"Here, I think – maybe I'll be okay later, but right now I'd fall asleep with my face in the soup. Sorry."

"No problem – I'll fix something for you. Would you like steak? Or an omelette, maybe?"

"An omelette would be great."

"Fine. Just sit there, relax – it won't take long."

She could feel her eyes closing as he returned with the omelettes and salad. She ate quickly, refusing the white wine he offered.

"Thanks, but I'm feeling the effects of the champagne already. Old age!" She laughed.

"Jet-lag," he said. "Want to get some rest?"

She nodded. "Please. I'll be fine after a few hours. Do you want to go out or something? I don't want you stuck in here, waiting for me."

"I've been stuck in here two months waiting for you, Clare – another few hours won't hurt!"

She tried to gauge how serious he was but it was impossible. She made her way to the living-room door, Rick following just behind her. He stepped past her to open the door to the bedroom.

"I've put you in here," he said. "I'll take the study."

She nodded gratefully, barely registering anything about the room except that it was large, looked very comfortable, and she would apparently be occupying it on her own.

"Your bathroom's through there, and I've made space in the closet. Sleep as long as you like, I'll wake you if you're still not up for breakfast!"

She smiled. "No chance!"

She slept far longer than she expected, waking several hours later and wandering into the living-room where Rick was reading. A flute played *The Lonesome Boatman* softly in the background.

"I didn't know you liked Irish music – I'd have brought some CD's – "

"No need, I brought back quite a collection. Put on something else, if you'd prefer. Unless you want to go out? It's almost nine-thirty."

"Half-two in the morning for me!" Clare calculated. "I'm beginning to feel human again, but I'm not sure I feel like going out just yet. Maybe in a couple of hours?"

He rolled his eyes, smiled at her. "I don't suppose you'd settle for a coffee, and we'll go sit in the roof garden?"

"Sounds good."

She loved it, the warmth of the evening, the sense of being in a little oasis, close to the centre of things and yet in total privacy. She looked around at the lights, above and around and below her in the other apartment buildings.

"Not too noisy for you?" Rick asked.

"Not at all." In fact, it was surprisingly quiet, their conversation punctuated only occasionally by the sounds of the traffic on the streets below and in the far distance.

"I thought maybe, after the cottage – "

"Remember, I'm used to Dublin. I've got an apartment in Ranelagh, right at the front of a big old house on the main street. I couldn't sleep for my first few nights there but by the end of the week I didn't even notice the noise. And when I moved to Connemara I used to lie awake for hours, wondering what was missing!"

"When will you go back there, Clare? To Dublin?"

"To live, you mean? Depends. Maybe not for a long time – I love Rossdarra."

"I know," Rick said. "It's a wonderful place." He was quiet for a few minutes as the sipped their coffee. "I've thought a lot about going back there," he said finally, breaking the silence.

"To Rossdarra? But – "

"To Rossdarra. Yes, I know," he said, catching her expression. "My life is here. And yet it's not – nothing that matters, anyhow."

"What about this house, and your practice? And your family, what about them?"

"Mom is only sixty-five, and in good health. I know she wouldn't object to my going as long as it wasn't forever. She's been really happy since moving to the farm, and Uncle Joe is all set to join her there as soon as he hands the practice over to me. He and Mom get on, and he spent all his summers there, he and Dad, when they were growing up. He really loves the place."

"He doesn't have a family?"

"He divorced a long time ago. No kids. We're his family."

"And how would he feel if you came back to Rossdarra?" she asked quietly. "What about the practice?"

In the half-light she saw a fleeting look of pain cross his face.

"It was never my dream. It was my father's dream, and Uncle Joe's. I'm not even sure it *was* Uncle Joe's."

"So what's your own dream?" she asked softly.

He sat thinking for a moment. "Remember that day out on the bay, sailing that hooker with Kevin? A wonderful day. I love sailing, always have. That's what

429

I want, Clare, my own hooker with those big black sails. That's my dream." He paused. "Part of it, anyway."

"Better not tell anyone here you want your very own hooker!" she said, smiling at him. "What would you do with it, anyway?"

He laughed. "Sail it! Lease out the practice, go live in Ireland, buy a hooker and take people sailing. I wouldn't need to make a living at it, I've got money from Dad doing that for me. It's what I'd really love to do."

"How come you never did it before?"

"I couldn't quit the practice until Uncle Joe wanted to retire – it wouldn't have been fair, he needed me there. And besides – I never had a good reason before."

"Rick – " She bit her lip, wondering how best to continue. "Before you decide anything – I mean, if you're serious, I wouldn't want – "

"Clare, don't say anything, okay? You know what I'm saying, don't you? But you don't have to say anything. Not yet."

Chapter Thirty

She had the time of her life in New York. They made a list, and Rick made sure she saw everything she wanted and more.

"A bus tour would be a good idea," he said at breakfast on the Sunday morning. "They've got these open-top tour buses, and you can get on and off as you please – you'll get to see a lot of the city that way."

"Sounds great," she said. "As long as I can see Times Square, and the Statue of Liberty, and Ellis Island, and FAO Schwarz, and the Empire State Building – did you see *Sleepless in Seattle?* – and St Patrick's – "

He laughed as she paused for breath. "So maybe it'll take a couple of days."

It did, but by late Monday evening she felt she had seen a great deal of New York, at least from the outside.

"What did you like best?" he asked. They were at a little restaurant near his apartment, too tired to go further afield.

"Everything! I loved walking through the Village.

And Harlem wasn't a bit scary, even in an open bus –
not if you're used to Dublin!" She laughed. "Maybe I'll
go back there and get some hair extensions – they seem
to do them in every second shop."

"Your hair is beautiful just as it is, Clare."

She smiled, changed the subject. They had been easy
with each other over the two days, keeping it light, and she
wanted it to stay like that. For the time being, anyway.

"South Street Seaport looked interesting – I'd love to
go back there. And the World Trade Centre – and the
Winter Garden, that's near there, isn't it? I've heard it's
gorgeous inside, looking out over the Hudson. And I
want to get to one of those famous deli's – Katz, or
Delmonico's . . ."

He was smiling at her. "We'll get to them. But what
about the Statue of Liberty, and Ellis Island? You don't
want to see them?"

"You've probably been there a dozen times," she
said.

"So one more won't hurt. We'll go Friday, okay?
Tomorrow I'll take you shopping, if you'd like that, and
then I guess you'll need time out on Thursday to recover."

"Recover? I'll be dead!"

He laughed. "You wanted to see New York! And so
far this is only Manhattan I'm talking about."

"That'll do – I'll see the rest some other time – "

"Will you, Clare? Do you think you'll come back
here?"

"I'll see how it goes," she said lightly, and was glad
when he left it at that.

They hit Fifth Avenue with a splash the following day and she was glad for once that she possessed a credit card. She'd worry about the bills later, she decided. This was once in a lifetime. Maybe.

She refused Rick's offer to buy her a piece of jewellery, and was glad when he let it go gracefully. "You wanted to see St Patrick's," he said. "It's just along here."

"FAO Schwarz first?" she begged.

He laughed. "Those are your priorities? I know, you promised the twins."

He nearly had to prise her out of there once she got inside. It was absolute magic, as bright and noisy as any child could wish, and she was sorry the twins weren't there with her.

It was hard to choose what they might like, but she finally settled on some Batman figures and some kites, and a gorgeous Teddy Bear for her brother Dermot's little girl. She was about to go upstairs one more time when she saw Rick picking up a toy, looking at it with an expression of utter sadness, and immediately regretted bringing him in here.

She paid for the toys quickly and moved to his side.

"I'm ready for St Patrick's now," she said, reaching for his hand. If he was surprised he didn't show it. She led the way to the revolving door, letting his hand go as she reached it, and they headed to the Cathedral, further along on Fifth Avenue.

The crowds in the streets amazed her. People seemed instinctively to go with the flow, not bumping into each other. The same couldn't be said for cars and buses, she thought, watching as one of the hundreds of yellow cabs suddenly cut in front of a bus, clipping the front of it and bringing them both to a stop. She wondered how *that* would turn out.

They slipped into St Patrick's for a few minutes and then crossed the road to the Rockefeller Center where they sat for a while on one of the wooden benches beneath the palm trees.

"It completely stunned me," Clare said. "I didn't expect it to be so huge. Imagine coming from Connemara a hundred years ago, and going to St Patrick's thinking it would be something like the little church you were used to at home. It must have been terrifying, completely alien."

Rick nodded.

"Like New York itself, maybe. I often wonder if my great-grandfather felt like that, when he came."

"How long ago was that?" she asked.

"In 1880. Before Ellis Island was open. He was just nineteen when he got here. And he had guts – he knew nobody, had to make his own way."

Rick was silent for a moment or two, lost in his thoughts. Then he looked up and smiled at her. "Sorry. Guess I'm tired. What about an early dinner? I thought we might try *Flaherty's*, see what they've done with it since Kevin and I left. And maybe tomorrow we'll rest, get ready to do the Museum of Modern Art on Friday."

"Or we could just visit the shop?" Clare suggested

hopefully, looking at the MOMA shop just across from them.

He laughed. "I get the message. So no museums?"

"No museums. But definitely Ellis Island – I don't want to miss that."

They caught the Ferry from Battery Park on Friday morning. It was a lovely day, the sun bright in a blue sky. A perfect day for being out on the water, Clare thought, as she looked towards the Manhattan skyline across the Bay. It seemed unreal, like a Hollywood set. The soft cream and grey and tan-coloured buildings dominated by the soaring Twin Towers of the World Trade Center were as familiar, from films and postcards, as if she had seen them every day of her life.

She turned to watch the Statue of Liberty as it came closer, standing beside Rick at the side of the ferry.

"There she is, the lady herself," he said. What do you think?"

"I think there'd better be a lift to the top."

There was, or as far as they wanted to go, anyway. They spent a pleasant couple of hours on Liberty Island before crossing on the ferry to Ellis Island.

And there it was a very different experience, almost unbearably poignant. Clare moved slowly through the big rooms, looking at photographs, reading passenger lists, stopping at a display case full of children's shoes. Wonderfully-crafted, most of them. New shoes for a new world. She wondered how they came to be there, what had happened to the children who had worn them.

And everywhere, faces. Photographs on the walls, hundreds of them, immigrants from Eastern Europe, China – and the startled burst of recognition when she found the whitewashed cottage with ten or twelve people outside it, the women in shawls, men in caps and jackets. She felt a deep sense of sadness, was glad when Rick came up behind her and slipped his hand into hers.

They wandered through the rooms, found the bronze statue of Annie Moore, from Cork, who had passed through Ellis Island as its first immigrant. They began examining some small sculptures in a glass case nearby, and then Clare told Rick she wouldn't be long, and went again to stand in the big, bright baggage room with its tiled walls and terracotta floor, and its high, vaulted ceiling, and tried to imagine it filled with thousands of exhausted, frightened people, waiting to see whether they would be allowed to enter the United States.

She could almost hear their voices, feel their fear, their hope –

"Talking to the ghosts?" Rick asked softly, coming up beside her, and she could only nod.

"I shouldn't have brought you there," he said later, as the ferry neared Battery Park.

"Of course you should. Besides, I wanted to go."

"It's left you feeling a little down, hasn't it? But I know the perfect antidote."

He did. They went back to his apartment, showered and changed, and caught a cab to the Plaza Hotel for dinner.

"I'd already made a reservation," he said, enjoying

her delight as they went into the lobby filled with the scent of tiger lilies and the soft sound of a harp. The waiter took Clare's jacket, showed them to a table, handed them menus and returned a few minutes later to take their orders.

Clare could feel herself beginning to relax as they ate, lulled by the wonderful food, the quiet atmosphere and Rick's attentiveness. He was wooing her, she realised. As he had been wooing her all week, in a gentle, unobtrusive way, putting no pressure at all on her.

"I'm glad we went there, to Ellis Island," she told him as they drank their coffee. "It puts it all in context, somehow."

"I know what you mean," he said. "I've been thinking about Ned on and off all day. My great-grandfather, the man who bought the farm. He worked like a slave for that place, got it together field by field, practically. So he could have something for his family – something no-one could take from them. It was Ned who set the family up, somehow got my grandfather through college. Land and education, Grandpa told me. They were Ned's dreams. And he wanted to see the farm full of children. He wanted generations of Flahertys, in the place he had dreamed of for them."

"And did it happen?" Clare asked quietly as the waiter placed two glasses in front of them, scotch for him and Bailey's for Clare.

Rick reached for the glass, took a sip. "No, it never happened."

He paused, looked steadily at her. "It's part of what I

want myself. You remember we talked about dreams? That was part of my dream, Clare. That someday I'd see my children there, swimming, riding bareback, just like I did when I was a kid."

"Rick . . ."

"You know what I'm saying, Clare – don't you?"

He sipped the whiskey again, never taking his eyes from hers.

She wasn't ready for this, should have been ready for this. It was there again, the certain knowledge this time that he had been biding his time. Courting her. Barely touching her all through the week, careful not to presume anything. Carefully not noticing the sexual energy that sparked between them from time to time. Waiting for the moment to be right.

"I don't know how to answer that."

"Is it so difficult?" His eyes never left hers.

"Yes. And no." She sipped her drink, playing for time.

"You must know that I love you, Clare." He put down his glass, reached for her hand. "Don't say anything," he added quickly, as she began to speak. "Say nothing yet. It's enough that I've told you. I've waited a long time to tell you that."

They finished their drinks, sipping slowly, talking quietly, lazily almost, while energy danced between them, drawing them close. And then they were out in the soft night air and he took her hand to lead her across the street to where the carriages were waiting.

"I promised, remember?" He helped her up into the

carriage, and a soft-voiced man from County Kildare drove them through the Park.

Magic, Clare thought, listening to the jingle of the harness, the rhythm of the horse's hooves as she sat back in the leather seat, her head on Rick's shoulder, his arm holding her close, his words echoing in her head, exhilarating, terrifying.

He put some music on when they reached the apartment, poured another drink for them, led her up the narrow stairs to the roof garden where they sat together on a wrought iron bench, his arm around her, his face buried against her hair.

"I meant it, Clare." He said it quietly, almost a whisper. "I've loved you since that first time I saw you in Albatross. You were so beautiful. Full of life and energy, and I knew that I wanted you in my life." He raised his head, looked at her, his face almost touching hers. "And then, that night in *Wildwood*. I wanted to make love to you then, you know that. Just as I want to right now."

She wanted him to, she realised. It was almost a shock. And then she moved slightly and suddenly they were kissing, hungrily, hands caressing, arousing, and she was afraid he might stop, more afraid that she wouldn't. This was all wrong, her head was telling her. But her body was in charge, charged, relaxed, on fire, all at once.

He led her downstairs to the bedroom and then they were lying on the bed, still kissing, caressing, beginning slowly and then more urgently to undress each other, all the time kissing, holding, touching, stroking. Until finally they were naked, and he bent to kiss her breast, his right hand moving to her hip, her thigh, and then –

"*No!*" In an instant she had pulled back and was moving off the bed, reaching for her dressing-gown that lay on the chair.

"What – " For a second he didn't move and then he sprang from the bed and stood facing her from the far side. His face, in the moonlight, was taut with anger, his breathing as ragged as hers.

"Would you like to tell me what game you're playing, exactly? Because I'd really like to know, Clare. Once, I can understand. But not twice. Not now." His voice was cold steel, the tenderness of a moment ago completely gone.

"I'm sorry, Rick – I shouldn't have – it just doesn't feel right. I'm sorry . . ."

She finished almost in a whisper, sick with herself that she had let it go so far, that she had let it start in the first place.

Rick grabbed his clothes, holding them in front of him like a shield.

"So am I, Clare. Sorry that I believed you were an adult."

He was hurt, and deliberately hurting. He strode from the room, heading for his study, his back rigid with anger while Clare sat at the edge of the big bed, forcing herself not to cry.

This is really, really stupid, she told herself. He's a lovely guy, I really like him. Why couldn't I just . . .

Because I don't love him.

The telephone rang, startling her. It was almost 2 a.m. She didn't think it could be anything good. Rick returned to the half-open bedroom door.

"For you." He barely looked at her. His face was still tight, full of hard lines of hurt. "Take it in there." He gestured towards the study, turned his back on her and went into the living-room.

She crossed the hall quickly and lifted the phone, her heart in her mouth.

"Sorry for ringing, Clare – I know it's late." Donal's voice. Relief, fear, a sudden jump in her stomach that must have been panic. Kate? Or –

"It's Tish – she and Jody disappeared on Wednesday. It seems he met her from school – she was due at her grandmother's but didn't show up. They've been missing for two nights now. We've just come back from looking for them again and I'm at my wit's end, I suppose I'm hoping you might have some idea – "

"I'll get there as soon as I can," she interrupted. "The direct flight is in the evening, around seven, but maybe I can get one through Heathrow – I'll ring as soon as I find out. Niall will pick me up."

"No, don't come back, Clare. I shouldn't have rung – I just hoped – "

"I want to. Try not to worry. I'll ring once I've got a flight."

She hung up slowly, conscious of Rick standing behind her.

"Everything okay?" His voice was tight, but the

anger had lifted from his face, replaced by concern. He put a cup of coffee on the desk in front of her and stood in the doorway, drinking his own.

Quickly she explained what had happened.

"I'll come with you."

"No, there's no need. I'm sorry to be going back early, but – "

"Are you really?" Anger flared again, briefly.

"Rick, I – "

"I'm sorry, Clare. What happened earlier – " He gave a slight shrug, sighed. "I really thought it could have worked for us, Clare." He said it quietly, moved to place his cup on the desk, knocked against a photograph in a silver frame so that it fell face downwards. Idly she picked it up, glanced at it. Looked again, not believing what she saw.

Heart pounding, she turned it over. Nothing on the back. She stared again, finally forcing her attention back to what Rick was saying.

"I'd like to come, Clare. Please. I know I've blown it between us – I'm just not sure how. But I want to come and help find Tish."

"Rick." She was speaking slowly, carefully. "Where did you get this?"

He glanced at the photo, distracted. "I took it at Oxford, one time when Beth's sister was visiting."

"Beth?" she said, almost in a whisper.

"You remember – "

"Beth." She stood up, holding the photograph, facing him. "Elizabeth?"

"Right, Elizabeth. I called her Beth. But what – "

He looked at her, puzzled, trying to fathom her expression.

"Donal has a photograph like this," she said. "Exactly the same. Rick – this is Jenny and Liz."

He moved towards her, took it from her and stood staring at it as if he had never seen it before.

"You're sure?" His eyes were riveted to hers.

"Positive." She watched him carefully as he leaned back against the desk, holding the photograph, still looking at her. She waited.

"If Beth is *Liz*, then she's Donal's sister-in-law . . . ?"

She nodded, holding her breath, watching his expression as the realisation came a moment later, and he jammed his hand to his mouth, teeth biting against his fingers, holding grief at bay. "You told me – Jenny and Liz, they're . . . Beth is – she's *dead*?"

She had to strain to hear him, nodded, though he hardly saw her.

"And Tish – she's *Beth's daughter?*"

He banged his fist against his forehead, drove his fingers back through his hair, never taking his eyes from the photograph.

"Christ, she's almost fifteen. Oh, Christ." He stared at Clare, his voice raw, emotions exploding across his face. "It's not possible – she would have told me. Wouldn't she? She would have written. She never wrote – "

He looked wildly round the room, seeing nothing. Then back at her.

"Clare – do you know – ?"

"I don't. Really I don't. Donal never knew who Tish's father was. But – you're right, Rick – it seems possible."

He sat down slowly at the desk, his head on his arms, cradling the photograph. For a long, long time she stood behind him, her hands on his shoulders, holding him while he wept.

Chapter Thirty-one

Donal met them at Dublin Airport. His friend David was with him which meant there was no opportunity for any of the questions Rick wanted to ask, except the very immediate one. "No news?"

"Not yet." Donal looked tense, haggard. "We'll go back to my place, settle you in. Then David and I will go out again."

"I'm coming," Rick said. It wasn't a question.

Donal met his eyes in the rear view mirror. "You're exhausted."

"I'll get over it."

"We'll be fine, Donal," Clare added. "We'll feel better if we're doing something."

The house was quiet when they got there, with just the hall light left on.

Donal reached for the phone the minute they got inside. "I'll check again with Kate. Go on into the kitchen, have some coffee."

They followed David in, straining to hear Donal's voice above the sound of the kettle being filled. David made the coffee quickly and brought some sandwiches over to the table. They were beginning to eat as Donal came back into the room.

"No word," he said, pulling out a chair to sit down. "She says Kinsella's fit to kill someone."

"Jody must be terrified," Clare said.

"That's just it," Donal answered, taking the coffee David passed to him. "At this stage they're probably afraid to come home, even if they wanted to."

"And we're not sure they do," David added, sitting down. "We've spoken to a kid in Tish's class, she says Tish talked about looking for a job in Dublin, or in the Isle of Man, with her boyfriend. Her friend didn't think she was serious."

"The Isle of Man? But why – "

"She went there once on a school trip," Donal explained. "The Manx police are looking for them."

"And the guards?"

"They're keeping an eye out," Donal answered. "Checking the hostels, the streets. But there are hundreds of homeless kids in Dublin."

"Homeless." Rick's voice was strained.

"Missing. Whatever. The point is, a lot of kids go missing, for one reason or another. The guards think it might take a while."

"Surely there's something we can do?" Clare asked. "We can't just wait. What about the papers, TV?"

"It'll be in tomorrow's papers," Donal said. "Her

grandmother was more annoyed about that than about Tish going missing in the first place."

"She's in no position to comment." Rick's voice was steely.

"Let's not get into that now, " Donal said. "We'd do better to concentrate on what we can do to find Tish."

"What about bed-and-breakfasts?"

"Where would you start?" he asked, pushing back his hair. She noticed his face had the same strained look as when she first met him. "We're hoping the papers to-morrow might take care of that."

He looked at his watch. "It's after eleven, time to get going. Sure you want to come?"

Rick nodded.

"Would you know where to go?" Clare asked, surprised.

Donal's response was grim. "We're learning."

Pearse Street Garda Station, in the middle of the night, was a scene of organised chaos. The Desk Sergeant greeted Donal as they came in. "Sorry, no word. But we're on the look-out"

Donal nodded. "We'll call back later."

"Do that." The sergeant looked at Donal sympathetically.

"What now?" Clare asked as he came back over to them.

"Search the streets," Donal said. "It's all we can do. We'll start in Temple Bar."

They went in two pairs, Clare and Donal together, and David with Rick, arranging to meet up at 3 a.m. back at Pearse Street.

They could be anywhere, Clare realised as she walked down Westmoreland Street with Donal. She could feel a chill that had nothing to do with the cool September night.

It wasn't yet midnight, the pubs and restaurants were still open. They saw lots of young teenagers hanging around Temple Bar, sitting near the Central Bank and at various places in the small streets behind it, eating chips and burgers, drinking from cans, seemingly oblivious to the passers-by who gave them a wide berth.

Donal leaned down from time to time to ask questions, show photographs. The response was sometimes aggressive, often suspicious, always negative.

They walked through Merchant's Arch, pulling their collars up against the sharp breeze from the Liffey. They turned left along the quays and Clare moved slightly closer to Donal, glad of his warm, reassuring presence beside her. The quays after midnight were an alien place to her. She found herself watching every car that passed, looking sideways into narrow streets and laneways, holding her breath any time they saw someone approaching.

It was a side of Dublin she never knew existed. They continued along towards Heuston Station, glancing into doorways as they passed, seeing the occasional solitary figure huddled there.

Clare finally said what she was thinking, hating the sound of it. "She could be anywhere."

"I know." She saw a look of anger – or frustration – on his face as they passed under a street lamp. "Bloody little fool," he said, in a low, controlled voice. "She doesn't even know what she's getting herself into. I hope to God they had the sense to find somewhere safe to stay. I'm not sure how much money they had on them."

"Why did she do it, do you think?" Clare asked. "Her grandmother will never agree to her coming to Connemara now."

"She mightn't have a choice," he said. "Tish told her friend Aoife that she had to get away, that she hated the school and her grandmother, and couldn't stand it a minute longer. I wish to God she could have told me." He paused. "She said as well that she was going to look for her father."

Clare drew a quick breath.

"Ironic, isn't it?" he said, as they continued walking.

She didn't answer for a moment or two, then said "And do you think Rick really is her father?"

"I don't see how it could be anyone else. The photo is absolute proof that Liz and Beth were the same person. I knew from Jenny that Liz had an American boyfriend while she was in England. She never mentioned anyone else – and she came home pregnant. But what I don't understand . . . of course!"

"What?"

"All we ever knew was that Tish's father was named Patrick and he lived in New York. Liz wouldn't talk about him, wouldn't give us his full name in case we tried to trace him. I always assumed Rick was short for Richard, but maybe – "

"He's Patrick," Clare confirmed. "I heard him booking the plane ticket."

They were nearing Heuston Station. Clare saw a car parked in the shelter of Guinness's gate, its boot open and a huddle of people around it. Donal spoke quietly to her as she hesitated.

"Simon soup run. We were here last night."

He walked over, nodding to several people who were standing around with steaming paper cups in their hands. A man and woman stood at the back of the car, dispensing soup and sandwiches, looking up when Donal greeted them.

Clare stood back slightly, near the shelter of the wall. No-one looked at her. They were concentrating on the food and cigarettes, some talking quietly among themselves, others holding back just out of range of a nearby street-lamp.

One or two, she could see, were eyeing Donal suspiciously as he talked to the Simon workers. "Who's your man, Mick?" a man with a pepper-and-salt beard, who looked sixty but might have been younger, asked in a loud voice.

"Nothing to worry about, Paddy. He's looking for a young girl."

"Aren't we all."

There was a roar of laughter from somewhere near the back of the crowd, followed by a woman's voice.

"Ah, for Jaysus sake shut up, Paddy. Haven't you daughters of your own."

Clare couldn't see the speaker. She was surprised, she hadn't noticed any women in the group.

"What's the young wan like, mister?" the woman asked.

"Fourteen, but she looks a bit older. Her hair is short, bright red. Dyed. Her name is Tish and she's with a boy from Galway called Jody. He's the same age, black hair, about six feet tall."

"If I see them I'll send them home to you. They'll go, too, if they've any sense. You could try down around Charles Street, I saw a gang of kids down there earlier."

"Thanks." He nodded to her, looked around the little group and raised his voice slightly. "If anyone sees her could they tell the guards?"

"We will in our arse tell the guards." It was the man with the loud voice.

"There's a reward if she's found."

"Why didn't you say that in the first place? We'll think about it."

They left the cluster of people and crossed the river, heading back along the quays in the direction of O'Connell Street. The streets were almost deserted at this hour with only the occasional car, and one or two other people walking.

"Are you afraid?" Donal asked, catching her hand. She noticed it was warm. Her own hands were freezing, like the rest of her. It was bitterly cold for September. God knows how Tish would manage if she was out in this.

"Not too much," she answered him. "A bit, maybe, back there."

"No need. They're decent, most of them. Like everyone else."

451

They had come to the end of the new apartments, were passing shops and dilapidated, boarded-up buildings. They searched the dark streets for more than an hour, finding no trace of Tish or anyone else. It was a terrifying place, all the same, and Clare was relieved when Donal finally said that they had better go back to meet the others. He sounded disappointed, absolutely exhausted.

They were walking down a side street on their way back to the quays when two figures stepped from the shadows, blocking their path. Young boys, she realised, not much older than Jody. She felt Donal tense as he let go of her hand. In case they went for him, she realised. Please, God . . .

"We're looking for someone, lads. A young girl called Tish – she's fourteen. She's with a fella called Jody. Maybe you can help us?" Donal's voice was warm, his tone conversational. He could have been chatting to friends.

The boys sniggered, an unpleasant sound, as they glanced at each other. Finally the taller of the two, a thin boy with lank, brown hair, spoke. "Why the f . . . should we?" "There's ten quid in it if you know anything." Donal reached slowly into his pocket, keeping his other hand visible as he extracted the banknote.

"And if we don't?" The smaller of the youths had a rasping voice.

Donal smiled. "I suppose you can have this anyway."

"Too bloody sure." The boy with the brown hair leaned forward to grab it. His eyes, Clare saw, had a vacant stare. "Any more where that came from?" he asked, stuffing it into his pocket.

"No, that's it." Donal's tone was still light. He never took his eyes from them.

"We might have a look."

"The cops know we're here, lads. They'll be picking us up in a minute. You don't need the hassle."

He reached out slowly for Clare's hand, began edging – infinitely slowly – past them, drawing her with him.

"Not so f . . . ing fast – we didn't say we were finished with you!" The taller boy reached forward and Clare thought she saw the glint of something in his hand. Donal moved quickly, grabbing the boy's wrist as the other boy moved forward. She looked around for something – a stick, anything – and then there was a squeal of brakes from the direction of the river, a muttered curse from the boys and they were gone, running up towards Smithfield.

Donal grabbed her hand and they ran as quickly as they could towards the quays.

"Don't even ask if I was afraid that time," she asked once she could catch her breath. "You were great."

"So were you. You didn't scream once."

"You think – "

"Joke. Come on, there's a taxi." He flagged it down and they ran for it. "We've done our bit for tonight."

Chapter Thirty-two

When they got to Pearse Street Rick and David were already there. Alone. Clare could hardly bear to meet Rick's eyes as Donal shook his head.

"Maybe tomorrow," David said. "That piece should be in the paper. We'll pick one up on the way home."

"I have it," Rick said later as he sat at Donal's kitchen table scouring the newspaper. They had dropped David home on the way, and Donal and Clare were making tea and toast though all three of them felt too exhausted to eat.

It was a small article, just a few lines, but the photographs were clear and it gave the Pearse Street phone number.

"Let's hope it does the trick," Clare said. "We'd better finish the tea and get some sleep so we can start early in the morning." She glanced across at Donal who looked ready to fall asleep in the chair.

"Not yet," Rick said. "Please. I know you're exhausted, Donal. But there's a couple of things I really need to know." He paused, and they both waited. His face was a mixture of anguish and hope as he said it. "Do you think I'm Tish's father?"

Donal didn't hesitate. "I'm sure of it. There wasn't anyone else, it has to be you. And, of course, there are ways of proving it now, if you want to do that."

But Rick wasn't listening now – he seemed lost for a moment, gazing into the distance, caught up in what Donal had said.

"And how do you feel about that? My being her father?" he asked finally, looking directly at Donal.

This time Donal didn't answer immediately.

"I don't know how I feel. I really don't. I mean, I think she could do a hell of a lot worse. But you have to admit, Rick, you haven't been much in evidence. Being a father should last a bit longer than one night."

"I didn't know – "

"You bloody well *should* have known!"

Clare looked at Donal, startled by the sudden burst of anger that seemed to come from nowhere. Then the two men were on their feet, facing each other across the big kitchen table, fury crackling between them.

"Where were you, for Christ's sake? You destroyed Liz. Do you know that? Do you give a damn?"

"Hold on – "

"No, *you* hold on. Jenny and I were the ones left picking up the pieces when she had to face that bitch of a mother of hers and tell her she was pregnant. You can imagine what that was like. Or maybe you can't. Believe me, it wasn't fun. And all the time she was hoping to hear from you. One rotten, bloody letter. That's all she wanted. And when she finally got up the courage to write, you hadn't the decency to answer. Oh, she knew what you were like. That you didn't want to get involved. But still she was hoping . . .

And now, what are you going to do to Tish, now? Where will you be for her? You're back here by sheer bloody chance, by a *fluke!* I'm glad, for her sake. But don't expect me to put out banners – I'll save my energy for picking up the pieces afterwards."

Rick stood there for a long time, saying nothing. Then slowly he sat down, never taking his eyes from Donal.

Donal took a deep breath.

"Look – I'm sorry. I didn't mean to say all that. Not yet, anyway." His gaze moved to include Clare. "I'll show you where the bedrooms are. I think we could all do with some sleep."

He turned to leave the kitchen and Clare was standing up to follow him when Rick spoke.

"Wait." His voice was low.

Donal half-turned in the doorway and looked at him.

"I wrote," Rick said. His voice was still low but very clear, and his eyes didn't leave Donal's. "You can choose not to believe me, if you want – but I wrote. A dozen letters, maybe more. I never had a reply. So finally I gave up, after maybe three or four months. I thought she didn't want . . ."

He stopped and Clare could see the glint of tears in his eyes. He had Donal's full attention now.

"She never got any letters," Donal said. "I know she didn't. She would have told Jen."

Rick looked steadily at Donal. One hand was stretched palm-down on the table in front of him, the white knuckles the only indication of the tension he was feeling.

"I wrote, Donal. To her address in England, and Debbie sent them to her. Beth never replied."

"She never got a letter," Donal repeated. "And I know she wrote to you at least once. I'm sure of it. I remember her mother taking it to – "

He stopped abruptly and all three of them looked at each other, appalled. "She couldn't have – "

"She must have." Rick's voice was hard. "The bitch!"

"Sweet God," Donal said. "I didn't think even *she* . . ."

He paused, brushed his hand back through his hair. "Rick, if I thought – God, I'm sorry . . ."

Rick looked at him, gave a slight shrug. "You were entitled. You couldn't have known. But would she do that? To her own daughter?"

"Oh, yes. She's well capable of it, if she thought she had a good reason."

"You mean, if she thought I might hurt Beth?"

"More likely because she felt Beth – Liz – had hurt her. She was punishing her."

Rick made a low. sharp sound under his breath. Clare watched as his palm curled into a fist on the table.

Finally he sighed. "Do you believe I wrote?"

"Yes." Donal came back into the room, sat opposite Rick at the table. "Yes, I believe you. I could kill Madge."

"Beth thought I abandoned her." There was a world of sadness in Rick's voice.

"No," Donal said softly. "No, actually, she didn't. She never stopped believing in you, Rick. She never stopped loving you. And she made excuses – she thought you were too busy to write when your father was ill, then she wondered what had happened, she thought you might have lost the address in England or something. That's when she wrote."

"And she wrote only once?"

"She didn't want to put pressure on you. She wouldn't let us try to contact you, either. She wanted it to be a free decision, if you came back."

Clare moved quietly to sit at the corner of the table, watching the expressions that flickered across Rick's face. She could feel the tears in her eyes, hardly dared breathe.

"She was named after you, you know," Donal continued. "Patricia."

Clare watched as, finally, the tears coursed down Rick's cheeks.

"What if . . ." He couldn't continue.

Clare moved to stand behind him, her arms lightly around him, cheek resting against his hair as he struggled to control the tears.

"We'll find her, Rick," Donal said. "I'm certain of it. Jody is sound – they'll be fine."

"But – "

"Shhh," Clare said gently. She moved towards the door. "Come on, you really need some sleep. Maybe there'll be some word tomorrow – someone's bound to see their photo in the paper."

"Clare's right – we'd better try and catch a few hours, anyway. And Rick – "

Rick had pushed back his chair.

Donal was smiling. "Tish could do a lot worse. She often told me she'd want her father to be just like you."

Clare was watching Rick's face. It was like watching the sun come up.

"Did you mind?" he asked, finally.

"Not a bit. As I said, she could do worse."

The two men smiled at each other. Donal stood up, put his hand lightly on Rick's shoulder. "Come on, I'll show you the bedrooms. We could all do with some sleep."

"I doubt if I'll sleep," Rick said.

"At least try and rest. We'll be starting early."

The phone call from Pearse Street came just after ten in the morning. Clare dragged herself from sleep, pulled on jeans and a jumper, and reached the landing as Donal was hanging up. Rick was already half way down the stairs.

"A bed-and-breakfast in Drumcondra," Donal said. "They've just left. Come on."

They were in the car and heading for Drumcondra in less than a minute.

"The guards are on their way," Donal said. "The landlady is fairly sure it was Tish and Jody – they'd just gone when she saw their photo and rang the guards."

"Is it far?" Rick asked.

"Ten minutes. We've a chance, if they didn't catch a bus."

"She's not expecting them back to-night?" Clare asked.

"No – they were there for two nights already. She said they didn't seem to have much money, they were counting it out to make up the cost. She dropped it by a couple of pounds so they'd have something left."

"And didn't she think of asking questions?" Clare said. "Two young kids with no money?"

"She asked them how they were fixed, the guards said. But she didn't realise they were so young, and anyway they said they were on their way to a relation – "

He pulled quickly into the side of the road and they sat in an agony of indecision.

"I'll go back," Clare said.

"Maybe you should – no, wait, David has a key."

He left the car and sprinted across the road to a telephone.

"He'll go straight there," he said a minute later as he started the car again and pulled out into the flow of traffic. "I said I'll ring him in half-an-hour. For the first time in my life I wish I had a mobile phone."

They reached the bed-and-breakfast and Donal ran in to speak to the landlady.

"Griffith Avenue," he said, jumping back into the car. "The guards have already headed up there."

He was making the left turn as he spoke and they cruised along the open, tree-lined avenue until the reached the squad car parked just before the junction with Mobhi Road.

"No sign," one of the guards said when Donal went over. "Any ideas? If they were headed for town they could have gone from Drumcondra. Do they know anyone around here?"

"No-one I know of," Donal answered. "Unless – her grandmother lives in Phibsboro. But I really doubt that they'd go there – she's the reason Tish ran away in the first place. And she wouldn't let Jody in the door."

"Do you want to try?" the other guard asked. "We'll keep cruising around. Will you check with the station later?"

"No go," Donal said, getting back into the car. "The guards suggested trying her grandmother – they could be headed for Phibsboro. And I haven't any better ideas."

He turned down Mobhi Road as he spoke.

"Might they be scared enough to go there, do you think?" Clare asked. "They don't know you're in Dublin, and it sounds like they haven't any money left."

"Or does Tish have friends nearby?" Rick asked from the back seat.

"One or two near Phibsboro, but their parents would – "

"You said the grandmother still lives there?" Rick interrupted. "In Phibsboro?"

"Yes, she's been there all her life. She's still in the same – Rick, what is it?" Donal asked as his eyes caught Rick's in the mirror.

Clare turned in her seat, startled at the anger on Rick's face.

"What address is she at?"

Donal told him. Rick swore. "That's the address I went to in May – the old lady who answered said she didn't know anyone of that name."

Donal swore. "That was Madge O'Brien, Rick. Tish's grandmother."

"That old woman is Beth's mother? Tish was living with *her?*"

"When she wasn't at school. Madge insisted. I fought against it, but there was nothing I could do. She's a law unto herself. And she was Tish's next of kin."

"Maybe. But not now." Rick's voice was low, tense.

"Right, not now," Donal agreed. "Now all we have to do is find her."

They stopped in front of a red-bricked, terraced house in a side-street near St Peter's church. When she glanced at the house Clare could see the face behind the lace curtain at one of the downstairs windows.

"Do you want to stay in the car?" Donal asked.

Rick was already out. "I'm coming with you."

"We won't be long," Donal said, following Rick up the short pathway. The door opened almost immediately, and opened again a few minutes later to let them out.

"What did she say?" Clare asked as they got back into the car.

"We didn't give her a chance to get going," Donal said. "Once we knew they weren't there we left, in the middle of her shouting that it was all my fault for luring Tish down to Connemara and 'giving her notions', as she put it. She was no help at all."

"Incredible to think she was Beth's mother." Rick said.

"And Jenny's. I know. The father was a decent man, but no match for her."

"I'm surprised she let you in," Clare said.

"She'd do that all right, on account of the neighbours. And in case she'd miss a chance to let fly at me. She's as vindictive as ever."

"No wonder Tish took off," Clare said. "You didn't ask her about the letters?"

"No," Donal said. "Because if she admitted destroying them I'd have killed her."

"And if she denied it?"

Donal gave a wry smile as he glanced at Clare. "I'd have killed her anyway."

"You'd have had to get in line," Rick said from the back seat.

Clare laughed, the first easing of tension since Friday night.

"Great. So you'd have been in jail, and Tish would have to live with Donal . . ."

"She could do worse," Rick said quietly, smiling as his eyes met Donal's in the rear view mirror.

"Do you think she recognised you from last time, Rick? When you went asking about Liz?"

"Maybe – but she doesn't know who I am. I didn't have a chance to give my name, either time."

"But she's probably guessed," Donal said after a moment. "I thought there was something a bit different about her, and it's certainly not concern for Tish. She knows who you are, all right – and she's afraid."

"She should be," Rick answered. "She should be very afraid."

They were cruising along almost aimlessly, beginning to feel exhausted, the lack of sleep catching up with them.

"They could be anywhere," Donal said finally. "Look, why don't we stop and have something to eat, and I'll phone Kate and David – and the guards."

They parked and went into a little restaurant, where Donal spoke briefly on the public telephone, shaking his head as he returned to the table.

"We ordered for you," Clare said as the waitress put a plate in front of him.

"Fine." He hardly seemed to notice what was on the plate, and nobody spoke as they concentrated on eating quickly.

"We'd better go back home and wait, I suppose, and let you two get a bit more sleep," Donal said as they were driving back towards Mobhi Road. "With luck someone else will recognise them and phone the guards."

"Or they might see the newspaper," Rick suggested. "She'll know you're not mad at her – "

"Turn left," Clare interrupted.

"Too late," Donal said. They were just turning off the road that swept left to Glasnevin and Finglas. "Did you – ?" He was already manoeuvring his way back around the small triangle to take the left turn.

"I thought – I'm not sure – " Clare said, straining to see as they rejoined the Finglas road. "Donal, where are Liz and Jenny buried?"

"What? Jesus!" A moment later he was speeding towards Glasnevin Cemetery, and they were out of the car almost before he stopped.

"This way," he said, racing along the gravel path, turning off once, twice. Rick kept pace with him, Clare was just behind. It felt wrong to be running among the graves – until she saw the two figures in the distance. And then she ran faster.

It was a pathetic sight. Tish, kneeling by the grave, tears teeming down her face, her mouth twisted in raw pain as she tried to stifle the sobs. And Jody, his arm around her, trying to comfort her, completely at a loss.

He glanced up at the running figures as they came to a stop a few yards away, then whispered to Tish and helped her up, his arm protectively around her, defiance battling with fear and exhaustion as he faced them. Tish huddled close against him, her expression so bereft that Clare struggled to hold back her own tears.

"It was my idea, Donal," Jody began. "The blame is all mine. Tish couldn't stay with that bitch of an oul' wan a minute longer. And she's not going back."

"You're right. She's not."

"They'll try to make her," Jody said.

"She's not going back," Donal repeated. "I promise you."

Tish moved, uncertainly at first, and then she was in Donal's arms and he was holding her, soothing her while she sobbed, a heart-breaking sound in the quiet of the cemetery.

"Why did she die, Donal? Why did she have to

die? I have no one of my own, no-one at all except –"

"You have, you know, Tish." He was still holding her tightly, smoothing her hair, speaking softly to her, trying to calm her.

"No, Donal. It's not the same. I love you and the boys, really I do, and Kate – but it's not the same, truly it's not. It's not like having a mother and father, someone of my own." The sobbing began again. "I want my mother and father."

Rick could stand it no longer. He had held back, standing close to Clare, his eyes moving back and forth between Tish and the grave with its inscription. But now he made a sound like a stifled sob and moved towards Tish and Donal.

"Tish," Donal said, holding her at arms length, reaching with his right hand to wipe her face. "Can you hear me, Tish? Good girl. Rick has something to tell you, Tish. Clare and I will wait in the car with Jody." He gave her a quick kiss on the cheek, reached to caress Jenny and Liz's names briefly where they shone on the black marble headstone, and moved across to where Clare was standing.

"I'll stay here," Jody said, but he moved back out of earshot and stood leaning against a tree as Tish turned towards Rick, her expression puzzled. Rick reached a tentative hand towards her and began to speak. And then she was in his arms, and as Clare walked slowly down the path with Donal she could hear Tish crying again.

She glanced back briefly as she and Donal reached

the cemetery gate. They were still standing there beside the grave, father and daughter, holding tightly to each other, as if everything they wanted in the world was there.

Clare could feel tears beginning to edge down her cheeks. She reached for a tissue and Donal took one from his pocket and gave it to her. She blew her nose and smiled at him through her tears as she stuffed it into her pocket.

He reached for her hand, squeezing it gently as they went through the cemetery gate, and as she turned to look at him she knew – suddenly, finally, and with absolute certainty – that she loved him.

Chapter Thirty-three

"So, it's just a question of what happens next!"

"And what do you want to happen next?"

Clare laughed. "Wanting and having are two different things!"

She and Dee were having coffee in Bewley's the following Thursday morning.

"I don't suppose you'd just tell him? Or would that make things too easy?"

"Dee, this is serious. I really don't want to blow it. I'm afraid to say a word in case I scare him off."

"You said he kissed you that night, when you came back from Albatross."

"Yes, and two minutes later he was tripping over himself apologising, and he's acted ever since as if it didn't happen."

"But it did. And I saw the way he looked at you when we were down there. The man's in love with you."

"I don't think so, Dee. Really I don't. If he was, surely to God he'd say something."

"Maybe. But he doesn't know how you feel. And he might be holding back because of Rick."

"God. Rick. He's the next problem. I've got to sort things out with him first. Tell him I don't love him."

Dee gave a wry smile. "I'd say he worked that out when you jumped out of his bed."

"You're no help at all." Clare was laughing. "Why do I bother telling you things?"

"I'd be a great help, if only you'd let me," Dee said. "I'm telling you what to do. Talk to Rick, and talk to Donal. It's dead simple. And it'll all work out. I know it."

Ruth said much the same that evening as they sat curled up on the floor in front of the fire in their parents' living-room. Their parents were out and Ruth was spending a rare evening without Conor.

"Go for it, kiddo," Ruth said once Clare had brought her up to date. "You've only got one life. Don't waste it!"

"I could make a complete eejit of myself."

Ruth laughed. "So what? It wouldn't be the first time! And Donal's mad about you – anyone can see that."

"You said the same about Rick."

"It was true. And it's true with Donal. So go and talk to him. Ring me when you sort it out."

"But, Ruth – "

"Talk to him."

"You know how he felt after his wife died. He's probably not ready for anything like this."

"Clare, he's an adult. He has a say in this too. And I told you, he's cracked about you."

"What if we're wrong?" She bit her lip. "No, it's too

469

big a risk. I don't want to hurt him. I don't want to get hurt myself. And then there's the twins . . ."

"What's the problem? You like them, don't you?"

"A lot. And they seem to like me. The thing is, if it got serious – "

"You're jumping the gun," Ruth interrupted.

"Not really. If it was anything at all, I'd want it to be serious. I'd want it to last."

"No guarantees, Clare. You know that. Let me know how it goes. Now, go and talk to him, sis."

Kate had a fire lighting when Clare arrived back home on Monday afternoon.

"You don't mind that I broke in?" Kate smiled as she opened the door to her. "I know the key is only for emergencies, but when you rang and said you were on the way, I thought you might want something to eat."

"You'd better believe it! I only had an apple for lunch, I'm starving!"

"Good enough for you, you know you should eat properly," Kate said, going towards the kitchen. "Now, tell me what you think of that," she added, as she came back with two plates of stew.

"Smells gorgeous, Kate" Clare said, sitting down and reaching for a fork. "You're spoiling me."

"Well, enjoy it. God knows I have to spoil someone, and I've hardly seen Donal or the twins since he got back last Tuesday. He's up to his eyes trying to catch up on work. I hardly see Kevin either. He's over in Donal's every single night."

"Why's that?" Clare asked, hoping her voice was steady. Even the sound of his name left her feeling as if all her senses were on full alert.

"Well. he's saying nothing yet, but I've an idea he's falling for Nan Kinsella. He takes her out every night, after she's finished minding the twins, and then brings her back to her cousin's."

"Are you missing the twins?"

"Don't mind me, I'm only giving out – they were with me all day on Saturday. But I miss being able to hop across here to see them. It was nice to know they were so near."

"How's Luke?" Clare asked.

"He's fine now, no nightmares or anything. It's a great help to them, having Nan there."

"And any word of Jody?"

"Donal didn't tell you?"

"No, I haven't spoken to him since he came down last Tuesday."

"A lot happened since then," Kate said. "Let me bring in the tea and then I'll tell you."

"You know Donal brought him back," she continued a few minutes later as she poured the tea. "And Jody was reluctant to go home, so he stayed with me that night and the following day Donal went over with Kevin and Jack to see Kinsella and prepare the ground for Jody."

"And how did Kinsella react?" Clare asked as Kate paused.

"No better than they expected. He ranted and raved

471

at Donal, saying he hadn't kept a tight enough rein on Tish. He said Jody would never have dreamed of going up to Dublin, and never would again by the time Kinsella finished with him."

She stopped for a minute to pour more tea.

"But then Jack lit into Kinsella and told him to leave Donal out of it. He said it was only a matter of time before Jody went anyway, the way Kinsella treated him, and that it was a wonder he stayed as long as he did. Kinsella hadn't time to get a word in edgeways, Kevin told me. It was as if a dam had burst, he said, and there was no stopping Jack. He told Kinsella that if he was a half-decent father instead of spending his time in the pub, his children might get some good out of him, and that he should be down on his knees thanking God he had a son like Jody instead of walloping him every time he got the chance."

"My God – *Jack* said all that?"

"He did," Kate said. "And Kinsella went mad and asked Jack what he'd know about it. And Jack said he knew that if he'd been lucky enough to have a wife like Sadie, and a son like Jody, he'd have given thanks to God every day of his life, and not have driven them away like Kinsella did."

"He was taking a risk."

"He looked as if he didn't care, Kevin said. And then Kinsella went for him bald-headed. He picked up the handle of a pick axe and lashed out, but Donal and Kevin caught him, one on each side, and held him until he quietened down a bit, and finally got him to sit down. And then they got an awful shock, because he started to cry. A man like Kinsella, as tough as old boots, and he was bawling like a baby, saying how much he missed Sadie, and how sorry he was about everything, and how he had tried to do his best for the kids."

"How did Jack react to that?" Clare asked.

"He hadn't a chance to react," Kate said, "Because Martin had come in without anyone noticing and was standing inside the back door while all this was going on. He walked over to his father and stood looking at him with an expression of pure disgust, Kevin said. And then he let him have it. Martin, who wouldn't say boo to a goose. He told him that he was fooling no-one only himself, and that as low as he stooped before, Martin never thought he'd attack the one man who had been a decent neighbour to all of them. A man who put food on their table more often than Kinsella himself ever did.

Jack looked a bit embarrassed at that, Kevin said. But Martin kept going, and told Kinsella that things would be different from now on, and that for a start he'd have to sign over the farm."

"He never agreed to that!" Clare said.

"Indeed he did. I don't think he had much choice. Martin pointed out that he's twenty-one now, old enough to manage it. He said himself and Jody were doing all the work anyway, and even the younger ones had to help because Kinsella wasn't pulling his weight. He said he'd give him three days to think about it, and that there was some kind of grant for farmers who sign over the land, and Kinsella could get that and drink himself to death for all Martin cared. And that Jody was coming home, and if Kinsella touched a hair on his head, Martin would kill him dead. Or better still, call the guards and get him barred from the place."

"And how did Kinsella take all that?"

"He was very shaken – he'd never have expected it from Martin. But it might be the best thing that ever happened, because he's a changed man. Jody went home, and Nan went back for a day or two to make sure things were all right, though she was always afraid of Kinsella, and with good reason. But she came back in great form, saying you wouldn't believe what it's like there now. Sheila is running the place, she's nineteen now and more than a match for him, and they'll keep him in line now between them. He was to see the solicitor to-day."

"And have you seen Jody since?"

"I have, and he's grand. He was a bit ashamed of himself, and kept telling me that himself and Tish didn't get up to anything while they were away, that they knew they'd be in enough trouble as it was. He still can't believe they got off so lightly. And neither can I."

"What do you mean, Kate?"

"Well, look at what they did. Vanished without a word to anyone, and poor Donal having to go scouring Dublin for them. Not to mention yourself and Rick having to come over."

"I don't think Rick is complaining," Clare said, smiling.

Kate's expression softened. "Well, no, I suppose not. All the same, it wasn't fair to you. Or to Donal, just when he was starting in the new job. Not that he'd say a word against her. I'd have strung her up."

"You don't mean that."

Kate gave a quiet laugh. "No, I suppose I don't. You couldn't be cross with her, not the way she is now. And it would lift your heart to see her with Rick. You worked a miracle for them, you know, even if it was by chance. You must be thrilled about that, though it leaves you a bit on the outside."

"How – oh, with Rick, you mean? That's no problem."

"Isn't it?" Kate asked, looking doubtful. "You had to cut short your holiday, and you've hardly seen him since he found her."

"It's not a problem," Clare repeated softly. "Really, don't worry about it. I'm delighted for them. When will they be back?"

"By the weekend. You know Tish is starting in Kylemore?"

"Yes – she was full of it when I met them in Dublin last Friday. She couldn't believe the grandmother agreed."

"You know, I nearly feel sorry for the woman. I know she did something terrible, but she's lost everything now. And at least she made things easier for them by agreeing so quickly. She could have held on to Tish instead of letting her move down here while Rick gets custody and sorts things out at home."

"I still don't think that woman deserves an ounce of sympathy, the way she carried on," Clare said. "And Tish refused to go back to her anyway."

"Oh, I know," Kate said. "But all the same – "

"She ruined their lives, Kate. Rick says he'll never forgive her – he could have married Liz and reared Tish with her."

"You're right," Kate said. "There's no answer to that. But I'm saddened at the waste of it all, I suppose, and the idea of that old woman with nothing now."

"Rick says he'll still bring Tish to see her, that she's still her grandmother. And Tish says she'll go if he wants her to."

"It doesn't surprise me," Kate said. "She'd do anything in the world for him, and he for her, from the look of things. Moving over here is a very big step."

"It is," Clare agreed. "But he was talking about that anyway, even before he knew about Tish."

"Oh?" Kate raised an eyebrow.

"It was probably just talk," Clare said quickly. "People say all kinds of things."

"And mean most of them," Kate said. "Would you like to see him living here?"

"Yes, of course. If it was what he wanted." She didn't meet Kate's eyes.

"I get the message," Kate smiled.

"I'm sorry, Kate. I'll tell you everything in a few days. Okay?"

Kate reached across to touch Clare's hand.

"You don't have to tell me anything, Clare."

"I know." Clare smiled at her. "That's why I will."

Kate stood up. "I'd better be going before it gets too late. Those poor cats of mine don't see enough of me at all."

"I wouldn't worry about them, Kate. If Mishka is anything like her daughter, she'll manage fine!"

The both turned to look at Minty, the sleek tabby curled up in front of the turf fire.

"You know, I was never into cats, but I'd be lost without her now. The place seems so empty with everyone gone."

"So you want them all back, do you? Even those people with all the wild kids – what was their name?"

"Don't remind me of them! No, it's Donal and the twins I'll miss." That brief flutter again as she said his name.

"You'll probably see them during the week. And if not, he'll definitely be at Niall's party on Saturday."

"What party?"

"His engagement party. Haven't you – ?"

"'f course. I forgot all about it. He told me on the way to the airport, but so much happened since . . ."

"You'll be there?"

Clare laughed. "It's manners to wait 'til you're asked!"

"Don't you know well you'll be asked. Wear that green dress of yours. It suits you."

A quick hug and she was gone, leaving Clare alone to absorb the stillness of the place.

She found herself listening every few minutes for footsteps, expecting to hear voices that weren't there. Her cottage had never felt so empty.

This was ridiculous, she told herself. She put on some music and went to make a cup of coffee she didn't want, for the sake of something to do. It was too early to go to bed, early enough still to go into Clifden and see what was happening, but then she'd have to come back to an empty cottage and she didn't think she could bear that.

She brought the coffee back into the living-room, pulled the phone towards her and sat with the receiver in her hand, running through the list of people she could ring. Ruth and Dee, of course, though she'd spoken to Dee only yesterday, and Ruth this morning. Niall, to tell him she was back. And . . .

Quickly she dialled the number before she could change her mind.

"Donal, hi. It's me." I love you, her mind was screaming. Quiet, take it easy, she told herself

"Clare! When did you get back?"

She loved the warmth of his voice, imagined him smiling as he spoke.

"Just a few hours ago. Kate has been here, filling me in on everything."

He gave a short laugh. "So you heard about Kinsella?"

"Yes."

"I almost feel sorry for the man," Donal said. "But he seems to be taking it in his stride now. I'm pleased for Jody – and Martin."

"I'd say Jody is pretty relieved – about everything. Has he seen Tish since she came back?" Clare asked.

"Briefly, just. But they'll both be at Niall's party on Saturday."

"Are you going yourself?" she asked, holding her breath.

"Probably," Donal said. "Nan's cousin has offered to stay with the boys – Nan will be going with Kevin."

"That seems to be getting very serious, from what Kate said."

He laughed. "Kate doesn't know the half of it. Look, I'd better go – I put the boys to bed an hour ago but it sounds like they're killing each other up there! See you Saturday?"

"See you Saturday." To her disappointment, and slight surprise, he didn't offer her a lift.

Niall phoned next morning, just after eleven.

"You'll come, won't you, Clare? It's in Kingfisher, and I've invited everyone. Should be a great bash. And you'll come for the wedding itself, won't you? It'll be just outside Paris, near Nogent-sur-Marne. February 17th, Nicole's birthday. I haven't had a chance to ask Rick yet, but when you see him – "

"I mightn't see him."

"Oh?"

"Well, I'll probably *see* him all right, he and Tish are due back on Thursday. But . . ."

"Something happened?" He sounded concerned.

"Yes and no. He's a lovely guy, but – "

"There's someone else."

"No!" Her response was too quick.

Niall laughed. "Keep telling yourself, and you might even believe it! It's about time you realised. See you Saturday, sweetheart!"

She was still protesting when he hung up the phone.

Ruth was next to ring. "Have you told him?"

"Which of them?"

"Either. Both."

"Neither, I haven't seen them. But there's a party on Saturday, Niall's engagement. They'll both be there."

"*That* should be fun! Let me know how it goes, first thing Sunday."

"Don't hold your breath. There'll be over a hundred people there, not much chance for a quiet word with anyone."

"Even better. All those smouldering glances across a crowded room, stuff like that!"

"Like I said, don't hold your breath . . ."

Kingfisher was hopping when Clare arrived just after eight thirty on the Saturday evening. She knew most of the people there, it would be a great night if she could only relax.

She threaded her way through the crowds towards one of the large, circular tables that were placed around the edges of the room.

Jim stopped to talk to her for a moment, on his rounds with a tray of wine. She took a glass of red, sipping it quickly.

"Steady with that, they'll be dancing later, you'll need a clear head. And I want the first dance!"

"Cheeky!" she laughed, as he went off with the tray. But he was right, she'd need a clear head for later.

And then she saw him.

He was wearing a soft blue linen shirt over a pair of chinos, and was sitting between Kate and Tish. He looked wonderful, somehow different. The light was catching his hair, picking up dark glints where it curled, still shower-damp, onto his forehead.

He was smiling as she approached the table. Her heart did a quick jump before she returned Donal's greeting and forced herself to look at the others. She hoped to God she wasn't blushing.

She glanced quickly round, smiling at Kevin and Nan, forcing herself to meet Rick's warm, relaxed gaze. If he, like her, had a sense of unfinished business, he was better at hiding it.

Tish jumped up to kiss her on the cheek.

"We were waiting for you. Sit down here, beside me."

Clare had no alternative, but for a moment she wished she was anywhere at all but there. The idea of sitting calmly at the table, facing Donal and Rick, seemed almost beyond her, but there was no way of avoiding it.

"I'll just go and say hi to Niall and Nicole first – " she began, but Kate nodded towards the next table and Clare could see them there, chatting to friends.

"They'll be here in a minute. You look really lovely, Clare."

Rick nodded his agreement, raising his glass in her direction. Donal, she noticed, seemed suddenly very interested in something Tish was saying, and was leaning across slightly to hear her. She had never seen Tish so chatty with him before.

"Are we waiting for someone else?" she asked Tish after a minute, indicating the remaining empty seat at the circular table.

The girl beamed at her. "Jody is coming – he'll be here soon."

Clare, glancing across towards Kate, saw that she was smiling, as were Rick and Donal. All was obviously forgiven.

Or was it? Clare wondered. She still wasn't sure that Rick had entirely forgiven her, though he showed all the signs of it. She wouldn't know until she had a chance to speak to him alone, and even then . . .

She chatted with Tish for a few minutes, moving up a seat when Jody arrived to let him in beside Tish. The look he and Tish gave each other was pure magic.

"If only I could bottle it," Clare thought.

Looking at them she felt . . . she wasn't quite sure what, and then it came to her – envious. She couldn't remember, for a moment, being quite so young, and quite so sure of what she wanted. It was obvious to anyone who looked at them that they were mad about each other. She hoped, as her mother would say, that it kept fine for them.

Suddenly it didn't seem too much to hope for, that things would work out well for them.

She turned to Nan, on her left, and began chatting about Niall and Nicole.

She hardly knew Nan, had only met her once or twice, briefly, but she looked transformed. Even her manner was different, more assured.

"Would you mind calling me Ann-Marie?" she asked Clare. "It's my real name, though I never used to use it – but Kevin thinks it suits me."

And when she turned to Kevin, laughing, to disagree with something he said, there was a spark there that was entirely new.

It was as if the Kinsellas were coming into their own, Clare thought. Sitting between them, pleased for them that they were so obviously happy, she was acutely aware of her own complicated emotions.

Rick, Donal and Kate, seated across from her, tried their best to draw her into the different conversations, but the table was slightly too large to do that with ease, even if she had felt relaxed enough to talk. So she sat there, isolated at her side of the table, thinking, I don't want to be here, I want to be here, dear God, I'm going to get this sorted out to-night, somehow, before I go mad.

She was rescued by Niall and Nicole arriving beside her, high as kites. She stood up to kiss them.

"You look wonderful, both of you!"

It was true. She had never seen Niall look happier, and he and Nicole could hardly take their eyes off each other. They went round the table, stopping for a word with everyone, basking in the warmth of it all.

"Now, come on, you lot," Niall said finally, smiling round at everyone. "I want to get the dancing going as soon as we can, and we need to get the food out of the way first. That's where you come in, Jody," he said, turning to him. "I want you to lead the way to the buffet, just remember to leave some for everyone else!"

Jody gave Niall a smart reply, grinning back at him. He was happy to oblige, and led Tish by the hand to take their place at the head of the queue, followed by the others at the table and from around the room, as Niall and Nicole continued on their rounds, encouraging everyone to do justice to the buffet so they could start the dancing.

"Are you all right, Clare?" Donal's voice was quiet as he stood behind her at the buffet.

"Fine. Well, a bit preoccupied, that's all."

"Deciding between beef or salmon?" His voice was gently teasing.

"Wish it were that simple!"

"It very often is, you know."

"But often it's not. And if you keep making the wrong choice, you end up afraid to choose at all – "

It wasn't what she meant to say. What was intended as light banter sounded suddenly more serious. She glanced at him quickly.

"Don't mind me. Like I said, I'm preoccupied."

This time, when they returned to the table, he sat beside her.

"Is everything all right between you and Rick? I was surprised when you didn't come with him," he said quietly, just before the others returned.

Jody and Tish were already sitting opposite them, but Jody was engrossed in the food and Tish was engrossed in him, and they were slightly too far away to hear the conversation anyway.

"I haven't seen much of him since the day we found Tish," Clare said. "Lunch on the Friday with them, that's all. But . . ."

She hesitated, not sure how much she wanted to say at this point, and the moment passed as the others came back.

The DJ was setting up in the corner just as they were finishing their meal.

"I can't wait to get up there dancing," she said to Donal.

She had never been more aware of his presence beside her. She felt nervous, yet relaxed, growing mellow from the wine and the company. Even with Rick she no longer felt awkward, chatting to him across Tish, who was now sitting between them.

Then the music started and it was as if all her senses came alive at once, willing Donal to ask her to dance, as Rick turned to Tish, saying, "Sorry, Jody. But we'll be right back."

Clare watched as he whisked her on to the floor, the two of the laughing, loving the music, hamming it up. She turned towards Donal as he began to say something, but Jim was at her side.

"Right, Clare. First dance – you promised!"

She laughed and went with him, glancing back in time to see Kevin and Nan – Ann-Marie, she reminded herself – following them.

Clare lost herself in the music, moving easily into the rhythm of it. From time to time, as she turned, she could see Donal sitting there watching her. She realised she had never seen him dance, wondered what he would be like, how it would feel to be with him . . . Her train of thought was broken by Niall who arrived just as the song finished.

"Okay, Jim, I'm borrowing her now."

He bent to whisper in the lad's ear, and Jim, grinning, touched Clare on the arm and went off.

"So what did you say to him?"

"That Tara Buckley is over there and if he wants to get to her before Matty Kane does, he'd better go now!"

"I didn't know he was interested in Tara Buckley."

"He wasn't. But he will be, she's grown up a lot this summer. And himself and Matty are arch-rivals."

"God, you're devious, Devlin. Did anyone ever tell you?"

"You did, hundreds of times! Anyway it's not deviousness, it's wanting to match-make for the whole world, now I'm in love myself."

"I thought you said you loved me?" she teased.

"I did, nearly ten years ago. And if you'd felt the same, who knows?"

"Admit it, Niall, you've never been happier."

"True." He whirled her round for a moment, drew her close as the music slowed.

"But what about you, Clare? What next?"

"What do you mean?"

"Come on, it's written all over you. At least, for someone who knows you like I do. You're going to have to choose, aren't you?"

"I've chosen."

"You'd better let him know."

"That's the hard part."

"No, Clare. I wouldn't say it's hard at all. He hasn't taken his eyes off you."

She danced away from him again, spinning round as the beat speeded up. He was right, she realised as she met Donal's gaze for the briefest of moments. He hadn't taken his eyes off her. She felt a fluttering in her stomach that had nothing to do with the wine.

Niall put his arm around her, leading her back to the table. He kissed her cheek, murmured "good luck" so quietly that only she could hear. Then he was gone, leaving her to sit beside Donal, with Kate and Rick at the far side of the table.

"Like to dance, Clare? Before you're whisked off again!"

She wasn't sure if she imagined a brief flash of disappointment on Donal's face as she stood up in response to Rick's invitation. The music was fast and loud, making conversation impossible. Clare was happy with that until the DJ announced a special request for Niall and Nicole, and as the slow number took off seamlessly where the previous song ended, Rick took her in his arms and drew her close.

I feel nothing, nothing at all, she thought, surprised. Not even embarrassment.

They danced like this for a minute or two, her head on his shoulder, and then he moved his head slightly to look at her.

"You know I love you, Clare."

He said it so softly that she had to strain to hear.

"Rick, I – "

"No, wait. Just listen to me first, okay?"

She nodded.

487

"I love you, probably always will, even though – "

"Rick – "

"Shhh." He held her a little more tightly, tenderly. "We need to talk. I go back Tuesday. Can we meet before that?"

"Yes, but – Rick, let's go outside. I'd prefer to talk now, okay?"

She led him towards the corner of the room, to the patio doors leading to the little garden at the back of the restaurant. She was glad to see, as she passed their table, that Donal was no longer there. She wouldn't want him to get the wrong idea.

There was a small fountain off to one side of the deserted courtyard, half-hidden by some shrubs, and she led him there, sitting on a low stone wall while he sat near her, their legs almost touching.

"Clare . . ."

"My turn, Rick – just for a minute."

She took a deep breath. "I don't want to hurt you. It's hard to know what to say. It's just that . . ." She hesitated.

"Let me make it easier, then." His voice was soft, gentle. "I know you don't love me."

She looked at him, relieved. Then she spoke again, choosing her words carefully.

"I didn't know that myself, until New York. I wasn't just stringing you along, Rick. I went there ready to see how it worked out – I wish it had been different."

"You don't, really, do you? Because if that's what you wanted, then it could have worked. You want something else. Someone else."

"How do you – ?"

"I've seen how he looks at you, how you look at him. It's – what's that expression Kate uses? It's written all over you."

"I didn't know, Rick. Honestly. I didn't realise that last night, when we were together, or I'd never have – I'm sorry."

"I'm not."

"No?"

"No. Because if things had been different that night, I mightn't have got to know about Tish."

"You would have. Not then, but it would only have been a matter of time."

"Maybe. But I've lost too much time already."

He stood up, held out a hand to her.

"I love you, Clare." He was looking into her eyes and she felt tears in her own. "I'll probably always love you."

He reached out, touching the trace of a tear on her cheek. "And I'll remember, always, that you brought me to Tish. And sometimes I'll maybe wish it could have been different. You're a very special woman, Clare Delaney."

"Rick . . ."

"And we can be friends, right? I'd prefer that than – nothing."

She nodded, not trusting herself to speak.

He put his hands on her shoulders. "I hope you have a happy life with him, Clare." He moved forward slightly, kissed her lightly on the cheek.

"Let's go back inside. It's getting cold." He took her hand and together they went back into the crowded room.

Donal was standing just inside the patio door, talking to a young woman Clare didn't recognise. He looked at them for moment, then leaned forward to say something to the woman and they moved together to join the dancers.

Rick turned to Clare with an apologetic half-smile. "Maybe I should leave – Jody will see that Tish gets back safely."

"No, don't be silly – you're enjoying it, aren't you?"

She hadn't taken her eyes off Donal as she spoke. He looked animated, laughing at something his partner was saying. He was, Clare noticed, a very good dancer.

"I'm loving it," Rick replied. "And part of that is just being able to stand here and watch Tish. I really can't wait to be back here with her." He paused. "Would you mind if I were living here?"

She didn't even hesitate.

"Not at all, not if we can be like this. And Tish will be thrilled."

He laughed. "While Jody's around she'll hardly even notice me. But she's agreed to spend Christmas in the States."

"That's great."

He smiled. "Great is too small a word. You've no idea how wonderful it is, finding a daughter I didn't even know I had. I'll always owe you that, Clare."

They began to move towards the table where Kate was

sitting alone, but were side-tracked by Jack who had just arrived. By the time the three of them reached the table Donal was already there, his jacket over one arm.

"You're leaving?" Rick asked.

Donal nodded.

Clare glanced quickly at Kate, who gave a slight shrug of her shoulders.

"I've tried to talk him out of it, but he won't be budged."

"If you're going, would you give me a lift?" Clare surprised even herself as she spoke.

Rick and Kate exchanged the briefest of smiles.

"You're sure?" Donal asked.

"Certain – if you don't mind." It was as if they were alone. The others no longer existed.

"No, of course I don't mind. But – "

Rick touched her lightly on the shoulder, saying "Bye, Clare," as he moved away. She barely noticed. Jack, aware that something was going on, but not sure what, told Kate that he was going in search of a drink, and asked if he should bring something back.

"I'll come with you," she replied.

Clare and Donal stood facing each other, alone on the edge of a crowded room.

"Are you all right, Clare?"

She nodded.

"So why are you going?"

She took a deep breath. "Because you are."

Her eyes never left his, watching the hope finally flicker.

"And if I stay?" He asked it quietly.

"Then I will."

"And – Rick?"

"It's over. It never began, really."

His smile was like the sun coming up. "So. Are you sure you want to go? Or . . ."

"I'd like to stay a bit longer," she said. "I'd like to dance with you."

Never taking his eyes from her, he dropped the jacket on the chair and reached out his hand. They were barely aware of the music, the soft lights, the buzz of laughter and conversation all around them. Right now, there were only the two of them, arms around each other, moving together, lost in their own private world.

And it felt like coming home.

Chapter Thirty-four

"Did you see it coming, Kate?" Niall asked as he sat down beside her for a minute.

"I don't know that I did, exactly. But it's what I hoped for since the first time I saw them together."

"Just look at them. And she says *I* look happy!"

"And so you do. She's a lovely girl, Niall. You couldn't have done better than Nicole."

"And Donal couldn't have done better than he's doing right this minute."

Kate nodded her agreement, smiling as she watched the two of them dancing. She'd hardly taken her eyes off them for the past hour.

He had left the table when Jack sat down beside her.

"You're a lucky woman, Kate." He spoke quietly, though there was no-one else at the table just then.

She looked at him for a moment before answering.

"Yes. I know that, now."

"Kate – "

He hesitated, not sure how to continue. He looked unsettled, not quite at home in the new navy suit, not quite himself without the cloth cap he usually wore.

She waited.

He cleared his throat, finding it hard to look at her.

"I'm sorry, Kate."

Again she waited, meeting his gaze steadily when he finally looked at her.

"It was a long time ago, Jack. We were young. It's water under the bridge."

"No, Kate." He hesitated again. She could see the effort this was costing him. "Not water under the bridge – that's gone and forgotten." He met her eyes, glanced away again, looking down at his hands. "But I never forgot you, Kate. All the years you were away, I never forgot."

"You did nothing about it." Her voice was sharp.

"What could I do?" he asked. "After letting you down, I was too much of a coward to face you. And I'll regret that for the rest of my life."

"There's a lot to regret, Jack. More than you know."

"How do you mean?" He was leaning towards her now, watching her intently.

"I can't tell you yet. Not now. But I will, very soon. I promise you that."

He nodded, only half-satisfied, then reached out and took a sip of the pint in front of him.

"I often wondered what it would have been like."

"The two of us?" she asked.

He nodded, and she followed his gaze to where the

Mahons, a couple they had known more than forty years ago, were dancing.

"It might have worked, Jack. I always thought it could have. You know that."

His look was wistful when he turned to her.

"Wasn't I the fool."

"More than you know. But it's past, now."

He smiled now, a slow smile that reached his eyes, and she realised, with some surprise, that he had probably never stopped loving her. She felt a sharp, fleeting pain at the waste of it all.

"Would you dance with me, Kate?" In the depths of his eyes there was a spark of devilment that she recognised.

She laughed. "Why not? Give them all something to talk about."

And they stood up, slipping into an old-time waltz as if they had been dancing together all their lives. Neither of them noticed when Clare and Donal finally left, just after one o'clock, though everyone else did.

Niall, dancing with Nicole, grinned as he saw them go. "About time," he murmured to Nicole, then forgot all about them as he kissed her.

Clare was vibrant with anticipation on the journey home. She wanted to kiss him, wanted to hold him, couldn't stop herself reaching out every minute or two to touch his arm as they talked.

And she couldn't stop talking.

It was as if they had known each other forever, yet didn't know each other at all. Now that she could finally admit to loving him, she wanted to know every single thing about him. Even the things she already knew took on a different meaning. Everything had changed. She had changed herself, seeing this man as if for the first time. She wondered how she could have been so blind. She couldn't take her eyes from his face as he drove.

It didn't take long to reach the cottage.

"You're coming in?"

"No, I'm not."

Before she had time to be upset his arms were around her and they were kissing, unable to get enough of each other, until finally she broke away and drew breath.

"Why not?"

He laughed, shakily. "Because of this. If I go in – "

"I don't want you to go. Come on in, we'll just have coffee, listen to some music . . ."

"And that's all?" He was smiling. "Who exactly are you trying to fool?"

He buried his face in the richness of her hair.

"God knows, I want you, Clare. I want to make love to you this very minute, if it's what you want. But . . ."

She waited, but he didn't continue.

"Donal."

"Mmm?" His face was still in her hair, his lips warm against her neck.

"No, wait. Stop," she said softly, pulling away from him slightly. "I have to say this, Donal, and I want you to listen."

He looked at her now, his eyes meeting hers in the soft light from the cottage window.

"Rick and I – no, listen," she said, as she saw his expression. "We didn't sleep together, Donal."

"It's none of my business."

"But I want you to know. We nearly did. I like him a lot, I got carried away. But I couldn't do it."

"Clare – "

"Because of you. That's what stopped me. I just didn't realise that – "

Her eyes never left his, and what she saw there gave her courage.

"I love you, Donal. I've loved you for a long time, I just didn't know it."

His lips were on hers and then he drew away, speaking softly against her cheek.

"I think I started loving you that first day I saw you struggling with the bench, yourself and Kate. And your hair was all over the place, and you had dirt on your face, and I wanted to reach out and rub it away. And then you laid into me for wanting to move the bench on my own – "

"I did not!"

"You did indeed. Your eyes were blazing, you were raging at me. But there was such a warmth about you that it was all I could do to stop myself reaching out and touching you. For the first time since Jenny, I knew I'd found a woman I could love."

He was holding her hands as he spoke, his long fingers curled against her palms.

"Why didn't you say something?" she asked softly.

"I couldn't. Even to think of someone else like that,

after Jen, felt – I don't know – like a kind of betrayal. And when I finally realised I loved you and that it was myself I was betraying, it was too late, you were with Rick. It nearly killed me when you went to the see him – I thought I'd lost my chance. And then, when Tish ran off . . ."

"You didn't use it an excuse?"

"God, no. No. I was beside myself – I wasn't thinking straight, I just knew I needed you there to help me get through it. And you did."

He reached to caress her cheek. "But I still wasn't sure how things were with you and Rick."

"You could have asked."

He gave a wry smile. "That would have been too simple, wouldn't it? No, I didn't want to put any pressure on you – "

"And I thought you weren't interested."

He laughed, leaned forward to kiss her gently. "Clare, are you sure – ?"

"I'm certain."

They kissed again, for a long time, before he moved slightly away.

"Come on, let's go for a walk on the beach."

"Are you mad?" She smiled at him in the half-light. "It's nearly two in the morning."

"It's not even half one yet," he said. "And there's a full moon. Where's your sense of romance?"

"It died of frostbite."

He laughed. "I'll lend you my jacket. Come on, it's not that cold. Just for a few minutes."

"Promise?"

"Promise. We'll come back if it's too cold for you."

"Okay. I'll just go and get some decent shoes – "

"No."

"But – "

"If you go in, I'll go with you, and I wouldn't trust myself to leave tonight."

She laughed quietly as she got out of the car. "There are worse things."

"True," he said, coming to join her, taking her hand to lead her towards the laneway down to the beach. "There are worse things, like getting too involved, and then regretting it."

"You think you might regret it?"

They had reached the end of the grassy laneway, were scrambling over the few rocks between it and the beach. He put his arm around her to steady her as she balanced precariously in her high heels on the last of the rocks. He lifted her down and they stood facing each other in the moonlight.

"Only if I lost you." They stood for a moment, arms around each other, before he took her hand. "Come on, let's walk. I promised you wouldn't get cold."

Clare bent to slip off her shoes. Then, barefoot, her shoes in one hand and the other still in Donal's, she walked with him through the soft sands towards the edge of the sea. His jacket around her shoulders protected her from the slight chill of the sea breeze. She felt as if she would stay there forever with the warmth of him beside her, the sound of his voice resonant above the quiet splashing of the waves, the light of the full moon making a pathway through the water, lighting up the two small fishing boats that rode at anchor in the bay.

They stopped to look out at the boats, arms around each other, enjoying the soft sounds and the smell of the ocean, the sense of absolute peace beneath the starry sky.

"Come on, we'd better go," he said finally.

"I'd rather stay. It's beautiful here."

"Another five minutes, before it gets too cold."

"I'm not a bit cold. I'd stay forever!"

He laughed. "You'll be on your own, so."

They walked for another few minutes, talking quietly, until a sudden sharp breeze from the sea caught them.

"Come on, before I freeze to death," he said. Laughing, he put his arms around her waist, surprising her by how easily he lifted her and swung her around. Then, hand in hand, laughing together like children, they ran towards the lane.

"When can I see you?" he asked, as they stood at the door of the cottage a few minutes later.

"Tomorrow?"

"Great. We could go to dinner in Roundstone, if you like."

"Niall would kill us."

"Niall won't know." He kissed her again, finally stopping to say that he'd go while he still could.

"Pity," she smiled.

"Clare, if – "

"No, go on. See you tomorrow."

After a last kiss she went in, feeling as if she were in a dream. She wandered round the cottage, switching off lights, getting ready for bed. The cottage seemed like home again. The empty feeling was gone.

She lay awake for a long time that night, thinking about him, planning how she would fill her day until she could see him again.

Chapter Thirty-five

Clare felt as if she were nineteen again. That sense of exhilaration, of every moment being magical – she couldn't remember when she had last felt it. It was like being in love for the very first time. Better, because this time she knew for certain how precious it was, how right it felt.

They spent every spare minute together, totally absorbed in each other. Though they dined out two or three nights a week they could hardly have said where, or what they ate. But they could have repeated every word the other had said, and given every detail of what they wore, and how they looked, and what it felt like when their hands touched briefly across the table.

And sometimes it seemed that nothing in the world meant more than this touching, and talking, and being together.

Everyone knew, of course, that they were seeing each other. They had left the party, apparently with Rick's blessing, leaving a trail of speculation behind them. But their friends were careful to give them space. Even Niall, when he phoned, made no comment, and Kate said nothing either but fussed over them quietly and went around with a smile of pure delight. They had a sense of being looked after, protected. It was as if the whole world was on their side.

Gradually their days fell into a pattern. After a few weeks they no longer went out so much, preferring to cook in one house or the other, usually Donal's during the week so that he could catch up on preparation for his classes. These times, when the twins were finally in bed, were for her and Donal alone.

"You're sure you don't mind?" he asked one evening, as they sat in front of the fire with glasses of wine, beginning to relax in the silence. "It's not the most exciting way to spend your time."

She leaned over, snuggling against him.

"Actually, right now it is," she said, smiling. "I don't need to go out every night, you know – I'm happy here."

And she was. She loved to watch him as he sat at the table in the big sitting-room with his books spread in front of him, remembering how she had done that when he stayed at the cottage. But now she knew she was doing it, and so did he. She would reach out to touch him from time to time, and he would turn and smile, and they would each go back to their reading, music playing softly in the background.

Sometimes they read to each other and she would curl up in the chair opposite him in the soft light, loving the rich sound of his voice, the words of poems she half-remembered from school. And when he read aloud words of love, new or hundreds of years old, it sometimes felt as if they had been written for them alone.

And always there was that slight, anticipatory tension between them, while they hovered on the brink of full commitment.

"What do you mean, you haven't been to bed with him yet?" Ruth had demanded during one of her frequent phone-calls.

"None of your business, Ruthie!" Clare had laughed. "We'll decide what to do, and when."

"You are my business, sis."

"Not that much, I'm not!"

"Clare . . ."

"Mmm?"

"I know you're finished with Rick – "

"He was never really in the running, Ruth. I just didn't know it."

"Right. Okay. But – you haven't let that bastard Tony totally spoil things for you, have you? I mean, what's stopping you? You're thirty-two, Donal's – ?"

"Thirty-five."

"Right. And you love each other, so where's the problem?"

"We're just taking it slowly, Ruth. No mad decisions. I've made enough mistakes."

"I don't think he's a mistake."

"Neither do I. But I'm still taking it slowly. And so is he."

"Well, okay, if that's what you want." Ruth still didn't sound convinced. "Just don't let him escape, okay?"

Clare was laughing as she hung up.

The weeks were full, and passed quickly, so that it was the middle of October almost before they realised. They still walked on the beach as often as they could, particularly in the early evening, or at night, when there was no-one else around. Kate was happy to mind the boys, or Annmarie and Kevin would stay with them if they weren't going out themselves.

Kate never commented, not wanting to put pressure on anyone, but it was obvious that she was pleased as punch about both relationships. The only thing troubling her world was her concern about Molly.

"She's not well at all, you know," Kate told Donal one evening as she sat in his kitchen with him. She had just come back from a few days in Dublin and the change in Molly had alarmed her.

"There's something up," Kate said, "but she won't tell me what. You know Molly, she's insisting everything is fine."

"I'll go up myself," Donal said. "She's put me off a few times on the phone, but I'm long overdue a visit."

"You told her about Clare," Kate said.

"I did, and in a way I'm sorry – that's her excuse now for not letting me go up – she says I'm too busy here. Did she mention her?"

Kate was just about to answer when the back door opened and Clare walked in. She looked from one serious face to the other and, apologising for the interruption, said she'd go and talk to the twins.

""We'll go for a walk in a minute," Donal said. "Can you stay with the boys, Kate? Just for half an hour or so?" he asked as Clare left the kitchen.

She nodded. "Take your time, love. I'm in no hurry."

They sat talking quietly until Clare came back in with the boys, then Donal got his jacket and they left the warm kitchen to go out into the dark evening.

They were silent on the short journey to the beach. The sky was threatening a storm, dark clouds blotting out the early stars, but the rain hadn't yet begun to fall. A stiff breeze was stirring the waves, and she was glad of Donal's arm around her as they made towards the shoreline.

She had to strain slightly to hear his voice above the sound of the sea.

"Maybe this wasn't such a good idea," he said. "Do you want to head back?"

"Tell me, first," she said. "I know that's why you brought me out here."

He hesitated for a moment, then stopped and turned to face her.

"Molly's not great. You know Kate was up with her. She's insisting herself that she's fine, but . . ." His voice trailed off.

"How long since you've seen her?"

"Too long, five or six weeks. I know she's hiding something, she won't let me come up. Even on the phone, sometimes, I feel she's making an effort."

"So you'll go up?" Clare asked.

He nodded, looking away out over the sea. "I should have gone before this and not let her put me off. But you know I've been up to my eyes with classes, and then – "

He turned back to smile at her.

"I've taken up every minute. God, I'm sorry, Donal, I should have – "

"Clare, I wanted to spend every minute with you. You know that. I'll go up next week, at mid-term break."

The rain began to fall, big, soaking drops.

"Come on," he said, taking her hand as they ran back to the car. He drove for only a few minutes before stopping outside a small pub.

"A quick drink?" he asked. "Or are you wet? Do you want to get back and change?"

"No, I'm fine. A bit damp, that's all. I wouldn't mind sitting in front of a fire for a few minutes."

They found a quiet corner of the pub, beside the smouldering turf fire. At this early hour there were only two or three other customers there, local farmers by the look of them, in the well-worn suits and cloth caps that were almost a uniform. Clare glanced over at them, returning their nods of greeting, while Donal got the drinks.

"That should help," he said, putting a small glass of whiskey in front of her. "It wasn't one of my better ideas, in that weather, but I wanted to get out into the fresh air, and have a few minutes on our own as well."

Clare grimaced as the first sip of the burning liquid caught at the back of her throat.

"I don't know why I like this stuff, but I do. Especially on a night like this."

She took another sip, savouring it this time. "So, will you take the twins with you?"

"No. I'm sure Kate will be happy to keep an eye on them. I haven't planned anything, I just decided to go when I was talking to Kate earlier. I'll probably stay a few days, go up on Friday, see her that night, then see how it goes. I don't have to be back until Monday night." He sipped his drink, his expression distant. "I have to admit I'm worried about her."

They finished the drinks and left, not wanting to delay Kate.

She was delighted when she heard he was going to Dublin.

"It's a good idea. I don't want to frighten you, but I wasn't happy at all with the look of her."

"You don't mind having the boys?"

"Not a bit, you know that."

"I'll give you a hand with them," Clare offered.

"I'll be fine. But thanks, I'll shout if I need you," Kate answered, getting up as they heard a knock at the door. "Kevin, he said he'd call in for me," she said as the door opened. "And he's on time for once, because he's rushing to see a match."

"Be good, you two," Kevin said as he whisked Kate out the door before they had a chance to say a word.

"Look who's talking," Donal laughed as he took Clare by the hand and led her to the couch in front of the big open fire that dominated the kitchen. She leaned her head on his shoulder, watching the sparks as they flew upwards. There was silence except for the crackle of the flames. Kate had worked magic – the twins were sound asleep.

Donal stretched his legs out towards the fire, put his arm around Clare, then glanced at her jeans.

"They're soaked," he commented. "Sure you don't want to take them off?"

"And then what?"

"Oh, we'll think of something." He had a wicked grin, she decided, as his other arm went round her and he kissed her, touching her cheek, her arm . . .

"Clare – " It was a ragged whisper.

"Mmm?" she said, willing him to go on kissing her, reluctant to pull herself away from the sensations, the melting warmth.

"Clare – " He kissed her again, briefly, before pulling back, his hands on her shoulders. "Would you come to Dublin with me?"

"Of course." She moved towards him, ready to kiss him again.

"No, wait. Hold on. I mean, would you stay with me? Somewhere outside Dublin, for a night or two . . ."

She laughed. "I thought you'd never ask!"

"You're sure?"

"Positive. And you?"

He looked into her eyes. "Oh, yes."

They were lost in each other for a few moments, until a sound from the top of the stairs made them spring apart. Donal laughed ruefully.

"You see why I need to get you away from here?"

Clare smiled at him, brushing back her hair, straightening her blouse.

"I do. It reminds me of when I was sixteen, in the front room at home with my first boyfriend, and my father knocking on the ceiling in the middle of the night to remind him it was time to leave!"

"The middle of the night?" He was laughing at her.

"It was all very innocent," she said, grinning at him. "You'd better get on up to those scamps of yours. Ring me tomorrow?"

"Of course. You wouldn't prefer to stay tonight, in the spare room?" They could hear the rain still pelting against the windows.

"You know we wouldn't do that. I'll be fine, I'll be home in a few minutes."

"Well, if you're sure – " He brushed back a strand of her hair. "Clare, if you change your mind about coming with me . . ."

"I won't."

They kissed again, briefly this time, and she slipped out the door as he went to see to the twins.

He rang the following evening just as she came in from feeding the animals. She thought she might ask Jack or Jody to look after them while she was away; Kate would have enough to keep her busy with the boys.

"I've booked somewhere," Donal told her. "A country house, just off the motorway, a lovely place. About ten miles out. I thought you might prefer that to somewhere in the city."

"It sounds perfect. I was going to ring Ruth and tell her I'd be around, but I had second thoughts."

"Good – I want you all to myself for a few days, as much as we can, once I've seen Molly. I thought about us staying in my own place, but . . ."

"No, you were right," she replied firmly. "This is better."

"Fine. Can I pick you up on Friday, early? I'll be up to my eyes tomorrow, sorting stuff for the boys – "

"Need a hand?"

"Thanks, but I have a system – of sorts!"

"Friday, then."

"Friday, at about ten. Love you, Clare."

"And I love you." She was glowing as she hung up the phone.

Chapter Thirty-six

Thursday morning was busy as she sorted out what she wanted to bring. Normally when she went home for the weekend she just took jeans and some jumpers, and maybe one decent dress. And an old tee-shirt for a night-dress.

But this was different .

She packed and unpacked the bag three times before she was happy. When it was finally done, and the animals were looked after, she decided to cycle over to Kate. She found her in her big, bright studio, surrounded by canvases.

"My God, Kate, it all looks wonderful," she said, stunned as much by the studio itself as by the multitude of paintings. Kate made a wonderful picture herself as she stood, paintbrush in hand, her hair caught back loosely with a purple silk scarf that echoed the swirling pattern of her long skirt.

"You've seen it before, surely?" she asked, putting down the brush and leading the way through conservatory into the kitchen.

"No, not since it was finished. It's completely transformed. And the conservatory is brilliant – all that space for hanging the paintings. You'll have to mind when summer comes, though."

"That's a long way off," Kate laughed as she put on the kettle. "And the way things are going already, it won't be a problem. I hardly have time to hang them before they're bought."

"You must be dead pleased with Kevin."

"Oh, I am. And with Niall – he's sending me all my customers."

"Things have really changed for you, haven't they, Kate?" Clare said as she sat at the kitchen table, looking through the new window at the sea in the distance.

"Indeed they have. I don't know myself. I sit here in the mornings with a cup of tea, looking out at that view, thinking how blessed I am."

She made the tea and brought it to the table, sitting down opposite Clare.

"Sometimes I think about the people who built the cottage," Kate said. "How hard they had to work, how they had more on their minds than windows looking out on the sea. I feel I'm having the life of a lady here now."

"If you are you deserve it, Kate. You haven't always had it easy, have you?"

"No, I suppose not," Kate said, glancing through the window again as she idly stirred the tea. "But it feels as if everything is finally coming together now. Everything is beginning to go right, if only I wasn't so worried about Molly. I'm glad Donal is going up tomorrow."

"Me too," Clare said. "I think he's more worried than he's letting on."

Kate took a sip of her tea before asking casually "Is he going on his own?"

"Why, what did he say?" Clare asked her, burying a smile in her own tea-cup.

"Not a word. But it doesn't stop me jumping to conclusions."

The two of them were beaming openly at each other now.

"I'm delighted, Clare. I really am. It's what I was hoping for."

"It is?"

Kate nodded. "Better than I hoped for, even. I've been praying for a long time that he'd meet someone who'd be good for him. And the more I got to know you . . ."

She reached across the table to touch Clare's hand.

"You're nearly like a daughter to me, Clare, do you know that? I couldn't wish for anything better than to see the two of you together."

She paused as they heard a knock at the door, was about to get up when it opened and Jack looked in.

"It was on the latch . . ." he said, looking a bit embarrassed when he saw Clare.

"Come on in, Jack, have a cup of tea," Kate said, smiling as she stood up.

"I won't stop, I have to be back to let Jody get away. I'm just dropping in a few fish I got, I thought you might use them."

He dropped a bag just inside the door and a moment

later he was gone, pulling the cap down over his eyes as he went through the gateway to the road. They watched him through the open doorway as he went, a tall man in an old navy suit and heavy boots, as much a part of the landscape as the hills and the low stone walls.

"You're getting on well with him now, Kate?"

The older woman nodded a response, not meeting Clare's eyes.

"I used to have the impression you weren't that easy with each other," Clare added, pouring herself some more tea.

Kate stood up quickly. "I'll throw out that stuff – it's gone cold. It'll only take a minute to make a fresh pot."

"No. really, it's fine."

But Kate had already lifted the cups and teapot and was on her way to the sink. She seemed to take a bit longer than was necessary, and was silent while she made the fresh tea. Finally she brought it back to the table.

"Maybe I shouldn't have said anything – " Clare began.

"No, no, it's all right." This time Kate was able to look at her. "You're right, we haven't been this easy with each other in a long time."

"Do you know him well, Kate? I was never sure – "

Kate lifted the tea-pot, began pouring the fresh tea, concentrating on it. She passed a cup to Clare and sat stirring her own for a moment, staring down into it, until finally she looked across at Clare and began to speak so quietly that Clare had to strain to hear her.

"There was a time I knew him very well. A long time ago. A time when he was all the world to me."

She took a sip of her tea, looking down into its depths as if she could see her past reflected there. "He was the first boy I ever went with. We were young, I was just gone nineteen and he was barely a year older."

"I thought – "

"What? That he was much older than me? That's how it seems now, he's worn down from that farm of his. I hope it was worth it to him."

There was a flash of bitterness that Clare had never seen before in her. She waited for Kate to continue, finally prompting her.

"What happened, Kate?"

"I loved him, that's what happened. And he loved me. We couldn't get enough of each other, we thought we'd spend a lifetime together. Oh, we had great plans. You can do that when you're young, make great plans. Only his family had other plans, and they didn't include me."

She sat quietly, lost in her thoughts. "So we did the only thing we could. We went away together, for ten wonderful days. And when they found us, in Dublin, they made us come back."

"And?" Clare asked gently.

"And that was the end of it. The end of everything."

"But, why did you agree to come? I mean, at that age – " Clare paused, not sure how to continue.

"We could have gone against them? Is that what you think?"

Clare nodded.

"I thought so too. I would have done anything to be

with him. But he wouldn't do it, he wouldn't stand up to them."

"Why not?"

Kate had a faraway expression now. "People didn't in those days, Clare. He said it would kill his father. Maybe it would have, I don't know. And maybe that would have been no harm."

"Kate, you don't mean that!"

"How do you know, Clare?" Her voice was tight with anger now. "How do you know what I mean? You don't know what it was like, that bastard running his son's life, and mine, and his son letting him do it! So don't tell me what I mean!"

"I'm sorry, Kate, I – "

"And I am." The voice was quieter now, gentle. "I shouldn't have gone off the handle like that. But it still hurts, even after all these years. The waste of it all, the loss of what we could have had. And all because he wouldn't stand up to that old man."

"What was their objection, anyway, Kate? Do you know?"

"Oh, I know all right – they made it very clear. I wasn't good enough for them, that was the problem. I came from a small bit of a farm, and they had notions of themselves. I wasn't what they wanted for their only son. They wanted someone with a bit of style who could grace that grand house of theirs, someone with money to her name. I wasn't what they had in mind at all."

"But if he loved you . . ."

"He loved me all right. I never doubted that. But love

didn't come into it. They wouldn't see it like that, and, as I said, he wouldn't go against them. Not completely, anyway. Not to the extent of marrying me."

"So he never married? Or – "

"No, you're right. He never married. They had a girl picked out for him, a friend of his sister's. An only child, all set to inherit a farm about five miles away."

Kate was lost again for a few moments, before looking up with a smile. "She was a grand girl, you know. I knew her well, and maybe she was a bit above herself, but she might have made a good wife for him."

"But he didn't marry her."

"No. No, he refused to do it. He stood up to them there, saying if he couldn't marry me, he'd marry no-one. But he wouldn't go the one step further and marry me anyway, in spite of them."

They were silent for a while, thinking of how different things might have been.

"Would it really have mattered so much to them, in the long run?" Clare asked finally.

Kate's smile was wry.

"Who can say, in the long run? But yes, I think it would have mattered. I think they would never have spoken his name again. They were like that."

"But that's awful!" Clare's expression was horrified.

"I know," Kate answered. "Awful. But they were different times, Clare. Ireland was a different place then. What we did wouldn't matter a jot now, going off to Dublin together; but then it was a scandal for both families. The wonder of it was that they didn't drag us in front of the priest when we got back. I suppose Jack was half-hoping for that, that he could force their hand and they'd get used to the idea. But it didn't work out like that."

"How did your own parents react?"

"My parents. God, my parents."

She sighed. "That was a different story. My father was a drunkard all his life, and as long as he had a few bob for the pub he didn't care what happened. So it was easy for the Stauntons to pay him off."

She paused, stirred the tea that was cooling in her cup. "It was my mother I was sorry about. She was my only regret, that she was mortified and heartsick at it all. But she never said a word against me, God rest her. Instead she took what little money she had and gave it to me, and I went up to stay with Molly for a while in Dublin, until it all died down and I could come back. Only I didn't come back, not then, not for a long time. I went across to England instead."

"And Jack stayed here."

"That's right, Jack stayed here," Kate answered, and her eyes were bright now, but with anger, not tears. "He stayed here, but he had no heart for the place after that. And his sisters married, and the other girl married, and his father never forgave him until the day he died, for not marrying that girl and getting her farm. And Jack has paid for it every day of his life. I've watched him, working his life away on that farm and keeping it for some niece or nephew who couldn't even find it on a map, let alone visit him."

"So what kept him here, Kate, after they died?"

"What else would he do, girl? He was in his fifties by the time they went. Too late for him to make changes – and besides, where would he go?"

"It's never too late, Kate. He could have sold the place – "

"After what it cost him? No, he could never do that. Though he doesn't know the half of what it cost him. And as for changing . . ." She made an impatient noise. "You have to want to change, Clare. If I know anything, I know that. And if he hadn't the courage for it back then, when he was young and I would have followed him anywhere, how could he do it now?"

"Are you still angry with him, Kate?"

The eyes that met Clare's were rimmed with tears.

"Not now. Not after all this time. Oh, I was, until I used to think sometimes that I could kill him with my bare hands, for what he did to me. But now . . ."

She sighed, stretched out her hands palms downwards, sat looking at them. "Now I'm just sad. The waste of it all, Clare. And what we lost, what we could have had, if he had only stood up to them."

Clare looked at her, slow realisation dawning as she remembered something Kate had told her a long time ago, a lifetime ago at the beginning of the summer. Surely not. But –

"Kate?" The urgency of her tone caught the older woman, made her stand up and start moving cups from the table.

"We'll leave it now, Clare. I've said too much already,

I never meant to. It's just that it's on my mind so much."
She turned and went to the sink with the cups, her back
stiff and heavy as she stood there rinsing them.

Clare hesitated, uncertain whether to say anything
more. She didn't want to upset Kate further, but if she
was right . . .

"Does he know, Kate?" She held her breath.

Kate turned sharply. "Does he know what?"

"Kate, maybe I've got it all wrong – and it's nothing
to do with me . . ."

She waited for Kate to object but she didn't. Instead
she said, warily, "Go on."

"You told me months ago that you had a decision to
make. And – well, that you had another son."

Kate stood there, wiping her hands over and over on
the red-and-white checked tea-towel. She said nothing
at all until finally she put down the towel and stood
with her arms crossed in front of her, protectively.

"I never told him, Clare. He doesn't know he has a
child."

"Kate! But why not? Surely – ?"

"He would have married me then? Oh, yes – I'm
certain of it. But I loved him too much to do that to him."

"But – did you never think of telling him?"

"Of course I thought of telling him. Every minute of
every day for seven long months when I knew for
certain. And even after that, until I finally decided what
to do. But telling him would have made no difference. It
would only have forced him into doing what he wasn't
prepared to do otherwise."

"He had a right – "

"Rights." Her voice sounded weary. "Don't talk to me about rights, Clare. I hadn't the luxury of rights. If he had to give up a child, at least he did it without knowing, without it tearing the heart out of him." Her eyes were bright with tears as she spoke. "We'll leave it now, Clare. I never meant to say any of this, not yet. Not until I talk to someone else first, and then I'll have to find the words to tell Jack what he lost. What all of us lost."

"Kate – "

"Leave it now, Clare. And promise you won't breathe a word. Not even to Donal, or to Kevin. He doesn't know, and maybe I shouldn't have told you. But it's a lot to carry on my own, all this time."

"No-one else knows?"

"Molly knew from the beginning. I'd have been lost without her."

Kate bit her lip and looked away towards the window.

"We'll ring you tomorrow night, Kate, after Donal has seen her."

Kate came over to her, a slight smile on her face now as she reached to touch Clare's cheek.

"I'm sure you'll have other things on your mind!" Her hand slipped to Clare's shoulder, and she stood, still smiling at her. "Take good care of each other, Clare. Don't leave any room for missed chances and regrets."

"We won't, Kate."

They turned to go out through the conservatory, Kate's arm still around Clare's shoulder, and as they passed by a little easel set up there Clare stopped, stunned by the power of the portrait that sat on it. Jack. Not a younger Jack – a Jack in his fifties, but without the cap, and with a different expression in his eyes. Not the defeated look he usually had, Clare realised.

And then she realised something else.

"You still love him," she said quietly, turning to Kate.

"I never stopped."

"Oh, Kate!"

Clare hugged her, looking at the sad eyes, then back at those eyes in the portrait, so different, yet familiar . . .

Kate caught her expression. "I didn't mean anyone to see it. Not yet, anyway. Now go on, you've to get ready and I've work to do."

"We'll ring you."

"Do that, and then maybe I can put my mind at ease."

She stood in the doorway watching as Clare mounted her bike and began free-wheeling down the hill. Then she went back into the conservatory and sat for a long time, looking at the portrait, thinking of what might have been.

She was still sitting there when Donal phoned. His voice was raw; she had to ask him twice before she knew what he was saying.

And finally she understood, and clutched the phone tightly to her and gave a long, low cry of pain.

And then he repeated it, in a voice as ragged as her cry.

"She's dead, Kate. My mother is dead."

Chapter Thirty-seven

The wind off the sea at Clontarf was sharp, but Donal was glad of it. He needed the stinging sensation on his cheeks, needed something immediate to take his mind off the scene in the cemetery. Another coffin, another grave – and two distraught little boys, crying their hearts out again.

That had been the hardest part of all, trying to find the words to tell them. When he got the phone call from the hospital he had wanted to sweep them up into his arms, run with them and keep going, anywhere, anything rather than have to tell them again that someone they loved was dead.

He'd never have got through it without Kate. She was back in his house now with Clare and Ruth, looking after the boys, clearing up, doing whatever she could. She hadn't stopped since Friday, helping him organise the funeral, preparing Molly's house for the neighbours who would call. And the relatives, some of them people he hardly knew, all sitting formally in the little front parlour, Molly's "good" room. All trying to think of the right things to say at a time when there were no right things, only awkwardness and, for him, a numbing sense of loss. A sense that nothing could reach him but this sharp pain, and nothing could lift the guilt of neglecting her these past months.

He turned to walk along the shoreline, shoulders hunched against the wind. If only –

"That's the surest way to go mad, love, thinking about all the 'if onlys'."

He jumped, as startled as if he had really heard her voice above the sound of the sea and the whistle of the wind. That's what she used to say to him after Jenny died. It's what she'd say now if she were here.

Sighing, he turned again and began the walk back to the house. It would take twenty minutes or so. He wondered if everyone would have gone, regretted his rudeness in leaving like that when they had all come back with him after the funeral. But he'd had no choice – he couldn't take another minute surrounded by everyone. He'd had to get out, to be alone.

He'd seen the hurt in Clare's expression, found he didn't really care. He couldn't care about anything right now. Except the boys. And Molly, and Jenny. Sweet Jesus, he didn't know if he could bear this all over again.

The house was quiet when he got there. Kate was sitting in the living-room, curled up on the couch with a child on either side, nestling into her.

"They've nearly all left, love," she said. "David said he'll ring later."

He nodded, barely taking in what she had said.

"Will you have some tea? Clare and Ruth are still in the kitchen, they'll probably be ready for some as well."

He went to the kitchen, noticing with some detached part of his brain that it looked better than it had for a long time. They had done a good job preparing it for the crowds of people who called – neighbours and Donal's friends, people who had worked with him in Dublin, and all their friends from Connemara who came for Donal, and for Kate.

They had opened Molly's own house for a few hours on Friday night, for her own neighbours and the distant relatives who called, second cousins Donal hardly knew about. They had sat and talked about her, while her coffin lay in the church, and they cried a bit from time to time, remembering the things they loved most about her.

"It's not that long ago since the corpse would have been brought home for a proper wake."

That was Mrs Downey, well into her eighties, sitting on the old armchair by the fire and sipping a glass of porter. Donal wanted to get up and walk out of the room, forced himself instead to pour some more tea for Mrs Cahill, another of the neighbours.

Sweet God Almighty, "the corpse". As if Molly had no identity at all now. He wondered briefly if she would have liked a wake at home, continued pouring tea, prayed for the moment they could lock up this house with all its memories, and leave.

It had been a relief to get back to his own house, where his own friends were waiting to sit through the night with him if necessary, and go with him to the funeral the following day. He could only hope they knew how he appreciated it. He hadn't the words to tell them, couldn't say anything at all when the funeral was over and they were back in the house and suddenly, with a sense of being stifled, he knew he had to get out, down to the sea.

"I'm sorry for running out like that," he said now, looking at Clare as Ruth turned to put on the kettle.

"No matter," Clare said. She knew better than to ask if he was okay. How in the name of God could he be okay?

They sat at the table drinking tea, and even when Ruth left them to see if Kate wanted some, they had little to say to each other. It was as if there was a barrier between them, as if Donal had retreated into his own private world, and no words or warmth from Clare could reach him.

Finally she stood up, rinsed the cup, picked up her bag from the chair.

"I'd better go. Will you call me if you need me?"

He stood up and faced her, looking into her eyes.

"I will. Clare, I'm sorry. I just don't know where I am right now."

She nodded, stepped forward to hug him.

He held her tightly for an instant. "I'll ring you," he said.

It was over a week before she heard from him. She was back home in the cottage, and had just locked up for the night when the phone rang.

"Could I come over tonight? Is that okay, or is it too late?"

"No. it's fine. Come on over." She felt tears in her eyes at the sound of his voice, the sadness in it.

He arrived half an hour later, looking haggard and exhausted. She wanted to fly into his arms. Instead, taking her cue from him, she sat down across from him in one of the armchairs.

"Would you like coffee? Or a drink?" she asked.

"I'd love a whiskey."

She went to the press, taking out the bottle of Black Bush and two glasses, putting them on the table in front of him, then went to the kitchen for a little jug of water. She waited while he poured a generous measure for both of them.

"How are you?" She hardly needed to ask, she could see how he was.

He didn't answer for a while, just sat sipping the whiskey.

"It's been very rough," he said, finally. "Worse than I could have imagined."

He paused to take another sip, looking at her directly this time.

"Clare, it's hard to say this, and I don't really know how to explain it."

She waited. She could see the upset in his face, wanted to reach out and touch him but knew she couldn't.

Her voice was quiet. "Go on."

"You know I love you, Clare."

She nodded.

"And if this hadn't happened . . ."

They would have spent the weekend together in Dublin. They sat looking at each other, neither of them needing to say it.

"But as it is . . ."

He reached again for his glass, sat holding it lightly with both hands.

"I really don't know how to put it," he said slowly. "But I need a bit of space."

He looked up at her, noticed the sudden tears in her eyes. Forced himself to go on anyway.

"This – Molly's death – it's brought up all kinds of things for me."

"Like what?" she asked, but she knew. She had already talked about it with Ruth on the telephone, wondering why he was acting so strangely, why he was turning away instead of towards her. There were two possible explanations. And he had said he loved her, so that left one.

He stood up, walked towards the window, looked out into the dark night.

"I thought I had moved on, Clare. Was sure I had. But this has brought it all back."

He turned to face her again, walked over towards her and sat on the coffee table just in front of her, reaching for her hand.

"I love you. I never thought I'd say that to anyone but Jenny. And now. . ."

He glanced towards the fire, still holding her hand, talking quietly, almost to himself.

"Now – well, I feel it's almost a betrayal. I know it doesn't make sense, but that's how I feel. As if I'm betraying her." He looked into her eyes, saw the tears there. "I'm sorry, Clare. I can't explain it any more than that. But I'm sorry."

"What are you saying, Donal? That's it's over?" Her voice was quiet.

He stood up abruptly, raking his hands back through his hair, pacing the room.

"NO!" He turned, stopped in front of her for a moment. "No," he repeated, much more quietly. "That's not what I want, Clare, it's not what I want at all. I just wish to Christ I could let go of this feeling . . ."

He reached the other armchair, sat down there, not looking at Clare at all. It was as if he was talking to himself.

"The funeral brought it all back. And then, in the house – both the houses, full of people. Another funeral. It brought it all back, Molly on the day of Jen's funeral, doing everything for me, feeding me, as if I was a kid, because I couldn't remember to eat . . ."

His voice trailed off and he sat silent for a minute.

"Jenny loved my mother," he began again. "Much more than she loved her own. She used to say she couldn't bear to think of a time when we wouldn't have Molly."

Suddenly he was crying, deep, racking sobs that shook him as he sat with his hands over his face. Clare stayed where she was, on the edge of her seat, tears in her own eyes, wanting to go to him but not sure what he would want.

Finally she couldn't bear it any longer and went to sit on the arm of his chair, her arm around him, and he leaned against her, and gradually the sobbing eased.

"God," he said eventually, taking the tissue she handed him. "It's a long time since I've done that."

"I know you didn't cry at the funeral. I wasn't sure about later."

He looked up to where she was sitting, still on the arm of the chair, slightly above him.

"I couldn't," he said. "Not in front of the boys, and Tish. That poor kid, I didn't want her to come to Glasnevin."

"Rick said she insisted."

He smiled faintly. "And there's no arguing with her when she insists. At least Rick was there with her."

She moved her arm from around him, wanted to brush his hair back where it had fallen across his forehead. "You okay?"

He nodded, managed a smile again. "I just let down my guard. Sorry."

"Don't be. They say it's better to cry."

"God, I thought I'd done my share of it. I thought – "

"Yes?" she said gently.

"I thought I had moved on, that things were finally going right for me. That I had a future, could make plans . . ."

She stood up and crossed to the other chair, watching him.

"You do have a future, Donal. If you want it."

He stretched back in the chair, looked across at her.

"I thought I had. Have. Until this. But now it's as if I'm right back there, just after it happened, after Jen died. As if I have to go through it all again."

"Would you think of talking to someone?" she asked gently.

"I talked to David until I thought we'd both go mad. I don't want to go through all that again."

"I don't know what to say, Donal. Really, I don't. Everything I think of sounds wrong. I wish – "

She paused and they both stayed quiet for a few moments, Clare sitting on the edge of her seat and leaning towards him, Donal sprawled back, legs stretched, his elbow on the right arm of the chair, hand raised to brush back the untidy hair from his forehead.

"What do you wish?" he asked her then.

"I don't know. That you could talk to me, that I could somehow make it better."

He smiled. "Thanks, Clare. I know. But it's not that simple. It's something I have to do for myself, and there are other things to do first, like clearing the house. I'm dreading that."

"I could – "

"No. Thanks, but no. I have to do it myself, on my own."

"What about Kate?"

"Molly wouldn't have wanted anyone going through her stuff. Even Kate, I think. Or me, for that matter, but I have to do it, I'm her executor. I'll need to sort everything out. I don't even know where she kept her will – the solicitor doesn't have it."

"Was there a sideboard, or something? Or a desk?"

"A bureau. But that was my father's, she never touched it."

Clare smiled as a thought struck her.

"Had she any old handbags? That's where my aunt used to keep everything."

"I don't know, but I'll have a look. I'm going up on Friday."

He stood up, reached for his jacket. "I'd better go."

She stood up but made no other move. He came towards her and touched her cheek gently.

"I just need a bit of time, Clare. I just don't know how long."

"It doesn't matter how long."

"I can't ask – "

"You don't have to."

She stood at the door as he left, tears spilling down her face, watching as the tail-lights of the car disappeared. Wondering how long it might be before she saw him again.

Chapter Thirty-eight

He sat in the car for a long time, looking at the red-bricked house, steeling himself to go inside and face its emptiness. When he finally knew he could delay no longer he left the car reluctantly and walked up the short pathway with its familiar pattern of black and terracotta tiles.

He put the key in the lock, dreading the musty smell, the clutter that he knew would be inside. He was sorry in a way that he hadn't let Kate come to help, but he was certain Molly would have wanted no-one going through her belongings. He would have to face this on his own.

The bigger task of clearing the house, preparing it to be sold, could wait; but now he must sort out Molly's papers. There were probably bills to be paid, he didn't know whether she had let things slip while she had been ill. And he had to find her will, so he could begin the process of administering her estate.

He entered the small, dim hallway, bending to pick up some letters from the mat inside the door. He glanced at them, put them in his pocket and opened the door to his left.

The front parlour was perfectly tidy, left that way by himself and Kate on the night of the removal. But there was still that faint musty odour of cold air and lingering polish that told, more clearly than anything else, of its function as the "good" room. It was used, as Molly always said, for "state days and holidays".

And funerals, he thought, feeling the sharp jab of pain.

He crossed to the long sash windows, opening them to let in the chill November air. Across the street he could see Mrs Downey, his mother's elderly neighbour. He hoped she wouldn't come in when she saw the car. He didn't think he could face anyone right now.

He left the room and went to the big kitchen at the back of the house.

This was a very different room from the parlour. It was the heart of the house, Molly's little kingdom, full of the evidence of her long years there. He remembered how he used to think when he was growing up that his mother never, ever threw anything away, and that some day they would all be buried under a heap of newspapers and plastic bags and old bits of twine, all kept because it might come in useful some day. A day that would never come, now. There were still newspapers sitting on two of the kitchen chairs, and under the table there was a box of delph she had packed, in readiness for the next jumble sale.

In the back scullery scores of old jam-jars and wine-bottles lined the high shelves, testimony to Molly's belief, against all the evidence, that she would one day get around to making her own wine and marmalade. She had long since let go of the idea, but hadn't been able to get rid of them. It would have seemed to her like giving in.

Donal bent to pick up her apron which had slipped to the floor from its hook on the back of the kitchen door. Without warning his eyes filled with tears and he found himself sitting at the kitchen table, head in his hands, as he wept in a sudden, uncontrollable torrent of rage and pain and helplessness.

Here, where he felt her presence most, he suddenly felt her absence.

For the first time since the night in Clare's he gave himself up to the deep sense of loss.

The funeral hadn't had power to do this to him. He had no sense of Molly in Glasnevin; there was only a hole in the ground, and a wooden box, and acres of flowers. His mother hadn't been there, not at all. Couldn't possibly have been there.

But here, in her beloved kitchen where she had fed him and held him and bandaged him and loved him – here, her loss was a deep wound, an open gash bleeding tears that wouldn't stop.

He sat, the sense of her all around him, crying for the loss of her, wondering if she had known how much he loved her.

It was beginning to get dark when he finally forced himself to move from the table. He stood up wearily, stretching, and glimpsed his haggard face in the small, mottled mirror above the kitchen sink. He looked wrecked, wanted nothing more than to go home and sleep, but he knew he couldn't, not until he found what he was looking for.

He went to the dresser drawer where Molly kept her household bills, paid and unpaid. Sifting through them quickly, he took up the unpaid ones and left them in a little pile on the kitchen table. Then he reached into the back of the deep drawer, rummaging around to see if there were any other envelopes there. Nothing.

He supposed he should try in her bedroom. There wasn't really anywhere else, except the small bureau in the parlour. He decided to begin there and went out again through the dim hall-way, still shaken by the unexpected onslaught of grief.

The little mahogany bureau was locked, as he had expected, and he had no idea where to find the key. He realised he had never actually seen it open, even when his father had been alive. He slid open the pedestal drawers, one after the other, finding only a clutter of pens and paper clips, and a few coins.

He tried the big centre drawer that spanned the width of the bureau.

It was locked, and so was the roll-top. If there was anything to be found it would be in one of those. He needed to find the key, thought about what Clare had said about handbags. Wondered if that's where Molly might have kept the key.

He went slowly up the stairs and into the room that

faced him across the small landing, his mother's room. Taking a deep breath he turned the brass knob, opening the door on flowered wallpaper, the old double bed with its faded bedspread, the picture of the Sacred Heart on the far wall.

It felt like desecration to be in her room without her, and he had to steel himself to cross to the wardrobe and open the door. The smell of mothballs wafted out as he moved her clothes aside. He hadn't realised she had so many.

He almost laughed at himself then, for being surprised. He should know well that his mother kept everything. Dresses long out of fashion, an evening dress in a midnight blue silky kind of material. When, and where, had she ever worn that? He couldn't remember seeing her in anything like it, couldn't even imagine her wearing it. It was a dress for a young woman, and to him she was old, had always been old.

Again he felt tears. I never saw her as a person, he thought with a stab of shame. I only saw her as my mother.

Brushing impatiently at his eyes, he squatted down, reaching into the back of the big wardrobe. He moved aside shoes, feeling his way into the far recesses, past long dresses, folded shawls and an old fur stole.

He brought out a brown leather bag, looked at it for a moment, opened it. Nothing much inside, just a musty smell and rosary beads and some old memorial cards. Briefly he examined them. They were for people long dead, strangers, people he'd never even heard mentioned.

A pink bag was next, full of photographs and letters. He'd go through those later, burn the letters and probably most of the photographs.

He tried again, groping in towards the very back of the wardrobe, and this time he found a black patent handbag, one he remembered his mother using for Sunday Mass when he was a child. Must be twenty-five, thirty years old, he thought, opening the clasp.

For a moment he thought it was empty and was about to put it aside when his fingers brushed against the fastener of an inside pocket. He reached in, finding some envelopes there. Three of them. As he took then out his fingers touched cold metal. He withdrew a small brass key, placing it carefully on the bedside locker. It had to be for the bureau, he couldn't think what else it might be for. He'd have a quick look at the envelopes before going back downstairs.

The first held several more photographs, mainly of a toddler with curly hair. Himself, he supposed, putting them on the bed.

The last photo caught his eye briefly. Two small babies, lying side by side in a cot. Only a few days old, he judged, wondering who they were. They looked like twins, but not his twins. The photograph was old, black-and-white, turned up at the edges. He put it with the others, replaced them all in the envelope.

He reached for the smallest envelope which, like the first, was unsealed. Inside were two locks of hair, two tiny, tight little blond curls. Just like his mother to have kept those, he thought, smiling for a moment before replacing the envelope on the bed beside the other two.

He picked up the final one, turned it over, saw that it was sealed. Noticed for the first time that his name was on the front in his mother's slanting hand. Just one word, *Donal*.

He sat holding it, looking at it, turning it over. For no reason that he could explain, he was afraid of what he might find inside.

He slit the envelope, took out several sheets of closely-written paper and began to read. He paused, stared at the paper, his heart racing. He read it again, quickly, his knuckles tightening on the sheets. Then he folded them carefully, putting them into his pocket. He took a deep breath to relax the tension in his jaw and went downstairs, the key to the bureau in his hand. The words of the letter echoed in his head, almost as if she were speaking them.

"Don't hate me," she had begged. *"I should have told you long ago, I promised Father Tom I would, but I was too afraid you would hate me. That I would lose you, when you are my whole life, the moon and the stars to me. I pray for the courage to tell you before God takes me. We only ever wanted what was best for you. Believe that, Donal. Please believe that, love. We always loved you, we were only afraid you would stop loving us."*

His mind was in turmoil as he went into the parlour and inserted the key in the bureau. He went quickly through it, finding the documents he wanted. He barely glanced at them. There were no surprises there now. No answers, either. For those, he would have to go to Kate.

He could get there tonight, he'd be there by midnight. He felt as if a lifetime had passed since late afternoon, when he had come to the house. Barely two hours ago. Long enough for his world to turn upside down again.

He locked the bureau, taking the documents with him, and pulled the hall door carefully after him. It was just past seven when he picked up the rain-slicked N4 and headed for Galway.

* * *

He arrived at Kate's cottage just as Clare was leaving. It was well after eleven, but they had been so glad of each other's company and the chance to relax and talk over a meal, that neither of them had been in any hurry to finish the evening.

They looked up, surprised, at the sound of the car, the sudden sharp rap on the door. He came in, barely greeting them. He looked tense, brittle. As if it would take very little to push him over some invisible edge.

"I need to talk to you, Kate."

"I'll go," Clare said, picking up her jacket quickly from the arm of the sofa.

He turned as if he had just noticed her. "I'm sorry, Clare. I didn't mean to interrupt. But I have to talk to Kate, and it can't wait."

She nodded a farewell to both of them. Kate, she noticed, hadn't said a word. She was looking anxiously at him. She seemed to be waiting for something, hadn't taken her eyes off him since he came through the door.

"You'll be all right getting home?" he asked Clare, half-turning to her.

"I'll be fine. Thanks."

As she pulled the door behind her and stepped out into the pouring rain she could hear his voice, with a sharpness in it that she didn't recognise.

"Why didn't you tell me, Kate? Why in the name of Christ didn't you tell me, all these years? Don't you . . ."

He sounded as he had looked, devastated and furious, all at once. No wonder Kate had looked worried, if she knew anything at all about what was upsetting him.

Clare reached the car, put her hand in the pocket of her jacket, felt in the other pocket, then in her jeans. Back to the jacket again, but it was clear that there was no point, her car keys weren't there. And then she remembered dropping them on the little table just inside the door, when she came in through the conservatory earlier this evening.

She would have to walk. The prospect of going two miles in the dark, in the lashing rain, seemed easier to face than going back into the house.

And then she told herself not to be ridiculous, that it would be dangerous to make her way home alone, on foot, even in this quiet corner of Connemara. Neither of them would want her to put herself at risk like that.

She went back up the path, meaning to slip in through the conservatory door, pick up the keys and go before they even realised she was there.

She had eased the door open and was reaching for the keys when she heard Donal's voice grow louder from just inside the door to the kitchen.

"You have to tell me, Kate! I have a right to know who my father is! Just as I had a right to know that you . . ."

A gasp from Clare interrupted him and brought them both to the inside door of the conservatory.

"What are you doing here, Clare? I thought you were gone!" His face was flushed with anger, his eyes hard.

"The keys. I . . ."

She stood there, unable to move, her mind spinning. Like well-oiled cogs the jigsaw pieces were shipping into place. The look on Kate's terrified face told her she was right. Begged her not to say a word.

"I'll go," Clare said. In her haste as she turned, she brushed against the cloth hanging over a canvas on the easel and it slipped to the floor. She bent to retrieve it, stood up to find herself looking again at the portrait of Jack. The unfamiliar, familiar eyes, the line of the jaw that had reminded her of . . .

Turning, she saw that he saw it too. Kate, her teeth digging into her knuckles, looked from one to the other of them, from Clare's anguished expression to Donal's look of disbelief, and recognition, as he stood gazing at the image of himself. Older, and with straight, grey hair – but the face, without question, was his.

He stood for a long moment, looking from the portrait to Kate, and back again. His eyes were those of a man in shock. Clare found that she was holding her breath.

"So when were you going to tell me?" he asked finally, turning to Kate. "After you had finished telling the rest of the world? No," he said, and his voice was like steel now, hard and cold, cutting through her protests. "At least have the decency not to deny it."

He turned back to look at Clare. "I can see that you know the full story, Clare. Which is more than I did, until now."

She took a breath to speak, decided it was better to say nothing yet as he turned to Kate.

"Does he know?"

"No," she said. Her eyes were pleading, her voice barely above a whisper. "I wanted to tell you first, Donal. I never meant to keep it from you . . ."

"Which is why I had to find out in a letter, at this stage of my life! I'll say this for you, Kate – for someone who never meant to keep it from me, you did a bloody good job! What else haven't you told me?"

She sat, collapsed almost, unto the sofa, her hands to her mouth, vainly trying to stop the wrenching sobs. It was a while before either of them could understand her. Finally the crying lessened and they were able to make out the words.

"Two of you, Donal – a sister – my little Maire. Oh, she was beautiful, Donal. I used to sit for hours just looking at the two of you. Loving you. But it wasn't enough, all the loving. After she died. . ." Kate was crying again, enough to make a heart break. "After she died, I was afraid to keep you. Afraid I couldn't look after a child, afraid I'd lose you too."

She looked up at him, and her eyes were still full of tears which poured down her face as she said, "But I lost you anyway, didn't I? I had to live my life away from you, when my arms ached to hold you and my heart ached to tell you, only I promised Molly I'd leave that to her. And I lost you anyway."

"Oh Kate. Kate." His tears mingled with hers as he crouched on his knees in front of her, gathering her into his arms, their cheeks touching. They didn't even notice as Clare slipped away quietly into the darkness, closing the door gently behind her.

Chapter Thirty-nine

"And I haven't seen him since."

Clare looked so dejected that Ruth wanted to go straight over there, walking the six miles if she had to, and shake some sense into Donal. But even she realised it wasn't as simple as that.

The sisters were curled up on the couch in Clare's living room, leaning back against its arms, feet drawn up under them. They had lit candles and put them on the mantelpiece, the scent of them mixing with the turf-smoke from the blazing fire. One small lamp was lighting in a corner of the room. They could hear the wind rising and were glad of the warmth inside, the stout walls that kept the December weather at bay.

"What does Kate say?" Ruth asked, reaching for more wine and re-filling their glasses.

"I think Kate is afraid to say anything much to me. Donal hasn't really forgiven her for telling me about Jack . . ."

"But she didn't . . ."

"She told me enough that I could guess the rest. So Donal's still a bit angry about that, and annoyed with me too, that I knew before he did."

"But that's not fair," Ruth burst out, sitting up straighter. "I mean, he can be angry with her all he likes, he's entitled, but it's not fair to drag you into it!"

"I don't think he's even thinking straight. That's what Kate says, anyway. He's all over the place, keeping to himself for days on end, then calling over to her with the boys and acting almost as if nothing has happened."

"God, Clare, but you pick them. Why couldn't you fall for someone uncomplicated, like a mad axe murderer? At least then you'd know where you stood!"

They burst out laughing, drank some more wine.

"And I thought you liked him!" Clare said. Then she bit her lip, looking serious again.

"But you're right, it's driving me mad. Half the time I feel I could kill him for staying away. But I think I understand why he's doing it."

"I'm glad one of us does." Ruth changed position on the couch, half-lying back against the cushions as she waited for Clare's reply.

"Molly's death brought it all back to him. That's what he told me in Dublin, remember? So now it's as if he has to face it all over again, losing Jenny as well as his mother. And finding out that she wasn't his mother after all, and that Brendan wasn't his father and that they had kept it from him – it's a lot to deal with all in one go."

"Couldn't he share it with you then, at least try to explain a bit?"

"I wish he would. I feel I could cope with anything except being shut out like this. You've no idea the number of times I wanted to go over there and talk to him."

"So, why didn't you?"

"For fear it would complicate things more for him. He's already said he feels as if he's betraying Jenny."

"Jesus, *that's* a bit much. How long ago was it – three years?"

"I don't think time comes into it. He thought he was getting over her, until Molly died."

"So, what now? You can't just sit here for the rest of your life, waiting for him to get his act together."

"Why not?"

"Come on, sis, don't be ridiculous. You're locking yourself away like a hermit. You haven't seen or heard from him in over five weeks."

Clare hesitated for a moment before replying.

"Actually, I did see him early last week, on the beach at Dog's Bay. He was a good bit away from me."

"You told me a few minutes ago you hadn't seen him since the night in Kate's house. So what happened?" she added impatiently.

Clare brushed a long strand of hair back behind her ear. "Well, nothing, really. That's why I didn't mention it. When he saw me he just waved, and I stood for a minute but he didn't move, and I turned back."

"You know, you're acting like a seventeen year old. You went over there hoping to see him, didn't you?" She knew from Clare's expression that she was right. "And it still got you nowhere. You can't just cocoon yourself up here, sis, waiting for something that mightn't happen. You'll have to decide what you're going to do."

"I've already decided."

"And?" Ruth asked.

"I'm going to wait for him." Clare's voice was firm as she said it.

"But what if things don't change for him?" Ruth, who had never in her life had to wait for a man, was beginning to sound impatient.

"If things don't change, I'll wait anyway," Clare said. "I'll wait until he comes, or until I'm absolutely certain that he won't."

Ruth didn't answer, but her expression said clearly that Clare was mad.

"I love him, Ruth. I think he loves me – he said he does. And I want to be with him, more than I've ever wanted to be with anyone."

"Only you're not, are you?" Ruth's voice was gentle. "You're sitting here on your own, and he's over there with the twins, and you've no idea when you might see him. Or anyone else either. I bet you haven't seen a single soul except Kate for the past week."

"No. Well, Jack, but I only saw him for a minute. He called in yesterday."

"Does he know?" Ruth asked. She picked up the empty wine bottle, grimaced at it.

"I don't think so," Clare said. "He wouldn't say anything anyway, and I could hardly ask. Want some more wine?" she added as Ruth drained her glass and put it on the small side table.

"I don't think so. No, better not. A cup of tea would be great, then bed." She stretched as Clare stood up and crossed into the kitchen to put on the kettle.

"Kate told me the other day that she was trying to find a way to tell him," she said as she came back and settled herself into the couch again, facing Ruth.

"She'd better find it fast then, before someone else does. It's only a matter of time before people put two and two together."

Clare considered. "If it was that obvious the word would be out already. It's only when you already know that you can see the similarities. And even then, you'd have to see Kate's painting."

"All the same . . . well, it's up to them."

"It is. And not a word, Ruth. Not even to Conor. I shouldn't even have told you . . ."

"Trust me. You know I'll keep it to myself. Come on, let's have the tea and get to bed. You're coming home with me tomorrow." She stood up as she spoke, went to the kitchen and came back with two mugs.

"I can't . . ." Clare began as Ruth handed her one.

"Come home with me? What's stopping you? Jody will look after the animals, won't he?"

"Probably. He's at a loose end since Tish went to the States with Rick for Christmas."

"Well, then. Phone him to-morrow and get it settled. You need a few days at home, with Mam spoiling you. And I bet you haven't even done any Christmas shopping."

"Not yet," Clare said. She had the grace to look a bit embarrassed.

"So what are you waiting for, the January sales? Come on, finish the tea and let's get some sleep. I want to be on the road by ten, and you're coming with me. And don't make any plans for Tuesday, I've the day off and we'll hit Grafton Street."

* * *

They did, with a vengeance, and Clare found she was enjoying herself for the first time in almost six weeks. She spent a fortune, buying presents for Kate and the twins as well as her family and her friends in Dublin, until finally there was only one present left to buy. The hardest one of all.

"Are you sure it's a good idea to get him something?" Ruth asked uncertainly as they sat in the mezzanine in Bewley's, surrounded by bags. Clare pulled her attention back from the crowded, colourful street below, which she could see through the tall window beside her. She could have sworn she saw Donal making his way through the crowds, told herself to stop imagining things.

"I don't know," she answered Ruth. "I don't know if it's a good idea or not. I don't suppose I'll even see him, but I'd hate not to get him anything."

"You didn't want to put any pressure on him," Ruth reminded her.

"No. But if I got him something small, that would mean something only to him . . ."

"You'd remind him that you still exist."

Clare smiled. "That's exactly it. Okay, finish the coffee. There's a book-shop I want to go to."

"Can I give it a miss? It's nearly five, and Conor is meeting us outside Brown Thomas, he wants me to help him pick something for his Dad. Unless you want me to come?"

"No, it's fine. It won't take me long, and I'll get the bus home."

"You could meet us at the Molly Malone statue at about six, we'll give you a lift . . ."

"Maybe. But if I'm not there, don't wait, okay? I'll probably be home by then!"

"Okay. Leave me the bags, Conor will carry them."

"Hardly fair."

"Don't worry, he won't mind," Ruth answered.

"That poor man is doing his purgatory!" Clare laughed, as they picked up the bags and made their way into the street past groups of carol singers, a string quartet playing valiantly outside a shop window brightly decorated in red and gold, children gazing awe-struck at fairy lights and window displays.

For a moment Clare wished the twins were with her to see it all. Then they reached Brown Thomas where Conor was already waiting, and she handed him her bags at Ruth's insistence, kissed them both briefly and was gone.

She walked with a graceful stride, threading her way quickly through the crowds. She knew exactly where she was going.

The little book-shop was a fifteen minute walk and a hundred years away from the bigger, brighter ones on Grafton Street and neighbouring Dawson Street. The front of it looked as if it hadn't changed in all that time, with its hand-lettered gold sign outside reading "Antiquarian Books."

It was quiet and dimly-lit inside, with only two or three other customers. A man with white hair and glasses glanced up from behind the counter as she entered, smiling a welcome as the little bell inside the door tinkled.

"Can I help? Or would you like to look around?"

"Thanks. I'm not sure what I'm looking for exactly, something special, but not too expensive. I want something for a friend – he told me he's bought several books here."

"And what category would your friend be interested in? Biography? Fiction? Or . . ."

"Poetry," Clare said, suddenly knowing exactly what she wanted. "Have you heard of a poet called Penelope Abbott? Early nineteenth century, I think. She's not very well known, she wrote love poetry, mostly . . ."

She held her breath, remembering the evening, barely two months ago, when they had sat in her cottage in the soft light of the lamps while Donal read to her from a book of nineteenth century poems. An evening that seemed a lifetime ago.

"That's quite incredible," the bookseller was saying. "Hardly anyone ever asks for her work anymore, and now there are two of you within the hour! Christmas, I suppose!"

"And do you have any?" She hardly dared hope, realised she was holding her breath again.

"As it happens, I had two very fine first editions of her collected works, up until an hour ago. And now I have one left."

He lifted a slim volume from the shelf behind him and handed it to her. She rubbed her hand gently over the fine leather cover, opened it, breathing in the rich scent that was only found in very old, well-preserved books.

"Could I have a quick look through it?"

"Of course. There's a chair at the back, and a little table. Just through there."

She took the book, sat at the table, scanned the index. And there it was, just as she remembered it. She could almost hear Donal's voice as she read the words.

Unravelling

I cannot ask that you will wait for me
As sorrows lay their burden on my soul,
As every thread in life's rich tapestry
Seems to unravel ere I reach my goal.

I would surround you, love, with roses sweet
But all I have to offer now are thorns;
And though life without you is incomplete,
I bring no fair winds with me, only storms.

My hopes lie all in tatters, and my dreams
Are cast adrift, no anchor to be found –
Although my love for you is all it seems,
There is no telling where I might be bound.

I cannot ask that you will wait for me;
I only hope, and pray, that it may be.

There were other poems in the book that she preferred, but this was the one he had read to her the night he introduced her to Penelope Abbott's work. And it bore a message she knew he would understand.

"I remember it from college," he had said. "I thought, even then, how wrong she was not to share her sorrows with the man who loved her, instead of trying to work though them on her own and hoping he'd still be around afterwards. There never was an afterwards for them, because she died just three months after she wrote it."

"How did she die?" Clare had asked. "And what happened to him?"

"She had scarlet fever or something, I'm not sure exactly. That's what the burden was, ill-health, and she refused to let him stay with her for fear of destroying his life."

"Maybe she was right?"

"No. No, she wasn't. She may have destroyed his life anyway. She should at least have let him be part of that choice."

Clare closed the book now, remembering what Donal had said next, how he had wanted to re-write the ending of the poem.

"What would you have done?" she had asked, amused at him, sorry for the unknown young poet and her lover. "How would you have ended it?"

"I wanted her to ask him, plead with him if need be, to

stay with her. And I wanted him to come to her, and to bring her dozens of roses. Hundreds of them, thorns and all. I wanted her to be surrounded by them, to drown in their scent and realise that this was what life was about, that if you shared love at all, then you shared everything, whether it was good or bad. I wanted her to know that the most important thing – the only important thing – was to be together, whatever life threw at them, or offered to them."

Clare sat at the little table with tears in her eyes, remembering how she had teased him, calling him an old romantic, and how they had gone into each others arms, forgetting the poetry book and everything else.

She stood up with a small sigh as the bell at the door rang again. It must be almost time for the shop to close. She reached into her bag, searching for her purse, and was stepping through the archway to go to the till when she heard the voice. She stood there unable to move, hardly able to breath.

"I wonder if I left my bag here? There were some toys in it, and children's books . . ."

"I have it here for you, sir, quite safe. You must have left it down when you were paying for the poetry book. You know, there was someone else asking for the very same book just now. Quite remarkable, such a little-known poet, and in the space of an hour. I was just saying so to the young lady . . ."

Clare came through the archway and she and Donal stood looking at each other for what seemed like a long, long time.

And then they were in each others arms, and the bookseller, beaming, turned away discreetly as they kissed, oblivious to him and to his remaining customers. He was tempted to applaud, but it would hardly have been appropriate. He wondered when he might close the shop, since it looked as if they had no intention of leaving.

And then he decided that such a reunion, as it obviously was, was worth staying all night for if necessary. He was humming softly to himself as he waited patiently for the moment, whenever it might be, when he could lock up his shop and go home.

Chapter Forty

They were sitting in an out-of-the way pub by the Quays, away from the madness of the Christmas shopping crowds. Their drinks were untouched as he sat holding her hand in both of his, running his fingers gently from the fingertips to her palm and back again..

"I want to take you to Paris. I want to find a little hotel near the Sacre Coeur, and make love to you for the whole weekend."

She laughed in delight, thinking of those hands stroking her back, in some little hotel in Paris. "Only a weekend?"

"To begin with. Clare . . ." He was still stroking her hand, looking into her eyes. "I'm sorry for cutting myself off like that. I didn't know how else to get through it all, I was trying to hold myself together. And I know now that I just made it harder – for both of us. I shouldn't have done it like that, but it seemed to be the only way I could survive. Can you understand?"

"I can imagine how rough it must have been."

"I made it worse than it already was, by blocking you out. But there was so much going on for me, so much to take on board. I was all over the place. Bad enough losing Molly, but the whole thing about Kate . . ."

He paused, took a sip of Guinness. "I just never expected that. I must have been blind."

"How could you have known? It's not unusual to look like your aunt, or get on well together. And if they never said anything . . ."

"That's the hardest part," he said. "Not a word, no clue at all, in all these years."

She hesitated. "Are you still angry with them?"

"No, not now. Life's too short. I've learned that, if I've learned anything. But I wish to God they had told me while Molly was still alive. I wish she could have trusted me enough to know that I loved her, no matter what. That she was my mother in every way that mattered, and that knowing about Kate wouldn't have changed anything."

"Maybe it was hard for her to feel sure of that," Clare said, "I mean, when you've kept a secret for so long . . ."

"It's hard to find the right time. I know. Kate told me that was the main reason she went to see Molly last summer, to persuade her to tell me, or let Kate tell me. But she asked Kate to wait just a while longer . . ." His voice broke, and Clare squeezed his hand gently.

"I wish she hadn't been afraid," he continued after a while. "She had no reason to be. I always loved her and I wouldn't have stopped. Molly was my real mother, she reared me. And I've always loved Kate anyway, we always understood each other and always got on together. I couldn't have loved her more even if I'd known."

"She must be glad to know that."

"She is. She was afraid too, and she's still dreading having to tell Jack."

"She hasn't done it yet?" Clare was shocked.

Donal shook his head. "No, she hasn't told him yet, and I'm probably as much to blame as she is. I should push her into doing it, instead of letting her wait for the right time. God knows, there'll never be a right time, she'll just have to tell him."

"I'm still puzzled by one thing. Your birth certificate. Why didn't you know from that?"

"Because Molly's name was on it all along. And my father's – Brendan's."

"She used Molly's name? Isn't that illegal?"

"Probably, but we haven't gone into the finer points. I was born in England and nobody knew her there, so there was little enough risk of it coming out. And I suppose, even then, she hoped Molly might rear me, and my sister. She knew they wanted children badly. Even before my sister died, she might have thought of leaving one, or both of us, with Molly. I'm guessing. I don't really know. They might even have planned it together – I think Kate would have needed Molly's marriage certificate to register Brendan's name. I'm not sure. And I'm not about to ask Kate – this has all been hard enough on her."

"What about Kevin? How did he take it?"

"He took it well. Much better than we could have expected. He said it explained a lot, why he always felt Kate was closer to me and why he felt jealous enough to kill me, sometimes. Why he grew up feeling second-best, as if he was never quite good enough for her . . ."

"God! That must have been hard for him!"

"Impossible. And it was true, you know. I always got on better with Kate than he did. I never understood why – all I could do was try not to get in their way."

"They seemed to me to get on fine together."

"Since you've known him, yes. Since he came back from the States. He grew up a bit while he was there, and stopped being so demanding and resentful. And Kate learned to appreciate him while he was gone. And, of course, having Ann Marie helps now. Kevin says he's not going to dwell on the past, when he has a great future in front of him."

"Sounds like he really *has* grown up!"

Donal gave a wry smile. "He could teach his big brother a thing or two!"

They were quiet for a few moments, sipping their drinks.

"And how are you now, Donal?" she ventured, finally.

"About the past, you mean? About Jenny?"

She nodded.

"Much better than I was. It hit me all over again, when Molly died. You know that. It was like losing her again. And I began to believe it wasn't worth it, loving people and then losing them. I felt that if I held back, then I couldn't get hurt. Something like that. I hadn't thought it out properly, but the feeling was there."

"And do you still believe that?"

"There's probably a part of me that does. It's hitting me all at once, losing people, and then finding people. Strange. Like my father dying eight years ago, and then suddenly he wasn't my father at all, my father is living not ten miles

561

from me and I've met him dozens of times, not knowing who he was. I never knew I had a brother, or a sister who died. It's all taking a bit of getting used to."

"I wonder how different things would have been, if you'd known all along? Would it have been easier for Kevin? And for Kate?"

"Who knows? Kevin says now that he's always wanted a big brother – pity it has to be me! Oh, and he wants me to be his best man."

"Donal! That's brilliant! So they're serious?"

"Absolutely. They're talking about getting married at Easter, when we've all had a chance to recover from Niall's wedding. I'm to be his best man as well – did he tell you? At least now I know I can face it, with you there." He paused, looked into her eyes. "You *are* coming, aren't you?"

"Try and stop me! I was dreading it until now. I didn't know how I'd go if you were there and we hadn't begun to sort things out."

"We're doing that, aren't we? I know I still have things to do – talking to Jack, and Christmas with the kids . . . and New Year's Eve. I always find that impossible – worse than anything. The sense of leaving people you've lost behind, moving into a year they've never been part of . . ." He smiled at her. "You can see why you don't need to be with me on New Year's Eve. But afterwards . . . I feel that this year, finally, I'll be able to let go. I know it. When are you coming back down?"

"I was thinking of the second or third. Ruth's having a New Year's Eve party, we'll still have people around the next day, but I thought I'd go down after that."

He nodded. "And Paris? I meant it, you know, about the little hotel somewhere."

"I've been wanting to go back to Paris for ages."

"I remember. You said you'd go with the right person."

"And I will." She smiled at him as they sat there, cocooned in a world with just the two of them, oblivious to the pub filling up with regulars, the rain beginning to fall heavily outside.

"I can't promise you'll see much of Paris."

"Don't make me any promises at all. Just that we'll get there."

"I promise you that." He lifted her hand to his lips, kissed the palm of it. "I wish I could ask you to stay with me tonight. But it doesn't feel right, not just yet."

"You're staying in Clontarf?"

"Just for to-night. I'm putting the house on the market after Christmas. I wanted one last night there, on my own."

"You're sure you want to sell it?"

"Certain. I'll keep Molly's house, that can be home for the boys if they ever come back to Dublin."

"And what about you?"

"I don't think I'll ever be back. Not to live. Connemara feels like where I should have been all the time. I love the job, the kids are settled. And everyone I love is there."

He smiled at her, squeezed her hand gently. "Come on, I'll get you home. They'll be sending out search parties."

She laughed, standing up with him. "I'll tell them I'm not one bit lost. Not anymore."

Chapter Forty-one

Clare had always loved Christmas Eve. She remembered her excitement as a child, counting the days from the beginning of December. She loved all the rituals of Christmas, the Advent calendar, the wrapping of the presents, the moment when the Christmas-tree lights were switched on and her father would hug them all, and gather them round the piano for a raucous, enthusiastic round of carols.

More than anything, she remembered her fear that Santa would forget whatever it was she longed for, and bring her the wrong present.

She laughed now, thinking about it, and Ruth and her brother Dermot grinned back at her.

"Is there a joke?" Ruth asked, stretching out against Conor on the big sofa. "Or are you just getting delirious again?"

"I am *not* delirious!" Clare was laughing, picked up a cushion, ready to throw at Ruth.

"It's the only word for it," Ruth assured her. "You've

been delirious ever since you met him, and that's two weeks ago."

She ducked as the cushion flew, so that Conor bore the brunt of it. Which was par for the course, Clare thought, smiling across at them.

"Talk about getting what you want for Christmas!" Ruth added. Then she looked serious for a moment as she snuggled up against Conor. "Pity you can't be with him," she added.

"I know," Clare said. "But he's going to ring tomorrow, sometime after lunch."

"Him, and the rest of the world! He'll never get through."

"Come on, Ruthie. You're supposed to be the optimist round here!" Conor said, giving her a playful punch on the arm. "Shut up and leave the girl alone!"

He turned to look at Clare.

"You didn't think of going down there yourself for Christmas?"

"No. I want to be here, and he needs to be there, with the kids and with Kate. It'll be a tough day for them. And there are still things he needs to sort out."

"But you're going down afterwards?"

"After your party – I'll stay for that."

"Great," Ruth said, a big smile on her face. "You can help with the cooking."

"Good to know I have my uses," Clare said, grinning back as she picked up the tray full of empty cups from in front of the fire. "I'll put the kettle on – they'll be home from Midnight Mass any minute."

Her parents had gone, as they always did, accompanied by her Aunt Ginnie.

"God, look at the time," Ruth said, standing up. "Go on home, Conor O'Malley, before your mother sends the guards out for you!"

"Happy Christmas to you too, Ruth."

Ruth laughed in reply, hugging him. "Sorry. Happy Christmas."

"Happy Christmas," Clare added, smiling as she went through the door to the kitchen to make some sandwiches before the others got home. They'd be starving, she knew from past experience, but in great form. As she was herself, ever since the day she met Donal in the book-shop. She hoped Christmas would be okay for him, wished she could make it easier. Realised she already had. And in only a few short days she'd be with him again.

Chapter Forty-two

The air was still and there were a million stars. The small grey granite church was packed to over-flowing, people who never graced its doors for the round of the year coming for the Midnight Mass on Christmas Eve. Donal smiled down at the twins, sitting in the pew between himself and Kate.

They were on a high, gone beyond exhaustion with the pure excitement of it all, mesmerised by the crib, and the sound of the familiar carols, and the warmth of all the friends and neighbours they had met on the way in, some of whom had pressed coins into the eager little hands.

Their only fear was that Santa wouldn't know where to find them in Connemara and would go looking for them up in Dublin, and Donal had to reassure them again and again that Santa knew exactly where they were.

"Anyway, Mammy will be sure to tell him, and Granny," Luke had told Michael as they made their way up the gravel path to the church. Donal, moved to tears by their innocence, had felt Kate's arm slip through his as they followed the boys through the small doorway and found a seat inside.

He could finally sit in a church again without feeling the great, raging anger about Jenny's death. As the music lifted him and the familiar rituals began, and he looked down at the two pale little faces beside him with their big dark eyes shining, wonder-struck, he felt the beginning of a kind of peace.

And when the boys went, afterwards, to light candles ("Mammy's Christmas present, Daddy, remember? And one for Granny now.") he was able to smile, where last year, and the year before that, he had felt as if his heart would break.

He followed the boys down the aisle with Kate, and as he stepped into the cold night air he felt a sense of ease, of calm that was completely unexpected. He half-turned to hold the door for the person following behind, and found himself looking straight at Jack.

"Happy Christmas," he said, smiling at the older man.

They moved together away from the door and Jack nodded at Kate.

"I won't wish you the same, in your time of trouble. But I hope the young fellas will get some good out of it. I've a few bits and pieces I meant to bring over for them."

"Why don't you come to-morrow, Jack?" Kate asked, on impulse. "Though I suppose you have something planned already . . ."

"Little enough. I'll cook myself a bit of dinner, and

take a walk afterwards. I'm not much of a one for celebrating Christmas."

It hadn't always been the case, Kate knew. "You could come to us for dinner – we've plenty of food in the house."

"Thanks, Kate. Maybe I'll come in a day or two, but not tomorrow. Tomorrow is a time for families."

"You'd be very welcome, Jack." She was looking at him as if time had stood still. "We'd love if you could come."

He stood, saying nothing, as the people still drifting from the church passed by them on either side, some casting sidelong glances at them, aware of the intensity between the two of them.

"That means the world to me, Kate," he said, finally.

"You'll come?" she asked.

"For a while only, to bring the few things for the children. I'll come over after the dinner." He nodded to them, put back on the cap he had been holding in his hand, and made his way towards the gate. Kate and Donal stood for a moment, smiling at each other in the soft light that spilled through the church doorway.

"That was a great idea," he said, putting his arm around her shoulders and hugging her to him.

She smiled up at him. "Let's hope it works!"

"It'll work," he said, suddenly sure that, somehow, it would. He bent to kiss her cheek before turning to the two little boys.

"Come on, lads, let's get a move on or Santa will get there before us!" He was laughing as he raced them down to the car.

Chapter Forty-three

Christmas Day was easier than he had expected. There were moments when he found himself laughing with the children, marvelling with them at their wonderful new acquisitions, with none of that heart-tugging sense that it had all lost its meaning after Jenny died. He had been dreading the day without her. And without Molly, who had somehow got him through it last year and the year before.

And now, instead, there was Kate, preparing the food, chatting to the boys, making sure to include Ann Marie in everything without being too obvious about it. Donal was smiling as he watched them from a corner of the big, warm kitchen. He had the poetry book from Clare in his hand, idly caressing its leather cover with his thumb while the boys played at his feet, well away from the cooking area.

He and Kevin had been banished too, told to save their energy for the washing-up, so Kevin was busy opening bottles and taking Kate's best glasses down from the dresser. Donal had never felt more at home there, hadn't expected this sense of contentment to be any part of the day for him.

Kevin came over and handed him a glass of whiskey.

"Well, big brother, whatever I wanted for Christmas, you're what I got. I suppose I'd better make the most of it."

Donal laughed. "You could do a lot worse, let me tell you. Slainte!" He raised his glass, and Kevin grinned as he returned the toast.

Kate looked across at them just at that moment, and they smiled back, raising their glasses to herself and Ann Marie. She felt her heart lift. May it always be like this, she prayed silently, seeing the look of affection that passed between her sons.

They had finished the dinner and were clearing the table when Jack arrived. Donal was surprised at the force of his own reaction, his sudden desire to tell Jack the truth there and then. Instead he shook his hand, offered him a drink, watched as the older man gave presents to Luke and Michael.

"I won't stay long," Jack said, taking a glass of whiskey and sitting in one of the armchairs by the fire. And, though he seemed relaxed enough, and spoke easily about the weather, and the goose he had had for dinner, and about some of the old Christmas traditions that had all but died out, he stood up after barely half an hour, telling them he had one or two other people to call into on his way back.

It was obvious that he was reluctant to intrude any

further on their day, and it was all Donal could do not to tell him why he had every right to be with them, and ask him to stay.

"I'll call over for a while tomorrow afternoon, Jack, if you'll be there," Kate said as he was leaving.

Donal sensed the tension in her as she waited for the reply.

Jack didn't hesitate. "Come over, and welcome. I'll be there all day."

They stood and watched as he got into his car to drive the short distance home.

"I was hoping you'd get the chance to tell him," Donal said.

"Not with all of you there, love. Even if I got him on his own, it wouldn't be fair. He should hear this in his own place, when he has a chance to take it in. And I've waited this long – I can wait one more day." She smiled up at him. "But it made my Christmas to see the two of you together. If only Molly . . ."

He hugged her as she blinked back the tears.

"Thank God I have you, Donal. You and Kevin. I shouldn't even dream of wanting more."

* * *

St. Stephen's Day was bright and clear, a perfect day for cycling.

"I won't be too long," Kate announced once they had finished lunch, and taking her cape and a flat, brown-covered package she slipped out through the back door with Donal beside her. She took the bike from the shed and began wheeling it down the path towards the road, stopping for a moment to balance the parcel in the big wicker basket at the front of it.

Donal walked down the path with her as far as her front gate. He wanted the chance of a quiet word with her, and that wasn't possible around the twins, who were high as kites with the excitement of having stayed the night in Kate's house.

"You're sure you don't want me to come with you?" Donal asked Kate as he opened the gate for her. "I'm sure Kevin and Ann Marie would mind with the boys."

"Thanks, love, but no. You stay here. I'll do this on my own."

He stood watching as she got up on the big, old-fashioned bicycle and began the steady cycle up the hill. Then, turning, he went back into the house to play with the twins.

"You're not paying attention, Daddy," Luke accused him when Donal gave the wrong response for the second time. And it was true, he hadn't a hope of paying attention when his mind was on Kate and Jack.

Finally he could stand it no longer.

"Would you mind if I abandon ship for a while?" he asked Kevin. "Or were you thinking of going out yourselves?"

It didn't look like it. His brother and Ann Marie were curled up on Kate's big couch, looking as if they hadn't a notion of moving.

"Off with you, old son, and take your time, we're staying put. And the lads will mind us, won't you, boys?"

"Only if you promise to be good, Kevin!" Michael said, and the sound of their laughter followed Donal as he went out the door.

He drove the short distance to the beach below Jack's farm. There was a light breeze blowing as he got out and started to walk down towards the water's edge. It was a gorgeous day, the sun strong enough to draw brightness from the blue-grey ocean.

At a distance he could see a boat scudding along the creamy wave-crests and he was reminded of one of Kate's paintings, wondered again how she was getting on.

He began walking along the shore-line, keeping an eye on Jack's house in the far distance, watching for Kate to reappear. Wondering how Jack had taken it. Thinking of what he might say to his father, what his father might say to him.

Knowing that it would all work out for them.

Chapter Forty-four

The sun was slanting across the stand of trees behind the house when Kate finally came to the doorway. Donal watched as Jack followed her out into the little front garden and they stood there talking. He wished he was close enough to see their expressions, watched as they moved closer together for a moment.

Then Kate turned and walked down the short pathway to her bicycle, turning again to look at Jack as she got up on it and began to freewheel down the hill.

As Donal moved towards the car he could see Jack in the distance, still standing in his garden, looking after her.

He reached the car just as Kate came round the bend that hid it from the house, and she pulled in as soon as she saw him.

"I didn't know you were here."

"I didn't want you to. But I couldn't stay in the house."

She nodded as she got off the bike and stood holding it.

He waited.

"He wants to see you," she said.

He felt his heart jump. "What did he say?"

"We'll sit into the car for a minute." She leaned the bike against the stone wall as she spoke. He opened the car door, waited again until she was settled beside him and ready to speak.

"He saw it himself, Donal. As soon as I gave him the painting. He looked at it, and thanked me and said he was delighted. And then he put it on the table, leaning against the wall, with the sun shining through the window on it. And then he turned to me suddenly, and the question was in his eyes, only I wanted him to ask it.

And then he just said "Kate?" and I nodded, because I didn't need him to say the words any more, it was enough for him just to know."

She had been looking through the windscreen, back towards Jack's house which was hidden from view, but now she stopped speaking and turned to look at Donal.

"He started crying, Donal. No warning, nothing, just tears coming down his cheeks. I never saw him doing that before, never once. And I didn't know what to do, because it seemed like something so private I felt I shouldn't be there at all. And then, after a long while, he stopped, and we talked. We had a lot of talking to do. Because he saw something else as well, as soon as he saw his portrait."

"What was that, Kate?" Donal asked quietly.

"He saw how he could have been. How he still is, to me." She paused. "He saw that I still love him."

"You wanted him to see that, didn't you?"

She smiled. "Yes. Yes, I did. Because I know he still loves me."

"And . . . ?"

"And that's enough for me. For now. He's coming over in a day or two. But first he wants to see you, love. Will you go?"

"I'll go. Of course I'll go."

He reached for the door handle. "Do you want to come back up with me? Or will you wait here?"

"Neither," she said as they stepped out of the car. "I'll go on home and wait for you there."

She retrieved the bike, turning it towards the road, and then paused and turned back to look at Donal where he stood by the car in the fading light.

"Don't let him be too hard on himself, will you, love?"

"What do you mean?" he asked softly.

She looked directly into his eyes.

"I mean it was my fault, as much as his. More, because I knew and he didn't. And I'll be sorry for the rest of my life that I didn't tell him."

"You did what you thought was right, Kate."

"Maybe I did, though no-one but a fool would do what they thought was wrong. And no-one but a fool would let their pride get in the way of their happiness, and other people's happiness. I've learned that pride can be a foolish thing, a lonely thing."

"You told me not to be hard on him, Kate. Look how hard you're being on yourself."

"Don't you see what I did to you?" she asked, and he could see the soft glint of tears in her eyes.

He reached for her hand.

"Yes, I see it. I see that you gave me the very best chance you could. And that you loved me all these years, and wanted the very best for me, always. I couldn't have asked for more than that. Well, maybe one thing more."

"What's that?" She looked at him anxiously, but he was smiling.

"That you'll forgive yourself." He bent to kiss her cheek. "Now, go on home – I won't be long."

He turned to walk the short distance up to the house. Kate was smiling again as she watched him for a moment before beginning her journey home.

* * *

The door was open wide when Donal walked up the path, and Jack was standing just inside. "I saw you coming up the hill," he said, moving back to let Donal into the warm, bright kitchen. The kettle was singing on the range and there were cups and saucers waiting on the table, beside the portrait that was still poised there, its back against the wall.

"I was hoping you'd come," he said quietly, gesturing to Donal to take a seat. "You'll have some tea?" he asked, and then he brought it to the table and poured it and sat across from Donal, saying nothing, just smiling, as if there was no need for words.

"I would have come sooner . . ." Donal began, and

then stopped as he saw the sudden twist of Jack's lips as he tried to control the tears.

"I wish you did," he said finally. "I wish to God you came a long time ago. I wish . . ."

He stopped, swiped at his eyes with the back of his hand, quickly got up from the table.

"I have something for you," he said abruptly, going across to the old sideboard under the window. The next minute he was on his knees, rummaging in its depths until he pulled out a small cardboard box and began searching in it, carelessly tossing envelopes aside until he found the ones he wanted.

He brought them back to the table and put them in front of Donal before sitting down again opposite him.

"It's yours," he said quietly. "It's all yours – the farm, and what's in the bank. I don't need much for myself. The house and a few acres, that's all I want. The rest is yours."

"Jack . . . "

"Listen to me." Jack's voice was firm, and then he smiled. "Let me be a father to you just this once, and let you listen to me."

Donal nodded, waited.

"You have no idea, no notion in the world what this means to me. You couldn't have. You have those two young gasurs of yours to rear, and every day you can see that what you're doing is for them. Whether it's what you want to do or not, it's for them. So that even if there's something else you'd sooner be doing, it has a meaning and a value in it, because it's all for them."

He paused for a moment and sat, just looking across at Donal, who nodded but didn't say a word.

"And that's what I feel now, Donal, after all this time. I feel there was some good in it all along. So don't refuse me, Donal. I've made enough mistakes and wasted enough time. If you don't want the farm now, at least promise me you'll take it when the time comes, so you'll have it for those young lads of yours. And no-one need know why you're getting it. There'll be no shame on you. Though for myself, I don't care what they think – that time is long gone. I wish to Almighty God I was the man then that I should have been."

Donal felt tears in his own eyes.

"I see the man you are now, Jack. That's enough for any man to be proud of. You and Kate can tell the whole world if you want to, and the last thing I'd feel is ashamed."

Jack nodded, tears in his eyes again, and stretched out a hand across the table as Donal reached to grasp it. Not a handshake, man to man, but the firm, warm touch of son and father, father and son.

Chapter Forty-five

Clare was curled up in the armchair by the blazing fire, reading again from the poetry book. The bottle of wine stood open beside her, though she didn't intend drinking more than this second glass. She had music playing and candles burning on the hearth. Two larger ones, as yet unlit, stood together on the mantelpiece.

New Year's Eve, almost midnight. She wondered how the party was going, knew she had made the right decision in coming down here.

"You'll be on your own!" Ruth had said, horrified that anyone would choose this on New Year's Eve.

"I'll be fine, Ruth. It's where I want to be. Even though I can't be with him, I want to be near him. Don't worry, I'll be fine," she repeated, when Ruth looked unconvinced.

"And she won't have to help with the party," Conor had added. "Maybe I'll join her myself . . ."

She stood up and stretched, bent to put some more turf on the fire, smiled as she remembered this morning's conversation with them.

In spite of Ruth's concern she was delighted to be back home. The living-room looked a bit dusty, but wonderful anyway. And it had warmed up beautifully once the fire got going by early evening. She wondered if Jack would see the smoke and come to investigate, wondered whether Kate had spoken to him yet.

She had had a moment, nearing Kate's cottage, when she had wanted to call in, knowing Donal would probably be there. She had forced herself to keep going, telling herself that she would see him in just a few more days, maybe even tomorrow.

For tonight she would leave him with his memories.

She thought of turning on the radio or television, but watching or listening as other people celebrated had no appeal for her. She planned to mark the ending of the year, the beginning of another, by lighting the two candles that stood waiting. That would be symbol enough for her, until she and Donal could celebrate together.

She watched the final moments tick by, struck the match to light the first candle, smiling as the flame took hold.

For an incredible year, she said silently, watching as the shadows danced along the wall.

She reached for the matches again, paused as she heard the dogs bark, just once. She thought she heard a sound in the yard, began moving towards the window, then stopped as the telephone rang.

"Happy New Year, sis! You're missing a great party!"

"I'm having my own. Wine, candles, the lot."

"Mmm. Well, you know best. I suppose. Say hi to Conor."

She heard the knock as she hung up the telephone, hesitated for a moment, flew to the door as she realised who it had to be.

And then she burst out laughing at the sight of him, standing there struggling to balance champagne, and a sod of turf, and a heap of the wild pink roses that were still scattered about the garden even in late December.

"Well, can I come in? Or should I just keep standing here for Madam's amusement?"

"Tell me first what the turf is for!"

"First-footing. You know, where the first visitor of the New Year is a handsome dark-haired man carrying a lump of coal, for luck. I couldn't find any coal out there in the dark. Or red roses, so these will have to do for the time being."

"And no handsome men, either?"

"None. You'll have to settle for me. And the roses."

"Thorns and all?"

"That's the deal."

She pretended to think for a moment.

"It's a good deal," she said, moving back as he stepped over the threshold. She took the roses from him, breathing deeply of their scent, and he reached past her to put the champagne on the table, the sod of turf on the hearth.

"I'll put these in water," she said. "And I must light the other candle."

He followed her gaze.

"For the future," she added.

"The future," he said, closing the door firmly behind

him, and she put the roses down on the table and moved forward into his arms. "The future starts now," he said, his breath warm against her cheek. "We've waited long enough."

He was right, she thought. And from where she was standing their future looked just about as perfect as those roses. Thorns and all.

THE END